LETTERS
FROM THE
DEAD

A Jefferson Tayte Genealogical Mystery

Other books in this series

In the Blood
To the Grave
The Last Queen of England
The Lost Empress
Kindred
Dying Games

LETTERS
FROM THE
DEAD

A Jefferson Tayte Genealogical Mystery

by

STEVE ROBINSON

THOMAS & MERCER

Text copyright © 2018 by Steve Robinson

Published by Thomas & Mercer, Seattle

www.apub.com

Amazon, the Amazon logo, and Thomas & Mercer are trademarks of Amazon.com, Inc., or its affiliates.

ISBN-13: 9781503903104
ISBN-10: 1503903109

Cover design by @blacksheep-uk.com

Printed in the United States of America

For my wife, Karen

Prologue

October 1869

Dear Robert,

Further to my recent correspondence, I write to you with great anticipation and excitement over your interest in the aforementioned matter. I have in my possession several letters written by my great-aunt Jane concerning her travels in India. By themselves they mean little. Taken as a whole, however, I believe they represent an extraordinary tale that could prove priceless.

It is in respect of this that I hope to secure your patronage to facilitate an expedition to Jaipur in search of a gemstone of unparalleled size and worth. In return, notwithstanding a favourable outcome, I assure you an equal share of said gemstone in addition to the full return of your investment.

Should these conditions meet with your approval, I am most keen to bring the letters in question to you at your earliest convenience so that you may see for yourself the uncommon opportunity they represent. Needless to say, your discretion in this matter is of the utmost importance.

Your most humble servant,
Cornelius Dredger

Chapter One

Present day

'Tickets, please!'

Jefferson Tayte stirred reluctantly from the heavy slumber he'd been lulled into by the rhythmic motion of the train. His eyelids peeled open momentarily, and then he closed them again, hoping the conductor had already passed by. A few seconds later, he felt a tap on his shoulder.

'Your ticket, please.'

Tayte opened his eyes again, more fully this time. He'd been using his suit jacket as a pillow. He yawned as he unrolled it and fished inside the pockets for his ticket. As he did so, he glanced out of the window and noted that the sunlit countryside that had been there when he'd last looked was now replaced by industry and housing. It had also started to rain.

'April showers,' he said to the conductor, handing him his ticket. 'Where are we?'

'Northumberland. We've just left Berwick-upon-Tweed.'

Tayte sat up. 'Thanks,' he said, taking back his ticket.

He checked his watch. It was almost one thirty in the afternoon. Having left London at ten that morning, he quickly calculated that his remaining journey time was still around two and a half hours, assuming a smooth changeover at Edinburgh for his onward journey to Perth, where he'd been told a car and chauffeur would be waiting for him. It might have been quicker to fly, but whenever he had an alternative, he preferred to take it on account of the stress he knew his phobia of flying would cause him.

Tayte put his ticket away again. As he did so, he felt the letters that had necessitated his trip to Scotland. He took them out, pinched the sleep from his eyes, and glanced over them again. One had been written by his client, Damian Sinclair, who had contacted him after seeing one of the advertisements Tayte had placed as soon as he'd felt settled enough in his new environment to start rebuilding his career. Sinclair's letter described a tantalising genealogical brick wall that was all but impossible for a man in Tayte's profession to ignore. Although brief, it spoke of British India, an illegitimate child, and an unknown four-times-great-grandfather who, despite many years of searching, no one had been able to identify. The other was a copy of an apparently related letter penned by another hand, dated almost 150 years earlier.

Business had been very slow of late. Tayte had only received a handful of calls in recent months, and he'd taken a few assignments as a result, but none had proved to be very interesting to a genealogist with his breadth of experience. The letters from Damian Sinclair, therefore, represented a welcome change, although mention of a valuable gemstone in the older of the two letters was still of some concern. The last thing Tayte wanted to get involved in since leaving his old life in Washington, DC, behind him was a trivial treasure hunt, but of all the assignments he'd taken on lately, this was the only one that excited him. He only hoped his skills as a genealogist hadn't become too rusty.

He closed his eyes again and recalled his initial meeting with Sinclair, the man he was now travelling to see at his family home near Comrie in Scotland's Southern Highlands. Sinclair was a stockbroker, and because he largely conducted his business affairs in London, he'd asked Tayte to meet him at the East India Club on St James's Square, where he was a member. Tayte pictured the lounge bar he'd been taken to by a smartly dressed member of staff wearing black-and-gold livery. The room was plushly decorated, with the high ceilings that were typical of the Regency style. It had cream walls adorned with gold stucco work and gilt-framed portraits, with several chandeliers hanging over a blue-and-yellow carpet, on to which was set an array of red leather Chesterfield chairs and settees.

There had been several other people in the lounge when Tayte entered, largely sitting in pairs, with one or two noses buried in the morning newspapers. Tayte was led towards the leftmost of several tall windows that faced the small parkland at the centre of St James's Square, where the man he had come to meet was seated in the corner of the room. He rose as Tayte arrived, his posture erect, head high, accentuating his aquiline features. Like Tayte, Damian Sinclair was over six feet tall, although unlike Tayte, Sinclair was very slim, with pronounced cheekbones that gave the skin beneath them a hollow appearance. Tayte's initial assessment of the man was that he'd recently been unwell, or that he simply wasn't getting enough calories in his daily diet.

Sinclair extended a bony hand. 'Mr Tayte, I presume?'

They shook hands and Tayte nodded, returning his smile. He thought Sinclair a particularly well-spoken man, who perhaps made it a point of pride to pronounce every letter of the words he spoke in a soft Scots accent.

'Do take a seat,' Sinclair continued. 'Given the personal nature of our meeting I thought a quiet little spot in the corner was appropriate.' He paused and smiled. 'I hope you'll forgive me, but I'm too frugal to hire one of their meeting rooms. I'm afraid that where money's concerned, I conform to all the stereotypical attributes you've no doubt heard about Scotsmen.'

Tayte smiled. 'This is just fine,' he said as he sat on a small settee with his back to the wall, adjacent to the window. He set his briefcase down beside him and continued to take his host in.

Damian Sinclair looked to be in his early fifties. He was wearing a dark pinstripe suit with a light-blue shirt and a bright candy-stripe tie. There was a gold pocket-watch chain running to his waistcoat pocket, which told Tayte he was perhaps a man of old-fashioned hankerings. His immaculate appearance caused Tayte to wish he'd run an iron over his own suit and buffed his loafers before he'd left home, or selected another of his tan suits altogether. One that wasn't made of easily creased linen.

'You don't like ties, do you?' Sinclair offered, clearly getting the measure of Tayte in return. 'I can tell. It doesn't sit well on you.'

Neckties for gentlemen was a requirement of the club, and Tayte was wearing the only one he owned, which was funeral black. He'd been pulling and fiddling with it since he'd put it on outside the Tube station at Green Park that morning. He thought Sinclair an astute man to have so quickly noticed his discomfort at wearing it.

Tayte grinned, opting to make light of the observation. 'I believe neckties to be little more than a necessary evil.'

Sinclair sat back and laughed. 'Good man!' he said. 'I admire your honesty. Let me get you a drink. Then we'll get down to business.'

Sinclair raised a hand. A moment later a waiter in a red velvet jacket and bow tie came to their table.

'I'll have a gin and tonic, and my friend here will have . . .' Sinclair trailed off, gesturing to Tayte.

'Coffee, please,' Tayte said. 'Strong and black.'

'Espresso, sir? Americano?'

Tayte nodded. 'That sounds great. I'll have an Americano with an extra shot of espresso.'

The waiter's eyes narrowed on Tayte briefly, as if questioning whether he'd heard him right.

'I have a young son,' Tayte said, as if to explain his need for the extra caffeine. 'He's five months old.'

'Very good, sir,' the waiter said. Then he turned on his heel and headed back to the bar.

'Now then,' Sinclair said, leaning closer to Tayte. 'What do you make of that old letter I sent you? I trust it's piqued your interest?'

'Very much so,' Tayte said. He opened his briefcase and took both letters out. 'Before we discuss it, though, I'd like to address the elephant in the room.'

'The elephant?'

Tayte looked Sinclair in the eyes. 'I think you know what I'm referring to. If this is just some kind of treasure hunt, I—'

'Ah, the gemstone,' Sinclair cut in. 'I see what you mean.'

'Well, is it?' Tayte asked. 'Because if it is, you should know right now that I don't do treasure hunts.'

Sinclair crossed his legs and began tapping his bony fingers together, as if contemplating how best to answer the question. A moment later he said, 'Not exactly. What I mean to say is that in essence this is connected to a potentially priceless gemstone, but that's not the reason I wish to solicit your services. As I said in my letter, I'd simply like to know who my paternal four-times-great-grandfather was. Surely, as a genealogist, you of all people can understand my need to find such a missing link in my family tree.'

Tayte understood the need very well. Not knowing who his biological parents were had eaten away at him for most of his adult life. He didn't quite buy Sinclair's motives, though. From what he'd read in the letters Sinclair had sent him, it seemed that the gemstone in question and Sinclair's four-times-great-grandfather were intrinsically linked. That said, if Sinclair wanted him to identify his unknown ancestor, what he did with that information afterwards was his own business.

'Let's talk about your ancestor,' Tayte said. 'Your letter says you have no idea who he was.'

'That's correct. The family's knowledge of my paternal bloodline ends there. All we know is his first name, which you'll have read in my letter.'

'Robert,' Tayte said. 'The man the letter from 1869 was sent to.'

Sinclair smiled to himself. 'Aye, Robert, for what good that does us. There were fewer names more popular in Scotland during the early nineteenth century.'

Tayte opened his copy of the letter that had been written in October 1869. 'So how exactly did you come by this in the first place? I mean, if the man it was sent to was unknown to your family, how did—'

'I didn't mean to imply that my ancestor in question was unknown to everyone in my family,' Sinclair cut in. 'I believe his son, my three-times-great-grandfather, must have known who he was. For some reason, though, he kept the identity of his father to himself. It's a logical explanation for how the letter from 1869 came into my family's possession. I knew nothing about it until my father died. It was one of the many things expressly left to me in his will.'

'I see,' Tayte said, becoming more and more curious about who this mysterious ancestor was—and, in light of what he'd just heard, why the man's son, if he had known who his father was, chose to keep his identity a secret.

Their drinks arrived and Tayte sat forward, placing both letters on the table. 'You said in your letter that you believe the man who wrote the letter from 1869, Cornelius Dredger, is the key to finding out who your four-times-great-grandfather was.'

'Aye, well he clearly knew him, didn't he? And well enough to be on first-name terms.'

'There's no address written on the letterhead,' Tayte said. 'I guess it's too much to hope that you have the original envelope.'

Sinclair shook his head. 'No such luck, I'm afraid.'

Tayte sat back with his coffee. 'So, just to be clear, all you're asking me to do here is to identify your ancestor?'

'That's it. Nothing more. And from what I've heard about you, Mr Tayte, you're just the man for the job. Are you still interested enough to hear what else I have to say?'

Tayte was. In truth, he'd have liked nothing more than to get started right away. 'Sure,' he said. 'Please, go on.'

Sinclair took a large sip of his gin and tonic. He smacked his lips as he set the glass down again. 'That wets the old whistle,' he said. 'Now, you may have been wondering why I chose to meet you here at the East India Club.'

'It had crossed my mind.'

'Good, because there's a very important connection to be made concerning my membership credentials. The club was created in 1849. Its original purpose was as a club for the servants of the Honourable East India Company, and for commissioned officers of the army and navy. Nowadays, by virtue of its constitution, the East India is a gentleman's club with a strict membership policy of election and nomination. I was nominated by my father, who was nominated by his father, who was nominated by—'

'And so on,' Tayte said, getting the picture, thinking that the club's records could perhaps tell him who Sinclair's unknown ancestor was. People researching their own family history often overlooked such minor historical documents in favour of the more obvious records.

It was soon clear, however, that Sinclair had not. 'No,' he said, raising his eyebrows. 'My three-times-great-grandfather was called Angus Fraser. He had a wee girl who married a Sinclair, but that's by the by. I've already checked Angus's membership with the club. His father made no such nomination. If he had then I'd have no need of your services, would I?'

'So who did nominate him?'

'His stepfather. His name was Lachlan Fraser. He was an officer serving in India when Angus was born in 1825. Having raised Angus as his own, it is to Lachlan Fraser that I owe my membership of this club today.' Sinclair paused, smiling to himself. In a low voice he added, 'Technically speaking, it seems I may have no right to be a member. You see, it's common knowledge in the family that my paternal four-times-great-grandmother, Aileen Fraser née MacGregor, had an affair. I've come to believe it was with the man I'm trying to identify—this man called Robert, whom Cornelius Dredger wrote to in 1869. I'm a descendant of their offspring.' He put a finger to his lips. 'Don't tell anyone, will you?'

'Your secret's safe with me,' Tayte said, wondering how much research Sinclair had already conducted, and whether there was anything left for him to look into. 'Have you seen a copy of Angus Fraser's birth certificate?'

'Aye, of course. Aileen Fraser is listed as Angus's mother, but there's no father listed.'

'That's unusual,' Tayte said. 'I mean, if Lachlan Fraser raised Angus as his own son, surely he would have added his name to the birth certificate when the child was born, to hide his wife's indiscretion.'

'I'm sure he would have done just that—if he'd been around at the time to do so. You see, when Angus was born, Lachlan was feared dead. According to family legend, which has since been backed up to some extent via Lachlan's East India Company service record, he went missing in 1824, during the First Anglo-Burmese War. His wife, Aileen, had been told her husband had fallen in battle, but that wasn't the case. Lachlan had been taken prisoner. He wasn't released until 1826, following the Treaty of Yandabo, which made provision for the release of all British prisoners of war. That was a year after Angus was born.'

'I see,' Tayte said, thinking that explained it.

'My research has been extensive,' Sinclair continued. 'As has the rest of the family's. Aileen married just the once, and she was married to Lachlan Fraser when Angus was born. Given what I've just told you, and the lack of any father listed on Angus's birth certificate, it's clear that Aileen must have had an affair during the time Lachlan was thought to be dead.'

'The rest of the family?' Tayte said, raising an eyebrow as he held on to Sinclair's words. He doubted the rest of Sinclair's family, the legitimate Fraser bloodline, could all be interested in their family history by chance. The reason seemed clear enough to him. 'Are other members of your family looking for this gemstone mentioned in the letter?'

'They are, and they've been looking for many years—it's an integral part of the family legend I mentioned. They all believe they have a right to it, but it's my belief that it once belonged to someone in *my* paternal bloodline, not theirs. And so, it seems, did Cornelius Dredger, or why didn't he send his letter to their ancestor instead? It's a treasure hunt to those greedy buggers, I can tell you.'

Tayte noted the resentment in Sinclair's voice at the idea that another member of his family should find the gemstone. It made him all the more wary of Sinclair's true motives for hiring him. He turned his thoughts back to the letter from 1869 and the reason Dredger had sent it.

'In his letter,' he said, 'Dredger is essentially asking for money.'

'That's right. To fund an expedition to India.'

'To search for the gemstone?'

'Aye.'

'And the other letters he mentions, from his great-aunt Jane in India. He believes her letters are the key to finding it?'

'Apparently so.'

Tayte may not have been interested in a treasure hunt when he first sat down to talk about the assignment with Sinclair, but given the obvious extent of Sinclair's research, and of the rest of his family's for all Tayte knew, it occurred to him that there could be a way to identify Sinclair's four-times-great-grandfather via the letters written by Dredger's great-aunt. Maybe they could give him a name or some other piece of information that might prove useful in identifying who this man called Robert was.

'Do you have those letters from Dredger's great-aunt?' Tayte asked, a hint of doubt in his voice, supposing that if Sinclair did have them he would have scoured them for clues and would perhaps have already found the answer he was looking for.

'Sadly, I have just one letter,' Sinclair said. 'No more than that. I believe my unknown ancestor came into possession of the rest—which, as I've said, is how I come to have one of those letters today, by way of a family heirloom, if you will. As an overly curious wee bairn, I once came upon a thick bundle of old letters in a golden-clasped album that was in my grandfather's possession at the time. I suspect that album contained the letters from Dredger's great-aunt.'

'You've no idea where the rest of the letters could be?'

Sinclair began to shake his head before Tayte had finished speaking. 'No, but if you're prepared to accept the assignment, you must come to Scotland and stay as my guest. You can talk to the rest of my family. Maybe one of them knows where those letters are.'

'Stay in Scotland?' Tayte said, surprised by the suggestion.

'Of course. Where else?'

Tayte didn't particularly like the idea of spending the duration of the assignment in Scotland. It wasn't that he had anything against Scotland; it had always been on his list of places he'd like to visit someday. It was simply because Scotland was several hundred miles away, and he didn't want to be so far from his family just now. If he accepted the assignment, however, he knew that Scotland was where he needed to be. He had to talk to Sinclair's family, if they would agree to see him. He drew a deep breath and held on to it, thinking. A couple of years ago he wouldn't have hesitated. He'd have been on the next train out of London, keen to get started. Now it was different. Now he had a family to consider.

'I'm going to have to sleep on it,' he said, and Sinclair nodded.

'Of course you must. Just let me know once you've made your decision.'

That afternoon, he'd explained the situation to his wife, Jean, who'd said that as much as she would miss him, she thought he should go.

'It's only for a week or so,' Jean had said. 'I'll be fine.' Then she'd squeezed his hand and added, 'You need this more than you know.'

An announcement stirred Tayte from the half-sleep he'd slipped back into since leaving Berwick-upon-Tweed, letting him know that the train would soon be arriving at Edinburgh, where he had to change for Perth. The letters Sinclair had sent to him had fallen into his lap as he'd drifted off. He put them back inside his jacket pocket beside his travel tickets and stretched, wondering what he'd let himself in for this time. As the train came to a stop, Tayte rose to collect his briefcase and the light luggage he'd brought with him, supposing there had to be more to this gemstone and the letters that spoke of it than met the eye.

Chapter Two

To Tayte, Damian Sinclair's family home near Comrie seemed more like a castle. As he stepped out of the car that had collected him from Perth station, into the cool, late-afternoon sunshine, he paused, briefcase in hand and mouth agape while he stared at the Scottish Baronial architecture. He took in the grand main entrance, over which was suspended what he imagined was an imitation portcullis, although given the apparent age of the place, it could just as well have been the real thing. His eyes drifted up over the grey stone walls, over the layers of small mullioned windows set high up on the first level, presumably as a defensive measure, to the ornately carved corbels and conical bartizans that adorned the towers. He looked back across the stream the car had just crossed, which the driver had told him was called a burn, and then out over the countryside, to the trees in one direction and the far hills in the other. There wasn't another house in sight.

'This way, sir,' the driver said, his broad Scots accent sounding more gruff to Tayte than he imagined was intended.

Tayte turned to face him, noting that he already had his suit carrier over one arm and his holdall in the other. He'd introduced himself as Murray. He was a short, stocky man with grey caterpillar eyebrows and a bald pate. Tayte thought him older than Sinclair, closer to sixty than fifty, perhaps, although it was difficult to tell on account of his weathered appearance. He was like no chauffeur Tayte had ever seen. He wore sagging blue corduroy trousers that were too short for him, scuffed tan boots, a navy-blue jumper with threadbare elbows, and no collar at his neck. The man's appearance and general demeanour had done nothing to prepare Tayte for the grandeur of the house he was about to enter. He followed Murray towards the entrance, his loafers crunching on the gravel, thinking that the chauffeur and the old car he'd just travelled in, with its faded silver paintwork and well-worn seats, were oddly conflicting with his expectations.

Inside the house, however, everything became clear. Sinclair, it seemed, was not as well off as Tayte had imagined. At least, things had apparently slipped a great deal since the family's heyday. The first thing he noticed was his breath swirling in front of him, the air inside the entrance hall being much cooler than outside. It gave Tayte his first clue that this was perhaps not a well-kept house. The decor left him in no doubt. He saw a once-grand oak staircase that had been varnished some time ago and was now patchy and flaking. The same was true of the carved wainscoting that covered the lower half of the walls, above which were lighter patches on the otherwise dark-cream paintwork, where paintings, tapestries and other wall-hangings had once been.

'Mr Sinclair has instructed me to help settle you in,' Murray said, scratching at the side of his nose as they arrived at the bottom of the staircase.

'You mean I can't see him now?'

Murray shook his head and very slowly began to climb the stairs. 'I'll take you up to your room. Keep to the left going up. Right side coming down.'

'Why's that?'

'Woodworm. The old place is riddled.'

Tayte didn't much like the sound of that. 'Is it safe?' he asked as they made their way up. 'My room, I mean.'

'You'll be just fine as long as you don't wander about too much.'

They came to the top of the staircase, where Tayte saw more evidence of missing family portraits and other artwork, which he imagined must have been sold off at one time or another, perhaps to pay for the estate's upkeep. There was also very little furniture, and what there was had seen better days.

'Stay clear of the east wing,' Murray said, pointing along a dark, unlit corridor to their right. 'The wee buggers have made a feast of the floorboards. We don't want any accidents now, do we?'

'No,' Tayte agreed, taking his new environment in with a degree of both fascination and concern. 'You have damp, too, I see,' he added, pointing up at the ceiling as they made their way along the opposite corridor, which in contrast was pleasantly lit by a large sunny window at the far end.

'Aye, and wet rot, dry rot. You name it.'

They stopped at the last door before the window. Murray put Tayte's holdall down and produced a large key from his trouser pocket. 'Here we are,' he said, opening the door. 'Mr Sinclair asked me to make up the corner room for you.'

Tayte followed Murray inside, not expecting much. He was pleasantly surprised. It was warm, spacious and flooded with sunlight from tall, leaded windows on two sides, one of which faced directly west. The mellow oak floorboards and rich yellow decor made it all the more cosy, and in the centre of the room was a carved, heavy-framed, four-poster bed.

'I've made up the fireplace,' Murray said, the floorboards creaking beneath him as he went further in. 'It can be a wee bit cool come evening time. There are matches on the mantle if you're one to feel the cold. If you need anything, there's a bell-pull beside the bed there. I can't guarantee you the kind of service you're no doubt used to, but I'll do my best.'

'Thank you,' Tayte said, smiling, having warmed to the man already. He went to give him a tip for his service, but though he imagined Murray could have used the money, he flatly refused it.

'It's nae bother,' he said, waving the money away, pulling a sour face as he did so. He set Tayte's bags down and handed him the room key. 'Dinner's at seven. You'll find the dining room easily enough. Turn right at the bottom of the stairs and follow the corridor. You can't miss it.'

'Got it.'

Murray made for the door. When he reached it he paused and turned back. 'And remember what I said about the staircase,' he added. Then he left Tayte alone.

Tayte checked his watch. It was just after five, giving him two hours to unpack his things and freshen up. What had he let himself in for this time? He paced over to the sunlit window and looked out. The sun was low in the sky, but there were still a few hours of daylight left. It felt hot through the glass, which he welcomed. He turned to the other window, which faced more to the south. It looked out over the burn to the front of the house, and he was reminded of the isolation he'd felt when he'd first taken in the landscape upon his arrival. Coming into the house had done little to change that. He'd imagined Sinclair lived with his family when he was home in Scotland, but he'd seen no evidence that anyone else was there, or anywhere nearby for that matter.

Thinking of family caused Tayte to check his phone. He was glad to see it had a signal, which prompted him to call Jean to say he'd arrived safely. As he waited for her to answer he looked up again, still facing the window, and realised he was wrong about there being no one else around. There was a figure on the other side of the burn. He thought it was a woman, but he couldn't be sure. He supposed Sinclair must have family living there after all, or perhaps it was another member of staff. Whoever it was, he or she was standing perfectly still, staring up at the house as if directly at him. So much so that it began to unnerve him and he turned away. When he glanced back a moment later, the figure was gone.

—⏜—

At dinner that evening, Tayte was pleased to see the familiar face of Damian Sinclair again. Gone was the suit and tie from their meeting in London, in favour of a heavyweight, grey cable-knit jumper, attesting to the coolness of the air, which Tayte had felt as soon as he came downstairs. He didn't mind. He usually felt too hot anyway, especially while he was eating, and he figured he could always keep his jacket on. Sinclair was already sitting at the dining table when Tayte entered the room, which, being on the ground level, was dimly lit from the small, high-level windows he'd seen on his arrival. The oak wainscoting ran floor to ceiling in this room, further darkening the environment, but there were electric lamps here and there and plenty of candles on the table, which helped to brighten the place.

'Ah, there you are,' Sinclair said, pointing a bony finger at him. 'Welcome to Drumarthen House.'

'Good evening,' Tayte offered.

'It is that. I trust you had an agreeable journey?'

'Yes, thank you.'

Sinclair gestured for Tayte to sit in the chair opposite him, and Tayte pulled the chair out and sat down. He hadn't expected it to feel so heavy as he slid it back over the flagstone floor, but he thought it matched well with the immense thickness of the dining table.

'The dining room never used to be down here,' Sinclair said, 'but I'm sure Murray has warned you about the old place by now. You won't be surprised to hear that I've chosen to stay clear of the upper floors until it's time for my bed. The house once had a grand dining room. You could comfortably seat a hundred people in it, but those days are sadly long gone. This relatively small room provides more than enough space now.'

'More than enough is a waste,' Tayte said with a smile as he poured himself a glass of water from the jug.

Sinclair laughed to himself. 'I see you're a man after my own heart. I only wish I could heat the place better, but it's near impossible with ceilings thirty feet high. Of course, I'm not here all the time, but Murray is—luckily he seems not to mind the cold so much.'

As if summoned by the mention of his name, Murray appeared through another doorway, carrying a beaten pewter tray that looked as if it had been in the family for generations.

'Murray's prepared us a hearty stew for supper,' Sinclair said as Murray arrived at the table. 'I trust you like rabbit? It's fresh off the estate.'

'I can't say I've eaten it before.'

'Then you'll have to let me know what you think once you have.'

Murray set their meals in front of them in wide, steaming bowls. Then he set down another bowl, full of boiled potatoes.

Tayte drew the steam in. 'It sure smells good.'

'And I'm sure it will taste even better,' Sinclair said. 'Murray's a fine cook.'

'Thank you, sir,' Murray said. 'I've lit the fire in the drawing room. Will that be all this evening?'

'Of course, Murray, off you go. I'll see you tomorrow.'

'The faithful family retainer,' Tayte said once Murray had left them. 'He must have his work cut out in a place like this.'

'Aye, he's invaluable. I've had to let the rest of the staff go over the years and Murray has stood in for every one of them. I don't know what I'd do without him.'

'It must be reassuring to know you have someone here you can trust to take care of things while you're in London.'

Sinclair nodded and spooned a few potatoes into his stew. 'Well, do tuck in. We've much to talk about this evening.'

Tayte tried the stew. If he hadn't been told it was rabbit, he thought he could easily have mistaken it for chicken. 'It's delicious,' he said, taking another mouthful. He hadn't realised how hungry he was.

'So, you're an American living in London,' Sinclair said a moment later. 'Is your wife American?'

'No, Jean's an Englishwoman—a history professor. We met in London a few years back. I now have dual citizenship, but we decided to live in London at her apartment until we're more settled and the baby's older.'

'Ah yes, you have a wee bairn. Five months old, I believe you said. I'll wager he keeps you and your wife busy.'

'You can say that again. His name's Benjamin.'

'As in Franklin, no doubt,' Sinclair said with a smile.

Tayte nodded. 'It was my wife's idea to continue the American Founding Fathers theme. She thought it sat well alongside Jefferson, and we both liked it. Even before little Ben came into the world, setting up the baby room and decorating the rest of the apartment along with it turned into a full-time occupation for a while. During what little spare time I've had, I've been looking into my own family history, which is something I've only recently been able to do.'

'Why only recently?'

'I was given up for adoption as a baby. It's taken this long to discover who my parents were, which opened the door to the rest of my family history.'

'Have you found anything interesting? Any skeletons in the closet?'

Tayte didn't answer straight away. He'd uncovered terrible things in his recent family history, having been told that both of his parents had been murdered, but since identifying his bloodline, his further research had turned up nothing out of the ordinary. He wasn't sure that he wanted to talk about his parents and the discoveries he'd made in Germany with this man he barely knew, so he decided to keep his answer simple.

'I don't know about skeletons in the closet,' he said. 'I found that my parents and grandparents on both sides are dead, which is too bad. I'd like to have known them. It's wonderful to finally be able to trace my own family history, though.'

'You must have some living relatives,' Sinclair said. 'Cousins, at least.'

'I'm sure I have, but for one reason and another I've not gotten around to them yet. I found I have a brother who's very much alive. He had this idea that I should start a school where I could teach family history, but I'm not ready for that yet.' Tayte paused and smiled to himself. 'It might sound crazy, but I love my work too much. I've really missed the challenges assignments like this can offer.'

'Well, I've no doubt whatsoever that you'll face a great many challenges with your assignment here in Scotland before you go back to your family. As for myself, I don't have any children,' Sinclair added, no regret in his voice. 'My wife wasn't keen from the offset, so we focused our time and energy on other things.'

Talking of other close family members, Tayte was reminded of the figure he'd seen by the burn earlier. 'I think I may have seen her.'

Sinclair gave a hearty laugh that rocked his shoulders. 'I very much doubt that. My wife left me several years ago for an Italian toy boy. Last I heard she was living the life of Riley in Capri.'

'I'm sorry.'

'Don't be. I'm not.'

'It's just that I saw someone from my bedroom window. When you mentioned your wife, I assumed it was her.'

'Where exactly was this person you saw?'

'Across the stream.'

'The burn,' Sinclair corrected.

'Yes, the burn. Do you know who it's likely to have been? From what you've told me it seems you live alone here with Murray.'

'Aye, it's just Murray and me, and now you, of course. There's a public right of way that runs alongside the burn, close to the estate. It was no doubt just someone out for a stroll. It's a grand evening for it.'

'Yes, it is,' Tayte agreed. 'Whoever it was stood there for quite a while, though.'

'Did they now?' Sinclair said. 'Mind you, Drumarthen's a fine-looking house from the outside. I'm not surprised to hear someone was taking an interest in it. We get plenty of tourists stopping by to take pictures in the summertime.' Sinclair smiled to himself. 'I should levy a charge for it.'

Tayte thought that was probably all it was, but he couldn't shake the idea that the person he'd seen was staring up at him rather than the house, as if he or she knew he was there, and perhaps more importantly, why.

They continued to eat their meal. No wine was offered, not that Tayte particularly wanted any, but as with the general state of the house, the old car Sinclair ran, and the fact that they were eating free rabbit shot on the estate, he wondered whether the lack of wine was also on account of Sinclair apparently being far less well-off than he had imagined on first meeting him. The man's London-based life seemed entirely at odds with what Tayte had learned about him since arriving in Scotland. Sinclair hadn't baulked at Tayte's fee, however, which told him that he had to consider it money well spent. The notion caused him to think about the gemstone mentioned in Cornelius Dredger's letter again. Sitting at the table opposite him was a man who could evidently use the money from the sale of such a gemstone should it be found. Once again, it caused Tayte to question whether Sinclair had been entirely honest about his motives for wishing to identify his mystery ancestor.

Chapter Three

After dinner, Sinclair ushered Tayte through a stone archway that led along a short corridor to what Murray had previously referred to as the drawing room. It was apparent to Tayte as soon as he entered the cosy space that, just like the dining room, this was also no more than a pale imitation of the room it had once been. There were two wing-backed chairs sitting on a worn rug in the middle of the room, facing an open inglenook fireplace that seemed to dwarf its surroundings. Above the stone mantel, Tayte saw an assortment of antique shields and other items he imagined had once formed part of the family armoury. Sinclair tossed another log on to the now-dwindling fire and they sat down. There was a circular table between the chairs, on which were set two glasses and a decanter containing a rich, honey-coloured liquid.

'Can I offer you a dram of whisky?' Sinclair said. 'It's a fine single malt, distilled in Aberfeldy, just north of here.'

'That would be great. Thank you.'

Sinclair poured their drinks and tapped his glass against Tayte's. '*Slàinte!*' he said, toasting Tayte's good health.

As they settled back with their drinks, before Sinclair could begin his spiel about the original grand drawing room that had likely once existed at Drumarthen House, Tayte got straight down to business. 'You told me you have one of the letters written by Cornelius Dredger's great-aunt. What does it say? Can I see it?'

'I was wondering when you'd ask,' Sinclair said. 'Anticipating it wouldn't take long for you to get around to it, I brought the letter down to dinner with me.' He twisted around in his seat and produced several off-white folds of paper from his back pocket, which he handed to Tayte.

'The letter was written in September 1822,' Sinclair continued. 'It is, by its own account, the first letter written by Dredger's great-aunt to her brother concerning her time in India. The mail service from India in those days largely relied on the East Indiamen—armed ships of the East India Company. Given that the letter's journey to England could have taken the better part of a year from Jaipur, it would have taken a considerable time to receive a reply, although I expect Dredger's great-aunt was in the habit of writing home as frequently as she cared to, without waiting to hear what her brother had to say.'

Tayte unfolded the letter. The handwriting, though faded, was tall and neat, written with care and precision, as if the writer took great pride in her letters home. He scanned over the names and addresses at the top of the page and began to read it out. '*Having arrived in Bombay at great length via the Cape of Good Hope, some six months after setting sail from Southampton aboard the East Indiaman,* Repulse—*a magnificent merchant ship of more than sixty guns—we prepared for the overland journey to our destination in Rajputana.*'

'As can be seen in the following lines,' Sinclair said, 'after a degree of uncertainty as to whether she and the rest of the party she was travelling with would make it to their destination unharmed, she has arrived in Jaipur with her friend and her friend's seventeen-year-old daughter.'

'Who were sent for by her friend's husband,' Tayte said as he continued to read the letter to himself. 'It seems that Dredger's great-aunt is there as the other woman's travelling companion.'

'That was also my take on the situation,' Sinclair said. 'Further down she also mentions certain duties of care as far as her friend's daughter is concerned. You'll also note that this was not her first time in India.'

Tayte found the passage that mentioned the letter-writer's return to India, noting that she had spent much of her childhood in Bengal. His eyes drifted back up to the top of the letter. On one side was the name and address of the recipient, William Dredger of Chesterfield in Derbyshire. On the other was the sender's return address in Jaipur.

'Her surname was no longer Dredger by the time she went back to India,' Tayte said. 'Jane Hardwick,' he added, almost to himself. 'She was clearly married, but there's no mention of her husband. Maybe she was widowed, else why was she in India without him?'

'Very good, Mr Tayte. Jane Hardwick was widowed in 1820, two years before she made the journey.'

Tayte smiled to himself. He glanced at Sinclair, who was smiling back at him. 'Now why did I imagine for a minute that you hadn't already looked into the family history of Jane Hardwick née Dredger?'

Sinclair's smile broke into a small laugh. 'I'm sorry, but I did warn you that my research has been extensive.'

Even so, Tayte had to remind himself that Sinclair had not been able to identify his four-times-great-grandfather, which told him that this assignment was not going to be easy. With so much research already carried out, he knew he was going to have to think his way around the problem. He also thought that Sinclair's research could prove useful in helping him to do that.

As if to pre-empt Tayte's next question, Sinclair said, 'I'll make all my research available to you, of course. I'll have Murray bring everything to your room in the morning. You'll see that I've only been able to go so far where India is concerned. As for Jane Hardwick, from parish registers I've managed to find information about her birth and marriage in Derbyshire, but I've been unable to locate any information about her death. From that, an obvious conclusion springs to mind.'

'That she never returned from India,' Tayte said.

'Aye. You'll no doubt wish to go over my research to confirm my findings. Maybe I missed something, but perhaps you'll find a record of her death in India.'

Tayte gave a nod, thinking that the odds of Jane having died during her travels in India in 1822 were certainly higher than if she'd stayed at home. On the other hand, it was possible that she'd simply chosen to remain in the country she had known, and possibly come to love, as a child. She may well have lived there to a ripe old age. Either way, Tayte was curious enough about Jane Hardwick to want to find out what had become of her.

He turned his attention back to her letter, and began to wonder why she had chosen to return to India. She was recently widowed, which accounted for her being free to do so, but what had driven her to make such a long and arduous journey? He thought a simple and likely scenario was that, after the death of her husband two years earlier, she had jumped at the chance to make a fresh start when the opportunity arose. From her letter it seemed that she was travelling as a companion to a friend who had gone to Jaipur with her daughter to be with her husband. He wondered who the other family was. No surnames were mentioned in the letter. What was their story, and how was it all connected to the gemstone mentioned in Cornelius Dredger's letter? Tayte sensed it was an important question to answer.

As he read on, he learned that Jane Hardwick's ongoing journey to Jaipur had been an eventful one, bordering on catastrophic as they neared their destination some months after arriving in Bombay. The letter gave some little account of the many towns and settlements they had passed through, having to wait at each for safe escort, often travelling with supply carts and soldiers of one regiment of foot or another. Then Tayte read that, having left the district of Tonk in eastern Rajputana, Jane and the entire party she was travelling with were soon in fear of their lives.

Chapter Four

India, September 1822

As Mother India had once been a part of her, so was she again now. Sitting with her travelling companions in an open horse-drawn carriage, with nothing more than parasols to shelter them from the relentless sun, Jane Hardwick could feel her presence like no other land she had known. It covered her skin, seeping deeper and deeper into her pores with every mile, knotting her hair and parching her throat. With every breath, she could taste the eternity of her dust.

They were on the Tonk Road, still some fifty miles south of Jaipur according to one of the soldiers leading the escort, and how Jane longed to be there. The road, like all roads she had travelled in India, was no more than a well-beaten route, born of necessity, connecting one town or river-crossing with another. She understood that to stray too far from such a road was to become all too easily lost amidst the unvaried open plains, having by day only the sun and the distant, barren hills for reference.

They were travelling in a four-seater carriage—a kind of barouche that on this occasion had no canopy. Jane looked across to her friend, Elspeth, and her seventeen-year-old daughter, Arabella, who had been her close companions since Southampton. Turning to her left, she glanced at the man sitting beside her who had joined them at Kota, many stages and as many days ago. He caught her eye and smiled at her, as he often did.

'Not far to go now,' he said. He had a yellowing, dusty piece of cloth on his head, no doubt having found the tall, black silk hats that were so fashionable in London impractical for travel in such climates. He removed the cloth temporarily to wipe the sweat from his brow. 'Shall I see you again once we've arrived in Jaipur? I should very much like to.'

The man's name was Albert Faraday, and he had made no secret of his affections towards Jane, pressing them at every opportunity.

Jane smiled politely, easing herself away. 'I'm sure I shall be too busy,' she said, looking across at her young charge. She decided to strike up a conversation with her so as to avoid further discourse with Mr Faraday.

'Yes, Bella. Not far to go now,' she said, sounding high-spirited as she repeated Faraday's words. 'I'm sure your mood will be much improved once you're with your father in Jaipur.'

Arabella continued to frown. She had a beautiful smile, Jane thought, if only she would show it more often. But she understood what a wrench it was for her to be uprooted from the only home she had known at such a young age, leaving her friends behind. She had felt much the same way when she'd been forced to leave Calcutta after her father died.

Elspeth gave a loud sigh. 'I'll certainly be glad when this wretched journey is over,' she said in her soft Scots accent. She sounded exhausted, although they were only a few hours into this particular stage of the journey.

Jane watched her open the reticule she wore on a black velvet tape around her neck. It stood out against her lace dress, which, as with all of their once-white dresses, had become tainted by the dust. Elspeth had taken to her opium pills again, perhaps to relieve the monotony of their seemingly endless journey. Or, as Jane sensed from their conversations over the past months, perhaps she took them for another, more personal reason. Elspeth removed one of her pills and placed it into her mouth. She drew a slow breath and sighed again, only this time she did so quietly and with satisfaction, no doubt taking comfort in the knowledge that her little opium pill would see her through.

Jane cared nothing for such things. She'd read of its effects, and she'd seen them manifested often enough. She had noted how it could, for a short time, replace misery with happiness, how it excited and enlarged the senses, and in many cases, when the dose was high enough, led to both moral and physical debility. Ultimately, however, it appeared to leave one all the more disconsolate. She had read that it was rare to find an 'opium-eater' over thirty years of age if the practice had been started early enough. To her knowledge, however, this was a new fixation for Elspeth, which had begun soon after their arrival in Bombay. She prayed that Arabella would not take to it as her mother had.

Interrupting her thoughts, Faraday sat forward and said, 'I shall report of our journey together, the four of us, just as soon as I'm settled in Jaipur. You shall all receive a favourable press, of course. No finer travelling companions could I have wished for.'

At Kota, Faraday had introduced himself as a newspaper correspondent with *The Times*. Originally from Yorkshire, he'd said he was now travelling the length and breadth of India reporting on everyday life under Company rule. He was rarely to be seen without a pencil poised in his hand. When not in his hand, it could usually be found balancing atop his right ear, where it was now.

'You're too kind,' Jane said. 'And what will you write of the lovely Arabella?' she added, winking at her. 'Will you mention her musical accomplishments with the recorder?'

Although she tried to hide it, Arabella began to smile at the flattery.

'Or perhaps you'll say that she's the bravest among us for making such a journey at her young age?' Jane continued, determined to see Arabella happy again.

'Yes to all of those fine merits,' Faraday said. 'And of you, Mrs Hardwick, rest assured, I shall note with great pride your expertise in the multifarious languages and dialects of India, having heard you speak them so fluently first-hand. You are an asset to all who travel with you.' He paused, averting his eyes as he began to flick at the hem of his jacket. 'A man predisposed to the reporting of life in India would do better than he deserves to have such a fine woman at his side.'

Jane feigned a smile, but inside she was exasperated. Could she not converse with the man at all without the threat of some furthering of their acquaintance? She feared not, and it was hopeless to suppose otherwise. She didn't want to hurt Mr Faraday's feelings, but she had to say something to let him know that she had no romantic interest in him. If she did not, she imagined he would make it his duty to seek her out once they reached Jaipur, and he would become quite the nuisance.

She was about to speak her mind on the matter when a cry went up ahead. A second later, a single gunshot rent the air and their horse began to whinny and rear up on its hind legs, bringing the carriage to a standstill. Another shot quickly followed the first. Orders were shouted by the officers and shots were returned. Jane noted that the terrain was more hilly here, ideal for an ambush, she thought. She looked to the hills, where she saw plumes of white powder smoke as more shots were fired on their position.

'Dacoits!' she said to her companions.

'Bandits?' Faraday said with surprise, as if scarcely able to believe it. 'The audacity! Don't they realise they're firing on at least fifty Company riflemen?'

The dacoits' confidence worried Jane. 'The reward must be worth it,' she said. 'Does anyone know what cargo we're carrying on those ox-carts?'

The faces around her were blank, except for Elspeth's, who seemed to smile with delight every time a shot was fired, as if she were watching fireworks explode around her. Her opium tablet had clearly taken its desired effect.

'Munitions?' Faraday offered.

'Or perhaps opium,' Jane said, the substance fresh in her mind at seeing its effect on Elspeth. 'I read an account of one such attack in recent months. The dacoits took off with around twenty maunds. The guard was much the same size as this.'

'Then we're for it,' Faraday said, sinking lower in his seat.

Looking around her again, Jane could see that the guards, with their Brown Bess muskets, had taken positions at the head of the convoy and were returning volley after volley of gunfire up into the hills, presumably as a show of force in the hope of warning off their attackers. From what she could see, it did them no good. She saw one of the riflemen fall, and then another. With no cover and no clear target to fire upon, their situation appeared hopeless. As she saw things, it wouldn't be long before their number was significantly reduced. Then it would be all too easy for the dacoits to come down from the hills and make off with the ox-carts and the cargo they had clearly come for.

A bullet splintered the carriage to Jane's right, so close that it startled her, despite the thunder of the now-constant gunfire. She could see in Arabella's eyes that she was afraid, and rightly so. She rose, only half-standing, and went to comfort her, knowing her mother could not currently be relied upon to do so. At that moment, their carriage driver, an elderly Rajput who had also been with the party since Kota and was earning his passage home, rose out of his seat with a shrill cry. He turned to face them and Jane witnessed the terror in his eyes as he clutched at his bloody throat and fell.

'He's been shot!' Faraday exclaimed, still full of surprise that this attack was going on around them and that he was caught up in it.

Jane didn't hesitate for a second. She knew that to sit there and do nothing was to share the old Rajput's fate, and she had no intention of adding her blood, or the blood of her companions, to the dust alongside him. She stepped up to the reins, and now with a clearer view of the proceedings, she saw that the dacoits were already coming down from the hills. There were so many of them. They would not be frightened off. Jane had only one thing in mind as she sat down again and flicked the reins hard against the horse's flanks: she had to get everyone aboard that carriage to safety.

'Yah!' she called to the horse, flicking the reins harder.

The horse whinnied and reared up again. Then it took off, breaking away from the formation. Jane pulled hard on the reins to regain control. She turned the horse to their left, steering them back along the line of ox-carts at speed. Dust churned and billowed in the carriage's wake.

'Look!' Arabella called.

Jane turned around to see that Arabella looked more afraid now than ever. She was pointing back towards the hills. The view was partly obscured by the cloud of dust the carriage had kicked up, but Jane soon saw what Arabella had seen. Dacoits on horseback, in their pale, billowing garments and pointed cloth hats, were now riding out from their cover, charging the remaining soldiers. More worrying for Jane and her companions was that a handful of dacoits had broken free from the main attack and were galloping directly towards them.

She flicked the reins harder still, but she knew they would soon be outrun. One horse, pulling a carriage of four people and their possessions, was no match for a single determined rider, let alone a half-dozen or so of them. The dacoits had clearly seen the carriage break loose from the formation, and Jane realised too late that they no doubt thought she was making off with some of the cargo they had come for. She chanced another look back and saw no Company troopers coming to their aid. There were only the dacoits, and as she had supposed, they were gaining ground fast.

'Yah!' she cried again, spurring the horse on.

They quickly passed the last of the ox-carts, heading back along the road towards Tonk, but she knew it was hopeless to expect they could make it. It was too far, and it was foolish to try. She pulled hard on the left rein, cutting away from the road, meaning to circle back around the line of carts and lead their pursuers towards the guard into a volley of gunfire. It was soon apparent, however, that there were too few soldiers left to be of any help, and those that hadn't already fallen or fled were too busy trying to fend off the main attack to pay her any attention as she passed them.

Jane made for the hills. What other choice was there but the open plain and certain death? She had to keep going. She thought the hills, if only she could reach them, might at least offer places to hide. The dacoits were surely only interested in the carriage. If they could disembark in time and flee into the hills on foot, she felt sure they would not follow.

The dacoits, however, were closing in. They were so close now that through the cloud of dust behind the carriage Jane could make out the whites of their eyes. She also noticed that their number was fewer than it had been, and she supposed that some had rejoined the main attack on the guard. She counted three riders and wondered why they weren't shooting at them. Whatever the reason, it was a blessing. It seemed to Jane that, having seen mostly women in the carriage, they were certain of their success in bringing it to a standstill without wasting a single round.

As hopeless as their situation now seemed, Jane kept going. She drove her horse hard, back on to the road that led to Jaipur as the hills began to rise either side of them. Then the first dacoit rider appeared beside her, his dark eyes set on hers. At the same time she heard a scream behind her. It was Arabella. The other two riders were close to the carriage, grabbing at Arabella while her mother, sensible to the situation at last, tried to fend them off with her collapsed parasol. Now that they were on top of them, Faraday could do no more than cower in his seat, curled over his knees with his hands on his head. Even if the man had managed to win his way into Jane's affections before now, he would have lost them again that instant.

Jane felt a tug on her reins, and her attention was drawn back to the lead dacoit horseman, who had grabbed them and was pulling her horse into his, forcing it to slow down. She was powerless to stop him. In a matter of seconds, the carriage had been brought to a standstill.

Chapter Five

Now on their second glass of whisky in the makeshift drawing room at Drumarthen House, Tayte's reading was interrupted by Sinclair's apparent impatience to talk to him about the gemstone. It forced Tayte to put Jane Hardwick's letter down in his lap for the time being, though he was eager to get back to her account of the attack on their party on the Tonk road.

'In Cornelius Dredger's letter to my as-yet-unknown ancestor,' Sinclair said, leaning closer to Tayte so that he had his full attention, 'you'll recall that Dredger was asking for money.'

'To fund his expedition to India in search of the gemstone,' Tayte said, recalling the letter very well.

'Aye, well, it's my strong belief that he accepted Dredger's offer.'

'It was quite a gamble.'

'Was it now?'

'You don't think so?'

'No, I don't. I believe Robert already knew of the gemstone in question, and that he believed the letters from Dredger's great-aunt in India represented the best chance of finding it.' Sinclair scoffed. 'No ancestor of mine would have put up so much money if the odds of a good return were anything less than highly favourable.'

Tayte couldn't question Sinclair's logic on that count. The more he thought about the gemstone, the closer he came to the conclusion that it could be key to the success of his assignment, whether he liked the idea of a treasure hunt or not. The person he needed to identify in Sinclair's family history was clearly wrapped up in the gemstone's story, and he was now beginning to feel the need to better understand that story.

'What do you know about the gemstone?' he asked. 'Can you tell me about it?'

Sinclair took a sip of his whisky. When he lowered his glass he was smiling. 'I knew your curiosity would get the better of you soon enough,' he said. He settled back in his chair again, and the glow of the fire danced across his face as he added, 'I can tell you about it all right—to a point, that is. To properly do so, however, I must first take you back seven hundred years to the fourteenth century and the time of the great Turco-Mongol conqueror, Timur, or Tamerlane as he's also known, although you can be sure that the gemstone's bloody history predates him by a good many more centuries. Timur was the first ruler of the Timurid dynasty in Persia, and the last great conqueror of the Eurasian Steppe. He was a man bent on restoring the Mongol Empire of Genghis Khan. It's believed that the gemstone in question, a huge ruby reported to be the size of a man's fist, came into his possession during his conquests in Egypt and Syria. In the years that followed, Timur became the most powerful ruler of the Muslim world, having amassed great wealth.'

'And, I imagine, a great number of precious gemstones from his years of plunder.'

'Aye, but few that compared to the ruby I speak of. So little is known about it that it's taken me years of meticulous research to trace its course through history. I could find no further mention of it until the late sixteenth century, when it's believed to have arrived in India by way of another conquest. This time the conqueror was Babur, a direct descendant of Timur, and the first of the Mughal emperors. In 1527 Babur defeated Rana Sanga of Mewar, a powerful leader of a Hindu Rajput confederacy in Rajputana, which largely encompasses Rajasthan as we know it today. In the years following Rana's defeat, many of the Rajput leaders formed alliances with the Mughal emperors, and many gave their daughters to the emperors so that their marriages would strengthen bonds between them.'

'You said the ruby came to India by way of another conquest,' Tayte said, 'yet the conqueror, Babur, already owned it.'

'Indeed I did,' Sinclair said, his eyes sparkling with enthusiasm as he spoke. 'You see, this time the ruby changed hands by way of a gift. Fast-forward a few more decades and we come to Akbar, the third and arguably the greatest of the Mughal emperors. He gave the ruby to one of his most trusted generals, Man Singh, for his loyalty. Singh was the Rajput Raja of Amber, or Amer as it's also known. He was the princely ruler of the Indian state we now call Jaipur.'

'Some of this is starting to sound a little familiar,' Tayte said, his eyes narrowing on Sinclair. 'Does this gemstone have a name?'

'Aye, it does, but it wasn't named by any of the Mughal emperors, or by Man Singh. You see, not all of the Rajput leaders accepted Mughal sovereignty. Chief among them was Maharana Pratap Singh, grandson of Rana Sanga, who, as I've said, was defeated in battle by Babur. It was he who first called the ruby the *Blood of Rajputana*, and rightly so as he saw it, because to him it represented the blood of the Rajputs who fought to defend their land against the Mughal invaders.'

'Of course,' Tayte said. 'I knew the word "Rajputana" rang a bell. I came across it a few years back, while reading an article about the British Crown Jewels and the Koh-i-Noor diamond. This ruby you're talking about is nothing more than a myth.'

'Is it?' Sinclair said, his eyes widening. 'Perhaps if no one had seen nor heard tell of the Koh-i-Noor diamond in hundreds of years, then that, too, would be no more than a myth by now. But would that make it any less real?'

Tayte thought back over the contents of Cornelius Dredger's letter from 1869, certain that the name of the stone had not been mentioned. 'Dredger doesn't name the gemstone,' he said. 'Come to think of it, he doesn't even say it's a ruby. Assuming for now that the Blood of Rajputana is real, why do you believe it's the same gemstone Dredger mentions in his letter? If it is, why doesn't he refer to it as such?'

'I don't know why he doesn't name the gemstone in his letter. Under the circumstances, perhaps he had good reason not to. I'm sure plenty of people have been interested in its whereabouts over the years, myth or no myth. As for why I believe Dredger is talking about the Blood of Rajputana, I have just one word for you—Jaipur. The ruby was given to Man Singh, remember, who—'

'Or so you read,' Tayte cut in. 'Did what you read confirm that the gemstone given to Man Singh was the Blood of Rajputana?'

'Not specifically, no, but then the name given to the stone hadn't long been circulating at the time. All I know is what I choose to believe, given the facts as I see them—that Akbar gifted a large ruby to Man Singh of Jaipur.'

'And that was the last anyone saw of it?'

'Not quite. Singh was a known devotee of Shri Krishna. It's believed that he set the stone into the forehead of a golden statue of Krishna and that it resided at his palace in Jaipur for many years as a symbol of peace, not war. Towards the end of Singh's life, it's said that he gave the statue to a prominent family in the neighbouring state of Kishangarh, on the occasion of the maharaja's first daughter's marriage to one of Man Singh's favourite grandsons. The gift cemented relations between these neighbouring states, and at the same time kept the ruby in the family, so to speak.'

Sinclair finished his drink and reached for the bottle again.

'The connections are all there, Mr Tayte. You see, Angus Fraser, my three-times-great-grandfather, was born in Jaipur. His mother, Aileen, with whom I believe Robert had the affair I previously mentioned, was married to an officer of the East India Company. You'll recall his name was Lachlan Fraser. From his military records we know he was stationed in Jaipur around the time the Blood of Rajputana was known to have been in the area. Now we have a letter about a priceless gemstone written, not to my step-four-times-great-grandfather, Lachlan—the man who brought Angus up as his own—but to the man I'm convinced is my biological four-times-great-grandfather, Robert. Between him and Cornelius Dredger lies the ruby's ongoing story, which I firmly believe, if carefully unravelled by expert hands such as yours, will lead to its whereabouts.'

Tayte drained the last of his whisky and stared at the flames in the fireplace, thinking that Sinclair had just admitted his real motive for hiring him. Sinclair wanted him to identify his unknown ancestor so he could go on to find the gemstone. It came as no surprise to Tayte—he'd suspected as much since their meeting in London. He said nothing about it. After all, he was hundreds of miles from home, having accepted the assignment, knowing full well what it was really all about.

There was a lot of speculation and hearsay in what he'd just been told about the ruby. He dealt with facts in his line of work, and he liked to keep it that way. For now, though, he concluded that he had little choice but to take the existence of the Blood of Rajputana on faith, and go about finding those facts, the first of which was the letter sitting in his lap. Could Jane Hardwick's letters home to her brother really help to identify not only Sinclair's unknown ancestor, but the location of the Blood of Rajputana itself? Did one somehow lead to the other? Tayte had no idea at this point, but as the letter was currently all he had to go on, he picked it up again and continued reading.

Chapter Six

India, September 1822

The carriage had been forced to a standstill, and it quickly became apparent to Jane that the dacoit horsemen who had pursued them were interested in far more than their possessions. As soon as the carriage stopped, Jane heard Arabella scream again. Ignoring the murderous glare from the dacoit ahead of her, she turned to see his two friends pull Arabella from the carriage, tearing her from her mother's arms and throwing her over one of the rider's saddles. Arabella continued to scream and kick until her bonnet flew off, loosening her red-brown hair, but it did her no good.

'Give back my daughter!' Elspeth cried. 'Mr Faraday! Won't you do something?'

At last Faraday raised his head, but Jane knew he could not be counted on to act. She was proved right a moment later when Faraday raised his hands in surrender and sank lower, until he was sitting on the carriage floor. He looked close to tears. It occurred to Jane now that the dacoits knew who Arabella was. Was she a part of the cargo they had come for, expecting that her father would pay a great many rupees to have her back? She thought that had to be why their pursuers had not fired at them.

Jane stood up. She had no idea what she was going to do next, but she had to do something to stop this if she could. No sooner was she on her feet than she saw the dacoit nearest her draw a pistol from the leather belt around his waist. He raised its long barrel towards her and Jane was all too aware that, while the dacoits would spare Arabella's life for the ransom they deemed it to be worth, they cared nothing for hers.

A shot was fired, but it was not Jane who fell.

The sound caused her to close her eyes momentarily. When she opened them again, the dacoit's pistol had dropped to his side. She saw a look of anguish in his eyes before he slowly began to slide off his horse. He hit the ground with a thud as another shot was fired, and Jane's attention was drawn further along the road, not to the south, where the guard was still trying to fight off the main dacoit attack, but to the north, in the direction of Jaipur.

'Troopers!' Jane called for the benefit of those who could not yet see them.

The remaining two dacoits each gave a cry. They kicked their heels hard into their horses' flanks and made off towards the hills, taking Arabella with them. The troopers, Bengal Army Light Cavalry sowars of the Honourable East India Company, arrived in a thunderous roar of blue tunics and stamping hooves, their battle cries designed to instil fear into the hearts of any dacoit who dared to oppose them. They paid Jane and her companions little attention as they passed, and she feared for Arabella all the more, but the two dacoits who had made off with her had not done so unnoticed. Jane saw four riders peel off from the main charge, heading into the hills after them. At that moment she offered a prayer to God that they would bring Arabella back unharmed. She went to comfort the now tearful Elspeth as Faraday got to his feet at last and raised a cheer for their saviours. It was with baited breath that they awaited the outcome of the cavalrymen's pursuit.

Gunfire in the hills soon joined the cacophony of the battle. Jane could no longer see the two dacoit riders, or the sowars who had followed after them. To think that poor Arabella was caught in the midst of their fury sent a chill through her despite the hot sun. Several minutes passed. Then the hills fell silent. A moment later she saw four horses returning, but only three riders. One of the sowars must have fallen.

But where was Arabella?

Jane placed her arm around Elspeth's shoulders as they watched the troopers return. Their horses drew closer, then one turned sideways and a smile spread across Jane's face.

'Look!' she said to Elspeth, pointing. 'There she is. There's Arabella!'

She was sitting on a dappled grey horse behind its rider, clutching him so tightly she seemed afraid to let go. The troopers with him soon left to rejoin the rest of their company as the other continued towards the carriage.

'Merciful God,' Elspeth said under her breath.

She clasped her hands to her mouth, and Jane could see they were trembling. When Elspeth reached for the little black purse around her neck again, Jane felt it her duty to caution her. She held her hand over her friend's as she tried to open it, and it only took a concerned shake of Jane's head to wake Elspeth from the spell her opium pills seemed to have over her. Elspeth nodded back, lowering her arms as the rider and her daughter drew close to the carriage.

'*Namaste*,' Jane said to the young sowar in greeting, bowing her head slightly as she pressed her palms together in front of her chest, her fingers pointing skywards.

'*Namaste*,' the sowar said in reply. Then he turned his horse to the carriage so that Arabella could climb off. He smiled and, in Hindi, said, 'I believe the young memsaab belongs with you.'

As Elspeth and Faraday helped Arabella back into the carriage, Jane studied the young sowar, curious to understand how such courage could manifest itself so readily in one so young; he looked little older than Arabella and cut a fine figure in his tunic and breeches. His dark features were sharp, his eyes a piercing green, and there was no sign of the beard and twirling moustache that were so prevalent among the older sepoys and sowars she had seen. She concluded that he was both a courageous and handsome young man.

Still speaking in Hindi, Jane asked, 'What is your name? How is it that you happened upon us at such a fortuitous time?'

When the young sowar answered, his eyes were not on Jane as he spoke, but on Arabella, who did nothing to avert her own gaze from his obvious attentions. 'I am Naresh Bharat Singh of Kishangarh. I carry important papers to Muhammad Amir Khan, the Nawab of Tonk.'

'Tell him my husband will hear of his bravery,' Elspeth said.

Jane conveyed the message, adding, 'You have rescued the daughter of the Resident at Jaipur.'

Naresh Singh bowed his head towards Arabella, and in reply he said, 'It was my great honour to do so.'

With that, he tugged at his reins, turning his horse away from the carriage before he galloped off to join his company in fending off what remained of the dacoit attack. Everyone watched him leave, but none so intently as Arabella, who was smiling to herself, moon-eyed, despite her ordeal. Then, as if her wish had just come true, the gallant young sowar turned his head back to her, and in that instant Jane had the feeling that this was not the last they would see of him.

Chapter Seven

Present day

Jefferson Tayte spent the morning of his first full day at Drumarthen House poring over Damian Sinclair's extensive research. He had become so engrossed that when he hadn't gone down for lunch, Murray had kindly brought it to him. The meal was a lighter offering than he or any man of his size might have liked, consisting of a bruised apple and a sparingly filled boiled ham sandwich, but he supposed that at this rate, once his assignment was over, he would at least go home to his family a few pounds lighter than when he'd left. All the same, as his appetite was never more healthy than when he was trying to break through a genealogical brick wall, his stomach was soon groaning in protest.

Tayte couldn't fault the work Sinclair had carried out on his family tree. The records he'd seen were as thorough and impeccably organised as if he'd carried out the research himself. Nothing he'd seen came close to shedding any light on who Sinclair's four-times-great-grandfather was, but Tayte was experienced enough to know that such brick walls were rarely, if ever, broken down by looking at the obvious. He had to think his way around this particular problem, hoping to arrive at the answer via alternative, perhaps obscure, means, which was exactly what happened. Yes, Sinclair's research was extensive, but he hadn't thought of everything.

It was mid-afternoon by the time Tayte left his room and headed for the stairs, eager to tell Sinclair about the discovery he'd made. He had one of Sinclair's records in his hand. If he was right, he knew he could have this assignment wrapped up in no time. Jefferson Tayte, the genealogist who cracked a family history mystery no one in the family had been able to solve in years.

'If you're right, JT,' he told himself as he reached the top of the stairs. He was as keen to prove he'd still got what it takes to himself as much as his client.

He was about to head down, keeping to the right as Murray had warned him, when an angry, raised voice coming from the hallway below stopped him in his tracks. The voice was deep and difficult for Tayte to understand at first, on account of the man's heavy Scots accent and the speed at which he spoke.

'He was your brother,' the man said. 'As far as I'm concerned, his debt is now your debt. I'll give you a week to pay or I'll take it out on your hide!'

Tayte wondered whether he should go back to his room. He wasn't one to eavesdrop on other people's conversations, but the visitor's threatening tone told him to wait where he was in case Sinclair needed any assistance. Sinclair, however, did not seem afraid of the man.

'Your bully-boy tactics don't frighten me, Callum Macrae,' he said. 'Jamie's business was his own and nothing to do with me, so you can take your threats elsewhere. If he owed you money, he took that debt to his grave with him, and may God rest his soul.'

'I'm not the only one Jamie borrowed from,' Macrae said. 'The rest of the family will want their money back, too. You can be sure of that.'

'The rest of the family?'

'Aye, and don't stand there and tell me you know nothing about it.'

'About what?' Sinclair said. 'Whatever are you talking about?'

'The syndicate, and the fanciful story your brother had us all believing. Perhaps it's a good thing he is in his grave.'

'Get out of my house, Callum Macrae!' Sinclair said, clearly angered by the other's words; rightly so, as far as Tayte was concerned.

He began to descend the stairs, thinking that a fight might break out at any minute, but then he heard what he thought was the front door being opened.

'I'll go, right enough,' Macrae said. 'But I want my money. You've been warned!'

With that, Tayte heard the door close with a thud.

'Mr Sinclair?' he called, concern in his voice. 'Is everything all right?'

Sinclair turned away from the front door, and as Tayte reached the bottom of the stairs, Sinclair's eyes met his. 'Mr Tayte,' he said, 'I assume you heard all that?'

'Some of it. Where's Murray? It sounded like you could have used his help.'

Sinclair waved a dismissive hand. 'I don't need any help where my cousin Callum Macrae is concerned. He's a bully, nothing more. He was always picking on my Jamie when they were at school, but he knows better than to try it on with me. Murray's out on the estate replacing some old post-and-rail fencing, which is just as well. Those two would have come to blows.'

Sinclair put a hand on Tayte's shoulder and led him to the front door. Opening it, he added, 'It's another fine afternoon. Take a walk with me, won't you? I've not been entirely honest with you and I think it's time I gave you an explanation.'

Tayte was in his shirtsleeves, so he folded the piece of paper he'd brought down to show Sinclair and slipped it into his trouser pocket for now. There was clearly more to this assignment than he knew. Did Sinclair's true motive have something to do with his brother—his late brother—and perhaps the syndicate he'd heard Macrae speak of? As he followed Sinclair outside, he was eager to hear what the man had to say.

'My brother, Jamie, died just two weeks ago,' Sinclair said as he and Tayte began to stroll along the flagstones to their left, in Drumarthen's cool shadow. 'There was a fatal accident inquiry, which has delayed his burial.'

'I'm sorry to hear that,' Tayte offered, thinking it helped to explain Sinclair's drawn appearance.

'Aye, well, Jamie was never bound for old age, that's for sure, although no one expected him to die the way he did. He was something of an adrenaline junkie, you see—an extreme-sports fanatic. Everyone in the family believed it would get the better of him sooner rather than later, but as it turns out, he fell to his death from the top floor of an apartment block in Glasgow, drunk to his eyeballs by all accounts. I had to deal with the nasty business of helping to identify his body, which wasn't easy given the circumstances.'

'No, I'm sure it wasn't.'

'The police told me he'd taken a short-term lease on the apartment barely a month before he died. Apparently, he'd been drinking heavily all that night and into the early morning, which was when he died. There had been complaints about his loud music from some of the other tenants. He wasn't having a party as such. He was all by himself. When the police went in, the French doors that led on to the balcony were wide open. They believe my brother somehow became caught up in the billowing net curtains, which caused him to panic and trip over the railings. The nets were still partially wrapped around his body when he hit the ground.'

'That's just dreadful,' Tayte said, wondering why he detected a degree of doubt in Sinclair's voice. 'So it was an accidental death? Misadventure?'

'So the police say. Jamie's door was deadlocked and bolted. Given he was alone, how could it have been anything but an accident?'

'But you have your doubts? You think he was murdered somehow?'

'Aye,' Sinclair said with a nod, his tone firm and grave. 'For all his faults, Jamie was no drinker for starters. That's not to say he couldn't have taken to the bottle recently. The toxicology report showed an excessive amount of alcohol in his bloodstream, and the apartment was littered with cheap whisky bottles.' Sinclair paused and reached into his trouser pocket. He withdrew his wallet, and from it he produced a small photograph, which he handed to Tayte. 'That's my wee brother, Jamie. I've carried his picture since he died. It was taken around five years ago, soon after Jamie turned forty. As you can see, he was never one to act his age, but I felt this picture best summed up what he was like.'

Tayte studied the photograph. It showed a dark-haired man of good physique, smiling for the camera in nothing more than a pair of skimpy swimming trunks and what appeared to be skiing goggles pushed high up over his forehead. He was covered in brightly coloured paint and there were several large red welts on his skin. He was posing for the camera with his chest stuck out and one hand on his hip. In his other hand was a large paintball gun.

Tayte had to smile at the image. 'That certainly looks like an extreme way to play paintball. He must have been covered in bruises afterwards.'

'Aye, well, that was Jamie for you—always looking for ways to make life more intense.'

'So why do you think he was murdered?'

'For the letters I told you about—the letters written by Jane Hardwick that I believe came into my family's possession via my four-times-great-grandfather. I'd seen them as a child, although I had little interest in them at the time. I never read them, but I knew they were here at Drumarthen. Then, one day, they were gone. As we grew up my brother became something of a wastrel, blowing every penny he could scrape together on surfing and skiing and the like. He bummed his way through life believing, I'm sure, that he'd someday inherit an equal share of this house, but our father saw Jamie for what he was, and he rejected him for it. Murray was more of a father figure to Jamie than his real father ever was. When it came to Drumarthen, our father knew Jamie would sell his share as soon as he could lay his hands on it, and I was inclined to agree with him. So, Drumarthen and all its chattels were left to me alone—minus those letters, of course, which had disappeared by then.'

'Surely you can only speculate that your brother took them.'

'It was speculation, aye, for a very long time. But close to a year ago now, Jamie told me to my face. It was the proverbial straw that broke the camel's back. We quarrelled and I said some hateful things, and that was that. We've not spoken since, which, of course, I fully regret now. They were just letters, or so I thought, but he believed they were more than that. He was of the opinion they were going to lead him to the ruby—to the Blood of Rajputana. That's why I believe someone killed him for them, and somehow made his death appear to be an accident to stop the police asking questions.'

'Have you told the police all this?'

'Of course, but even I can see it for the wild story it appears to be. As far as the police were concerned, my brother's death was an accident. Given the circumstances I can't rightly blame them.'

They came to the corner of the house and passed through a gate into bright sunshine, arriving in a walled parterre garden that showed the same degree of neglect as the rest of the house. It was overgrown with weeds and unkempt climbers, with fallen iron obelisks scattered here and there, quietly rusting away.

Sinclair paused as they entered, turning to Tayte with apologetic eyes. 'I'm sorry I didn't tell you all this in London, Mr Tayte. In truth, my brother's death is the real reason I hired you. After hearing what Callum Macrae had to say just now, I'm all the more certain that Jamie was up to something that ultimately got him killed.'

'Macrae mentioned a syndicate,' Tayte said. 'Do you know anything about it?'

'No. As I said, my brother and I hadn't spoken in a while. It seems he needed money, though, and by all accounts he went to the rest of the family to raise it.'

'To go and look for the ruby?' Tayte offered. 'Just like Cornelius Dredger planned to do when he wrote to your four-times-great-grandfather?'

'Aye, perhaps. It would take the promise of something as valuable as the Blood of Rajputana to get my family to part with their money.'

Sinclair stopped beside a grey oak bench and they both sat down. They were facing the overgrown garden, looking along a weed-ridden pathway that led the eye to the glens and mountains of the Southern Highlands.

'If I'd told you all this when we first met at the East India Club,' Sinclair said, 'I'll wager you'd have run a mile, wouldn't you?'

'Probably,' Tayte said, nodding as he thought about Jean and his son, and how much his life had changed in recent years. Not so long ago, he knew he wouldn't have been put off by the potential risks involved in such an assignment, but that was back when he was living alone in his one-bedroom apartment in DC, with nothing to lose and no one to care if he never came home again.

'Mr Tayte, I was telling you the truth when I said I wanted you to identify my four-times-great-grandfather. As I've said, because of the letters I believe this man called Robert is the key to locating the Blood of Rajputana. It's my hope that if it can be found it will draw my brother's killer out so that he or she can be brought to justice for what they've done. That's my real motive for hiring you.'

'I see,' Tayte said, wondering how he felt about continuing in light of what Sinclair had just told him. If a man had been murdered because of the ruby Sinclair wanted him to find, there was every chance that he would be in harm's way, too.

He drew a long, thoughtful breath before answering. Sinclair had told him that he and the rest of his family had been looking for the gemstone for some considerable time, especially Sinclair, judging from all the records he'd gathered together, yet no harm had come to him or to the rest of his family. The police remained convinced that Jamie Sinclair's death was accidental, and nothing Tayte had just heard gave him reason to believe otherwise. For now at least, that was good enough for him. He thought about the piece of paper in his pocket that he'd brought down to show Sinclair. He was excited about the discovery he'd made. He wanted to continue.

'I don't know whether your brother was murdered or not,' he said, 'but if it'll give you peace of mind over the matter, I'll do my best to help you find out what became of this ruby you've all been looking for.'

'Splendid!' Sinclair said, smiling broadly. 'Now tell me, what have you made of my research so far? You've been in your room all day. I trust you've found it interesting.'

Tayte reached into his trouser pocket and withdrew the piece of paper he'd brought down. He was smiling now, too, as he unfolded it. 'I came across this newspaper clipping from *The Times*. It's dated April 1823.' He handed it to Sinclair who studied it briefly.

'I recall it, yes,' Sinclair said. 'It was written by a journalist called Albert Faraday.' He looked back at Tayte, his expression confused. 'He writes about Jane Hardwick, but it's little more than a glowing account of her accomplishments—the many languages and dialects she speaks and how fine a travelling companion she was. What of it?'

'In itself I'd have to agree that it's of little interest to us,' Tayte said. 'The date caught my attention, though. Given the time it took to send a letter home, or a newspaper report in this case, Faraday's article would have been written around the same time Jane wrote the letter you showed me last night. We know Jane was travelling as companion to a friend and her daughter, and I've been racking my brain trying to think how I might find out who they were. I think it's important, because when Cornelius Dredger wrote to Robert, the man we're trying to identify, he must have done so knowing that Robert was in some way connected with Jane's story, or how would he have known who Robert was in the first place?'

'Aye, that makes sense. Go on.'

'Well, I figured that connection had to come from Jane's letters, which wound up with her great-nephew, Cornelius, and then with your family via Robert—still assuming for now that Robert was your four-times-great-grandfather. If that's true, there has to be a family connection, possibly with the family Jane was travelling with and staying with in Jaipur. At least, that's the idea I'm running with for now.'

Sinclair's forehead began to crease. 'But this newspaper article gives no other names. I can't see how you could possibly learn anything more from it.'

A slow smile spread across Tayte's face. 'I already have. You probably didn't see it because you were so focused on Jane Hardwick at the time.'

Sinclair studied the article again. 'Technically speaking, this is not my research.'

'It's not?'

'No. I have it in my records, but it wasn't my discovery. I wasn't really focused on it at all.'

'Whose was it?'

'I've previously collaborated on our family history research with another cousin of mine—Gordon Drummond. Like Callum Macrae, he's a descendant of one of Lachlan and Aileen Fraser's legitimate sons. He's also the doctor in the family. As such he had the similarly unfortunate job of identifying Jamie's body, and, in his case, dealing with the procurator fiscal—that's the Scottish equivalent of a coroner.'

'Does he have research of his own?'

'Aye, quite a collection, I'm sure. Although you'll no doubt find it similar to my own.'

'Similar perhaps, but I'd like to take a look at it. Maybe there's something in his collection that's not in yours.'

'I'll see if I can arrange it,' Sinclair said. 'He lives in the village, along with most of my family. I'll give him a call. Maybe I can introduce you to him this evening.'

'That would be great.'

Sinclair's eyes returned to the article. He began to shake his head. 'Go on then, Mr Tayte. Tell me what I'm not seeing here.'

'It's going to seem obvious when I tell you,' Tayte said. Then he reached across and tapped the name at the top of the article.

'Albert Faraday?'

Tayte nodded. 'Faraday wrote this article for his travel column about Jane Hardwick, but only Jane Hardwick. He goes on and on about her merits for so long that he's filled the entire article writing just about her. There's no room for anyone else. That set me wondering whether he'd written about his other travelling companions in another article—written about the people who would also have been travelling with Jane at the time.'

'Of course,' Sinclair said. 'And I take it he did just that?'

'Yes, he did,' Tayte said. 'Jane Hardwick was travelling with her good friend, Lady Elspeth Christie, and her daughter, Arabella. They were on their way to meet Elspeth's husband, Sir John Christie of Glentrave.'

'Christie,' Sinclair repeated. 'So it's possible that my four-times-great-grandfather was called Robert Christie. My God, man, I'd heard you were good, but that's quite something. You only arrived yesterday!'

Tayte laughed. 'I brought twenty-plus years of experience with me,' he said, 'and let's not get ahead of ourselves. I've not looked for Robert Christie in the archives yet, let alone proved his relationship.'

'Just the same, it's a fine start.'

'Yes, it is,' Tayte agreed, still smiling to himself as he sat back, and began to wonder who the members of this Christie family were. Given their titles he imagined he would easily be able to find out more about them in *Burke's Peerage*. Then he would dig deeper into their family history, building a picture of their lives in the hope that it might help to unravel the past and reveal the location of the Blood of Rajputana.

Chapter Eight

The Rajmahal Palace had originally been built in 1729 by Maharaja Sawai Jai Singh II on the outskirts of the city, as a private garden-retreat for his beloved wife, Maharani Chandra Kunwar Ranawatji. In 1821, following an alliance between the East India Company and Jaipur State, the palace had become a British residency, home to the Resident at Jaipur, who was the Company's political agent for the area. One morning soon after their arrival at the residency, Jane Hardwick and the young Arabella were enjoying the palace gardens, taking a stroll in the grounds beneath their parasols. Following eagerly after them were the personal servants that had been appointed to them. They were Rajputs, each wearing the red turban that was common to their people.

Arabella's mother was not with them, having made her excuses immediately after breakfast and taken to her bed with some new malady that she would have everyone believe India was entirely responsible for. Having seen Elspeth with her husband on a number of occasions by now, however, it was apparent to Jane that it was he, rather than the country in which Elspeth now resided, that was to blame. Jane did not yet know why the air in this hot climate seemed so cold between them, but she imagined that, given the close company they all shared, it was inevitable that the cause would reveal itself soon enough. She recalled their reunion vividly.

'Arabella!' Sir John had bellowed, a lively spring in his step as he came out to the main gate to meet their carriage.

Sir John had swiftly helped Arabella down, full of smiles as he embraced her. Then, never once letting go of her hand, he blatantly ignored Elspeth's when she offered it to him. Instead, he gave her only the slightest nod to acknowledge her presence as he gestured to the rotund Rajput standing behind him, and said, 'Your servant, Kamala, will take you to your room, madam.' And that was that. As far as Jane was concerned, it was no reward at all for the many months of hardship and toil her friend had endured to get there.

As she and Arabella made their way across the well-tended lawn to the pergola tent that had been erected for them, their arrival at the residency still playing on her mind, Jane asked, 'Before we came to India, how many years was it since you last saw your father?'

Arabella pulled a face as she thought on her answer. Several seconds later she shook her head, and in her gentle Scots accent said, 'I don't exactly know.'

'You mean you were too young to remember?'

'Aye, I suppose so. Why do you ask?'

Jane smiled. 'I was just curious,' she said, although it was the root of her curiosity that had led her to ask the question. Given the obvious lack of affection she had witnessed between Arabella's mother and father, it had occurred to Jane that Arabella was entirely the reason her father had sent for them, rather than his desire to be with his wife again after what was evidently a lengthy absence of several years.

They came to the pergola and sat down beside one another, facing the white-painted palace, with its colonnaded verandas and walkways. Cool drinks were brought to them by another of the many household servants.

'*Dhanyavaad,*' Jane said, thanking the man in his native tongue. Then to Arabella she said, 'You seem so much happier now the journey's over and you're here in Jaipur. Didn't I say you would?' She squinted at her. 'Or is there some other, more romantic reason?'

Arabella fidgeted. 'I'm sure I don't know what you mean.'

'Is that so? Then why are you blushing from ear to ear? You've been thinking about the young sowar who came so gallantly to your rescue, haven't you?'

Arabella's cheeks continued to flush, and Jane laughed. She knew she was teasing Arabella.

'Don't worry,' she said. 'Your secret's safe with me.'

At that moment, voices drew Jane's attention and she turned around to see Arabella's father, Sir John Christie, walking towards them. There was another man with him, a soldier whom she had not seen before. How Sir John could bear to be wrapped so snugly in so many layers of dark clothing on such a hot morning was beyond her. She imagined he must either have become accustomed to it, or was simply too strict in his standards of dress for his own good. He wore knee-length boots over his trousers, a silver-grey waistcoat over his shirt, and a heavily woven forest-green tailcoat over that. At his neck, flowing from his tall shirt collar, was a bright purple cravat. He was a short, stout man, made to appear shorter still by the height of the man standing beside him, despite his top hat. As they approached, Jane and Arabella set their drinks down and stood up.

'Good morning, ladies,' Sir John said, smiling warmly as both men removed their hats. His broad Scots accent and quick manner of speech was at times difficult for the untrained ear to understand. 'I was sorry to have missed you at breakfast this morning, but duty first, eh?' He leaned in and kissed Arabella's cheek. Then he stepped back and gestured to the man standing beside him. 'Arabella, Mrs Hardwick, this fine gentleman is Captain Donnan Fraser. We've been talking about Company affairs all morning and now I'm bored to distraction.' He paused and laughed to himself. 'I told him your company would be just the tonic, so here we are.'

'Good morning to you both,' Fraser said with a bow, his eyes set on Arabella. His accent, although still Scots, was far more pleasing to the ear. 'You've timed your arrival in Jaipur quite well, having missed both the hottest and the wettest months.'

'I can assure you we've had more than our share of both since we arrived in Bombay,' Jane said, drawing his attention from Arabella at last. 'With the monsoon season almost past, we must now bear the humidity that follows.'

Here was another dashing young soldier with eyes for the resident's daughter, she thought, although he was not as young as the gallant sowar they had met on the Tonk road. Jane put Captain Fraser in his early to mid-twenties, several years older than Naresh Bharat Singh. He was dark-haired, tall and slim, with full elongated sideburns framing his angular face. He did indeed cut a fine figure in his red-and-gold braided tunic and his predominantly green tartan trews.

'Have you been long in India, Captain Fraser?'

'A wee while, for sure, Mrs Hardwick. I've found it both a savage country in parts and quite beautiful in others.'

Jane couldn't help but notice the captain's eyes drift back to Arabella again as he finished speaking. 'I fear that's because you must often see a side to India that others do not.'

'Very true,' Fraser said, 'although I hear you've recently witnessed such savagery yourselves. The dacoits are proving to be quite a bother in the area. All the more so, the further north one travels.' He turned to Arabella. 'I hear the blackguards tried to kidnap you. It must have been a terrifying ordeal.'

'Aye, Captain Fraser, it was,' Arabella said. 'I thought I would never see my family again.'

Sir John picked up on the tremor in Arabella's voice as she finished speaking. He placed an arm on her shoulder for comfort. 'Come now, child. That's all in the past. You're here in Jaipur with your family now, under the protection of the Honourable East India Company and this fine house. I'll see you safe, don't worry your pretty little head a moment longer.'

'As shall I,' Fraser said. 'I only wish I'd been there to dispatch those cowardly devils myself. They'd have felt the sharp end of my sword, I can tell you.'

Sir John gave a hearty laugh. 'That's the spirit, captain. You do your regiment proud.'

'Thank you, Captain Fraser,' Arabella said. 'I'm sure you would have been every bit as courageous as the man who did save me.'

'I should like to meet the fellow and shake his hand.'

'He was a young sowar,' Jane said, expecting the information to dampen Fraser's enthusiasm. She wasn't wrong.

'Was he indeed?' Fraser said. 'Well, I suppose they have their uses. Although in my experience the majority of sowars and sepoys in the Company's pay need a solid lesson in hard work and good manners.'

Jane could have laughed at his prejudiced appraisal of the Company's native regiments, who would clearly never measure up to the far superior British in his eyes.

Fraser quickly moved the conversation on, turning his attention back to Arabella. 'Miss Christie,' he said, brightly. 'May I ask how you intend to spend your time in Jaipur now that you've arrived?'

'I really hadn't given much thought to the matter, captain.'

Fraser inched closer to her. 'You would do me a great honour if you would call me Donnan.'

Arabella's blush returned to her cheeks. 'I hardly know you well enough.'

Fraser smiled, playfully. 'Maybe not yet, but it is my hope to rectify that disadvantage as my duties allow. Perhaps you would permit me to escort you on a tour of the city.'

'That's a splendid idea,' Sir John said. 'You must arrange it at your earliest convenience.'

'I shall be most glad to,' Fraser said, without waiting to hear whether Arabella wished to accept his offer.

Noting her father's enthusiasm, Jane had the feeling it was not an offer Arabella was at liberty to refuse. She was about to say that it would be good for both Arabella and herself to become better acquainted with the area, letting the captain know that she fully intended to join any such excursion, when out of the corner of her eye she saw three lizards scurrying towards them. They reminded her of an Indian superstition she'd heard as a child: three lizards for marriage. Was this the cause of Sir John's enthusiasm, and the real reason for this journey to India? Did an understanding exist between him and Captain Fraser over his daughter's hand that Arabella was as yet unaware of?

The thought had no sooner crossed Jane's mind than she saw something that made her shiver, despite the heat of the morning. A fourth lizard had joined the others, and all were now scurrying towards the pergola. According to the superstition this was another matter altogether, but then it was just a superstition, wasn't it?

Four lizards, Jane thought. *Four lizards for an upcoming death.*

But whose?

Chapter Nine

'You're visiting a lovely part of Scotland,' Sinclair said as he drove Tayte along a narrow, stone-walled road that was bordered by trees to their left and the River Earn to their right. The car windows were wound all the way down, which amplified the unhealthy clatter of the old car's engine as the sound reverberated between the stonework. 'Comrie's an historic conservation village,' he continued. 'It's won many awards for its outstanding natural beauty.'

'It's like stepping back in time,' Tayte said, marvelling at the lack of people and motorised vehicles. He wouldn't have been surprised to see a horse and cart coming their way, or a coal barge heading along the river.

'Aye, I suppose it is. It's always nice to come home, and all too easy to take for granted. You might be surprised to hear that we experience more than our fair share of earth tremors here in Comrie.'

'Earthquakes?' Tayte said, associating such things more with places like California and the Pacific Northwest. 'Are we sitting on a fault line?'

'We are indeed. The Highland Boundary Fault to be specific. Comrie's not nicknamed the "shaky toun" for nothing.'

They came to the village and Tayte's eyes immediately fell on a white building with a slate-tiled roof and steeple, glowing in the early-evening sunshine. 'Is that the parish church up ahead?' he asked, pointing towards it.

'It's the Comrie Community Centre these days,' Sinclair said. 'The parish church is further along the road. A wee bit further still and you'll come to St Margaret's Catholic Church.' Sinclair pointed out of the window to his left. 'The mountain you can see directly behind the village there to the north is called Ben Chonzie. It forms part of the Grampian mountain range, which you've no doubt heard of.'

Tayte hadn't, but he didn't want to disappoint Sinclair, so he just smiled as they turned off the main road to their right, crossing the river. 'I saw the main road back there was called Drummond Street,' he said, 'and here we are on our way to see Dr Drummond. Any connection?'

'Quite possibly,' Sinclair said. 'The Drummond bloodline in this area goes back a fair way.'

The car slowed down and Sinclair pulled over outside a stone townhouse. It had four mullioned windows set close together on two levels, and a central front door that was no more than a few feet from the road on the other side of a narrow pavement.

'Here we are,' Sinclair said. 'When I spoke to Gordon earlier, he sounded keen to make your acquaintance.'

Tayte had brought his briefcase with him, in which he now had printouts of the further records he'd spoken to Sinclair about, written by Mr Albert Faraday of *The Times*. He'd made a note to look into what else Faraday had written, but for now he intended to focus on trying to find out if there was anyone called Robert in the Christie family. Perhaps the doctor had come across the name during his research, even if he hadn't been able to connect it at the time. He picked up his briefcase and followed Sinclair out of the car, joining him at the front door as he knocked.

'A cup of tea would go down well about now,' Sinclair said. 'Or perhaps something a wee bit stronger, eh?'

'A hot drink sounds good,' Tayte said, not wishing to cloud his head while he was on the job.

Sinclair checked his watch and knocked again. 'It's six o'clock sharp. We're bang on time. I do hope he hasn't had to go out on a house call.'

Not waiting for an answer, Sinclair left Tayte on the doorstep and went to one of the windows to look inside.

'No lights on. No sign of activity. It doesn't look good. Give that knocker another bang, would you.'

Tayte knocked again, loud enough for anyone inside to have heard. Sinclair checked the other window.

'Same this side,' Sinclair said. Then he came back to Tayte, opened the letterbox and called, 'Gordon! Are you in there?'

Tayte thought he heard Sinclair's voice falter as he finished the sentence. As Sinclair stood up again and turned to Tayte, his expression had darkened, as if he'd seen something as he looked through the letterbox and couldn't quite believe his eyes.

'What is it?' Tayte asked. 'What's wrong?'

Sinclair's mouth was agape, his features suddenly lined with confusion. 'I think it's Gordon,' he said. 'I think he's dead.'

A short while later, the immediate area around Gordon Drummond's house had been cordoned off by the police. Tayte and Sinclair were standing in the street outside, waiting to speak with the senior officer, Detective Inspector Alastair Ross, who Sinclair appeared to know. Behind them, the crime scene examiners in their white overalls were recording the scene and gathering potential forensic evidence, leaving little doubt in the minds of the onlookers watching from beyond the police cordon tape that they were dealing with a murder.

'Thanks for your patience, Damian,' DI Ross said to Sinclair as he joined them. 'Who's this you have with you?'

'I'm Jefferson Tayte,' Tayte said, introducing himself with a firm handshake that was well met.

'Mr Tayte's a family historian,' Sinclair added. 'I've hired him to try to identify my four-times-great-grandfather.'

'Have you indeed?' Ross said, running a thumb and forefinger slowly out and down over his 1970s walrus moustache as he took Tayte in. 'From what I've heard you'll have your work cut out for you there, Mr Tayte.'

'Detective Inspector Ross is an old friend of the family,' Sinclair told Tayte, as if to explain how the detective knew about Sinclair's family history brick wall.

'I see,' Tayte said. 'I take it the man we saw through the letterbox when we arrived earlier was murdered?' No one had formally told them and he wanted clarification.

'He was,' Ross said. 'The good doctor was stabbed in the chest with what appears to be one of his own kitchen knives.'

'I knew it as soon as I saw him lying there at the foot of the stairs,' Sinclair said. 'Will you listen to me now, Alastair? Gordon was closer to my brother than most. Now they're both dead. There has to be a connection.'

'Aye, and you'll no doubt want me to believe it's connected to this fabled ruby you're all after. I've told you many times before—Jamie's death was an accident. He was alone when he died. His apartment door was locked and bolted. The only way in or out was via the balcony your brother fell from.'

'What about the balconies to either side of his?' Sinclair protested. 'Surely someone could have left via one of those.'

Ross shook his head. 'You know full well we checked with every occupant on your brother's floor—the only balconied floor of the building, I might remind you. No one saw or heard a thing, and there was no way down from there other than to go through someone else's apartment. Your brother had his problems. He was drunk to his hind teeth that night, and he met with a fatal accident as a result. It's time to let it go.'

'I can't let it go,' Sinclair said. 'Especially now Gordon's been murdered. Just why do you think that is, inspector? He was a well-liked and respected man. Who would want to do such a thing? Why?'

Ross drew a deep breath and sighed. 'I can see you're upset, Damian, and rightly so. Your brother's death was a tragedy, and now this. You want answers and I promise I'll do my best to get them for you. I'll even keep an open mind about Jamie, although heaven knows I've already lost more hair than I can afford to over the matter. Right now, though, I've no reason to challenge the procurator fiscal's verdict.'

'An open mind is all I ask for,' Sinclair said, his tone softening. He turned away, looking back along the street momentarily. 'I only spoke to Gordon a few hours ago. I can't believe he's gone from us so soon after my brother.'

'It's a terrible business,' Ross said. 'What did you and Mr Tayte come to see Gordon about?'

Tayte answered. 'I wanted to talk to him about his family history research. I thought the records he'd gathered over the years could be useful to me.'

'Did anyone else know you were coming here?'

'Only Murray,' Sinclair said. 'Why do you ask?'

Ross took out a small notebook from the inside pocket of his navy-blue suit jacket. 'It just strikes me as odd that he should be murdered just as you're on your way to see him. There are no signs of forced entry. Nothing appears to have been disturbed. I've little doubt Gordon knew his killer, but that doesn't help us too much on this occasion. As the village doctor it's fair to say that Gordon Drummond knew just about everyone.'

Sinclair scoffed. 'Surely you don't think Murray had anything to do with this?'

'It's just a name to write in my wee book,' Ross said. 'That's all it is for now.'

Tayte began to wonder at the timing, too. Perhaps the detective was right. Perhaps Tayte's visit had triggered Drummond's murder. 'You might want to check that the doctor's research hasn't been stolen,' he said, supposing it could be the reason Drummond was now dead. 'Maybe someone didn't want me to see it.'

'Aye, we'll do that,' Ross said, and before he could continue, Sinclair cut in.

'If you're looking for suspects to write in your notebook,' he said, 'you should know that Callum Macrae came to Drumarthen to see me this afternoon.'

'Callum knew you were coming here, too?'

'Perhaps. Maybe he parked alongside the burn after he left and came back. If he did, he might well have overheard my telephone conversation with Gordon. I was out on the drive at the time.'

'There are plenty of ifs, buts and maybes in there,' Ross said. 'What did Callum want to see you about?'

'He wanted money. He said something about a family syndicate my brother was tied up in, and that he died owing him and the other syndicate members money. He came to Drumarthen insisting I was now responsible for Jamie's debts. I told him where to go, despite his threatening behaviour.'

'That sounds just like Callum Macrae,' Ross said. 'Did he say why Jamie owed money to him and the rest of this syndicate?'

'No, but knowing Jamie and the family as I do, I have a pretty good idea. They certainly wouldn't lend him money to go off kite-surfing. It had to be something with a payout at the end of it, and the only thing that springs to mind is the ruby. I told you Jamie had those old letters from India. He must have seen something that made him believe he knew where the ruby was, and he borrowed money to go off and find it. Maybe he did. Maybe that's why he's dead.'

'Or maybe he didn't. Maybe he took his own life because he came back empty-handed and couldn't face the music, owing money to the wrong kind of people. As much as I hate to say it about your family, Damian, I wouldn't choose to borrow money from the majority of them, especially if I knew there was a risk I wouldn't be able to pay it back.'

'And that's coming from a policeman,' Tayte interjected, although his comment seemed to fall on deaf ears. It made him feel that his opinion where this particular family was concerned was unwelcome. He knew that if he was to continue with the assignment he would have to tread carefully.

If he was to continue.

That Jamie Sinclair had been murdered because of the ruby that was bound up in his assignment was pure speculation at this point. The doctor, however, had most certainly been murdered, and whether his death was because of the assignment or not, it cast a whole new light on the matter. He had some serious thinking to do.

Ross stepped back towards the house. 'I want to know who these syndicate members are,' he said as he went. 'I'll speak to Callum. Maybe we can get everyone together at Drumarthen tomorrow evening. It'll save me visiting them individually and I don't think I want to bring them all into the station just now.'

'It's been a long while since we've had a family gathering at Drumarthen,' Sinclair said, sounding none too keen. Then he began to nod as he seemed to come around to the idea. 'But perhaps it's high time we did.'

'Very good then,' Ross said. 'I'll be in touch.'

Chapter Ten

After dinner that evening, Tayte and Sinclair retired to the drawing room for a glass of whisky, which Tayte was coming to believe was something of a ritual with Sinclair. On this day in particular Tayte wasn't about to turn his offer down. Neither had shown much of an appetite during dinner, despite Murray's considerable efforts in the kitchen, having prepared a tasty dish of haggis and mashed swede, served with steamed cabbage.

'I thought you might appreciate some traditional Scottish fare,' Murray had said as he'd set Tayte's plate down in front of him.

On any other day Tayte would have devoured it, but not today.

They sat facing the fire, as they had the night before. Tayte noticed that Sinclair was studying him more than usual. 'What is it?' he asked. 'Did I get haggis on my shirt?'

Sinclair gave a small laugh. 'No, I've just been thinking you were very quiet during dinner, and with good reason. Gordon's death is going to shock the entire community.'

'I take it he lived alone?'

'Aye, his wife died around five years ago now. They were happily married for close to thirty. It's a blessing she didn't have to endure this.'

'Did they have any children?'

'Just the one. A girl. She married and moved south to England some time ago. Birmingham, I believe. The news will devastate her, as it will all the family. I expect most of them will have heard by now.'

Sinclair picked up the whisky bottle, eyeing the level as he did so. 'We're going to need another one of these in a wee while,' he said as he measured out what was left into their glasses. He sat back and began to study Tayte again. 'You're wondering whether or not you want to continue with this, aren't you?'

'Yes, I am,' Tayte said. There was no use being coy about it. 'What if Dr Drummond really was murdered because of what I'm looking into here, or because of what he might have been able to tell me? If that's the case, who's to say I won't also be in danger if I carry on?'

'But it's not necessarily the case now, is it?'

'How do you mean?'

'I mean, if it were, why kill Gordon now? He's been looking into our family history longer than I have. And I've spoken to him a great many times about it during my own research. No one has wanted to kill him over it before, and no one has tried to kill me, either, for that matter. I have to remind you that most of my family have conducted such research at one time or another. So why kill the doctor over it? And why now? I can't believe it's because his killer thought he knew who my four-times-great-grandfather was, or that he might tell you something that would lead you to the Blood of Rajputana. Gordon didn't know. I'm sure whoever killed him did so for another reason, although it's possible that our going to see him today may have triggered it.'

'But why?' Tayte said, thinking aloud.

'At this point, who can say? What I'm getting at here is that Gordon's death could be entirely unrelated to your assignment. If his records aren't missing, will you at least consider that while making your decision as to whether or not you want to continue?'

Tayte thought about it. If the doctor's records were still at his house, then it seemed logical that Sinclair was right—going to see the doctor to talk about his records wasn't the reason he was dead. A big part of him still wanted to continue, and he concluded that until they heard more from DI Ross about the matter, he had no idea whether the doctor's murder was connected to his assignment or not.

'I'm going to have to sleep on it,' he said. 'Before I do I want to talk to my wife about it, too. See what she thinks.'

'Of course you must. It's not a decision to be made lightly.' Sinclair picked up his glass and added, '*Slàinte!*'

'*Slàinte!*' Tayte repeated, and they both drained their glasses.

'I'll fetch that other bottle,' Sinclair said. 'That wee drop barely touched the sides.'

Sinclair stood up, and Tayte's eyes followed him to an old oak sideboard that was set against the wall beneath a threadbare tapestry behind them. As Sinclair opened one of the cupboards, Tayte thought he heard him catch his breath. When he returned, he seemed to have forgotten all about the whisky. Instead, in his hand were several pieces of paper—old paper by the look of it.

'I found this at the back of the shelf,' Sinclair said, sounding bewildered. He unfolded the sheets of paper and glanced over them. 'It's one of Jane Hardwick's letters.'

'You didn't know it was there?' Tayte said with a sense of creeping scepticism.

'No, it's an old sideboard. The letter could have been there for some time. I go to it regularly for my whisky, though. I'm sure I'd have noticed it before now.'

'Yes, I'm sure you would,' Tayte said, suddenly wondering whether Sinclair had conveniently produced the letter at this opportune moment simply to draw him further into Jane's story—a hook to help sway his decision in favour of carrying on with the assignment.

'You don't think I put it there, do you?' Sinclair said, clearly reading Tayte's body language. 'Why on earth would I do that?'

'So how did it get there? Murray?'

Sinclair shook his head. 'No, but I'll be sure to ask him whether he knows anything about it just the same.'

Another explanation occurred to Tayte then, and he was reminded of the figure he'd seen by the burn the evening he'd arrived. It sent a shiver through him. 'This morning you told me you thought your brother may have been murdered for these letters, which you said he told you he had.'

'That's right,' Sinclair said, clearly understanding what Tayte was thinking. 'So maybe whoever took the letters from him put this one in there, knowing I'd find it as soon as I went for another bottle of whisky, which wouldn't have been long given the other bottle was sitting there almost empty.'

'What if your brother gave them to someone else before he died?' Tayte offered. It was another possibility he thought Sinclair might have overlooked given his determination to prove his brother had been murdered.

'Aye, it's possible,' Sinclair said, a little tentatively. 'The bigger question for now, however, is why put it there at all? Someone clearly wants us, or rather wants you, to read it.'

'But why only one letter? I mean, if whoever put it in your sideboard wants us to know Jane Hardwick's story, why not put them all in there?'

'That's another very good question,' Sinclair said, 'and one to which I'm afraid I have no answer. Here,' he added, passing the letter to Tayte. 'Perhaps you'd better read it.'

Tayte took the letter and noted it was dated September 1822, the same month in which Jane and her companions, whom he now knew to be Lady Elspeth Christie and her daughter Arabella, arrived in Jaipur. As he began to read, he became so caught up in Jane's story again that he soon forgot about the letter itself, and the implications of how it had suddenly turned up at Drumarthen House.

Chapter Eleven

Jaipur, September 1822

'There really is nowhere better to discover India than through the sensory delights of the bazaar,' Jane said to Arabella as they ambled towards the tents and stalls of the city's largest street market, their white, high-waisted dresses gently flapping in the light breeze.

'It smells awful,' Arabella said, raising a scented handkerchief to her nose.

Jane threw her head back and drew a deep breath, taking it all in as they entered the bazaar's bustling periphery. 'It smells of India,' she said. 'The livestock and the honest sweat of the traders, the spices and the hot dust at our feet combined. I've always thought it a homely smell.'

'There you have the advantage of growing up in India, Jane. I'm sure I shall never become accustomed to it.'

'Give it time, Bella. India is full of surprises.'

The bazaar was a bright and colourful place, with swathes of silk, cotton and other textiles in all colours of the rainbow, flapping in the breeze in every direction Jane looked. Their vibrancy was matched only by the spices of the food stalls, and the prolific Indian beads—a string or two of which a young Indian boy would every now and then try to sell to them until he was chased away by one or the other of their personal servants, who were never more than two steps behind them. Beggars, young and old, were a permanent presence in such places, and Jane had come well prepared for them, handing out a few rupees here and there as if gradually buying their way into the heart of the bazaar. The air buzzed, not only with flies, but with the cacophony of ages boiled down into one steaming pot of ordered chaos.

'I do hope my father won't be upset at our having come here today,' Arabella said as they paused at one of the textile stalls. 'Perhaps I should have waited to ask him.'

'Your father is a very busy man,' Jane said, brushing the back of her hand over a piece of cloth she was admiring. 'We might have waited all day.' She turned to Arabella. 'Don't worry yourself. Sometimes it's better to seek forgiveness than to ask permission. Besides, your mother said it was all right, didn't she?'

Arabella frowned. 'My mother would have agreed to just about anything. I do wish she would stop taking those pills. She hasn't been herself since Bombay.'

'No,' Jane said, concern in her tone. 'I'll make a point of talking to her about it. I'd hoped she would give them up once the journey was over, but now we're here I see she has another need for them.'

'My father?'

Jane wasn't surprised by Arabella's reply. She thought the entire household must have observed the bitterness between Sir John and Lady Elspeth by now.

'I heard them quarrelling again this morning,' Arabella continued. 'Did your parents love one another? Please tell me they did. I have to believe it possible.'

Jane gave a small sigh. 'I'm afraid I couldn't say. I never really knew my English mother. India took her soon after I was born.'

'I'm sorry,' Arabella offered. 'So why is it you still love this country so much?'

'It wasn't India's fault. I suppose if I were looking to apportion blame for my mother's death, I would blame my father for bringing her here. I'd say he should have left her in England with my brother, who was attending boarding school at the time. But it wasn't my father's fault, either. How was he to know what the future held?'

'Your English mother?' Arabella said, seeking clarification.

'Yes, she was my birth mother, of course, but I was raised by a native woman called Sumana, whom I regarded as my Indian mother. She and my father never married, but I do know that they came to love each other very much indeed. My father died when I was about your age, and although I was no longer in India when Sumana died, I know from her letters that she continued to love his memory to her dying breath.'

'That sounds very romantic,' Arabella said, her faith in love seemingly restored. 'I wish my father loved my mother, even just a wee bit. I really don't know why he wanted us here.'

Since meeting Captain Donnan Fraser, Jane thought she knew well enough, but she didn't go into it. 'Perhaps things will soon settle down,' she said. 'Your father has become too accustomed to his own company, and your mother needs time to adjust to her new life in India. It's been a terrible wrench for both of you.'

'I'm not taking pills.'

'No, but you're young,' Jane said. 'And something else has lifted your spirits, I'm sure of it.' She smiled at Arabella. 'I had thought it was on account of the young sowar, Bharat Singh. Now I can't decide whether your continued good nature is because of him or Captain Fraser.'

Arabella's face broke into a smile. Then she rocked her shoulders self-consciously and turned away. 'I should like to buy something to remember our day out by,' she said, changing the subject. 'Perhaps some beads.'

They moved on, quickly coming to a food stall, where Arabella paused. She turned to their servants and said, 'Rashmi, Pranil, whatever is this odd-looking dish?'

Rashmi, a tall, middle-aged Rajput with a twirled moustache and a long grey beard that was tied at the back of his head, stepped closer to see what Arabella was pointing to. 'It is called *Eri Polu*, young mem-saab,' he said, his accented English very good. 'It is a delicacy from Assam, made from the pupa of the Eri silkworm.'

Arabella pulled a sour face at the thought of eating such a thing. 'Thank you,' she said, and quickly moved on. To Jane, she whispered, 'I thought they were sausages,' and they both laughed.

'Beads!' Arabella said a moment later, and Jane followed her excited steps to a colourful stall full of dangling beads and trays of bangles.

'If you're going to buy some,' Jane said, 'let me do the haggling.'

Arabella gazed up at the vast array of beads on offer, full of smiles and wonder. 'I should very much like to, but it's overwhelming. Which to choose?'

'How about these?' Jane said, indicating a string of blue-green stones. 'They match your eyes perfectly.'

At that point, a brightly dressed girl, no older than Arabella, rose up from behind the stall, her midriff exposed between her red *gagra* skirt and the cropped hem of her yellow *choli* blouse. As with so many Hindu women, she had a red *bindi* mark between her eyebrows, although Jane was drawn more to the long branch in her hand, which she used to lift the blue-green beads down for Arabella to try on.

'*Sundar!*' the girl said, smiling broadly as soon as they were around Arabella's neck.

Arabella looked to Jane for translation.

'She says they're beautiful.'

Arabella nodded and smiled back at the girl.

'How much?' Jane asked in Hindi.

'Only seven rupees,' the girl answered in her native tongue.

'I'll give you four.'

The girl's head began to wander from side to side. 'I can accept five, and not one rupee less or my mother will beat me.'

Jane reached into her reticule and handed five rupees to the girl.

'*Bahut dhanyavaad,*' the girl said, thanking Jane very much.

They were about to leave when a man in dusty, tattered apparel stopped at the bead stall beside Arabella. Jane took him for a beggar at first, but when he turned to them she saw his bright young eyes and recognised him at once. It was the young sowar, Naresh Bharat Singh. He smiled at them, his teeth bright against his dark skin, which was as dirty as his dust-covered sandals.

Arabella gasped at seeing him. Then she returned his smile, scrunching her brow in confusion as she said, 'It is you. But however did you find me? Surely you're not here by coincidence.'

Bharat Singh answered in words Arabella could not understand. Then he reached a hand towards her and between his slender fingers was a folded piece of paper. Arabella took it, just as her servant, Pranil, a younger, stockier man than Rashmi, similarly moustachioed with a full dark beard that tapered to a point on his chin, placed his hands on Bharat Singh's shoulders and turned him away. Clearly he had taken the sowar for a beggar as Jane initially had. Bharat Singh was still smiling at Arabella as he left, despite Pranil's angry face and the threatening tone of his voice.

'I should have liked him to stay long enough to thank him for rescuing me,' Arabella said to Jane as Bharat Singh became lost to the crowd. 'What did he say?'

'He simply said that you are the resident's daughter.'

'Of course. He therefore knew I'd be staying with my father at the residency?'

Jane nodded. 'He must have followed us when we left this morning, which is no doubt why he's disguised as a beggar.'

Arabella unfolded the note in her hand. 'Here,' she said, whispering as she handed it to Jane. 'What does it say?'

The note was written in Hindi. Jane had no trouble reading it. 'He'd like very much to see you again.'

'Where?' Arabella asked, sounding more than a little excited.

'He says to look for him by the stream outside the main gate of the residency tomorrow evening at five o'clock. He'll be looking for you.'

Arabella clasped her hands together and drew them to her chest. 'I can thank him then,' she said. 'You'll come with me, of course.'

'Of course,' Jane said, as if there were no question about it. 'I could hardly let you go without a chaperone, and however would you hold a conversation together otherwise? But aren't you going to ask your father's permission first?' she added, smiling playfully, already knowing the answer.

'Heavens no!' Arabella said. 'I'll take your advice and seek his forgiveness afterwards if I have to.'

Jane laughed, and as they made their way out of the bazaar, she continued to smile to herself. Arabella's obvious excitement at seeing Naresh Bharat Singh again had fully satisfied her that it was the young sowar, not Captain Fraser, who was the cause of her improved mood of late. But how were they to meet Bharat Singh the following evening without the presence of their personal servants? Rashmi and Pranil had barely left their sides for a moment since their arrival in Jaipur.

Jane put that little problem to one side for now as she began to wonder what repercussions Arabella's interest in the young sowar might have, especially in light of the arrangement Arabella's father seemed to have with Captain Fraser over his daughter. Jane would do nothing to help decide Arabella's affections for her—as far as she was concerned they were Arabella's alone to make—but she sensed that the path ahead, should Arabella choose to take it, would not be an easy one.

Chapter Twelve

Jaipur, September 1822

It was several minutes after five in the afternoon when Jane and Arabella slipped out through the residency's main gate, which meant that Arabella was already a few minutes late for her meeting with the young sowar, Naresh Bharat Singh.

'I hope he hasn't already left,' Arabella said as they headed towards the stream that ran its course a hundred yards or so to the front of the residency, where several people could be seen coming and going.

They were both peering ahead, beneath shawls that were draped over their heads and shoulders, trying to single Bharat Singh out. But how would he appear today? Jane found herself wondering whether he would be in disguise again.

'My dear Bella,' she said. 'I have little doubt that he would wait here all night before giving up on the chance to see you again. If you really want something to worry yourself about, spare a thought for poor Pranil, who is diligently waiting outside your bedroom, where you have apparently retired for the evening having taken too much sun. Worry instead at how your father will react should it be discovered that you are no longer there.'

'I'm not worried about my father,' Arabella said as they drew closer to the water—close enough to hear its gentle course as it babbled over the rocks.

'Really?'

Arabella paused before answering. 'Well, perhaps just a little.'

Jane smiled at her. 'Exciting, though, isn't it?'

Arabella giggled. 'Aye, very.'

It was just over an hour before sunset, the orange sun sinking inexorably over the plain, lending its golden aura to everything it touched. There were a number of *dhobi wallahs* at the edge of the stream, tirelessly washing clothes. On the other side an old man with a long stick was leading his goats to a suitable place to drink from. There appeared to be no sign of Bharat Singh.

'You see. He's not here,' Arabella said, sounding dejected.

'Well, even if he isn't, it's a lovely evening for a stroll beside the stream. Perhaps his duties have kept him away.'

'Or he's changed his mind.'

Jane shook her head. 'I doubt that very much.'

They watched the washerwomen as they waited, then they began to amble along the bank, which was dotted here and there with lemon trees and firebush shrubs with their clusters of scarlet-orange tubular flowers. Arabella noted movement among the flowers, and as they came closer her face lit up.

'They're sunbirds,' Jane told her as they looked on at the colourful display.

'They're tiny.'

Jane nodded. 'They're the only birds in the region small enough to drink the firebush nectar.'

At length they turned back towards the residency. The sun dipped lower and their shadows grew longer. Jane was about to suggest they return home, when on the other side of the stream she saw a cloud of dust rising. She thought at first that it was a small dust devil whirling on the plain, but a moment later she heard the unmistakable sound of galloping hooves. She pointed, drawing Arabella's attention to what was now clearly a lone rider on a fine dappled grey horse.

It was Naresh Bharat Singh.

When he reached the stream, his horse did not stop. It leapt clean over it, whinnying as it came to an abrupt stop on the near side, not ten feet from Jane and the now palpitating Arabella. Its rider was quick to dismount, and he was on his knees before them in seconds.

'Humble apologies, memsaab,' he said to Arabella, bowing his head.

'*Namaste*, Naresh Bharat Singh,' Arabella replied, having picked up a few Hindi words from Jane. 'I had no idea you spoke English?'

Bharat Singh got to his feet, standing tall and handsome in his blue trooper's uniform. He removed his hat and tucked it under his arm. 'Only little and very poor,' he said. 'But for you, I try.'

'That's very sweet,' Arabella said. 'But you spoke Hindi at the bazaar yesterday, and your note—that was also written in Hindi.'

'I was too—' Bharat Singh paused, as if searching for the right word. Then, seemingly unable to recollect it, he said, '*Sharminda.*'

'Ashamed,' Jane said, helping him out.

'Yes. I was too ashamed.'

'There's really no need to be,' Arabella said. 'Your English is far better than my Hindi. I hardly speak a word. Perhaps we could teach one another.'

Bharat Singh looked to Jane for translation.

'You must speak more slowly, Bella,' she said. Then she translated Arabella's words.

Bharat Singh was smiling broadly by the time Jane had finished. 'Very much would I like that,' he said, 'for I have much to learn.'

At that point, Bharat Singh lurched forward until he was almost touching Arabella. He paused momentarily, gazing into her eyes. Then, as the shock of what had just happened registered on his face, he backed awkwardly away again, stooping to pick up his hat, which had been knocked to the ground by the muzzle of his horse as it nudged him.

'Humble apologies once more,' he said, turning to his horse, taking it firmly by the reins. 'Nilakantha is very bad horse. She will have no supper.'

'I think she's a lovely horse,' Arabella said, stepping closer to stroke her mane. 'She just wanted to be introduced, that's all.'

'It is you who are lovely,' Bharat Singh said. '*Sundar*.'

Arabella had learned what *sundar* meant from the bazaar the day before. To hear Bharat Singh say that she was beautiful caused her cheeks to glow. She averted her gaze from his, using the horse as a screen until the young sowar's eyes found hers again.

Jane came to her rescue, although she wasn't convinced that Arabella wanted to be rescued from Bharat Singh's attentions. '*Nilakantha* means sky flower, if I'm not mistaken.'

Bharat Singh turned to her. 'Yes,' he said. 'She is called Sky Flower, after *jhaadee*.'

'After the shrub,' Jane said, translating the word for Arabella's benefit.

Arabella came around to the horse's muzzle again. She held her hand close to its nostrils, allowing it to draw in her scent. 'Sky Flower,' she said, smiling at the horse as she nestled her head into the soft hair of her neck. 'I like that name very much.'

'Miss Arabella! Mrs Hardwick!'

Startled at hearing their names, both turned away from the stream in unison towards the call that had come from the direction of the residency. Three men were marching with purpose towards them. There were two guards. At their head was Captain Fraser.

'It is you,' Fraser said as he and the guards approached. 'Thank heavens. The whole household was worried for your safety. Didn't Sir John explicitly tell you not to leave the residency without a guard or escort, and certainly not without telling anyone?' He paused, studying the young sowar and his horse. 'Who's this you're with?'

'Respectfully, sir, I am Naresh Bharat Singh of Kishangarh.'

'Bharat Singh?' Fraser said as he seemed to recall the name. They continued to converse in Hindi. 'Well, what are you doing here, man? Shouldn't you be with your company?'

'I am on very important business.'

'What business sees you loitering here at the stream, bothering these fine ladies?'

Jane wanted to correct Fraser's assumption that they were being bothered by the sowar, but she bit her tongue.

'I am delivering dispatches to the Resident at Jaipur from the Governor-General of Rajputana himself. My horse has ridden long and hard and was in need of water.'

Fraser gave a low harrumph. 'Well, get about your business, man, or I shall have words with your commanding officer.' He turned to Arabella. 'Now, if you'd care to follow me, Miss Arabella, I'll see you safely back to your father.'

Arabella was about to comply when Jane spoke. 'We're in no danger here, captain. We'll come back when we're good and ready.'

Fraser's eyes bored into hers. 'I don't believe I was addressing you, madam. You can do whatever pleases you, but I have my orders to take the resident's daughter back to her father where she belongs.'

Arabella put a hand on Jane's arm, as if to tell her it was all right—that she would return with the captain as he had commanded. Before she did, however, she turned to Bharat Singh and whispered, 'When shall I see you again? How?'

To know that Arabella wanted to see him again must have filled the sowar's heart with joy, because his eyes were smiling more than ever as he replied, 'Do not worry, memsaab. I will find a way.'

Chapter Thirteen

Present day

Jefferson Tayte awoke to the sound of a shotgun being fired. The first loud boom caused him to twitch in his bed as he stirred. The second woke him more fully. He'd had such a fitful night, dreaming of India, of being chased by unseen figures, and of murder, that at first he was unsure whether or not he was still in the dream. As he took in his surroundings, however, he quickly realised that the shotgun was not being fired at him, but was coming from somewhere in the near distance outside. He imagined Murray must be out on the estate trying to bag something for their dinner.

Tayte wondered what he would serve today, and whether he'd still be around to find out. When he'd called Jean the night before, she'd told him she was worried about him—of course she was—but sensing his desire to continue, she'd said it was up to him, that he should do whatever felt right. A part of Tayte had wanted her to tell him to come home. It would have removed the burden of having to make the decision for himself. Now it was all on him. Was he overreacting to the situation? He told himself again that Jamie Sinclair's death could well have been an accident, and Dr Drummond's murder could be completely unrelated to his assignment. And yet, given the way in which another of Jane Hardwick's letters had turned up at Drumarthen the night before, he wasn't so sure. One way or another, there was certainly more going on here than he could as yet see.

As far as the letter was concerned, Tayte could only conclude that someone was trying to help him. Why else leave one of Jane's letters in the sideboard for Sinclair to find? If that was the case, then Tayte perceived no immediate threat to himself from whoever had put it there. He was, however, curious about their motive. In the letter, he'd read of a blossoming romance between Arabella Christie and a young Indian boy, and he'd been able to add another name to his list of people to look into: Captain Donnan Fraser.

Was he in some way significant? The Fraser name was hard to ignore. It connected generations of Damian Sinclair's family. After reading the letter the night before, Sinclair had told him he'd never heard of Donnan Fraser, which was perhaps not surprising as his research had been more concerned with his biological bloodline. Was Donnan Fraser related to Sinclair's step-four-times-great-grandfather, Lachlan Fraser? Perhaps that was the connection someone wanted Tayte to draw from reading the letter.

He pinched the sleep from his eyes and swung his legs out of bed, stretching and yawning as he did so. He stood up and went to the window where he threw the first of the curtains open, noting that the weather had turned, settling the area with mist. He opened the next curtain along, still trying to decide what to do. He was certainly invested in the assignment by now. There were so many questions he wanted to know the answers to, and he hated the idea of walking away from unfinished research.

When he reached the last curtain and flung it open, a folded slip of paper fluttered from the windowsill on to the floor. He stooped down and picked it up, curious to know what it was. When he opened it, he saw that it was a note, and as he began to read it his heart rate quickened.

'*Find the ruby,*' he said under his breath. '*Restore the Blood of Rajputana.*'

After the message there was a series of symbols he didn't recognise, although he knew it had to be some kind of language—Hindi, perhaps. As with Jane Hardwick's letter, he wondered who had left it for him. He was sure it hadn't been on his windowsill when he'd drawn his curtains the night before, but then he'd gone down to dinner. He thought someone must have put it there during that time, and he imagined it had to be the same person who had left Jane's letter. He went to the bathroom, eager to wash and dress and go down to speak with Sinclair about it. The note left no doubt that someone wanted to help him find the ruby.

But to what end?

———

'It's Sanskrit,' Sinclair said as he studied the note Tayte had passed to him across the table. 'You don't mind porridge for your breakfast, do you?' he added, looking up at Tayte, as if wondering whether he considered it adequate. 'It's simple but hearty, and it was also quick and easy for Murray to prepare for us before he went out shooting this morning.'

'I don't mind at all,' Tayte said. 'In fact, there was a time when oatmeal was my go-to breakfast of choice. This is very good.'

'Aye, Murray makes fine porridge. Perhaps if you ask him, he'll share his secrets with you.'

'I'll do that,' Tayte said, then getting back to the note, he added, 'Do you know what the Sanskrit means?'

'I do. It's a word I've seen before, during my research into the Blood of Rajputana. I don't know whether to feel excited or afraid about seeing it here at Drumarthen.'

'Afraid? Why? What does it mean?'

'It means that a fabled group of Rajputs may be real after all. I read that these men, each carrying a tattoo bearing the Sanskrit written on this note, were once charged with protecting the Blood of Rajputana. Since it was taken they've been honour-bound to recover it and return it to its rightful place.'

'To the forehead of the golden statue of Krishna it was taken from,' Tayte said, glad that he'd been paying attention when Sinclair first told him about the ruby.

'So the story goes,' Sinclair said. 'I've found no evidence to support their existence, until now perhaps,' he added, looking at the note again. 'These Rajputs are said to be patriots to their cause, which is more or less my understanding of what this Sanskrit word means.'

'If that's true,' Tayte said. 'If this note was left by these fabled patriot Rajputs, their cause has been passed down through several generations.'

'Aye, which is where my concern at reading this note comes from. They're clearly very determined.'

Tayte's brow furrowed. 'How could they have gotten in here? The ground floor to this place is like a castle. Have any doors been left unlocked? Are any of the windows broken?'

'Not to my knowledge,' Sinclair said. 'Murray may not be in the habit of locking every door behind him each time he steps a foot outside, but I certainly lock up whenever I go out for any duration. Murray's either here or out on the estate most of the time, of course, so maybe that's it. I'll be sure to tell him to lock the doors behind him when he goes out in future, and to ensure they're bolted at night.'

That much was reassuring, but Tayte's brow remained creased. 'How could these people know what I'm doing here? How do they know you've hired me to look for this ruby?'

'Given their cause, I imagine they've taken great interest in the pursuits of my family, in which case I suspect they've had their eye on us all for some time.'

Tayte was again reminded of the figure he'd seen by the burn the evening he arrived at Drumarthen. Had they been watching him then?

'This could very well be connected to my brother's death,' Sinclair added, thoughtfully. 'If he did borrow money from the syndicate Callum Macrae mentioned, to fund a trip to India in search of the ruby, it could well have drawn their attention. Maybe they didn't like what my brother was doing. If we're to take it that these Rajputs left you this note, then we can also suppose that they left us Jane Hardwick's letter, which to my mind, given that I know my brother had them, means they took them from him.'

'Or from Dr Drummond,' Tayte offered. 'You said that your brother and the doctor were close.'

'Aye, perhaps. Who can say at this point? It's an interesting turn of events, that's for sure.'

'We need to tell the police about this.'

'Leave that to me,' Sinclair said. 'I'll let DI Ross know what's happened. As for the ruby, you must believe me when I say I don't care for it. I simply wish to bring my brother's killer to justice. My determination in the matter gained all the more strength when I saw Gordon Drummond lying dead at the foot of his stairs. I need your help, Mr Tayte. Do as the note says, won't you? Find this accursed ruby if you can. Perhaps in doing so you can put a stop to what's going on here.'

Tayte sighed. It was clear to him that, for now at least, whoever was doing this had no interest in harming him. If that situation changed, he knew where the front door was.

'Okay,' he said. 'I'll keep going for the time being.'

'That's the spirit,' Sinclair said. 'So where will your research take you today?'

Tayte had already thought about that, which in itself was enough to tell him he was keen to continue. 'I figured I'd start where I left off yesterday,' he said. 'I want to look into the Christie family I identified from Albert Faraday's newspaper reports.'

———⌣———

Sitting at the desk in his room, facing a painting of the Scottish Highlands with its ubiquitous mist and purple heather, it did not take Tayte long to prove his inklings about the Christie family were correct. By late morning his laptop screen was displaying a page from the UK Genealogy Archives, showing information he'd searched for in *Burke's Peerage*. The heading he was interested in was 'Christie of Glentrave,' which matched with the information he'd found in Faraday's article in *The Times* newspaper archive.

Beneath the heading was all the information Tayte could hope to find. Sir John William Christie of Glentrave in the county of Fife was born on 11 August 1778. Died June 1826. In December 1799, he married Elspeth Macleod. Beneath that information Tayte read the names of their issue—and there was Robert, along with his sister, Arabella, whom he'd read about in Faraday's newspaper column and in Jane Hardwick's letters. In this instance, no dates of birth or death for Robert or Arabella were listed.

There was little doubt in Tayte's mind that this had to be the right Robert—the very same man Cornelius Dredger had written to in 1869 about his great-aunt Jane's letters. Jane, Tayte now knew, had been in India with this Christie family. It stood to reason that Jane's great-nephew, who had clearly been left her letters, would have written to John and Elspeth Christie's son about them.

Tayte had to remind himself, however, that Robert was a popular name. While he could feel Sinclair's genealogical brick wall beginning to crumble, due to the illegitimacy of Robert's as-yet-supposed offspring, he knew it would be difficult to fully prove that Robert Christie was Sinclair's four-times-great-grandfather. All he had for now were the letters, which according to Sinclair had been passed down through his family, leading him to suspect that Robert was his four-times-great-grandfather—Robert having come by them himself via Cornelius Dredger. It all stacked up well enough, giving Tayte the confidence to keep digging. He thought it was sure to be exciting news for Sinclair when he told him, but he hoped to find some solid proof.

Next, Tayte looked up Robert Christie, once again turning to *Burke's Peerage*. Having quickly found that Robert had inherited his father's titles and estate when Sir John Christie died, Tayte was keen to read about Robert's marriage and subsequent offspring. He was surprised to learn, however, that Robert Christie had never married, and that with no legitimate heir to his title, the peerage became extinct. Tayte thought this information was telling in light of the affair Sinclair had spoken of. It was yet more supporting evidence to suggest that Robert Christie had fallen for a married woman, and that any children he may have fathered were therefore illegitimate.

Tayte sat back and began to ponder where to take his research next. He knew little of the interaction between Dredger and Robert Christie, so he thought that merited further exploration. Had Robert given Dredger the money he sought to fund his expedition to India in search of the Blood of Rajputana? Or had Dredger been forced to look elsewhere? That was if he'd managed to raise the money at all. It would be difficult to accurately draw out the events that took place from the archives alone, but Tayte thought the ship indexes could be useful. Maybe Cornelius Dredger's name would appear on them, dated soon after he wrote his letter to Robert Christie, or perhaps they took a voyage to India together, which would be very telling indeed.

Then there was Captain Donnan Fraser, the man he'd read about in the letter someone had clearly wanted him to read. Donnan Fraser would certainly have to be looked into further, but for now Tayte was keen to prove the connection he'd just made between Robert Christie and the man he knew from Sinclair's existing records to be Sinclair's three-times-great-grandfather, Angus Fraser. As Angus's birth certificate showed no father's details, however, Tayte knew he needed to find a way around the problem. He sat forward on his elbows, contemplating how best to do that, when his thoughts were interrupted by a knock at his door.

'Come in!' he called, turning around to see who it was.

It was Murray, as shabbily dressed as ever in a pair of dirty old jeans and a sagging green jumper that had seen better days.

'My apologies for interrupting your research,' Murray said, remaining in the doorway as he spoke. 'Mr Sinclair asked me to pop up and tell you that he's spoken with Detective Inspector Ross. There's to be a family gathering here at Drumarthen at seven thirty this evening and he'd like you to attend.'

Tayte smiled. 'Who would, Mr Sinclair or DI Ross?'

Murray, whose dark eyes always seemed to be set in a permanent squint, looked confused. 'I couldn't say, sir.'

'It's okay. I was just fooling around. It's one thing to be invited to a gathering by your host, but perhaps another altogether to be asked to attend by the police.'

'Aye,' Murray said, scratching at his ear. 'I see what you mean.'

'Tell Mr Sinclair I'll be there,' Tayte said, thinking that he wouldn't have missed it for all the Hershey's Miniatures in the chocolate factory. The chance to meet and hopefully talk to so many family members at the same time was an opportunity too good to pass up.

'Very good, sir,' Murray said, and closed the door again, leaving Tayte to his research.

While Tayte felt that distractions were often unwelcome in his line of work, when he turned back to his laptop he began to smile to himself. Perhaps the intrusion had helped to clear his mind, or maybe his next step seemed so obvious to him now that he would have arrived at it sooner or later regardless. Whichever it was, as he began tapping keys, bringing up the National Records of Scotland's associated online records website, Scotland's People, he knew exactly how he might prove that Robert Christie was Damian Sinclair's four-times-great-grandfather. If he was right, he imagined that Sinclair was going to be a very happy man indeed.

Chapter Fourteen

Having wrapped up his research for the afternoon, Tayte arrived in the dining room at Drumarthen House half an hour early for the family gathering DI Ross had set up. He was excited to share his findings with his host, yet at the same time he was aware of the nervous energy rising within him at the thought of meeting so many of Sinclair's relatives under such awkward circumstances that they warranted the presence of the police. He'd put on a fresh white shirt and his best tan suit for the occasion. It was the suit he typically reserved for visiting clients and their families for the first time, considering that his everyday research suits were always far too crumpled to make a good impression, which on this occasion he was keen to do.

'Ah, there you are,' Sinclair said as Tayte entered the room. More chairs had been brought into the dining room, which Sinclair was arranging around the table. 'I'm glad you're early. It won't be so overwhelming for you, as long as everyone doesn't arrive at once.'

'That's kind of what I was thinking,' Tayte said, counting the chairs. There were nine. 'I was also keen to share some of the results from my research with you before the proceedings began.'

'Don't tell me you've found something else already?'

Tayte gave Sinclair a wide smile. 'Actually, I have.'

Sinclair laughed. 'Good man!' he said. 'Although you're putting my humble efforts to shame. You'll be telling me next that you've smashed through my family history brick wall and found my four-times-great-grandfather.'

Sinclair was laughing as he finished speaking, and Tayte laughed with him. When the short burst of laughter subsided, Tayte didn't speak. He just held on to his smile until Sinclair understood his meaning.

'You haven't?' he said.

'I think I have.'

Sinclair couldn't have run around the dining table faster. When he reached Tayte he slapped him heartily on the back. 'I knew you were the right person to hire for this. Was it finding the Christie name that did it?'

Tayte nodded. 'That was the way in. Once I had that, the rest was pretty simple. I found Sir Robert Christie, son of Sir John Christie in *Burke's Peerage*.'

'Sir Robert Christie,' Sinclair said, slowly, as if feeling proud to be associated with the name and title. 'Given we know that Jane was travelling with the Christies to stay with Sir John Christie in Jaipur, there's little doubt then that Robert Christie is the man Cornelius Dredger wrote to?'

'It seems highly likely,' Tayte said, 'but just because Dredger's letters wound up with your family here at Drumarthen, it doesn't prove that Robert Christie is your four-times-great-grandfather. I wanted more, so I spent the afternoon looking for proof.'

'And you found it? How?'

'Did you ever wonder how Drumarthen came to be in your family?'

'It was purchased by my three-times-great-grandfather, Angus Fraser, with the inheritance money he received following the death of his stepfather. There's a copy of the will bequeathing a generous sum of money to Angus.'

'Yes, I've seen your copy of the will,' Tayte said. 'But Angus didn't buy this house with the money he inherited.'

'He didn't?'

Tayte shook his head. 'Testaments for the period 1514–1925 have been digitised. You can view them at the Scotland's People Centre in Edinburgh, and online. This afternoon I was able to see a digital copy of Sir Robert Christie's last will and testament. Drumarthen belonged to him. He left it all to Angus Fraser.'

'That's very interesting indeed, Mr Tayte. I had no idea.'

'Without the Christie name to open the door, how could you? Given that Angus was born illegitimate, and that, for reasons as yet to be discovered, he appears to have distanced himself from his biological father, or at least his biological father's name, I think this will I've found is about as much proof as we're likely to get that Sir Robert Christie was your paternal four-times-great-grandfather, and it could be enough. As Robert died without legitimate issue, you may even have a right to the peerage titles that became extinct when he died. Illegitimacy today is looked upon rather differently from how it was back then.'

'This is wonderful news indeed, Mr Tayte,' Sinclair said. He turned towards the door that led into the drawing room. 'Now, if you'd care to follow me, I think we've time to celebrate with a wee dram of the good stuff before the clan arrives. Then I shall have to lock it away, or that'll be the last I'll see of it.'

As Tayte followed Sinclair into the drawing room, he thought a small glass of whisky was just the thing to help settle his nerves before meeting Sinclair's guests, especially if Callum Macrae was anything to judge by. Tayte hadn't even seen the man yet, but he'd heard enough to know that he wasn't someone he particularly cared to acquaint himself with.

'So, who else is coming this evening?' Tayte asked as he sat in his usual armchair by the fire and watched Sinclair pour their drinks. 'Apart from Callum Macrae and DI Ross, of course.'

Sinclair sat back with his whisky and stared up at the ceiling as he thought on his answer. 'Well now, there's Callum's mother, Moira Macrae. She's been a widow for a good many years. After her long-suffering husband passed to a better place, she never remarried.' He paused and scoffed to himself. 'No man in his right mind would have her!' He sipped his whisky. 'All the family you'll meet tonight are descendants of Lachlan and Aileen Fraser. Unlike myself, they're from the legitimate Fraser bloodline, which brings me to Niall and Mairi Fraser. Niall's the only member of the family who carries the Fraser name today, all others having changed through marriage at one time or another. The Frasers are a touch pretentious for my liking.'

'I should particularly like to talk to Niall about his family history,' Tayte said, thinking that as he was the only direct descendant of the male bloodline from Lachlan Fraser, Niall was perhaps best placed to tell him more about the captain he'd read about in Jane Hardwick's letter.

'Aye, perhaps we can arrange that,' Sinclair said. 'You'll certainly have better luck with the Frasers in that area than you will with the remaining two guests coming to Drumarthen this evening. Chrissie MacIntyre's from the same Fraser bloodline as Niall, via a common great-great-grandfather, but she hasn't had anything worthwhile to say to anyone in years. Then there's Ewan Blair. He's more closely related to the Macraes than he is to the Frasers. He likes the sound of his own voice, so I'm sure he'll have plenty to talk about this evening. I'd take it all with a good pinch of salt if I were you.'

'I see,' Tayte said, his thoughts returning to Callum Macrae. One way or another he sensed there were sure to be fireworks, and he was thankful DI Ross was going to be there to manage the proceedings. All he had to do was be polite, sit back, and listen to what everyone had to say.

The first of the guests to arrive at Drumarthen House that evening did so fifteen minutes early, interrupting Tayte and Sinclair's fireside whisky with a thud from the heavy front-door knocker. Murray was showing the guest into the dining room as they both went to see who it was. The man had a trilby hat in one hand and a wet raincoat over his arm, telling Tayte that the mist, which had clung to Drumarthen all day, had now turned to rain. He was smoking a roll-up cigarette, which he drew deeply on before looking around for an ashtray. Seeing nothing suitable, he handed it awkwardly to Murray to dispose of.

'Mr Ewan Blair,' Murray announced, his mouth twisted with distaste as he took the wet end of the still-smouldering cigarette.

'Damian, you old bugger!' Blair said. 'It's good to see you again.'

'Hello, Ewan,' Sinclair said, showing nothing to suggest the feeling was mutual. 'I trust business is good?'

'I can't complain,' Blair said, lifting the cuff of his pinstripe suit jacket to reveal a heavy-looking gold watch. 'So, what's all this about? Frankly, I've better things to do. Time is money, and all that.'

'If Detective Ross hasn't told you already, I'm sure he'll do so when he arrives,' Sinclair said. 'Now, before I forget my manners, this is Mr Tayte. He's staying at Drumarthen while he works on my family history.'

'Got you looking for that ruby, has he?' Blair said with a wry smile and a wink as he reached out and shook Tayte's hand.

Tayte looked at Sinclair, unsure whether he wanted any of the other family members to know his business.

'That's all right,' Blair said, smiling more fully, revealing a gold incisor. 'Mum's the word, eh?' he added, tapping the side of his nose.

'Have a seat, won't you?' Sinclair said, and Blair sat down, further flattening back his black hair as he did so.

Next to arrive was a woman Tayte thought was about sixty years old. Over a blue floral dress, she wore a clear plastic raincoat and hood that she wouldn't let Murray take, despite the fact that she was dripping rain everywhere she walked. She only said one word as she entered the dining room.

'Damian,' she acknowledged with a slight nod of her head.

She had a small voice that Tayte barely heard, perhaps hinting at a demure nature or otherwise nervous disposition. She made little eye contact with anyone as she crossed the room, except Tayte, whom she looked up at briefly from beneath her hood. Then she sat down, alone for now, at the opposite end of the table from Blair.

'That's Chrissie MacIntyre,' Sinclair whispered to Tayte as the woman removed her hood, revealing short, mousy hair that bore the awkwardly chopped signs of a do-it-yourself haircut. 'She keeps to herself most of the time. I'm surprised she came.'

'I'm not sure I like the way she keeps staring at me through those thick glasses of hers,' Tayte said.

Sinclair laughed to himself. 'Oh, don't mind Chrissie. I'm sure she's just curious to know who you are and doesn't like to ask.' He looked over to her and called, 'This is my guest, Chrissie. His name's Mr Tayte—a family historian.'

Tayte smiled at her, but instead of smiling back she pulled an awkward face and turned away.

'I very much doubt Detective Ross will get anything out of her tonight,' Sinclair said as another thud from the heavy door knocker echoed in the main entrance hall. This time it was accompanied by a distant rumble of thunder. He checked his watch. 'It's almost time,' he added, turning to find out who Murray would bring in next. 'Perhaps that's Alastair now.'

'Niall and Mairi Fraser,' Murray announced from the doorway.

As Murray stepped back, Tayte saw a couple he thought were in their mid-forties enter the dining room. Unlike the previous guest, they were both full of smiles, the man sporting a full but tidy brown beard, and wearing blue jeans and a fitted ink-blue shirt, the woman looking somewhat overdressed for the occasion in a short, low-cut black dress and patent-leather high heels. Tayte wondered whether they were going somewhere fancy afterwards.

'Niall,' Sinclair said, offering no smile or warmth in his tone. 'Mairi. Sit yourselves down. I'm sure DI Ross will be along shortly.'

Tayte smiled politely at them, nodding his head as they passed him on the way to their seats. He wondered what had happened between them and Sinclair in the past to warrant such a cool reception. He also sensed that Ewan Blair's appearance at Drumarthen was similarly unwelcome, and it was patently obvious to him that for one reason or another there was little love lost between Sinclair and the rest of his family. Another rumble of thunder sounded, louder and closer this time. Now that half the table was seated, Tayte began to feel awkward standing at Sinclair's side, so he went over and pulled out a chair and sat down, drawing the attention of those already seated.

Niall Fraser shot a hand across the table. 'I'm pleased to meet you,' he said as they shook hands. 'This is Mairi, my lovely wife of twenty years and counting.'

Mairi extended a pale and slender arm towards Tayte, her hand palm down, as if expecting Tayte to kiss the back of it.

Tayte gently shook her fingers and smiled. Then everyone sat back. 'I'm Jefferson Tayte. I hope you don't mind my being here. Detective Ross asked me to attend.'

'He's a genealogist,' Blair said from one end of the table, his eyes fixed on the roll-up cigarette he was making. 'So you're caught up in all this nonsense, too, are you?'

'If by "nonsense" you mean the Blood of Rajputana,' Tayte said, 'then yes, it looks that way.'

'Poor you,' Blair said, laughing to himself. 'It's obsessed this family for decades.'

'So I've heard.'

'I suppose Damian's hired you to find it, has he?' Niall said, pulling thoughtfully at his beard. 'Well, good luck with that. I hope you like Scotland. You may be here for some time.'

At that point, Murray made another announcement. 'Detective Inspector Alastair Ross,' he called, far too loudly for the size of the room, as if he thought he was still in the Drumarthen of old, announcing guests in a far larger space.

Everyone turned to the doorway as Ross entered, brushing rain from the shoulders of his navy-blue suit. 'Good evening, everyone,' he said, straightening his tie. 'Thanks for turning out in this foul weather. Are we all here?'

'Not quite,' Sinclair said. 'We're missing Callum Macrae and his mother.'

'Well, let's get started,' Ross said. 'I've other duties to attend to, and I'd like to see my wife and wee baby girl again before they forget what I look like. I don't want to be here all night just because the Macraes can't tell the time.'

Ross pulled out a chair and he and Sinclair sat down.

'I'll listen out for the door,' Murray said, making to leave.

'You take a seat, Murray,' Ross insisted. 'This may concern you, too. We'll hear the door sure enough from in here.'

Ewan Blair purposefully coughed into his hand. 'Any whisky before we get started? My throat's parched.'

'Then it'll be water you need,' Sinclair said. 'I've accommodated you all here at my house at the detective's request, but I'll be damned if I'll share my Scotch with you as well.'

'Still tight as a drum I see.'

'I'm generous enough with those I care for,' Sinclair said, at which point DI Ross stepped in.

'Gentlemen, please! I should remind you why we're all here this evening. Let us start by paying our respects to the good Dr Drummond, who I'm sure will be greatly missed.'

There were nods of approval from everyone around the table, all except Chrissie MacIntyre. Instead of nodding and lowering her head as everyone else did, Tayte thought he heard her scoff through her nose at the suggestion that Gordon Drummond was a 'good' doctor. Several seconds of silence followed, which was punctuated by a bright flash of lightning at the high windows, and a crack of thunder so sharp and so booming that Tayte jumped in his seat. The lights flickered momentarily, then as he began to relax again the thump of the door knocker and the scraping of Murray's chair legs as he went to answer it startled him further. Why did he feel so nervous this evening?

Murray came back a few seconds later with the formidable sight that was Callum Macrae. He was an obviously overweight man, but he looked strong with it. Macrae arrived alone, and this time Murray made no announcement, nor did he need to. The man lumbered into the room, half staggering as he did so, his hair wild and wet, his long, waxed coat glistening in the lamplight as he took it off and practically threw it at Murray.

'My bloody car's broken down!' he said, his coarse Scots accent befitting his size and surly disposition.

Half the table immediately began to snigger to themselves.

Tayte leaned close to Sinclair. 'What's so funny about a man's car breaking down? Especially on a night like this.'

'He's a mechanic,' Sinclair said, whispering back. 'He owns the local garage.'

Mairi Fraser was smiling more than most at the irony, enough to draw Macrae's attention.

'Do you find that amusing, woman?' he said, leaning aggressively over the table. 'I've just had to walk half a mile in the pissing rain, and in case you hadn't noticed, it's blowing a gale out there!'

At that point, Niall stood up. 'You leave my wife alone. Your car broke down through no one's fault but your own. Everyone knows you're a lousy mechanic, Callum Macrae. It's no wonder your business is on its knees.'

Macrae's face began to glow red. He looked as if he were about to leap across the table at Niall.

'Sit down, Callum,' Blair said. 'Have a drink.' He laughed. 'Oops, sorry. I forgot our host has locked his whisky away for the night.'

Ross stood up, loosening his tie as he did so. 'You look like you've had enough to drink already, Callum. Now calm down, the pair of you. Where's Moira?'

Macrae sat down at last, slumping into his seat as Niall and Murray sat back in theirs. 'My mother sends her apologies. Her leg's been playing her up more than usual today. Given the weather she decided to stay home, which, as it turns out, is just as well.'

Ross plucked at his moustache. 'I didn't think she'd come. She's always been one to have others come to her, hasn't she?'

The lightning continued to flash at the windows. The thunder continued to crackle and rumble above them. Macrae gave no answer.

'Very well, I'll call on her tomorrow,' Ross said. 'Now that we're all here, I'd like to get the obvious question out of the way. Do you know of any reason why anyone should want Gordon Drummond dead?'

A few heads began to shake. No one gave Ross an answer.

'Okay, then,' he said. 'Let's get down to business. What's this syndicate I've heard about concerning Jamie Sinclair? Was Gordon involved?'

'Aye, he was,' Macrae said. 'The good doctor was with Jamie when he came to me asking for money. He was clearly the first to sign up to Jamie's idea.'

There was another slight, but clearly audible scoff from Chrissie MacIntyre, and this time Ross turned to her. 'Have you something to say, Chrissie? That's the second time this evening I've heard you scoff. Is there something about Gordon you'd like to share with us?'

Chrissie looked suddenly shocked at the idea that she might have something to say about Dr Drummond. Her face flushed as she pressed her lips together and vigorously shook her head.

'Very well. So Dr Drummond was with Jamie when he came to see you about the syndicate.'

'Having Drummond on board added weight to Jamie's proposal,' Blair said. 'I for one was in all the way.'

'Exactly what did Jamie propose to you all?' Ross asked.

Mairi Fraser leaned forward, tucking her long blonde hair behind her ears as she did so. 'He offered us a share in his venture. He said he knew where to find the ruby we've all been looking for.'

'The Blood of Rajputana,' Sinclair said. 'I knew it.'

Mairi nodded and began to play with the string of beads that hung around her neck. 'He showed us several letters from India, written by a woman called Jane Hardwick.'

Tayte and Sinclair exchanged knowing glances.

'We weren't allowed to read them,' Mairi continued, 'but Gordon told us he had. He vouched for Jamie when he said that the letters held a clue to the ruby's whereabouts.'

'So Jamie wanted money to go and find it?' Ross said.

Niall answered. 'He didn't have two pennies to rub together, but he did have those letters. He proposed we each give him as much as we could afford, up to a point, in return for an equivalent share of the ruby's street value once he'd found it and sold it. His take was to be thirty per cent, leaving seventy per cent up for grabs—ten per cent to each of the seven of us.'

'For those who could afford a ten per cent stake,' Macrae scoffed. 'I bought in, but I could barely scrape five per cent together.'

'We managed to find fifteen per cent between us,' Mairi said.

'And you, Chrissie?' Ross asked.

Chrissie didn't speak. Instead, and with an expressionless face, she held up both hands, fanning all her fingers and thumbs out as she did so.

'My mother also bought ten per cent,' Macrae said, sounding angry again. He thumped the table. 'It cost the poor woman most of her savings to do so.'

'And Dr Drummond?' Ross said. 'How much was he in for?'

Blair put his hand up. 'We bought the rest between us. Fifteen per cent each.'

'And what kind of money are we talking about here?' Ross asked. 'Hundreds? Thousands?'

'The total amount Jamie said he wanted from us was ten thousand pounds,' Blair said. 'It's not much money these days. Personally, I'd have been happy to give him the lot for a fifty–fifty share.'

'Aye, that's because you've always been a greedy bastard,' Macrae said. 'Apart from you, and maybe Gordon, it was a lot of money to the rest of us.'

The Frasers and Chrissie MacIntyre all nodded their heads in agreement.

'And you trusted Jamie?' Ross said with an air of disbelief.

'No,' Blair said, almost laughing at the idea. 'But we trusted Gordon, who was to go to India with him.'

Ross sat back in his chair and shook his head. 'I've got to ask why none of you came to me and told me about any of this when Jamie Sinclair died. Did it not occur to any one of you that it might have had some bearing?'

'The report said it was an accident,' Mairi said. 'Why would any of us think otherwise?'

'More likely you didn't want to get involved,' Ross said. 'You were too busy counting your losses. In case you haven't already worked it out, I can tell you now that you were all duped. When Damian told me what he suspected this syndicate was about, I had Jamie's movements prior to his death checked out. He made no such journey to India. As far as I can tell, he never left Scotland. He rented himself a nice penthouse apartment in Glasgow instead, presumably with your money, given that you just told me he didn't have two pennies to rub together prior to forming this syndicate with you.'

Everyone fell silent. Several seconds later, Sinclair turned to Ross and said, 'So, where does this leave your murder investigation?'

Before Ross could answer, there were several more flashes of lightning at the high windows, strobe-lighting the room with an intense white glare. It was closely followed by a thunder clap above them that shook the room. The lamps flickered several times, and then Drumarthen was thrust into darkness.

———

'I half expected that,' Sinclair said, as one by one the guests around the dining table took out their mobile phones, lighting the room with a harsh blue-white light. 'Murray, I think you'd better go and fire up the generator. The power's sure to be out for a while.' Sinclair stood up. 'I'll go and fetch some candles.'

Rising from the table with him, Murray made for the door, but Ross stopped him. 'Here,' he said. 'You'll need a torch.'

'Keep it,' Murray said. 'I'd know my way around this old place blindfolded. There's a torch in the generator room.'

With that, Murray left the dining room, his way lit by another flash of lightning.

'He doesn't like to depend on others for anything,' Sinclair said to Ross. 'It's been his way for many a year now.'

At one end of the table, Blair flicked at his cigarette lighter. 'Do you mind if I have a smoke while we're waiting?'

'Aye, I do.'

'I figured you'd say that. In which case I'm going outside. Storm or no storm, I'm positively gagging.'

Blair scraped his chair legs back over the flagstones and left the room. Sinclair went to fetch the candles. When he returned, he set them out at intervals along the dining table, lighting each one as he went. Then he lit a few more around the room, gradually filling it with a warm, flickering glow. He sat down again and a few more minutes passed before Blair rejoined them, bringing the smell of stale cigarettes back with him.

'Isn't this cosy?' he said. 'Can we carry on now? I don't want to be here all night either.' To DI Ross he added, 'Before we were interrupted, Damian asked you where all this leaves your murder investigation. I'm sure we'd all like to hear your answer.'

Ross sighed. 'It's a very good question, and one to which I'm afraid I currently have no solid answer.'

'You must have a hunch, surely,' Niall said. 'Detectives always have a hunch about things, don't they?'

'Aye, I have a hunch,' Ross said, 'but I doubt you'll like it. In trying to establish a motive for Gordon Drummond's murder and, I'll now concede, perhaps that of Jamie Sinclair, I find myself turning to each of you here and wondering whether you weren't satisfied with your part-share in the ruby. I'm wondering whether someone took it upon themselves to go to Jamie, and in turn to Dr Drummond, meaning to take the ruby they were supposed to have come back from India with.'

Macrae laughed derisively at the suggestion. 'You told us just now Jamie never went to India, in which case he couldn't have brought that ruby back, could he?'

'No,' Ross said. 'But then, none of you knew that Jamie never went to India until a moment ago, did you?'

Tayte, who had been no more than an observer until now, had something to add to Ross's line of thinking. 'Surely someone must have gone to see Jamie before he died,' he said, and all eyes turned to him. 'Clearly someone else now has those letters he showed you.'

'How can you know that?' Blair asked.

'I know it because someone left one of those letters here at Drumarthen yesterday evening.' Tayte thought about the note he'd found on his windowsill that morning. 'And I know it because I've received a note urging me to find the Blood of Rajputana. Maybe Jamie didn't have those letters when whoever's behind this went to see him. Maybe Dr Drummond did. Perhaps that's why they're both dead.'

'Because of the letters?' Niall Fraser said.

Ross nodded. 'Why not? Someone finds out where Jamie is. They go to see him and learn that he never went to India. Perhaps they went after the ruby and they're disappointed to learn that he didn't have it. Then they turn to the letters—letters Jamie has already said hold a clue to the ruby's whereabouts. They go to take the letters, hoping to use them to find the ruby for themselves. But perhaps this person discovers that Jamie no longer has them. They learn that he gave the letters to Dr Drummond. So Jamie is murdered, making his death look like an accident to buy his killer time. Then he or she waits for the dust to settle before paying Gordon a visit. The killer takes the letters from him, but this time he's in a hurry. Damian and Mr Tayte are on their way to see him, so the killer is forced to act, leaving no question this time that it's murder.'

'Only, his killer can't work out where the ruby is from the letters alone,' Tayte interjected, so caught up in Ross's supposition that he was unable to stop himself.

Ross nodded. 'So he or she turns to Mr Tayte here, the professional, asking him to find the ruby, leaving him another of Jane Hardwick's letters in the belief that the story they tell will help him to do just that.'

'That's a fancy supposition,' Blair said. 'Maybe it fits the scenario well enough, but how do you suppose whoever's doing this plans to get the ruby once this fella here's found it? That's assuming he's able to, of course.'

'Right now, Ewan, I have no idea. I don't even know if I'm barking up the right tree, but for now it's all I have.'

'And you think one of us is doing this?' Macrae said.

Ross's eyes roamed around the table. 'Have any of you spoken about this to anyone else?'

Heads started shaking. Then one by one they all said, 'No.'

'Then tell me,' Ross said. 'What else am I supposed to think just now?'

The room fell silent. In the background, the thunder continued to rumble, growing distant again. It was Damian Sinclair who eventually broke the silence.

'You're overlooking another possibility,' he said. 'On the phone earlier today, when I told you about that letter showing up at Drumarthen last night, and the note Mr Tayte found when he woke up this morning, I also told you there are people who have supposedly been looking for the Blood of Rajputana since it went missing two centuries ago.'

'Aye, supposedly,' Ross said, emphasising the word. 'Frankly, these Rajputs you told me about sound like a load of mumbo jumbo to me.'

'Maybe they are,' Sinclair said. 'But then again, maybe they're not. Is it something you can afford to overlook?'

Ross further loosened his tie. He sat back in his chair, giving no answer, his silence a concession to the fact that Sinclair could be right. As Tayte saw it, Ross couldn't know enough to rule anything or anyone out just yet.

'Murray's been gone a while,' Macrae said a moment later. 'Is it far to the generator?'

'No,' Sinclair said. 'But it's a temperamental beast. I expect it's giving him some bother. I'm sure he'll have it up and running soon enough. He always does.'

Macrae stood up. 'Where is it? I'll go and see if he needs a hand.'

'It's at the far side of the east wing, but you'd better go around the house if you're going. The east wing is far too dangerous unless, like Murray, you know exactly where to tread. Once you're outside, turn left and follow the walls around the building until you come to a steel hatch. The generator room's in the basement below. Give the hatch a good thump to let Murray know you're there. He'll let you in.'

'I'll be needing my coat then,' Macrae said as he activated the torch on his phone and shone it out into the darkness beyond the dining room door to see where Murray had put it. He closed the door behind him as he left.

As soon as he'd gone, Ross sat forward on his elbows and pushed back his thinning hair. 'Look, I don't know who's doing this, and I'm not accusing anyone here of anything just now. If I was, we'd be at the station and you'd all be telling me exactly where you were when Gordon was murdered.'

'Did your forensics team find anything useful at his house?' Sinclair asked. 'Any prints on the handle of that knife I saw?'

'The knife was clean, but there were plenty of prints and fibres elsewhere. Something may prove useful, although I believe the doctor not only made house calls, but had frequent callers visit him at home. That will undoubtedly complicate things.'

Tayte spoke then. 'Was Dr Drummond's research still there?'

'Aye, it was,' Ross said. 'So I think it can safely be ruled out as a motive for his murder.'

'Was it intact? I mean, did it appear to have been interfered with?'

'That's hard to say. There were no obvious signs that anyone had taken an interest in it.'

'Would it be possible to see it? While it may help my own research, having me go over it could also prove useful to your investigation.'

'How's that?'

'Well, if something's missing it might stand out to someone in my profession. Mr Sinclair previously told me that the doctor's research had been as thorough as his own. As an example, if there's now a hole in his research files, whatever's missing could incriminate someone for one reason or another.'

'I like your thinking, Mr Tayte. I'll see what I can do. Just how is your research going, by the way?'

Tayte glanced at Sinclair, wondering whether his client was comfortable with him talking about the assignment in front of the other family members. He knew they all had an active interest in the Blood of Rajputana. Now that Jane Hardwick's letters had come to light with the promise of a clue to its whereabouts, he figured they would be all the more keen to hear about the missing link he'd discovered in Sinclair's family history. Sinclair was quick, yet subtle with his response. Tayte noted the almost imperceptible shake of his head.

'I understand your reticence to talk about it here,' Ross said. 'But tell me, do you actually believe you have a chance of finding this ruby? Whoever's behind this clearly thinks you can.'

'I don't even know if it's real.'

'What about the letters?' Mairi Fraser said. 'Gordon confirmed they spoke of it.'

'It's not yet certain what part Dr Drummond played in all this,' Tayte replied. 'Who's to say he wasn't in on Jamie's scam?'

Almost everyone shook their head at the suggestion.

'Gordon Drummond was a good man,' Niall Fraser said. 'He wouldn't lie to us.'

'I'm sure you're right,' Tayte said. 'But no one here has actually read about the ruby for themselves, have they?'

Everyone shook their head again.

'I'm just saying,' Tayte added. 'Like you, I've yet to see any proof that this thing's real. I have a few lines of research I'd like to follow up on—a few names I'd like to look into further—but that's about it for now.'

At that point, the lights came back on.

'Ah, that's better!' Sinclair said. He got up and blew out the candles. 'Maybe Callum's not such a bad mechanic after all,' he added, directing his comment to Niall, who said nothing in return.

Ross stood up. 'I think I've heard all I need to hear for now.' He turned to Tayte. 'I'll get you those files to take a look at. If you do come across anything in there, or if your own research reveals anything you think might be useful to the investigation, I'd be more than glad to hear it.' Turning to the others in the room, he added, 'And if Mr Tayte here has any reason to speak to you about the family while he's here—your family history, I mean—I'd be grateful if you'd show him some Scottish hospitality and cooperate with him. If the good doctor's murder is tied up in all this, you could be doing both of us a great service.'

The dining room door opened then and Murray came back into the room, wiping his hands on his handkerchief. He was alone.

'What happened to Callum?' Ross asked.

'I've not seen him, sir,' Murray said.

'He went out to help you,' Sinclair said. 'I sent him around the house.'

Murray began to shake his head, just as Callum Macrae appeared in the doorway behind him, his hair and his coat once again dripping wet.

'I couldn't find the bloody hatch,' he said. 'I saw the lights come on again so I came back.'

DI Ross went to the door. 'Well, we're all done here,' he said. 'Thanks for the use of your home, Damian.'

He was about to leave when Macrae said, 'Any chance of a lift? I'll have to sort my car out in the morning. If it's nae problem, that is.'

'Of course it's nae problem,' Ross said, holding the door open. 'After you.'

———

Sinclair remained in the dining room with Tayte as his guests left, not caring to see them out personally. He left that to Murray. With the last of his visitors gone, Sinclair heaved a sigh as he turned to Tayte and said, 'Thank goodness that's over with. I don't care if they never step foot inside this house again. Now, how about finishing off that bottle we were enjoying before Ewan Blair's early arrival interrupted us? I know I could use a drink.'

'I don't know about finishing the bottle,' Tayte said, 'but sure, I'd be glad to join you.' He was keen to discuss the evening further, although he sensed Sinclair would sooner forget all about it.

Murray came back into the room, and Sinclair said, 'I don't suppose I can tempt you into joining us for a wee drop of the good stuff, Murray? You've certainly earned it tonight.'

Murray shook his head. 'It's kind of you to offer, but the Frasers' old MG roadster won't start and I've offered to see if I can get her running again. I'll close the place up after that and get to my bed. I've an early start in the morning. The storm's bound to have caused some damage somewhere on the estate.'

'Very well, Murray. I'll wish you a good night then.'

As Murray left them again, Tayte followed Sinclair back into the drawing room and sat down while Sinclair fetched the bottle of whisky and poured them each two fingers. The fire had gone out, leaving a pleasant, homely smell of woodsmoke in the air. It was still warm enough to be comfortable for the short while Tayte expected to be there.

'What's with Chrissie MacIntyre?' he said. 'She never spoke a word all night.'

Sinclair settled back and sipped his whisky. 'I wish I knew. She used to be a lively enough lassie when she was younger, although I suspect that was before her boy died. Maybe that's it.'

'How long ago was that?'

Sinclair drew a thoughtful breath. 'I suppose that would have been about thirty years ago now. Young Conall MacIntyre was fifteen years old when he died. He and Jamie were the best of friends at the time. It shook us all, especially Jamie, but none more so than his mother of course. The wee laddie's father had already abandoned them. Conall was all she had.'

'It must have been devastating,' Tayte said, thinking about his own son and wondering at all the worry and heartache he and Jean undoubtedly had in store. 'Do you mind my asking how Conall died?' Tayte expected Sinclair to say that his death was due to an illness, or an accident. He wasn't prepared for the answer Sinclair gave him.

'He killed himself,' Sinclair said in a cool, very matter-of-fact way. 'Chrissie came home from the supermarket where she worked one afternoon and found the poor boy hanging at the bottom of the stairs. He'd found some old rope and tied it to the top of the bannisters on the upstairs landing. Then over he jumped.'

Tayte took a good slug of his whisky. 'That's shocking,' he said, beginning to understand why Chrissie MacIntyre was the way she was.

'On to lighter subjects,' Sinclair said a moment later. 'Where do you plan to take your research next, now that you've found the missing link, as it were?'

'I've been giving that a lot of thought,' Tayte said. 'If the plan is to prove the existence of the Blood of Rajputana, and hopefully go on to find it so the doctor's killer, and perhaps Jamie's, can be flushed out, then my interest for now is with those people who appear to have been close to it in the past.'

'The Christies?'

'Yes, and this Captain Donnan Fraser I read about in Jane Hardwick's letter last night. He's been on my mind, and since Murray announced Niall Fraser when he and his wife arrived this evening, I've been thinking it would be good to go and talk to him. Are there any other Frasers in the family?'

'They have a son, but he moved away some time ago. Niall's the only family member I know of who carries the male bloodline from his four-times-great-grandfather, Lachlan Fraser. I suppose you'll be wanting to find out whether Donnan Fraser was related to him?'

'Yes, I would. I should be able to find that out easily enough from the records, but family members can often tell you so much more. I'd like to speak with Moira Macrae, too, if that's possible.'

'Ah, Moira! You'll love her,' Sinclair said, and Tayte noted the sarcasm in his tone. 'Why in God's name would you want to speak with her?'

'Her age for one. She's a generation back from everyone else. She may know things about the Fraser family others don't.'

'She may know a few things,' Sinclair said, laughing to himself, 'but she may not choose to talk to you about them, however much DI Ross wants everyone to cooperate with you.'

'It can't hurt to ask.'

'It can hurt a lot, believe me. If there were a branch of the mafia here in Comrie, people would be referring to Moira Macrae respectfully as Don Moira. She's a crabby old boot best left to the likes of DI Ross, if you ask me. I'm glad she didn't come this evening.'

'All the same, she could have something to say.'

Sinclair frowned. Then he sighed to himself. 'Very well. We'll drop by her house in the morning. Just don't go getting your hopes up. I doubt she'll even answer the door when she sees I'm there.'

Murray came back then.

'Changed your mind, have you?' Sinclair said.

'I'm not here for the drink,' Murray said as he approached.

'Did you manage to get the Frasers' car running again?'

'Aye, I did. The coil-to-distributor lead had come loose, but that's not why I'm here, either.' He held something up. 'I found this in the entrance hallway just now as I went to switch off the table lamp.'

Tayte twisted around in his seat to better see what it was. It was an envelope.

'It has your name on it, Mr Tayte,' Murray said as he handed it to him.

Tayte put his glass down and sat up. Sure enough, the envelope had the word 'Tayte' written on the front of it. Nothing more than that.

'What's inside?' Sinclair asked, sounding as eager as Tayte was to find out.

The envelope hadn't been sealed. Tayte opened it and saw a familiar style of paper—old paper. It was another of Jane Hardwick's letters. Unfolding it, he saw that it was dated October 1822, a month after the previous letter he'd read. He handed the envelope to Sinclair.

'Do you recognise the handwriting?'

Sinclair studied it. He shook his head.

Tayte began to wonder who had put it there, concluding that it could have been left by anyone who had visited Drumarthen that evening. Everyone had passed through the entrance hallway. Everyone had the opportunity to slip an envelope on to the side table in question.

To Murray, Tayte said, 'Is there any chance this was on that lamp table before the guests started to arrive?'

'None, sir. I switched the lamp on myself just before you came down. It wasn't there then or I'd have seen it, plain as I did just now.'

'It's one of the guests then,' Sinclair said. 'One of the syndicate.'

'Perhaps,' Tayte said, 'although as no one had to go and open the front door for Callum Macrae when he came back from trying to help Murray with the generator, he must have left the door off the latch so he could get back in. In which case, just about anyone could have slipped in and put it there.'

'Very true,' Sinclair said. 'If that's the case, we're dealing with someone who's very determined, waiting around outside the house on a night like this. Why am I thinking about those Rajputs I told you about again?' He drew Tayte's attention back to the envelope. 'I'll see to it that DI Ross gets this. Maybe his forensics people can make something of it. Now, what does the letter say?'

Tayte began to read it. 'Jane opens by telling her brother that she's been witness to an incredible turn of events. Something wonderful has transpired, which she can scarcely believe.'

'Does she say what it is?'

'Not yet. She says she'll come to it, but first she goes on to mention Captain Fraser again, and his promised tour of Jaipur.'

'He does seem to be cropping up rather often, doesn't he?'

'Yes, he does,' Tayte said, his interest in the man becoming further aroused. He quickly read on, keen to learn what else Jane Hardwick had to say about her time in Jaipur with the Christie family and Captain Donnan Fraser.

Chapter Fifteen

Jaipur, October 1822

The unusual perspective of everyday proceedings when viewed from high up on the back of an elephant was nothing new to Jane. It was, however, a welcome reminder of a happy childhood in India before her father's untimely death from cholera, which had forced her return to England to live with her aunt. Travelling by elephant on Captain Fraser's guided tour of Jaipur had certainly won him a degree of merit in Jane's eyes. She saw it plainly for what it was, of course, but on this occasion she didn't mind. The well-meant gesture was intended to impress Arabella, to bolster the profuse apologies he'd made for his surly behaviour at the stream the evening they had gone to meet Naresh Bharat Singh.

It was late morning by the time they left the city walls, the sun not far from its zenith. As the party slowly traversed the trail up into the Aravalli Hills, which rose high above Jaipur, heading towards Nahargarh Fort, Jane could see that the gesture had clearly hit its mark as far as Arabella was concerned. She had been all giggles since the excursion began, smiling and laughing with Captain Fraser atop their elephant as Jane and Elspeth followed after them on theirs, each being guided by a *mahout* sitting with his legs around his elephant's neck.

'They do seem to be getting along very well, Jane. Wouldn't you say?' Elspeth said as she continued to fan herself; their parasols alone offered little defence against the humidity and the direct heat of the sun.

'Evidently so,' Jane said, wondering what Arabella and Captain Fraser were talking about.

'I believe my husband was correct in supposing they would make a fine couple.'

There was Jane's proof, if any were needed, of Sir John Christie's intentions as far as the hand of his daughter was concerned. She imagined the match had been made long before Arabella had arrived in India. 'Captain Fraser can certainly be quite charming when he wishes.'

'Do I detect a note of cynicism, Jane?'

'Perhaps. I would sooner put my daughter's happiness first, that's all, and certainly above that of a soldier. I don't believe Arabella is aware of Sir John's arrangement with Captain Fraser, is she?'

'I'd hardly call it an arrangement. My husband has high hopes for them, that's all. The rest is down to them.'

'Are you entirely sure about that, Elspeth?' Jane said, wondering how Captain Fraser would react should Arabella not give him her hand when the time came to ask for it.

Elspeth gave no reply. Instead, she changed the subject. 'I'm told that when we reach the top, the view of the city will be quite unparalleled.'

Jane smiled at her friend, thinking it naive of her to suppose that Captain Fraser had been led to expect anything less than marriage to the resident's daughter, irrespective of Arabella's feelings. She said no more about the matter, however, moving on as Elspeth had.

'It should make a fine setting for our lunch,' she said, looking back at the servants, who outnumbered them three to one, as they followed after them on foot with their provisions. 'Look there,' she added. 'Your servant, Kamala, has a basket full of oranges.'

'Please don't talk to me about Kamala,' Elspeth said. 'He's a fat oaf. I find him all but useless. Did the captain say we were taking lunch at the fort itself?'

'No, I don't believe so. I can see two of the servants carrying what appears to be the makings of a pergola tent.'

'That's a pity. I'm sure it would have been much cooler inside the fort.'

At length they came to the summit, where the elephants stopped and knelt at the commands from their *mahouts*, allowing their passengers to climb down. They were in a clearing at the top of the trail, a lookout of sorts. The view as Jane gazed out over Jaipur was enough to take her breath away. The city, which had appeared so large and bustling from below, now seemed tiny and insignificant amidst the land that enveloped it. Being so high up and close to the edge, there was also enough of a breeze to put a smile on Elspeth's face. Captain Fraser and Arabella joined them as the servants went about setting things up for their lunch.

'I was just telling Arabella about the fort you can see yonder,' Fraser said, indicating the impressive sandstone structure to their right. 'It was built in 1734 by the founder of Jaipur, Maharaja Sawai Jai Singh the Second, as a retreat for himself and the royal ladies. It's almost a hundred years old, and do you know that in all that time it has never once been attacked? The defence walls run over the hills all the way to Jaigarh Fort. It's an admirable achievement.'

Jane noted that Arabella seemed to hang on Captain Fraser's every word, causing her to wonder what charm he'd worked on her while they had been alone together on their elephant. Whatever they had talked about, their conversation had clearly done him no harm in her eyes. Perhaps the contrary. Was it possible that Captain Donnan Fraser was for Arabella after all?

The pergola was quickly erected and Elspeth was the first to seek its shade, frantically beating her fan as she sat down on one of the four chairs that had also been carried up from the city on the back of one of the servants. Having grown up with many young natives, whom she had come to call her friends, Jane was at odds with the things they were often made to endure for the sake of their masters' leisure, but that was the way of things in India, where a few rupees could buy a man's untiring service and obedience.

Arabella was next to sit down, still smiling her innocent smile, which seemed to beguile every man who looked upon it. 'I shall remember this day forever,' she said, looking up at Fraser as he lowered himself into the chair beside her.

'Then we must do it all again someday,' Fraser said.

Elspeth stopped fanning herself. 'Perhaps we could take lunch at the fort next time, captain?'

'Aye, perhaps. I'll have a word with the maharaja the next time I see him. Maybe I can garner an invitation.' He smiled and winked at Arabella, who blushed in return.

Jane sat beside Elspeth, all facing the hilltop and the far-reaching views of the plains below. She had to smile to herself at hearing Fraser's words suggesting that he, a mere captain of the East India Company Army, was so acquainted with the Maharaja of Jaipur as to curry any favour with him. If any such arrangements were to be made, it would be down to Arabella's father, not Captain Fraser.

With the meal laid out before them, Elspeth reached for an orange. 'My throat is quite parched,' she said. 'If I attempt the bread and cheese first, or heaven forbid the boiled meats, I shall be sure to choke on them.'

Fraser smiled at her exaggeration. 'I can offer you tea or sherbet to quench your thirst, Lady Christie.'

'Sherbet!' Arabella said. 'You really have thought of everything.'

'Your father, Miss Arabella, kindly placed the residency kitchen at my disposal. Among the many and varied treats you see before you, including the fruit sherbet, I had the *khansamas* prepare a few native dishes for you to try—although I'm quite sure you'll find our own cuisine far more palatable.'

'Do the herbs and spices upset your constitution, Captain Fraser?' Jane asked.

'If I may make so blunt,' Fraser said, 'I find the native food no better than peasant food. We're not here in India, or any other parts of the world, to learn or adapt, but to civilise.'

Jane was not shocked by Fraser's opinion. She understood that it represented that of the majority of British officers and officials in India. Nevertheless, it was not her opinion. From that moment she determined to eat only local foods in his presence, to spite him and his damned arrogance.

'You must try the pickled mangoes,' Jane told Arabella. 'You'll find it excites your taste buds like nothing else and goes magnificently with the mutton pie.'

While they ate, Captain Fraser regaled them all with stories of his youthful adventures in India since he'd taken his commission with the Honourable East India Company, and Jane and Elspeth bored him to tears, or so it seemed, with stories of life back home concerning both Scotland and England, the latter of which, during Jane's account, he showed no interest in whatsoever.

With the meal over, they were left sipping tea beneath their hilltop pergola in the warmth of the afternoon sun, the shade and the gentle breeze giving no one cause to leave.

Arabella, whose cup was evidently empty, raised it and said, 'It's so lovely up here. Could I have another cup before we head back down?'

'Of course, Arabella,' Fraser said, turning at once to the servants. 'Chai wallah!'

'Thank you, Donnan,' Arabella said, and the informal manner of their address did not escape Jane's attention.

The chai wallah, a young, thin man, little more than a boy, was quickly beside Arabella with his urn of tea. Arabella offered her cup to him and he began to pour, but as he did so the urn slipped in his hands, spilling the tea on to Arabella's dress, staining the white muslin the colour of mud. She gave a startled yelp.

'You bloody fool!' Fraser shouted, instantly getting to his feet.

'Very sorry, sahib!' the boy said, backing away.

'I'll bloody well make you sorry!' Fraser said as he went after him.

Fraser grabbed the *chai wallah* by the neck and marched him out from beneath the pergola, causing him to drop his urn altogether with an almighty clatter. Fraser threw him to the stony ground, withdrew his pistol and proceeded to whip him violently with the butt. The boy curled into a ball and everyone looked on in horror as Fraser bent over him, not letting up. If anything, his savage blows against the defenceless boy became all the more excited.

Jane was well aware that officer brutality against the natives had been made legal by the East India Company, but she could not sit there and watch Captain Fraser beat the boy to death for something as trivial as spilling tea. She supposed the captain was incensed to such violence because in his eyes it had been *his* Arabella who had been affronted by the *chai wallah*. All the same, Jane would have none of it. As Elspeth and Arabella continued to sit with their hands to their mouths in shock, Jane stood up and ran to the captain.

'Stop this!' she demanded, but the captain did not seem to hear her. A moment later she took up her own teacup, which was still half-full, and threw the contents in his face.

Captain Fraser recoiled immediately, turning to Jane with wild, unseeing eyes as he raised his pistol to whip her with it, too.

'Captain Fraser!' Elspeth screamed. 'Have you completely lost your senses?'

The captain froze at hearing Elspeth's voice, his pistol held rigid in mid-air. He seemed to see Jane then as if for the first time since he'd turned to her. Their eyes met: hers full of scorn, his doleful and apologetic. He dropped instantly to his knees, clutching at the hem of Jane's dress.

'I'm so very sorry,' he whined. 'However can I expect you to forgive me?'

Jane tugged her dress free from his grasp. 'You can't,' she said, and then she turned back to the pergola, noting that Arabella had now averted her eyes altogether, seemingly unable to look upon Captain Donnan Fraser again.

Chapter Sixteen

Jaipur, October 1822

A week had passed since Captain Fraser's violent outburst in the Aravalli Hills. During that time he had been seen but once at the residency, at an awkward supper that saw him drunk by eight, profusely begging Arabella's forgiveness and failing miserably. It seemed that no manner of encouraging words from her father could bring Arabella to forget what she had seen, and neither should she, as far as Jane Hardwick was concerned. The captain had shown his true colours and he had been found wanting.

Today was a special day at the residency, and Jane was thankful that the loathsome captain, as she now saw him, was nowhere to be seen. It was late morning. Jane had finished her correspondence, having written home to her brother with news of recent events in India, letting him know exactly how she felt about Captain Fraser. She was now with Arabella in her room, helping her to get ready, the morning sun falling softly through the latticework, illuminating a predominantly white room that was punctuated by colourful mosaics.

'I'm glad Mother is feeling well today,' Arabella said as Jane continued to dress her hair. 'It's not every day one gets to meet a maharaja.'

'No,' Jane agreed. 'And I'm sure your father is eager to introduce you. We must hurry.'

'Tell me what you know about him.'

Jane pushed a silver hairpin through Arabella's hair to keep it in place. 'His name is Kalyan Singh,' she said. 'He's the Rajput ruler of Kishangarh, which borders Jaipur to the west.'

'He is friendly, isn't he?'

Jane smiled. 'He would hardly be here otherwise. Along with Jaipur, Kishangarh has been under British protection since the Marathas were defeated four years ago.'

'You know a lot about India, don't you?'

Jane laughed this time. 'I assure you there's plenty I don't know about India. Now come along. Stand up and let me have a good look at you.'

Arabella rose from her chair and straightened her dress—the whitest batiste dress she owned, adorned with fine yellow embroidery where it drew in beneath her bust and at the shoulders. At her neck was a dainty citrine choker.

'Wonderful,' Jane said through her smile, feeling as proud of her charge as her own mother surely would. Not for the first time, Jane wondered what it would have been like to have a child of her own. It had never happened for her, but at least she had Arabella, whom she had watched grow from infancy and had often cared for in her mother's frequent periods of absence, both in body and mind, over the years.

Jane led Arabella out of the room, heading for the courtyard garden where they had been told Sir John and Lady Elspeth would be entertaining the maharaja. As they approached, Arabella's brow began to knot, and in a low voice she asked, 'Who are all these people?'

'The maharaja's retinue,' Jane said. 'His personal servants and advisors.'

They passed around twenty people in all, recognising a few of the household servants among them, smiling and nodding politely as they entered the courtyard, which had been arranged with plentiful fruits and fresh flowers for the maharaja's visit. Though a little cooler than it had been in recent months now that autumn had begun, it was still hot enough to warrant the shade of the magnificent pergola tent that had been erected in the middle of the garden.

As they made their way towards it, Jane saw Sir John sitting in his finest white suit beside Lady Elspeth, who looked similarly distinguished in her white gown and pale-blue mameluke turban trimmed with an ostrich feather. There were two men with them, both in golden *achkan sherwanis*, a garment of trend among Indian royalty since its first appearance at Lucknow in recent years.

It was easy to see which of the two men was Maharaja Kalyan Singh by the sheer number and size of the jewels he wore. His headdress was of shimmering red-and-gold cloth, adorned with strings of pearls, with a diamond aigrette of three feathers rising from the centre, inset with a single ruby. Around his neck, layer upon layer of pearls covered his chest. As their seats had been arranged in a semicircle, the figure beside him was obscured for now, his face turned away.

'Arabella!' Sir John said, standing as soon as he saw them approach. 'Allow me to introduce you to His Highness, the Maharaja of Kishangarh.' He was full of smiles as the maharaja rose from his seat to greet them. 'Your Highness, this is my daughter, Arabella, and our good friend, Jane Hardwick. Arabella, Mrs Hardwick, this is Maharaja Kalyan Singh, and his brother, the crown prince.'

'*Namaste*,' Arabella said, pressing her palms to her chest and bowing her head as Jane had instructed her.

When Arabella looked up again, it seemed to Jane as if she were about to faint. Standing beside the maharaja, looking equally regal, though somewhat understated by comparison, was the young sowar, Naresh Bharat Singh.

Jane quickly ushered Arabella to the chairs that had been set out for them beside her mother, facing the maharaja and the young prince. As Arabella lowered herself into her seat, she couldn't seem to take her eyes off Bharat Singh, whose face held a puckish smile.

'His Highness has bestowed a fine gift upon me,' her father said. He clicked his fingers and one of the guards standing at the perimeter of the pergola came closer. He was carrying an embroidered silk pillow, which he lowered before the resident. 'This beautiful jewelled dagger,' he said, lifting it gently in both hands as if afraid to mark it.

'It is but a letter opener,' the maharaja said with a smile. 'Something with which to open your many correspondences.'

'Then it is both practical and beautiful,' Sir John said, 'although I'm not sure how I will ever bring myself to use it as such.'

'But you must, and every day you will remember our meeting.'

Sir John smiled at the maharaja, bowing his head towards him. 'If it is your wish.'

They continued talking together, largely about India and the politics of the Honourable East India Company, and Jane noted that the maharaja spoke good, if accented, English. On the other hand, the prince said very little, perhaps because by his own admission he did not, which surprised Jane given his status and the wealth of learning that was clearly at his disposal. She thought perhaps that Bharat Singh was more for adventure at his young age than scholarly pursuits. At twenty-eight years old, the maharaja was around ten years older than the prince. By the time the prince was that age, Jane had no doubt that his English would be just as good, especially now that it appeared he had good reason to learn, in the form of the young woman sitting beside her.

Every now and then the ladies would be drawn into the conversation, although even Jane had to confess that after thirty minutes of such talk, she began to tire of it. She imagined Arabella must be bored to distraction, or might have been had the young sowar-prince not been sitting opposite her. After several minutes more, Jane coughed into her hand.

'Would anyone mind if I took a stroll around the garden before lunch?' she said, not waiting for permission before slowly getting to her feet.

'That's a splendid idea,' Sir John said. He turned to Elspeth. 'Perhaps an amble would suit you, my dear?'

'Actually, I'm rather tired,' Elspeth said. She, too, stood up. 'If you don't mind, I think I'll go and lie down for an hour. I find the heat so tiring and I'm sure you have much to discuss with the maharaja.'

'Of course,' Sir John said. 'I'll send someone for you in time for lunch.'

Arabella was next to stand up. 'I should like to go,' she said, 'and perhaps the prince would care to join us.'

'Yes, very much,' Bharat Singh said, smiling as he rose.

They left Sir John and the maharaja to continue their discourse beneath the shade of the pergola, stepping out into the sunshine as one of the servants approached with a parasol for each of them.

'You're certainly full of surprises,' Arabella said to the prince as soon as they were out of earshot.

'Did I not say I would find a way to see you?'

Arabella laughed to herself. 'Yes, and I'm glad you did, Crown Prince of Kishangarh.'

They both laughed together as they walked, and Jane held back a little as they reached the courtyard border with its colourful flowering shrubs.

'I have gift for you,' Bharat Singh said, his broken English becoming quite endearing. He unbuttoned his sherwani, reached inside and produced a fold of crimson material, which he unwrapped to reveal a posy of small mauve flowers that were white at the centre. He handed them to Arabella and added, '*Nilakantha.*'

'After your horse,' Arabella said. 'Sky Flower.'

Bharat Singh nodded. 'I wish for you to see them.'

The flowers had wilted, but Arabella didn't seem to mind. She held them to her nose, drawing in what remained of their fragrance, smiling as if to suggest she thought it a lovely gesture all the same.

As Bharat Singh withdrew his hand, one of his rings sparkled in the sunlight, drawing Jane's attention. 'What a beautiful ring,' she said, noticing a familiar symbol that was set into the face of the ring with numerous small diamonds—ॐ. 'That's the ancient Sanskrit Aum symbol, isn't it?'

'Aum, yes,' Bharat Singh said, holding the ring up so that Jane and Arabella could better see it. In Hindi he added, 'It represents the most sacred sound, from which all creation was born. My father had two identical rings made: one for me, and one for my brother, His Highness the Maharaja. I wear it always, but I am afraid I will someday lose it in battle.'

Jane translated everything Bharat Singh had said. Then, continuing the conversation in Hindi, she asked him, 'How is it that you, a crown prince, are also a sowar in the Bengal Army?'

'It was my wish,' Bharat Singh replied, also in Hindi. 'I desire to fight as my great ancestors fought. My brother, however, indulges me only so far. Because I am young, he believes the experience will build my character and make me strong, but I have guards at my side always—guards who will give their lives to save mine should the need arise. That day on the Tonk road when you first arrived is the closest I have come to battle. I am charged mainly with the delivery of dispatches, to keep me from harm.'

Jane continued to translate their words for Arabella as they ambled beside the flower border. 'But you came alone to the stream when you were delivering your dispatches to the resident,' she continued. 'Where were your guards then?'

'Nilakantha is a very fast horse,' Bharat Singh said. 'And although strong men, my guards are very slow and fat.' He laughed to himself. 'She outran them easily so that I could come to the stream alone. The two who were with me that afternoon were not far behind.'

'I see. And the bazaar? Didn't your company miss you?'

'As I have said, I am indulged. I am not bound to the life of a regular sowar. I am allowed certain dispensations and am free to take my leave whenever I choose. I wear the uniform, but because of my position as crown prince, I cannot be a real soldier. I do not suffer their hardships. Because of this, I will never be accepted as one of them.'

Jane noted the sadness in Bharat Singh's voice as he finished speaking. When she translated his words, Arabella stood close to him and held his hand briefly, making sure no one could see them. His spirit seemed to lift instantly as they looked into each other's eyes, and in that moment Jane suspected that Arabella and the young sowar-prince might come to see a lot of each other over the coming months. But while Naresh Bharat Singh had proved to be most resourceful when it came to devising ways to be with Arabella, Jane knew there were great barriers ahead for the young couple if the spark of love she had just witnessed between them was to blossom.

Chapter Seventeen

Present day

When Jefferson Tayte awoke on the morning after the family gathering at Drumarthen, it was not to the booming report of Murray's shotgun, but to the equally unwelcome sound of car doors being slammed shut beneath his bedroom window. He checked the time on the retro digital watch Jean had bought for him. The glowing red LEDs told him it was just before eight. Thanks to last night's whisky, he'd gone out like a light as soon as his head had touched his pillow, and he'd slept like the dead.

His first conscious thought was to wonder who was there, so to satisfy his curiosity he swung his legs out of bed, went to one of the curtains and pulled it aside. The unexpected glare of bright sunshine after last night's storm made him blink several times as he tried to focus. Once he had, he saw a police car on the drive, which prompted his second thought of the day: what were the police doing at Drumarthen so soon after DI Ross's visit the evening before? The only way Tayte could answer that question was to get dressed and go down to see for himself.

As Tayte descended the stairs five minutes later, he was surprised to see DI Ross standing in the main hallway. He wondered why he'd come in a regular police car this time instead of his own unmarked car, which he'd arrived in previously. That, and the uniformed officer standing by the door, suggested a far more official visit, further arousing

Tayte's curiosity. Ross's moustache was twitching excitedly as he spoke to Sinclair, and Tayte could only imagine that there had been a further development in his murder investigation.

'Good morning, Mr Tayte,' Sinclair said as soon as he noticed him on the stairs. His face was lined with concern. 'You've arrived just in time to hear the terrible news.'

'Good morning,' Tayte replied, nodding to Ross and the uniformed policeman. 'What's happened?'

'Another murder, I'm afraid,' Ross said. 'Two more, in fact.'

'Two more?'

'Aye. Niall and Mairi Fraser were stabbed to death in their car a few miles from here.'

Tayte took a long, slow breath to calm himself. 'What happened?'

'It appears that someone ran their car off the road after they left here last night,' Ross said. 'It was found earlier this morning on the road to Carroglen.'

'That's just dreadful. Why? I mean, I'm still here, trying to find the Blood of Rajputana, just as whoever appears to be doing this wants me to. Why has this person killed again?'

'I wish I knew, Mr Tayte. I really do. We're trying our best to figure it out, believe me. Maybe their killer didn't leave those letters for you. Or maybe he did and he has another agenda I've yet to figure out. Whatever the reason, as soon as you find out what became of that ruby the better, in my opinion—before someone else dies.'

Tayte thought that was just great. Now, not only did Sinclair want him to find the Blood of Rajputana, in the hope that doing so might help to bring his brother's killer to justice, as he saw it, but so did the police. It seemed that because of this gemstone, people were now being murdered left, right and centre. If he'd had any prior inclination to walk away, how could he do so now?

He wished his sense of right and wrong wasn't always so strong, but it was an integral part of who he was. He couldn't change it. He thought back over some of the unexciting, everyday assignments he'd taken since moving to London, and considered that the humdrum that made up so much of his work perhaps wasn't so bad. But how could he have known? What he did know was that he had to help stop this if he could.

Ross looked up at the high ceiling, scanning the area from left to right. 'I've been thinking it would be a good idea to install a couple of wireless security cameras here at Drumarthen. Maybe next time we'll get some footage of whoever's leaving these letters—if that's agreeable to you, Damian.'

Sinclair nodded. 'It's a pity we didn't think to do it sooner. If the letters *are* being left by the same person who's behind these killings, it appears that whoever murdered the Frasers was also here at Drumarthen last night.'

'That's partly why I called on you this morning,' Ross said. 'I was the first to leave here, with Callum Macrae. It's possible that whoever left after the Frasers followed them from here, or their killer could just as well have been waiting nearby for them to leave. Did anything unusual happen after I'd gone?'

'Their car wouldn't start,' Tayte said.

'Aye, that's right,' Sinclair added. 'I had Murray see everyone out. One of the engine leads on the Frasers' car had come loose.'

'So they were last to leave?' Ross said.

'Aye, maybe fifteen minutes or so after you and everyone else.'

A quizzical expression washed over Ross's face. 'I have to question the odds of their car having arrived here perfectly fine, only to develop a fault while it was sitting out there on your drive. I mean, how does a lead come loose all by itself? Such a thing seems far more likely to happen while the car's bumping along the roads.'

'You think someone tampered with it?' Tayte said.

'It seems the more likely scenario to me. Maybe someone wanted to make sure they were the last to leave. With myself and the others gone, the roads around here would be empty on a night like that.'

'Callum Macrae,' Sinclair said. 'He's a mechanic. He'd know just what lead to tamper with, and he had plenty of opportunity when he went out to help Murray with the generator. It would also account for why he said he never found the hatch. Maybe he never intended to look for it.'

'I took Callum home, remember?' Ross said. He scratched at his head. 'That's not to say he couldn't have used another car from his garage and gone straight back out again. He could have tampered with the Frasers' car to buy himself time to get back out here.'

'He specifically asked you to take him home, too,' Sinclair said. 'What better alibi could he hope for?'

'Aye,' Ross said. 'I think it's time I had a word with Callum Macrae in a more official capacity.'

'What about Ewan Blair?' Tayte said. 'He went out for a cigarette.'

'Aye, and Blair too,' Ross said. 'Is Murray about?'

'Murray?' Sinclair said. 'What do you want with him?'

'He also left the gathering last night. You said he got the Frasers' car running again, and by all accounts it didn't take him long to do so. Maybe he already knew exactly what was wrong with it. Can you account for his whereabouts after the Frasers left?'

'He brought that letter in to us,' Tayte said.

'Then he went to his bed,' Sinclair added. 'He wanted an early night because of the storm. He was out early this morning checking the estate. We've a couple of trees down. No doubt you'll have heard his chainsaw buzzing in the distance when you got out of your car.'

'Aye, I heard it. Did you see him go to his room?'

Sinclair shook his head.

'Then if it's all the same to you, I'd like to come back later and have a word with him.'

'Of course,' Sinclair said, quickly adding, 'You know there could just as well have been someone else outside, watching the house, waiting for the opportunity to tamper with the Frasers' car and slip that letter on to the lamp table in the hallway while we were all talking in the dining room, especially when the lights went out.'

'By someone, I suppose you mean these Rajputs you keep telling me about?'

'Aye, maybe.'

Ross smiled wryly. 'I'll be sure to keep that in mind, although I'd sooner focus my investigation on more tangible suspects. I'm just heading over to Moira Macrae's house to see what she has to say for herself. I'm sure she already knows about the poor Frasers. She knows most things that happen in Comrie long before they're announced in the papers.'

As Ross headed for the door, Sinclair said, 'I was going to call and ask Moira whether I could take Mr Tayte to see her today. Maybe he could go along with you instead. She could hardly refuse to talk to him with you there, especially after what's happened.'

Ross turned back. 'I've got to drop by the station and pick up my car, but if you'd care to join me, Mr Tayte, that's fine by me.'

'That would be great,' Tayte said, at the same time getting the feeling that Sinclair couldn't have palmed his visit off on DI Ross quickly enough. 'I'll just grab my briefcase.'

Tayte wasn't quite sure what to expect from his visit with Moira Macrae, whose name alone had begun to fill him with dread. If Sinclair and Ross's poor opinions of the woman were anything to go by, he imagined he was in for an uncomfortable morning. On meeting Moira, however, apart from carrying a thick, knotted walking cane at her side, he didn't think she looked so intimidating. She was a full-figured woman with a round face and wiry grey hair that complemented her lilac velour loungewear.

When they arrived at her modest semi-detached bungalow in Dalginross, an extension of Comrie to the south, her hospitality and softly spoken Scottish tones also helped put Tayte at ease. As Ross had called ahead, she had a fresh pot of tea waiting for them, and any remaining concerns Tayte might have had were immediately dispelled at the sight of her fluffy slippers and tan support tights. They were seated in the lounge on a worn, paisley-print three-piece suite. Tayte and Ross were on the sofa in front of a low teak and smoked-glass table, while Moira sat opposite them in one of the armchairs.

'Would you like a shortbread biscuit, Mr Tayte?' Moira asked. 'They're particularly fine—made in the village to an old Scottish recipe.'

Tayte leaned forward, smiling politely as he took one. 'It's very kind of you to have laid on cookies for us,' he said. 'Thank you.'

'It's nae bother,' Moira said, smiling back at him. 'Cookies,' she repeated to herself, still smiling, clearly amused by Tayte's Americanism.

Tayte took a bite and tried to catch the crumbs without spilling his tea.

'I've heard about you, Mr Tayte,' Moira said, sipping her tea as she continued to take him in through her wide, cat-eye glasses.

'From your son, Callum?'

'Aye, he likes to visit his old mum. I think it must be my Scotch pies he comes for, but I don't mind. He helps keep me up to date with what's going on in Comrie when I can't get out myself.'

Ross sat forward and helped himself to a biscuit. 'Then you'll no doubt have heard what happened to Niall and Mairi Fraser. I take it Callum's been to see you this morning?'

'Aye, I've heard, but not from my boy. He's not been over to see me yet.' Moira turned to Tayte. 'You don't much care for my tea, do you, Mr Tayte?'

Tayte hadn't been aware that it was so obvious. He'd only taken a few sips, but he supposed it must have been written all over his face. 'It's fine tea,' he said, feeling awkward, not wishing to offend.

'Come now, Mr Tayte. I'm sixty-eight, not ninety-eight. You can't pull the wool over my eyes that easily. Too strong for you? Is that it?'

'I'm just not particularly partial to tea. I prefer coffee.'

'Ah, well, I can't help you there, I'm afraid.'

Ross settled back again. He crunched into his biscuit and the crumbs cascaded down over his suit. 'Mr Tayte would like to ask you some questions about your family history,' he said, his mouth still half-full. 'There's a chance his work may be important to my investigation, so it's equally important you answer him as best you can. I don't need to remind you how serious this is.'

'No, you don't,' Moira said, her expression darkening. 'As far as my side of the family goes, Mr Tayte, you've come to the right person. When it comes to our ancestry, I believe I know more than most. I've been an enthusiast for many years—more even than the good Dr Drummond, Lord rest his soul.'

'That's good to hear,' Tayte said. 'I'm hoping to see Dr Drummond's research soon,' he added, looking at Ross.

'I should have it for you tomorrow,' Ross said.

'Great,' Tayte said, turning back to Moira. 'In the meantime, for now at least, I'm particularly interested in your Fraser bloodline.'

'What would you like to know?' Moira said. 'Maybe we can exchange information. Help to fill in the blanks in each other's research, as it were. I hear you've made good progress with your work for Damian Sinclair.'

Tayte was beginning to wonder whether there was anything Moira Macrae hadn't heard about him since he'd arrived in Comrie. He ignored the obvious attempt at getting him to share his findings. The discovery of Robert Christie on Sinclair's side of the family seemed paramount to learning more about the Blood of Rajputana, and he wasn't about to hand that key piece of information over to anyone.

Addressing her question, Tayte asked, 'I'd like to know more about Lachlan Fraser's close family. I take it you know who he was?'

'Aye, of course I do. My research dates back many generations. Lachlan was my three-times-great-grandfather. He was a military man, as many of the Fraser men were. If it's him you're interested in, then more's the pity Niall Fraser's no longer with us. He had a particular interest in the family's military affairs.'

'I'm not so much interested in Lachlan himself,' Tayte said. 'I've come across another Fraser, whom I believe was from Lachlan's time. Scottish archives would no doubt provide the answer I'm looking for, but it would save me some time if you could tell me whether Lachlan had a brother.'

'Aye, Lachlan had two brothers,' Moira said, no need to reference her research. 'One died young, the other fared little better by today's standards.'

'Was one of them called Donnan?' Tayte asked, keen now to make the connection between this family and the man he'd read about in Jane's letters. 'He was a captain in the East India Company during the first half of the nineteenth century.'

'As I've said, I don't know much about the family's military history, but aye, that was the name of Lachlan's older brother. I say older, although there was barely more than a year between them.'

'Thank you,' Tayte said, smiling because he now had the confirmation he sought, and another name to add to the puzzle he was trying to unravel.

'Their father was a man called Dougal,' Moira continued, but before she could go on, Tayte stopped her.

'That's okay,' he said. 'I just wanted to confirm the connection for now. Unless there's anything more you can tell me about Donnan Fraser. Did he marry? Any children? Are there any of Donnan's descendants living nearby?'

'No,' Moira said.

Tayte smiled. 'No to which question?'

'All of them. As I said, Donnan Fraser died a relatively young man. I'd have to check my records for the details, but I'm pretty sure it was sometime during the 1830s, while he was serving in India. He had no wife and no wee bairns.' Moira paused, her eyes narrowing on Tayte. 'So you believe Donnan Fraser is somehow important in all this? Maybe he's the connection to this ruby everyone's been looking for.'

Tayte thought he'd said enough. 'At this juncture, I really couldn't say. It's just another name I'm interested in for now.'

'But wherever did you come across it?' Moira asked, and then her face lit up as she realised. 'It was in one of those letters Jamie Sinclair told us about, wasn't it?'

There was no use denying it, so Tayte gave Moira a nod. At the same time he got the feeling that the longer he spent talking with Moira Macrae, the more information she would gradually draw out of him. Despite everything that was going on, it was apparent that she was still looking for the Blood of Rajputana—still trying to work out this family history puzzle for herself.

Before Moira could probe Tayte further, DI Ross came to his rescue. 'I sense you're about done here, Mr Tayte. If you've nothing further to ask Mrs Macrae about her family history just now, I'd like to talk about Gordon Drummond. Moira, you know the people of Comrie. You hear plenty about what goes on around here. I can't think of a better person to ask whether you know of anyone who'd wish to harm him.'

Moira put her empty cup and saucer back down on the table. 'It's not just about the doctor now, though, is it?'

'No, it's not,' Ross said, 'but he's as good a place to start as any.'

Moira settled back again and stared into the gas fireplace to her right as she seemed to give the matter some thought. 'I'd have a word with Chrissie MacIntyre, if I were you. Unlike most in Comrie, she's never had a good word to say about Gordon Drummond. Perhaps you should ask her why.'

'Aye, I got that impression at Drumarthen yesterday. She was quiet as a church mouse all evening, but every now and then she'd give a little scoff when Gordon was referred to as the good doctor. She wouldn't say why.'

'No, she wouldn't, being the quiet type.'

'I'll go and see her. Maybe she'll talk to me without the family around her. Did you see your son last night at all?'

'No,' Moira said, her eyes narrowing. 'Why do you ask?'

'I need to speak with him, too. We called in at the garage on the way here this morning. His assistant told me he'd not seen him. Until I can ask him for myself, I wondered whether you could vouch for his whereabouts after I dropped him home last night.'

Moira began to fidget. 'And why should I need to do that? Do you think he's a murderer? Is that what you think? You've known him since he was a wee bairn.'

'Calm down, Moira. I'm not accusing anybody of anything just now. I simply want to talk to him, that's all. There's a chance the Frasers' car was tampered with last night, and—'

'And just because my son's a mechanic,' Moira cut in, sounding agitated, 'you think he must have done it?' She gave a sharp, derisive laugh. 'If you want to talk to someone about the Frasers, I'd suggest you go and see Damian Sinclair. He's a man with a motive when it comes to the murders of Niall and Mairi.'

'How do you figure that?'

'It's no secret that Damian's harboured a bitter dislike for the pair of them for some years now. You must remember when Jamie introduced Mairi to the family. They were engaged to be married, until Mairi none too gently broke the engagement off. Surely you recall how Damian nearly killed Niall when he found out he'd been having an affair with Mairi for several months behind his brother's back?'

'Aye, I remember, and better than you, it seems. Damian might have given Niall a good thumping on his brother's behalf, but he came nowhere close to killing the man.'

'Well, you remember it how you will, but Damian Sinclair's never been one to forgive and forget.'

Ross smiled to himself, as if seeing through Moira's plan to steer the conversation away from her son. 'You'd love it if I had reason to arrest Damian Sinclair, wouldn't you? It's also no secret that you hate the man, as you hated his father before him. All because of a family feud, and for what? A few trinkets left in a will.'

'Those paintings should have come to me,' Moira said with an indignant air. 'They were promised to my great-great-grandfather and the Sinclairs bloody well knew it!'

Tayte sat quietly on the sidelines, thinking that if he had a dollar for every occasion he'd come across a family quarrel over an ancestor's last will and testament, he'd be a rich man. He was content to stay out of this particular conversation, but it seemed Moira had other ideas.

She turned her head sharply to Tayte, her expression having long since lost its initial charm. 'When you go back to your client, Mr Tayte, you can tell him from me that I still want those paintings. I've not forgotten, and he'd better not have bloody well sold them!'

Tayte wasn't sure how to reply to that, but thankfully he didn't have to. Ross put his cup and saucer down on the table with a clatter, silencing Moira and drawing her attention back to him.

'Do I need to remind you that four members of this syndicate I heard about last night are dead? That's all I'm interested in just now. A syndicate, I might add, that you were a part of.'

'Well, maybe I'll be next,' Moira said with sarcasm. 'I'll be sure to keep an eye out for Damian Sinclair when he comes for me, don't you worry.' She turned back to Tayte, her eyes squinting and her lips thinning as she said, 'So, is Captain Donnan Fraser all you're going to give me? Are you going to tell me what other discoveries you've got in your briefcase there or not?'

'Most definitely not,' Tayte said, beginning to see now why others felt the way they did about Moira Macrae.

On hearing Tayte's answer, Moira stood up, needing no help from her walking stick. She picked it up just the same. 'Then get out of my bloody house, the pair of you,' she said, poking her stick threateningly in Tayte's direction.

Ross stood up, smiling to himself. 'You know, Mr Tayte, as soon as we sat down, I thought to myself, this is not the Moira Macrae I know. I'm glad to see you didn't let her sweet old lady routine fool you.'

'Get out!' Moira yelled, and this time she brought the tip of her walking stick down hard on to the table, rattling the crockery.

'Come along, Mr Tayte,' Ross said. Then, as they began to leave, he turned back to Moira and added, 'Tell Callum I'd like to speak with him when you see him. He knows where to find me. Or don't tell him. It's up to you. One way or another, I'll catch up with him soon enough.'

Chapter Eighteen

When DI Ross dropped Tayte back at Drumarthen, Murray was standing on the sunlit drive with a spade in his hand. He was covered in mud, from his elbows to his oversized wellington boots, suggesting that he was still busy dealing with the aftermath of the previous night's storm.

'Just the man I want to see,' Ross said as he brought the car to a stop.

They got out and Murray stepped closer. As well as the spade, Tayte now saw that he was holding a brown-paper package, which he handed to Tayte as he and Ross approached.

'This parcel just arrived for you, Mr Tayte.'

'Thank you, Murray,' Tayte said as he took it, wondering what it was. His eyes immediately fell on the postmark. It was from London and he supposed Jean must have sent it. Had he forgotten something?

Murray turned to Ross. 'Mr Sinclair said you wanted to see me about last night.'

'Aye, I do,' Ross said. 'Take a wee walk with me, will you? Do excuse us, Mr Tayte.'

'Of course,' Tayte said, still feeling the outline of his parcel, trying to guess the contents. 'Thanks for your help today.'

'Anytime, Mr Tayte. As I said, the sooner you find what you're looking for, the better.'

Tayte headed for the front door. As he reached it, Damian Sinclair appeared in the frame, a welcoming smile on his face, his cable-knit jumper also spattered with mud.

'I've been helping Murray,' he said by way of an explanation. 'Sometimes one pair of hands isn't enough around here.'

Tayte returned his smile and stepped inside. 'I'm sure a place like this must be quite a challenge. Ever thought about selling up?'

Sinclair looked shocked by the idea. 'Heavens, no. My father would turn in his grave. And who would buy the old place in this state? No, Drumarthen will stay in the family as long as there's a breath left in me.'

'But you don't have any children to leave it to,' Tayte said. 'Someone might buy it at the right price. You could be enjoying the money.'

'I've seen enough money through my work in London to last me a lifetime, Mr Tayte. I don't much care for it these days, as long as there's enough. If Murray's still around when I'm gone, the place will be his to do with as he pleases. He'll have earned it, believe me.'

'That's a very generous gift.'

'What good will it do me when I'm gone? Murray's as good as family—always has been. He's so much closer to me than my flesh-and-blood family are. I couldn't stomach the idea of Drumarthen falling into their hands.'

Having met a few of Sinclair's relatives, Tayte could understand why he felt that way. He began to walk towards the stairs, eager to carry on with his research now he'd confirmed that Donnan Fraser was Lachlan Fraser's brother, tying the captain from Jane Hardwick's letters to the family he was researching. He'd only taken two steps when Sinclair stopped him.

'If you've got a moment,' he said, 'there's a room at Drumarthen that a learned man such as yourself might be interested in seeing.'

Tayte turned back again. 'Sure,' he said. He was very interested in seeing more of the house. 'Lead the way.'

'It's here in the west wing, so we'll be quite safe,' Sinclair said as he led Tayte through a door to their right. It opened into a corridor that was dimly lit by several open doorways along its length. 'I had the contents of the original room moved down here some time ago, to help preserve it all. I was worried about the rotting woodwork on the upper floors.' As they headed along the corridor, Sinclair asked, 'How did you get on with Moira Macrae?'

'I found her a very calculated woman,' Tayte said. 'I managed to get what I wanted from her. Donnan Fraser was Lachlan Fraser's brother. As soon as she told me that, it was clear she wanted information from me in return.'

'You didn't tell her about the Christies, did you?'

'Under different circumstances I'd have thought it a fair enough trade, but no, I didn't give her anything beyond Donnan Fraser himself. She knows I'm interested in him, which could help her, assuming she's still looking for the Blood of Rajputana, with everything that's going on here.'

'You can be sure she is,' Sinclair said, scoffing to himself. 'She's invested too much time in trying to find it to let it go now, especially since you're here looking for it.'

They turned a corner to their left and the way was marginally brighter, lit by several high windows through which the midday sunshine beamed, illuminating dusty flagstones and the faded, threadbare carpet runner on which they were walking.

'Before I forget,' Tayte said, 'Moira told me to tell you she still wanted those paintings, and that you'd better not have sold them.'

'Did she now?' Sinclair said, furrowing his brow.

Tayte nodded. 'Ross mentioned a family feud. It had something to do with trinkets left in a will.'

'The paintings to which she refers are more than mere trinkets, and yes, I still have them—not that I'll ever let Moira Macrae get her hands on them. They're from the old days, when my four-times-great-grandmother, Aileen, was alive. She's in most of them, although there's one of her husband, Lachlan. I suppose that's why Moira's so keen to have them, and maybe why she feels they should have gone to her side of the family. Lachlan's her biological ancestor after all, not mine, but that's hardly the point.'

'I saw in your records that Aileen survived her husband. I guess the paintings were hers to do with as she pleased.'

'Aye, and while she and Lachlan had four legitimate children together, she wanted her illegitimate son Angus to have them. The feud between the two sides of the family has been going on for generations, but it was never greater than when my father was alive—when he had Moira Macrae to contend with. Jamie always said she finished our father off in the end, although he was already in poor health. Mind you, the stress she caused the man might well have put the last nail in his coffin, so to speak.'

They came to the end of the corridor and Sinclair stopped. To his left was a large oak door, which he slowly opened. It creaked in protest, clearly not having been opened in some time. Sinclair stepped back and with a wave of his hand, invited Tayte to go inside.

'It's a library,' Tayte said, stating the obvious as he gazed around at all the colourful, if dusty, book spines lined up on shelves that reached almost to the ceiling. 'There must be a thousand books or more in here.'

'I counted closer to two thousand,' Sinclair said. 'The house came with quite a collection to begin with, but as I'm from a long line of readers, the collection quickly grew.'

Tayte walked further in. There was little furniture in the room—not even a desk to sit and read at. He saw a tall wooden ladder at the far end of the room, but other than that, it was all about the books. He drew in their scent, and the many old pages combined to assault his senses.

'I love that smell,' he said, a wide smile on his face as he was reminded of all the old documents he'd had the privilege of seeing during his twenty-plus years as a professional genealogist.

'The original library was far more grandiose than this, of course,' Sinclair said. 'We managed to fit some of the old bookcases in, but as you can see, most of the shelving is comparatively crude. On the whole, I think Murray did a fine job.'

'Anything that helps keep such a collection safe is a good thing in my book,' Tayte said. 'No pun intended. Is it okay to take a few out?'

'Be my guest,' Sinclair said. 'What use is a collection of books nobody reads? If anything takes your fancy, you're more than welcome to take it back to your room with you, and you know the way here now should you want to try something else.'

'Thank you. I'd like that very much,' Tayte said as he put his brief-case and parcel down and began to read some of the titles on the lower shelves.

He was standing beside a section of books about architecture. He saw titles by John Ruskin: *The Seven Lamps of Architecture*, published in 1849, and *The Stones of Venice*, 1851. Moving along, he came to a section about landscape gardening and saw many books about the works of Lancelot 'Capability' Brown, whom someone living at Drumarthen in the past had clearly taken great interest in. Next there was a section on poetry, and then other, very old sections about geography and botanical studies. After that he came to a large section devoted to art.

'*Methods and Materials of Painting of the Great Schools and Masters* by Charles Lock Eastlake,' Tayte read from one of the spines. 'There's enough material in here to keep just about anyone content. I'll be sure to come back and take a better look when I have more time.'

'Of course,' Sinclair said. 'You have your research to do.'

He turned away, heading for the door, and Tayte followed after him, collecting his things as he went. When Sinclair reached the door he stopped.

'I meant to say, it's Jamie's funeral the day after tomorrow. You're welcome to come along with Murray and me if you wish. I doubt there'll be many there, and to be frank I'd appreciate your support.

Jamie didn't care much for the rest of the family. I'm sure he'd prefer to be in the hands of a stranger such as yourself when it comes to lowering his coffin into the ground.'

The invitation came as something of a surprise, but how could Tayte refuse? 'Of course,' he said. 'I'd be glad to attend.'

'Splendid,' Sinclair said as they headed back along the corridor. 'I'll let you know what time the car's due to arrive. We can all travel to the church together.'

***

Jefferson Tayte set his briefcase down by the desk in his room, took off his jacket and hung it over the back of the chair, eager to find out what was inside the parcel that had arrived for him. Without another moment's delay, he tore it open like an excitable child at Christmas, and what he saw put a wide smile on his face. The contents of the package were accompanied by a note, which he read out to himself.

'*I thought you might need these. Love Jean.*'

Tayte had purposefully left his Hershey's Miniatures at home, thinking to put them out of reach for a week or so, trying to break the habit. He held the bag up and continued to smile. Given what was going on here in Comrie, he thought he might just need them now. The note prompted him to take out his phone and call Jean. She picked up on the second ring.

'JT!' she said, sounding excited to hear his voice. 'I'm so glad you called.'

'Why? Is something wrong?'

'No, everything's great. I'm just glad to hear your voice. I miss you.'

'I miss you, too. How are you? How's Ben?'

'We're both fine. We're about to head out for lunch.'

'I wish I was going with you. I've decided I have to stay and help out here if I can. I don't know if what I'm doing will make a difference, but I have to try. Two more people were murdered here last night—a man and his wife. You might have heard about it on TV already. I know it's happening in Scotland, but I expect something this big would have national coverage.'

'I've not seen the news lately,' Jean said. 'I'll have a look later. Promise you'll be careful, JT.'

'I promise,' Tayte said. 'I don't believe whoever's doing this is after me. It all seems too personal—something to do with the ruby I'm after and this syndicate the victims were a part of. I'd better get back to it. I just called to say thanks for the candy. You must have read my mind.'

'I'm glad it arrived okay. Just don't eat it all at once.'

'I'll try not to.'

'Save me a couple of Mr Goodbars, will you?'

Tayte pulled a face. 'You're not serious.'

'Go on, you can do it. The discipline will be good for you.'

Tayte sighed. 'I'll give it a go, but I can't promise anything. You know Mr Goodbar's my favourite.'

'Why do you think I chose it?'

'There's a cruel streak in you, Mrs Tayte. You know that, don't you?'

Jean laughed. 'You're the one who wanted to cut back. If you can't save two chocolates for the woman you love, what hope have you got?'

Tayte sighed again. She had him there, but he had a plan. He opened the bag of Hershey's, took out two of the Mr Goodbar chocolates and walked over to the wardrobe where he'd put his travel case. *Out of sight is out of mind*, he thought as he dropped the chocolates inside, knowing he could now eat the rest of the bag without having to leave two of his favourites in the bottom, calling to him every time he saw them.

'No problem,' he said, smiling to himself. 'You have a great lunch. I'll call again soon.'

When the call ended, Tayte grabbed his bag of Hershey's, opened his briefcase and thrust them inside before temptation could get the better of him. 'Pace yourself, JT,' he told himself. 'You only have one bag, and it's not even full.' He pulled his laptop out and began to gather his thoughts. When he set it down on the desk and opened it, however, every thought in his head abandoned him. His breath caught in his chest. He was looking at another of Jane Hardwick's letters. The old paper was identical and there was clearly no need for an envelope with his name on it this time.

He opened the letter and saw that the year was now 1823, having been written several months after the previous letter he'd read. He quickly scanned the contents and saw mention of marriage, and of tears, but he was less concerned with the contents of the letter at this point. What concerned him most was how it had got into his briefcase, sandwiched between the keyboard and screen of his laptop. He'd had his briefcase close by him all day and he'd had no reason to open it before now. So who had? He considered who'd had the opportunity.

'Moira Macrae?' Tayte mumbled under his breath.

He shook his head. His briefcase had either been in his hand or by his side throughout his entire visit. The only time it had left his sight that morning was when he'd thrown it on to the back seat of DI Ross's car on the way to Moira's house, and then on the way back to Drumarthen again. He'd been holding it since then, apart from a short time while he was looking at the books in Sinclair's library.

'Damian Sinclair?' Tayte said, still thinking aloud.

Although Sinclair had every opportunity to leave these letters for Tayte, he had trouble comprehending how his host, his client, could be the one feeding Jane's letters to him like this. If Sinclair had them, he could just as well have presented them all to him upon his arrival at Drumarthen. What was to stop him?

The answer quickly presented itself. Whoever had the letters was in the frame for the murders of Jamie and Dr Drummond. Tayte also thought about the timing. Someone was releasing the letters to him one at a time. There had to be a reason for that, and Tayte now supposed it was connected to the murders. So far, a letter had turned up just before or just after someone had been killed. It was as if the killer was buying himself time to complete what he'd set out to do before Tayte knew Jane's full story.

Tayte thought back to the last time he'd opened his briefcase. Until a moment ago, he'd had no reason to go in there for anything since the afternoon before, when he'd finished his research into Robert Christie. It occurred to him then that whoever put this latest letter in his briefcase could well have done so the night before, when they left the previous letter on the lamp table in the main hallway. It could easily have been Callum Macrae or Ewan Blair, or anyone else who might have taken advantage of Macrae having left the front door off the latch when he'd gone out to help Murray.

Tayte sighed to himself. He had no way of knowing who had put Jane's letter in his briefcase, but he thought the fact that they had all turned up at Drumarthen was telling. He supposed there was perhaps a connection to the house itself, or were they simply being left at the house because that was where he was? The letters were, after all, intended for him to read. He shook his head, deciding it was best to stay focused on his objective. As he picked up Jane's letter again, his other hand subconsciously wandered down into his briefcase and withdrew one of his Hershey's Miniatures. Then he deftly unfurled the wrapper with one hand, popped the chocolate into his mouth and began to read.

Chapter Nineteen

Jaipur, March 1823

As the months came and went, Arabella and the young sowar-prince fell more deeply in love. But it was an ill-fated love. Jane was sure of that.

On one side, Naresh Bharat Singh had his Hindu religion to consider: Rajput marriages were arranged, and as the Crown Prince of Kishangarh, his marriage was to be no different. His bride was already determined, as was the date of their marriage. Since meeting Arabella, however, and coming to understand what real love felt like, it was a marriage he no longer desired. His brother the maharaja, and all his counsel, would tell him that love did not matter, and who was he to question their time-honoured customs? But to Naresh Bharat Singh, it mattered very much.

On the other side, Arabella's father was no different from the vast majority of British officers and officials in India, showing little more than contempt for its native people, however high their caste. He would also not let up on his own designs for his daughter's marriage as he continued to extol the virtues of Captain Donnan Fraser at every opportunity.

But these things did not deter Bharat Singh, whose English had improved considerably over the winter months. 'I believe that true love, once recognised, should be seized with all the heart, for it may never be found again,' he had told Arabella one evening as they sat holding hands by the stream.

Jane's translation services were hardly required any more, but Arabella seemed to enjoy her company, as a chaperone, a friend, and perhaps even as a mother in light of Elspeth's all too frequent absence from her daughter's life. As their time in India progressed, Elspeth had taken to her bed more and more with one illness after another, and had now come to rely on her opium pills to see her through each and every day.

Jane was with Arabella now, standing outside her father's study at the residency as Arabella tried to pluck up the courage to knock on his door.

'I can't do it!' Arabella said in a strained whisper. 'Can't you ask him for me?'

'You know the answer to that, Bella. You must find your courage if you mean to go through with this, or we'll be here all afternoon. You do want this, don't you?'

'Aye, with all my heart,' Arabella said. Then she drew a deep breath and knocked.

'Come!'

Her father's coarse tones sent a shiver even through Jane as she stood beside Arabella, whose hands, she noticed, were already aquiver.

Jane gave her a warm smile. 'Go on, dear,' she said. 'You can do this.'

Arabella nodded. 'Don't go away, will you?'

'I'll not move an inch. Now go on with you.'

Arabella stepped closer to the door and turned the handle. 'I'll leave the door open so you can hear us,' she said. Then she stepped inside.

Through the gap, Jane couldn't resist watching Arabella walk slowly towards her father. He was sitting at an intricately carved Indian rosewood desk of huge proportions, which made him seem small by comparison. Suspended from the high ceiling above the desk, a turquoise *punkah* wafted slowly back and forth. The *punkah wallah* operating it was out of sight, perhaps sitting outside beyond the lattice windows so as not to distract Sir John at his work.

'Bella, my darling!' Sir John said, his face lighting up at seeing her. 'What brings you here?'

'I–I hope I'm not interrupting you,' Arabella said, stammering slightly.

Sir John slapped his right hand down on to a pile of papers that sat a foot high on his desk. 'Company business would allow me no respite whatsoever if I let it,' he said. He removed his reading glasses and sat back in his chair. 'In truth, you're just the excuse I need to rest my eyes. Now, what troubles you so much that it can't keep until tiffin?'

Trouble was just the word Jane had in mind as Arabella stepped up to the desk.

'You recall the Crown Prince of Kishangarh, Father? He visited with us last autumn with the maharaja.'

'Yes, of course. A fine young man, although of very few words, as I remember.'

'Do you really think him a fine man?' Arabella asked, optimism in her voice.

'As fine as any Indian prince, I'm sure. But what of him?'

Arabella began to turn her heel back and forth. She was a long time answering. 'He would like . . .' she began, faltering.

'Yes, what would he like?'

'He would like to ask you a very important question. A question whose answer has been weighing heavily on my mind.'

'Well, get to it,' Sir John said, sitting forward on his elbows. 'What is it?'

Arabella coughed nervously. Then she stuck her chin out and said, 'The crown prince would like to ask you for my hand in marriage.'

There, it was done, Jane thought as she waited to hear Sir John's response, although she could guess at his reply. She had told Arabella many times in recent weeks that her father was unlikely to agree to such a union. Had she tried hard enough? She feared not, but who was she to stand in the way of two young people who had found a place for one another in their hearts?

Sir John fell back into his chair, his face suddenly lined with disbelief at what his own ears had just heard. 'Are you out of your mind?' he said, screwing his face up further. 'Has the heat affected your senses? Of course you cannot marry him!'

'But, Father,' Arabella protested. 'He's a crown prince, and—'

'I couldn't care less if he was the wealthiest maharaja in India. You're not marrying a native and that's final. Besides, what of Captain Fraser? You know full well by now that he has his heart set on you, just as you know it's my wish that you and he should marry.'

At that point Arabella burst into tears, and Jane couldn't stop herself from rushing to her side.

'Now it all becomes clear,' Sir John said. 'I suppose I have you to thank for putting my daughter up to this. You've been filling her head with romantic notions since the day you arrived, haven't you? If I thought I'd ever hear the last of it from my wife, I'd send you packing this instant!'

While there were a good many things Jane would have liked to say to Sir John Christie at that moment, she knew better. Instead, she put her arm around Arabella and led her out of the room as the girl continued to sob her young heart out.

Chapter Twenty

Jaipur, March 1823

Five days later, Jane was sitting at the supper table opposite Arabella. The evening meal was almost over, and Jane could see that her young charge was glad of it. The reason was sitting beside her in the form of Captain Donnan Fraser, whom Sir John had insisted join them yet again, for the second time that week. Since Arabella had told her father of her wish to marry Naresh Bharat Singh, it seemed to Jane that Sir John had gone out of his way to bring Captain Fraser and Arabella together even more than usual. Jane had no doubt that he did so in the hope that his daughter would soon give up her foolish notion of marrying the crown prince, but Jane knew she would not.

The table conversation had so far been congenial enough, although it had largely been dominated, as usual, by Sir John and Captain Fraser discussing politics and military matters, in which no one else seemed to have the slightest interest.

'What's your brother up to these days?' Sir John asked the captain. 'Last time you spoke of him he was fighting in the Punjab, and we all know how that turned out!'

'Every dog has its day,' Fraser said. 'The Sikh Empire may have won the war for now, but they can't hold out forever. I received a letter from Lachlan just a few weeks ago. He's not too far away. His company is currently stationed in Delhi, awaiting orders. He believes he'll be coming to Jaipur soon. It would be good to see him again. It's been too long.'

Fraser sipped his coffee and set the cup down again, turning to Arabella with a smile that had not been far from his lips all evening. 'Thanks to your father,' he said, nodding to Sir John, 'it is my sincere hope that you and I at least shall soon be able to see all the more of one another.'

'How so?' Arabella said, frowning as she continued to toy with her dessert, clearly in no mood for it. 'What of your duties?'

'That's just the thing. Pretty soon my duties will be limited to Jaipur and its neighbouring states. I'm to deal with the dacoit problem in the area, having been granted full autonomy to stamp it out once and for all.'

'And the area will be a safer place for it,' Sir John bellowed. 'As I told the Governor-General of Rajputana just last week, you're just the man for the job.'

'How convenient for you,' Jane said, smiling to hide her sarcasm.

'Aye, indeed,' Elspeth said, signalling to one of the servants to top up her brandy glass for the umpteenth time that evening. 'I look forward to your visits almost as much as Bella must. It's so nice to have someone of the opposite sex to talk to from time to time.'

At the other end of the table, Sir John sat up, his cheeks flushing. 'What's that supposed to mean?'

'Come now, John,' Elspeth said, smiling back at him, her head visibly wobbling as she spoke. 'You know full well what I mean. You barely know I'm here.'

'You barely are here! How many of your pills did you take this evening?'

'Enough to see me through another evening in your company.'

'You forget your place, madam!'

Before the conversation could decline further, Arabella got to her feet and said, 'I'm going outside.'

'That's a splendid idea,' Fraser said, rising with her.

'No, Captain Fraser. Unlike my mother, I've had quite enough of your company for this evening.'

'Arabella!' Sir John protested.

Arabella ignored him. 'Jane, would you care to join me?'

As Fraser dropped back down on to his seat, his expression bewildered, Jane stood up and neatly folded her napkin. Then she and Arabella left the room to the sound of Sir John's flustered voice.

'Now see what you've done, woman!'

It was a cool evening, the courtyard air sweetly scented with the subtle fragrance of amaryllis and a host of other colourful spring-flowering plants. Looking up as she breathed in the scent, the immeasurable night sky reminded Jane of such dark, clear nights aboard the *Repulse* on their voyage from Southampton, now over a year ago. There was an enormity to the sky that was difficult to comprehend, the myriad bright stars so infinite and intense.

'I have to leave here,' Arabella said as they sat against a low stone wall by one of the courtyard entrances.

'Leave?' Jane said, unsure whether she'd heard Arabella correctly.

Arabella nodded. 'I met with Naresh yesterday while you were out with Mother.'

'You went to meet him alone?'

'No, Pranil accompanied me. I've had his trust for some time now. Naresh has told his family he wishes to marry me.'

Jane picked up on Arabella's downhearted tone as she finished speaking. She turned to her with a sympathetic smile. 'You can't be too surprised by their answer, Bella. Naresh is a crown prince after all, and—'

'I'm not surprised,' Arabella cut in. 'I'm just disappointed, that's all. We're in love. Why can't that be enough?'

Jane drew a deep breath. She could find no reasonable answer.

'That's why I have to leave,' Arabella continued. 'Naresh and I are eloping.'

Jane had feared it would come to this, and as much as she wished otherwise, she doubted any previous attempt to intervene could have prevented it. Such things had to run their course. 'Are you sure that's wise?' she said. 'You're both young, and although Naresh has proved himself very capable, despite his age, he is after all a sowar in the Bengal Army. He could face a court martial for desertion.'

'He's a crown prince. His duties are not like those of other sowars. He's already made that clear.'

'Then if not that, his family would surely disown him the instant they found out that he's run away with you. What of his status then? Have you thought all this through?'

'Of course. Naresh said none of that mattered. Only our love matters. If it's our will, no one has the right to keep us apart.'

As right as that arguably was, it was a naive view as far as Jane was concerned, but she had to consider her stance carefully. To try to dissuade Arabella was to risk being shut out of her life. Arabella would leave just the same, and Jane would never know what had become of her.

'What do you plan to do?'

'Naresh said he would come for me at sunset, two days from now.'

'Two days,' Jane mused. 'If you really must go, promise me you'll write to let me know how you are, as often as you're able to.'

Arabella smiled at last. 'I promise. Perhaps someday you'll come and visit us.'

'I'd like that very much,' Jane said. She crossed her arms and rubbed her shoulders. 'It's getting chilly. We should go back inside.'

No sooner had they turned their backs to the courtyard than they saw Captain Fraser standing in the shadows beyond the doorway.

'I was just coming to find you both,' he said. 'Lady Elspeth has retired to her bed for the evening and Sir John and I were looking to play a hand of whist. Would you care to join us?'

Jane and Arabella gave each other a quizzical look that was not to ask whether the other wished to play cards, but how long Captain Fraser had been standing there. How much, if anything, of their conversation had he overheard? Jane couldn't know. The captain's charming smile gave nothing away.

'Yes, of course,' she said as she took the now somewhat confused-looking Arabella by the arm and led her back inside, having quickly decided that compliance would arouse the least suspicion.

Chapter Twenty-One

Present day

After showing the latest of Jane Hardwick's letters to Damian Sinclair and discussing its contents, Tayte fixed himself some lunch and returned to his room, keen to get stuck into some more research.

'Where next, JT?' he asked himself.

More and more he felt that Captain Donnan Fraser was somehow important in all this, but how? For the time being he had no clear idea what to look for. He wasn't interested so much in the man's birth, marriage or death records; he'd already heard from Moira Macrae that Donnan Fraser never married, and that he'd died sometime during the 1830s. He hadn't yet confirmed what Moira had told him, but as far as Fraser's vital records were concerned, nothing seemed important enough just now to warrant the time it would take to do so. The same was true of Fraser's military records. There would be Officer Cadet Registers and Entry Papers, Honourable East India Company army service records, military pension-fund contributions and more, but until he knew what he was looking for and why, he'd just be chasing his tail.

He stared down at the browning apple core on his lunch plate beside him, considering the most recent of Jane's letters again. He thought about Arabella Christie's desire to marry Naresh Bharat Singh, and of her plans to elope with him, and he wondered where their story was heading. He shared Jane's fears that their road to happiness would not be an easy one, if it was to lead anywhere at all. But what of the ruby? So far, the letters gave no mention of the Blood of Rajputana.

He threw his head back and closed his eyes, supposing that he would have to take its existence on faith for now. If he was to make any worthwhile progress with his assignment, he had to think beyond what he'd so far read of Jane's story—beyond the letters themselves and what they might yet come to tell him. To do that, he had to look into more recent events, to the lives of Cornelius Dredger and the man he'd written to in 1869, whom Tayte now knew to be Sir Robert Christie.

Firstly, Tayte decided he had to satisfy himself that Dredger did in fact go to India. If he could find a record to prove as much, perhaps dated soon after Dredger wrote to Robert Christie, then he could safely assume that Christie had agreed to fund Dredger's expedition. That would be a good place to start, but how to go about it?

Back then, Dredger would have travelled by ship, but Tayte knew he wouldn't be able to use the British outgoing passenger lists because they were only available from 1890, all previous records having been destroyed by the Board of Trade in 1900. Neither could he use the incoming passenger lists because they were only available from 1878. He thought it a pity that the year he was interested in, 1869, was so tantalisingly out of reach of those records. They might have offered him another way to confirm that Dredger had left the country soon after writing his letter to Robert Christie, by way of his return voyage.

As every journey has a beginning and an end, Tayte thought to search through everything he could find on India's passenger lists, some of which he discovered were recorded at the back of the *Bombay Calendar and Almanac* and the *Madras Almanac*. There was also the *Bombay Directory* and the *Bengal Directory*, but he quickly learned that the years covered were largely too early.

His next step was to try a website he'd used before. It was a genealogical organisation called the Families In British India Society. He accessed their website and read that FIBIS was founded in 1998 to assist families tracing their ancestors to and from British India. Although paid membership for added-value services was available, their online archive was largely free to access and boasted over one and a quarter million names. It was potentially just what he was looking for.

He pulled his bag of Hershey's Miniatures up on to the desk and poured several out of the bag within easy reach of his right hand. He unwrapped one and began to eat it as he studied the webpage in front of him, wondering where to start his search. He recalled that Jane Hardwick and her companions arrived in India via the port of Bombay, as Mumbai was then known. He supposed Cornelius Dredger would likely have arrived by the same route. Further down the webpage he saw the option to search the FIBIS database and he followed the link.

He thought Dredger an unusual enough surname, so he entered it into the quick search field and clicked the 'Go' button. There were several results from various records. Closer inspection, however, revealed that they were not for 'Dredger' at all, but for 'Tregear,' a variant spelling of the name with its origins in Cornwall. Tayte went back and clicked on the advanced search option, into which he added Dredger's first name, omitting the year range for now. He was disappointed to find that there were no matching results at all.

He popped another chocolate into his mouth, supposing there had to be another way to prove whether or not Dredger had gone to India. If he'd made the journey as intended, surely he would have left some kind of trail in the records that were available to Tayte today.

'One hundred fifty years ago, give or take,' he said under his breath.

He thought about the type of record he might hope to find from that far back, for an everyman such as he imagined Cornelius Dredger was. Headstones came to mind, then books and journals, and then one of the most useful genealogical resources there was beyond a person's vital records: newspapers. He thought the odds were slim that Dredger would have drawn enough attention to himself while in India to have made the news, but it was possible. And yet, there was nothing at all in the FIBIS database, which had entries from *The Times of India*, and the *Bombay Gazette*, and a great many more publications across India besides.

'Think, JT,' he told himself, just as there was a knock at his door.

It was Murray. He had a green bucket hat on his head and a garden trowel in his hand. 'I'm sorry to interrupt,' he said, 'but Mr Blair is here to see you.'

'To see me?' Tayte said, surprised.

'Aye, he asked for you personally.'

Tayte stood up. 'What's it about?'

'He wouldn't say, sir. He's waiting outside.'

Tayte supposed it was as good a time as any to take a break. 'Tell Mr Blair I'll be right down,' he said, wondering what the man he'd met at the family gathering the night before wanted to see him about.

Having passed two men in overalls, who were installing DI Ross's discreet wireless CCTV cameras, Tayte found Ewan Blair on the driveway outside, sitting against an old burgundy Jaguar XJS, puffing on one of his roll-up cigarettes. Tayte crossed the driveway to find out why Blair wanted to see him, hoping the reason was somehow connected with his research. Maybe there was something about Blair's family history that he wanted to share. In the background, towards the sunlit bridge that crossed the burn, Tayte could see Murray tending one of the estate's many ailing flower borders.

'Mr Blair,' Tayte called as he approached. 'Murray told me you wanted to see me. What is it I can do for you?'

Blair threw him a wide smile that Tayte immediately saw for the car salesman's greeting it was. He wouldn't have been surprised if Blair was there to try to sell his Jaguar to him.

'Perhaps the real question here, Mr Tayte, is what can I do for you?'

'What *can* you do for me?'

'I'll come to that in just a moment,' Blair said. 'Tell me, how's your research coming along? Are you any closer to working out where this ruby—the Blood of Rajputana—might be?'

The question told Tayte to be wary of Blair's intentions. He wasn't about to tell him anything more than he'd told Moira Macrae when he'd gone to see her. 'It's going okay,' he said, leaving it there.

'Good, good,' Blair said, nodding as he spoke. 'So, what do you think the odds are that you'll find it?'

'I really couldn't say. Look, where's this heading? I'm kind of busy.'

'Of course you are, Mr Tayte. Let's take a walk. I've a proposition for you.'

Blair reached a hand up on to Tayte's shoulder and turned towards the bridge. Tayte didn't appreciate the contact, but he went along with him, if only to find out what he had to say.

'I'm a businessman, Mr Tayte,' Blair said as they started walking, his hands back at his sides. 'I don't mind admitting that I also like to take a wee gamble now and again. Tell me, are you a wealthy man?'

'Not particularly.'

'I bet you'd like to be, though, wouldn't you?'

Tayte decided he didn't like where this conversation was going. 'Not particularly,' he said again.

'Well, hear me out anyway. You just might like what I have to say.'

As they came to the bridge they passed Murray, who did nothing to acknowledge their presence as he continued to dig weeds from the border. Blair didn't speak again until they were halfway across the bridge, as if not wishing Murray to overhear his proposition. He stopped and rested his elbows on the bridge wall, and Tayte stopped with him, each looking along the babbling burn that chattered over the rocks several feet beneath them.

'I'm not short of a few bob,' Blair said, 'but I wouldn't class myself as a wealthy man, either. What I have to say could be very good for both of us.'

Tayte was growing impatient. 'Can you get to the point?'

Blair drew a sharp breath. 'The point is that I want that ruby. I'm prepared to give you a cheque for a tidy sum right here and now, whether you find the thing or not. That's my gamble. If you do find it, we'll split the proceeds of the sale fifty–fifty. You don't have to tell anyone else you've found it, and—'

Tayte began to laugh, stopping Blair mid-sentence. 'I don't know what kind of person you think I am, Mr Blair, but my answer's no. Now, if you'll excuse me.'

Tayte began to walk away, but there was Blair's hand on his shoulder again.

'A thing like that won't be easy to sell at the right price,' Blair persisted. 'I know people.'

The suggestion that he was in this for the money angered Tayte. This time he shrugged Blair's hand off as he turned to him and said, 'I don't care who you know. I'm not interested. You got that?'

The fact that Blair's cheesy smile had returned told Tayte that he hadn't.

'Just think about it,' he said, deftly sliding a business card into the breast pocket of Tayte's jacket. 'I'm leaving Comrie in the morning. I'm not stupid. Three members of the syndicate have already been murdered, four including Jamie. Perhaps Damian was right about these Rajputs he mentioned. Either way, I'm not sticking around to find out who's next.'

'I don't need to think about it,' Tayte said, and at that point he heard another voice.

'Is he bothering you, Mr Tayte?'

It was Murray. He paced up on to the bridge in a surly manner, pushing his shirtsleeves higher up as if he were bruising for a fight. He had a penknife in his hand, which Tayte was pleased to see him close and put away as he arrived.

'It's okay, Murray,' Tayte said. He fixed his eyes back on Blair. 'Mr Blair here was just leaving.'

Despite Tayte's words, Murray kept coming. He walked up to Blair until there was no space between them. Then with aggression in his eyes he pushed his face closer to Blair's, forcing him to back away.

'Is that right?' Murray said to Blair. 'You were just leaving?'

'You'd love me to say no, wouldn't you, Murray?' Blair said. 'Any reason to punch me on the nose and throw me off the estate, eh?'

'I don't need any more reason than I already have,' Murray said, and Blair laughed at him.

'All these years and you still can't let it go, can you?'

Tayte didn't know what Blair was referring to, but there was clearly more going on here than he understood.

'I'll never let it go!' Murray said, almost shouting.

He grabbed a lapel of the leather jacket Blair was wearing, turned on his heel and practically dragged the man off the bridge, back towards his car. He was moving so fast that Blair almost tripped a few times as he tried to keep up. Tayte wanted to say something, but he felt he had no right to. Whatever had happened between Murray and Blair in the past, it was none of his business, and Murray hadn't actually hit the man. He didn't have to. Blair was now as quiet as the proverbial church mouse. They reached the car. Murray, still holding Blair by his jacket, opened the driver's door, and then he none too delicately shoved him headfirst inside.

'Now get away from here and don't come back!' Murray said as he slammed the car door shut. 'You're not welcome, you hear?'

Tayte heard the engine start up. Then the Jaguar's wheels began to slip on the gravel, churning loose stones all the way to the bridge. When the car reached him, Tayte stepped back.

Blair slowed and lowered his window. 'If you change your mind, just let me know. You've got my number.'

As the car sped away, Tayte had to smile at the man's tenacity. He shook his head, thinking that if Murray hadn't intervened Blair would never have let up. He made his way back to the house and Murray met him halfway.

'I'm sorry for my outburst, Mr Tayte,' he said, 'but there's only one way to deal with a man like Ewan Blair.'

'Are you okay? Is there anything you want to talk about?'

Murray shook his head. 'It's in the past. I must get back to my gardening. We'll leave the matter at that, if you don't mind.'

'Of course,' Tayte said, and they each went their separate ways: Murray back to his weeding, Tayte to his room.

As he made his way up the stairs an idea came to him, and he thought Blair's visit hadn't been quite the waste of time he'd taken it for when he first heard what the man had to say. The interruption had helped to clear his head, making room for other ideas to present themselves. Now, as he opened the door to his room, he was wondering whether, for one reason or another, Sir Robert Christie had made the journey to India instead of Cornelius Dredger.

Back in his room, Tayte was drawn to the window by the sound of another car on the gravel drive. He wondered whether Ewan Blair had returned. He wouldn't have put it past the man to come back and hound him over his proposal to split the proceeds from the sale of the ruby if and when he found it. He was, however, glad to see that it wasn't Blair, but Damian Sinclair, returning to Drumarthen in his beat-up old car from wherever he'd been that afternoon. Tayte smiled to himself as he went over to the desk, wondering how the old motor continued to run, supposing it was all down to Murray's mechanical know-how.

He sat down, opened his laptop with renewed enthusiasm and ran the Families In British India Society database search again, this time not for Dredger, but for the man Dredger had written to. Along with both parts of his name, Tayte entered the year range from 1869 to 1875, supposing that the event he was looking for would have been relatively soon after Dredger sent his letter. Within seconds he was looking at a very short but promising list of records. He opened the first entry. It was from *The Times of India,* under maritime, arrival and departure notices.

'Touchdown!' he said a moment later, smiling to himself as he slapped his palm on the desk. 'There you are,' he added, scrutinising the record that was now displayed in front of him. At the same time, he helped himself to another Hershey's Miniature to celebrate the find.

Tayte was looking at an entry that had been transcribed from *The Times of India* in 2015. It was titled 'Arrivals 1870.' He read his subject's first and last names back to himself to confirm they were correct, then in the title field he read 'Sir,' and it left him in no doubt that the record before him was for the man he was interested in. The name, title and date all fit perfectly. Here was a record showing that Sir Robert Christie arrived in Bombay from Southampton aboard the P&O steamship *Golconda* on 9 April 1870. It even gave him the name of the ship's commander: Captain A Coleman. It was a great discovery, although it raised a number of questions.

'Why did Christie go to India?' he asked himself. 'Why not Dredger?'

As far as Tayte could gather from Dredger's letter to Robert Christie, it had been Dredger's plan to go to India, equipped with his great-aunt's letters, offering Christie a share of the ruby if he could find it. Yet there was no mention of Dredger on the FIBIS database, no mention of his being aboard that ship with Christie, or any other ship bound to or from India around that time.

So what changed? Tayte wondered, supposing that the answer had to be because Cornelius Dredger, for some reason, had been unable to go. He imagined the reason had to be a considerable one. It was his plan, after all, and his letters that would supposedly point the way to the location of the Blood of Rajputana. Tayte doubted he would have backed out of the trip lightly, and yet here was proof that Sir Robert Christie had arrived in India six months after Dredger wrote to him in October 1869.

The odds of the two events being unrelated were close to impossible as far as Tayte was concerned. Christie, therefore, must have had Dredger's letters with him. He had gone to India, hoping to use them to locate the Blood of Rajputana in Dredger's place. It was possible that Dredger had contracted an illness soon after writing his letter, making him unfit for travel, facilitating the need for Christie to go instead. As far as the ruby Tayte was now trying to find was concerned, however, he began to suspect that greed might have played its ugly part, and he feared the worst for Cornelius Dredger.

Knowing there was one simple, surefire way to find out, and having previously noted that there was nothing of significance in Damian Sinclair's research for Cornelius Dredger, Tayte brought up another browser screen. This time he opened the FreeBMD website, which gave free access to the birth, marriage and death indexes for England and Wales dating back to 1837, when civil registration began. If Dredger had been unable to go to India with Christie in 1870 because he'd died, the death indexes would tell him so.

Tayte clicked the search button and selected the record type he was interested in: death. Then he entered both parts of Dredger's name. Given how unusual his name was, he figured that was probably enough, but he recalled from the address on Dredger's letter that he lived in the town of Chesterfield in Derbyshire, so for good measure he found Chesterfield on the list of districts and selected it before starting the search. There was only one result. It was beneath the heading 'Deaths Nov 1869,' the month after Dredger wrote to Christie. It was all Tayte needed to tell him that his hunch was right. Cornelius Dredger hadn't gone to India with Sir Robert Christie because by the time Christie had embarked on his voyage, Dredger was dead.

Tayte noted down the index volume and page number, then he opened a digitally scanned image of the original index to see it for himself. And there it was, halfway down the first column. The information was telling enough, but before Tayte could be sure of foul play on Christie's part, he needed to know the cause of death. How Dredger had died would tell him whether his death was due to illness or other natural causes, absolving Christie of the dark deeds Tayte had begun to imagine, or perhaps confirming them.

It would take time and a small sum of money to find out, but thanks to the Internet, Tayte knew it would take far less time than it used to. He quickly brought up another website, this time for the Ancestry Shop, where you could buy copies of birth, marriage and death records online. Armed with the index reference he'd just noted down, he knew he'd be looking at a digital copy of Dredger's death certificate within twenty-four hours, emailed to him while he waited for the paper copy to arrive.

Tayte pinched his eyes and sat back in his chair, thinking that it had been a productive day, but it wasn't over yet. He checked his watch and noted that it was a little after four. He still had a couple of hours or so before dinner, which was a good thing because he didn't have much of an appetite just yet. He looked at the scattering of empty Hershey's Miniature wrappers to the right of his laptop and it was plain to see why: there wasn't a single chocolate left among them.

'Some more research, then,' he told himself, thinking that might help to bring his appetite back. 'But where next?' he added, leaning over his keyboard, just as his phone rang.

'Jefferson Tayte,' he announced as he took the call. He didn't recognise the number, but it was clear who his caller was as soon as he spoke.

'Mr Tayte, it's DI Ross.'

'Detective Ross,' Tayte said. 'How can I help you?'

'I was wondering how your research is coming along.'

Tayte thought he sounded tired. 'Good, I think. I can't say I'm much closer to working out where this ruby is just yet, but I feel I've made some progress today.'

'That's good to hear,' Ross said, although he didn't sound very upbeat about it.

'Is everything okay?' Tayte asked, sensing that there was more to Ross's phone call than he'd as yet divulged.

'No, everything's far from okay, Mr Tayte. I've got forty police officers working on these murders and we're getting nowhere fast. Meanwhile, dead bodies are piling up around us. I was hoping to hear you were close. If finding out where that ruby is means the end of this killing spree, then the sooner you do so, the better.'

Tayte almost didn't want to ask his next question, but once the thought popped into his head, he knew he had to. 'Has there been another murder?'

'I'm afraid so.'

'So soon?' Tayte could scarcely believe it. He stood up and began to pace his room, his free hand clamped to the back of his neck as a wave of anxiety gripped him. 'Who?'

'Moira Macrae,' Ross said. 'She was beaten to death in her sitting room this afternoon with one of her own ornaments.'

'Moira Macrae?' Tayte repeated. He began to feel nauseous. He and Ross had gone to see her just that morning. 'Are the other members of the syndicate okay?'

'It doesn't look good for Chrissie MacIntyre,' Ross said. 'Officers were sent to her house. The glass in her back door was broken. No one knows where she is. A helicopter with thermal imaging equipment is searching the area behind her house now, but there's a lot of moorland to cover. As for Ewan Blair, there are two officers waiting outside his house now. His car's not on his drive so I expect he must be out somewhere.'

'He was here at Drumarthen,' Tayte said, sitting down again. 'He came to see me, offering to fence the ruby for me if I found it, for a fifty per cent cut. He left under an hour ago.'

'That sounds just like Ewan Blair,' Ross said. 'Well, maybe he'll be home soon. Callum Macrae's still nowhere to be found,' he added. 'His car's still out on the road to Drumarthen where it broke down last night. I don't know what he's playing at, but it's highly suspicious, if you ask me.'

'You think he's doing this—that he beat his own mother to death?'

'Mr Tayte, I still don't know what to think just now. One thing's for sure though—Callum Macrae's not the blue-eyed boy his mother no doubt believed him to be. If what's going on here is motivated by money, as it appears to be, I wouldn't put it past him to have killed her. He'd have taken the crowns from her teeth for the gold inside them given half the chance. Look, I have to go. Will you let Damian know what's happened?'

'Of course,' Tayte said, already heading for the door, suddenly wondering where Sinclair had gone that afternoon. It was pure fancy, but as the call ended and he went to break the news, he couldn't shake the idea that Damian Sinclair might have gone out to pay Moira Macrae a visit, perhaps in connection with the family feud he'd previously heard about.

———~———

Following an early dinner with Sinclair, having told him all about his call from DI Ross, Tayte had had one quick drink with him to help ease the shock of hearing that someone else had been murdered, and then he'd gone to his bed for an early night. He was restless. Someone was on a killing spree in Comrie, and while he was almost certain the reason had something to do with his assignment, he felt powerless to stop it. Sinclair's reaction to the news that Moira Macrae had been murdered was also keeping him awake. Despite their mutual dislike for one another, she was family. Tayte was surprised to find Sinclair so unmoved by her death, especially given the circumstances. When asked casually where he'd been that afternoon, Sinclair had also taken what Tayte thought was a long time to answer, especially given that he'd apparently only gone out for more whisky. Tayte hadn't liked to push the matter. Perhaps Sinclair's hesitancy in answering was simply because his thoughts were with Moira after all.

Tayte rolled on to his side and tried to fill his head with pleasant thoughts of Jean and their son. He'd called Jean before he turned off his bedside light, just to hear her voice again, and he replayed the telephone conversation over in his head as he drifted in and out of sleep. Then sometime in the quiet of the night he heard a scratching sound and his eyes shot wide open. As he lay there listening, he could feel his heart rate begin to climb. There it was again, a faint but clearly discernible scratching sound, coming from somewhere over by his bedroom door. His first thought was that it was probably mice, and he supposed the old place must be riddled with them. He imagined that such sounds had likely been present every night since his arrival at Drumarthen, only he'd slept too heavily to hear them before. He closed his eyes again and rolled over. Then they shot open again as he heard the unmistakable sound of a creaking floorboard.

Not mice.

He sat bolt upright, listening. His heart was now pounding. The sound appeared to have come from somewhere beyond his door, out in the corridor. He checked the time, noting that it was almost one o'clock in the morning—not an hour during which he expected Sinclair or Murray to be up and about. Someone was definitely out there, though, and he was determined to find out who it was and what they were up to. He flung his bedcovers aside and went to the door, trying to be as quiet as possible, but failing miserably. It seemed that every old floorboard he stepped on began to creak and groan under his weight until he reached the door and flung it open.

At first, the corridor seemed to be in total darkness. Then, as he stepped out of his room and looked to his right, towards the main staircase, he saw a faint amber glow that was rapidly growing fainter. In nothing more than his stars-and-stripes boxer shorts, Tayte followed after it, quickly reaching the top of the stairs where the pale glow of the moon through the narrow upper windows tinted everything with its silver-blue light.

He paused, listening. Beyond the sound of his own breathing, all was still. He looked below and saw nothing out of the ordinary, so he turned his attention to the opposite corridor, and there it was. There was that faint amber glow again. Whoever had been outside his bedroom door had clearly gone that way. Tayte followed after it, into the east wing.

The air here quickly began to smell damp and rotten, and it reminded Tayte that for his own safety Murray had told him never to go into the east wing. He'd taken several long paces before he realised where he was, blindly following the light and the occasional creaking sounds he heard. Then, suddenly, the amber light was gone.

'This is madness, JT,' he whispered to himself.

He stopped, wishing now that he'd brought his phone with him so he could have used it as a torch. He could just make out another pale trace of moonlight further ahead, which he supposed must be coming from a window or open doorway, but it was dim and distant, the space between them dark and potentially treacherous. He listened again, but beyond his own thumping heart, he could hear no other sound.

He turned around and slowly began to retrace his steps back towards the landing, drawn like a moth by the glow of the moon. He thought he was lucky to have made it as far as he had. He was sure to hurt himself if he continued his pursuit further into the east wing in the dark.

'Come back when there's daylight,' he told himself.

He came to the landing, thinking at first that Murray or Sinclair could accompany him. They knew their way around the old place. They knew where it was safe to tread and where it was not. Maybe they could find out where his night visitor had gone. Perhaps there was some other way into Drumarthen that had been overlooked. Then it occurred to him that it could have been Sinclair or Murray outside his bedroom door. How could he trust them? He resolved to take a look around by himself after daybreak when he could better see where he was going. If there was another way into the house and he could find it, it would at least go some way towards ruling them out.

Pacing back along the corridor towards his bedroom, he began to wonder why anyone was outside his room in the dead of night at all. His instincts told him they were up to no good. When he arrived back at his bedroom door he saw the reason. As he crossed the threshold, there beneath him, glowing in the faint moonlight against the dark floorboards, was a familiar envelope. Tayte had been so keen to follow after whoever had put it there that he'd missed it when he first opened the door, his eyes still adjusting to the darkness. He stooped and picked it up, knowing before he opened it that it was another of Jane Hardwick's letters.

'Another murder, another letter,' Tayte said under his breath as he closed his bedroom door behind him.

He went to his bed and switched on the lamp. Then he got back into bed and pulled the covers up around him, suddenly feeling the cold night air for the first time. Sitting up against the headboard, he opened the envelope and took out the letter, wondering what Jane had to say about her days in India this time. Then he began to read, and her opening words immediately grabbed his attention.

> My dearest brother,
> I hope you are quite well as I am the same. Today I
> write to you with a heavy heart and of such shocking
> news that I am barely able to believe it possible. . .

Chapter Twenty-Two

Jaipur, March 1823

Two days had passed since Arabella had confided in Jane about her plans to elope with Naresh Bharat Singh. They were sitting on the balcony outside Arabella's bedroom, waiting. The sun was already low on the crimson horizon. In thirty minutes or so Arabella would be gone, and Jane knew she would miss her as much as if she really were her own daughter. Having fought long and hard with her conscience during the last forty-eight hours, she could not bring herself to betray Arabella's trust and tell the girl's father, even if a part of her thought it would ultimately be for the best. And who was she to decide their paths for them? True love as strong as theirs would find a way, as it had for her own father and Sumana after her English mother died. She had to believe that.

Arabella got to her feet and stood at the balustrade, the soft evening breeze gently playing with the loose strands of her hair. 'I thought I saw him,' she said, gazing out over the residency walls to the west.

'How will you know it's him?' Jane asked. 'It's quite a distance.'

'He told me to look for him on the far bank of the stream. He said he'd be standing high in his saddle waving a burning sword as a signal.'

'That sounds very dramatic.'

'Aye, I suppose he means to tie a rag to his sword and set fire to it.'

'Can you see a flame?'

'No, not yet,' Arabella said, sounding disappointed as she turned back to Jane. She did not sit down again but continued to look towards the sunset for her prince.

Jane rose and stood beside her. 'I'll help you look,' she said. 'Then when he comes, we'll go to meet him together and say our goodbyes by the stream.'

Arabella shook her head. 'As much as I'd like to have you with me, Jane, I wouldn't want you to get into any trouble should anyone see us leave. Captain Fraser has been with Father all day. I'm sure he's been invited to supper again. I think it's best you don't come with me. That way, if I'm discovered, you can tell my father you knew nothing about it. I've written him a letter. Pranil is to deliver it once I've gone.'

'You mean to go out alone?'

'No, Pranil has offered to carry my travel bag as far as the stream. Then I shall be with Naresh.'

'I saw Pranil outside your room as I came in,' Jane said. 'Are you sure you can trust him not to alert your father?'

'I must trust to a great many things if Naresh and I are to be together.'

'Yes, I suppose you must. I thought Pranil looked nervous. If he doesn't control the sweat on his brow none of it will matter. He'll give the game away for sure.'

At that moment there was a knock at Arabella's door and they both turned back into the room. Jane's first thought was that Arabella's plans were already discovered, and here was her father come to put an end to them. The door opened slowly.

'Bella, darling!'

It was Elspeth.

'And Jane!' Elspeth added as soon as she saw her. 'I didn't expect to find you here.'

Arabella gave her mother a kiss, which seemed to surprise her. 'We were just watching the sunset from my balcony.'

'How lovely. Can I join you?'

Arabella cast a quick, worried glance back at Jane, who was still standing by the balcony doors. 'Of course,' she said, walking ahead of her mother and pulling a face at Jane, silently asking whatever was she going to do now?

As they all stood by the balustrade watching the sun dip ever lower in the hazy evening sky, Jane noticed that Arabella's eyes were fixed on the stream, watching for Naresh's signal. If it came now, she wondered what on earth Arabella would do. Jane had no doubt that Elspeth, should she discover her daughter's plans to elope, would hold quite the opposite view to her own.

Elspeth turned to her daughter. 'It's so beautiful, I almost forgot why I came to your room in the first place.' She held out her hand to Arabella, opening it to reveal a square of bright cerise cloth. 'I know your birthday is still a few weeks away, but as I've so little else to occupy myself with I've been making a few arrangements. I know your favourite colour is yellow, but I saw this at the cloth market the other day and thought it would brighten the place up a treat. What do you think?'

'It's lovely,' Arabella said, running her fingers over the material.

'I mean to make up for the meagre offerings of last year aboard that wretched ship,' Elspeth said. 'I'm putting a guest list together and sorting out the menus. I'll run through it all with you nearer the time, of course. I just wanted to know what you thought of this colour before I commit to it.'

'I think it will do very well.'

'Oh dear. You don't sound very excited about it. You're going to be eighteen. That's something to celebrate. I wish I was eighteen again.'

Jane had also picked up on the melancholy in Arabella's voice. Unlike her mother, she knew it was because there would be no birthday party. By the time Arabella turned eighteen, she and her prince would be long gone.

Arabella gave no reply. She looked almost tearful as she turned her attention back to the stream. Jane knew she had to do something to get Elspeth out of the room. The sun was almost over the horizon, the sky darkening rapidly. It was still a little early for supper, but for now that was the only excuse she could think of.

'Is anyone else hungry?' she said. 'I'm absolutely famished.'

'To tell the truth,' Elspeth said, 'I've had little appetite since we arrived in India. How about you, dear?' she added, turning to Arabella.

'I'm not hungry either,' Arabella said, clearly not wishing to leave her balcony until she saw Naresh's signal.

Jane gave her a gentle nudge to let her know she was up to something.

'That is to say,' Arabella quickly added, 'I've not been feeling at all well. I don't think I could eat anything just now.'

'Really? You poor child. I know just how you mean. I have some pills that should soon sort you out.'

'I think I just need to lie down and rest.'

'A drink before supper then?' Jane offered.

A pre-supper drink was nothing Elspeth didn't ordinarily practise every evening, but Jane rarely joined her and had never suggested it.

Elspeth smiled at the idea. 'That's a splendid suggestion, Jane,' she said, stepping back from the balcony as if suddenly keen to leave. To Arabella she said, 'You get some rest, darling. I'll pop in later to see how you're feeling.'

As her mother turned to leave, Arabella went to her and held her tightly in a show of affection Jane seldom saw between them. Elspeth slowly and somewhat awkwardly returned her embrace.

'Very well, dear,' Elspeth said, patting Arabella's back as she waited for her daughter to let go.

When she did, Jane offered her the warmest smile she could muster. Then she led her from the room, leaving Arabella to what she hoped would be a grand future with her young sowar-prince.

Supper that evening was a sombre affair. By the time they had finished their soup and started on the cold meats and cheeses, Elspeth had had too little of the wine and brandy she was so fond of to bring about the loquacious, if often uncharacteristically poor, behaviour that so unsettled her husband. To the contrary, she had said little since Sir John had joined them, and even he did not seem his usual self. As for Jane, her mind was preoccupied with Arabella, imagining that, as the sun had now long since set, she was sitting on the back of Nilakantha with Naresh Bharat Singh, riding hard and fast towards their destiny.

'No Captain Fraser?' she asked Sir John. 'I was sure to find him at supper again this evening.'

'Sadly, Captain Fraser has had to leave us on important Company matters,' Sir John said. 'But never fear, he'll be joining us again very soon.'

Jane was far from overjoyed by the prospect. She supposed that life at the residency was going to be very dull in Arabella's absence, although she did not expect that Captain Fraser would be as keen to keep up his attendance once he discovered that the object of his affections was no longer there, which was some blessing.

'I've been meaning to ask you, Sir John, how is your son?'

'Very well, last I heard, which was some months ago now. He's studying at the East India College at Haileybury.'

'That's in Hertfordshire, isn't it?'

'Aye. He wants to be an administrator, of all things.'

Jane helped herself to another slice of roast fowl. 'You don't approve?'

'It was his mother's idea,' Sir John said, grimacing as he pulled something from his teeth. 'It's a decent profession, of course, and the East India Company certainly needs administrators. Personally, I'd have preferred it if he'd taken a more active role with the Company, as befits a healthy young man of his age. He could have become a captain, perhaps even a lieutenant, by now. That's how I started.'

'Or he could be dead,' Elspeth cut in, her tone cold. 'Could you please pass the Madeira, Jane?'

Jane reached for the decanter, but she froze partway as the door opened. It was Arabella, her face fixed in a downcast expression.

'Is there any supper left?'

'Of course,' Sir John said. 'You know we keep a plentiful table.'

'I'm glad to see you have your appetite back,' Elspeth said. 'You do look rather peaky, mind. Perhaps something to eat will do you good.'

Arabella sat down, and Jane saw an almost imperceptible shake of her head as she did so, letting her know, as she already suspected, that her prince had not come for her. She wondered why, certain that the reason was not of Bharat Singh's own volition.

What, then, had happened?

Chapter Twenty-Three

Jaipur, March 1823

Four days passed without word from Naresh Bharat Singh. Until the end of the first day, Jane remained open to Arabella's certainty that his family must have heard of his plan to elope with her in time to prevent it. As the days passed, however, Jane began to have her doubts. As she saw it, there were a number of possible reasons why Naresh had not come for Arabella. Had her servant, Pranil, somehow betrayed her after all? Jane thought not, or Arabella's father would surely have locked her in her room. Had something else befallen Bharat Singh on his way to the stream? It was certainly possible, but the young sowar-prince knew the land well and had made the journey a great many times before.

By the fifth day, an unsettling thought had occurred to Jane. It concerned the absence of Captain Fraser from the residency the evening Bharat Singh was supposed to have come for Arabella. He had been there all day, yet he was not at supper, having been called away on Company matters. Was it a lie? Was Bharat Singh the real reason? Jane shuddered to think of the implications, but how could Fraser have known? Jane's mind circled back to Pranil, supposing it possible that Arabella's servant, if indeed he had betrayed her, could have done so in time for Fraser to intercept Bharat Singh that night. Or had Fraser simply overheard Arabella in the courtyard two days before she was due to leave, talking of her plan to elope? Jane couldn't know, but if either of the latter scenarios were true, what then for Naresh Bharat Singh?

It was late morning and Jane, having written to her brother after breakfast, as was her custom on a Monday, strolled quietly through the grounds of the residency beneath the shade of her parasol. At her mother's insistence, Arabella had gone to the bazaar with Elspeth to pick out something that could be used as a table favour for her upcoming birthday party, and for obvious reasons Arabella had been reluctant to go. Jane supposed they would be back soon. Then she imagined Arabella would continue to beseech her to find a way to take her to Kishangarh in pursuit of the answers she was so desperate to find. If Kishangarh had been closer to Jaipur she would have gladly taken a fast gig there with Arabella days ago. But it was a journey that would take three or four days, across more than sixty miles of unfamiliar and potentially dangerous terrain for two women travelling without escort.

At length she came to the main gate, having ambled thus far with no urgency in her step. When she saw the fine carriages and well-dressed Rajputs gathered in the quadrangle before the gate, however, her step increased with her curiosity. Someone of great importance was clearly visiting the Resident at Jaipur and she was eager to find out who it was. Sir John was always keen to say when anyone of importance was coming to see him, but she had heard nothing. This visit, then, had to be one of an impromptu nature. As Jane drew closer to the entourage, she recognised the finest of the carriages among them and caught her breath. She had seen this carriage at the residency before. It belonged to Bharat Singh's brother, the Maharaja of Kishangarh.

Jane did not proceed further. Instead, she backtracked briskly around the building, entering beneath a pillared terrace where she collapsed her parasol before going back inside the building via a side entrance. The maharaja's visit could only be in connection with his brother, she supposed, and in light of what she knew, she was desperate to hear what he had to say. Having had no time to prepare for the visit, she imagined Sir John would receive him in his study, where he worked most mornings.

She crossed the central courtyard where she and Arabella had previously met the maharaja, and then went through to the rear of the building to the west, where it was cooler in the mornings. Another door took her outside again, this time into a much smaller courtyard, where a bored-faced *punkah wallah* sat beneath the shade of a tiled canopy. That was a good sign. It meant that Sir John was indeed in his study, the room being fanned by the man sitting outside his lattice windows.

The *punkah wallah* paid her no attention as she stepped cautiously closer to the latticework. As wrong as Jane knew it was to listen to the conversation taking place inside, she could not let such an opportunity pass. If not for her own satisfaction then she would do so for Arabella's, whom she felt had every right to know what was being said if it concerned the man she intended to marry. At hearing Sir John speak, it was apparent that she had arrived in good time.

'I was not expecting you, Your Highness, or I would have laid on a more befitting welcome. That said, I believe I know why you're here.'

'I am here because of my brother,' Kalyan Singh said. 'Several nights ago, he came to me with wild dreams of marrying your daughter.'

'Aye,' Sir John said, drawing out the word. 'My daughter, Arabella, came to me with the same delusion. I, of course, told her that such a marriage was not possible.'

'No, it is not. My young brother is promised to another, as is our way.'

'I fully understand.'

'Good. Then perhaps you can tell me where my brother is. He was seen riding out of our palace at Kishangarh alone five nights ago. No one has seen him since. It is my fear that he has fled with your daughter on a most foolish endeavour.'

'I can assure you my daughter is here in Jaipur,' Sir John said. 'Your brother . . .' His voice trailed off.

Jane pressed her ear closer to the latticework window. Did Sir John know something of the whereabouts of Bharat Singh? From his hesitation to continue, she supposed he did.

'Before I go on, Your Highness, I must stress that I knew nothing of the matter for two days, at which time, word was sent to you immediately. But of course you were not at Kishangarh to receive it. You were on your way to see me.'

'What are you saying?' the maharaja said. 'To which matter do you refer? If you have something to say about my brother, then say it quickly.'

'Very well. I regret to inform you that your brother is dead.'

Outside the lattice window, Jane gasped so loudly she was sure someone other than the *punkah wallah* must have heard her. She clasped a hand to her mouth and felt it tremble as a tear fell on to her cheek. Inside the study, all was quiet. Several seconds passed before anyone spoke again. It was Sir John.

'His body was found in the hills southwest of here. Perhaps he was travelling to see Arabella, or perhaps he was on some other business. I know nothing of his reason for being there.'

'If he was found so close to Jaipur, then he was surely travelling to be with your daughter,' the maharaja said, his voice full of grief and at the same time tinged with anger.

'Who can know with any certainty?' Sir John said. 'The only thing we can be sure of is who was responsible.'

'You know who did this terrible thing?'

'I do.'

'Then tell me so that I may cut his heart out!'

'There'll be no need for that,' Sir John said. 'The matter has already been taken care of. Your brother was attacked by dacoits.'

'How can you say that with such confidence?'

'Because I've spoken with the man who was tasked to go after them. His name is Captain Fraser. At my recommendation, the

Governor-General of Rajputana has placed him in charge of a company of men to stamp out these wretched villains. Following the discovery of your brother's body, Captain Fraser was quick to act. It was he and his men who came upon an encampment of these dacoits the very next day. His judgement was both swift and decisive, I can tell you. Not a man, woman or child was left alive.'

'And you know these people were responsible for my brother's death? How?'

'We know they were responsible because your brother was robbed blind. They left him to die with little more than the clothes on his back. His horse was found among the wretched villains.'

'Nilakantha.'

'I don't know the beast's name, but Captain Fraser told me he'd seen it before. He knew it at once. Among other items that were seized after the attack was this.'

The conversation fell silent again, and Jane thought she heard a drawer being opened and closed.

'It is my brother's ring, identical to my own,' the maharaja said a moment later, his voice trembling with emotion. 'There is no doubt then. Justice is done.'

'As I said, Your Highness, Captain Fraser's response was both swift and decisive.'

Beyond the lattice windows, Jane slowly sank into a crouch, sliding down the wall until she was able to wrap her arms around her knees. The fact that Arabella's young sowar-prince was dead took time to sink in. She wondered how on earth she would be able to break the terrible news to Arabella when her own father clearly could not.

'What other items were recovered?' she heard the maharaja ask. 'My brother left Kishangarh with gold and many jewels that night. One jewel is most precious to me—a large ruby that has come to represent the blood of many fallen Rajput warriors. I believe he took it purely to spite me for refusing his marriage to your daughter. Where is it?'

'You have to understand that anything of value seized in such a manner becomes a spoil of war, subject to British law. This ring of your brother's was recognised, and so I've returned it to you as a gesture of good will. All else has become the property of the Honourable East India Company and His Majesty King George.'

'This is an outrage! The jewels my brother was carrying belong to me.'

'Can you prove it?'

'I do not need to prove ownership of what I know to be mine!'

'I'm afraid you do,' Sir John said. 'I'm sorry for your loss, but you'll have to take the matter up with the governor-general. I'm afraid I can't help you more than I already have.'

The room fell silent again, and Jane could imagine the maharaja's anger and frustration, intermingled with his grief. When he spoke again his voice was surprisingly calm, perhaps because his thoughts had returned to the loss of his brother.

'I wish to see my brother's body.'

'It was a most savage attack,' Sir John said. 'I would caution against it.'

'Let me see him!' Kalyan Singh said, this time with such assertiveness that Sir John made no further attempt to dissuade him.

'Very well. I'll make the arrangements.'

With that, Jane had heard all she needed to hear. She rose unsteadily to her feet and made her way back the way she had come, wondering whether Arabella was home from the bazaar, and whether or not she should tell her what she knew without delay, knowing that to do so would break her heart.

Chapter Twenty-Four

Present day

On the morning after Jefferson Tayte had read the latest of Jane Hardwick's letters, he wolfed down his breakfast of tattie scones and square sausage, taking only as much time as was necessary to eat his meal and to discuss the letter with Sinclair, before going outside for a stroll in the grounds. His reason on this occasion, however, was more exploratory than recreational, having decided overnight that he must satisfy his curiosity as to whether or not there was another way into Drumarthen.

First, he wanted to find the hatch to the generator room that Sinclair had mentioned on the night of the thunderstorm. He thought that was as good a place to start as any. Perhaps it offered a way into Drumarthen that had been overlooked or compromised. He recalled Sinclair's instructions on how to find it.

'Turn left and follow the walls until you come to a steel hatch,' he told himself as he stepped outside and closed the door behind him.

There was fine rain in the air, and it was cool enough today to make Tayte glad of his suit jacket as he set off, whistling a show tune to himself for company—just a guy out for a morning stroll should anyone wonder what he was doing out there in the drizzling rain. He wanted to keep his activity to himself for now, at least until he was satisfied that it had not been Sinclair or Murray who had come to his room in the night.

He followed the flagstone walkway around the house, keeping to the angled contours of the grey stone walls. There was little of interest to see. Having just discussed Jane's latest letter with Sinclair, his mind was still ruminating over its contents. It excited him to have read about the ruby for the first time—the ruby that, according to what Jane had overheard, represented the blood of so many fallen Rajput warriors. With such a description it could only be the Blood of Rajputana, and now at last Jane's words made it real. The ruby had been taken from the Maharaja of Kishangarh by Arabella's lover, Naresh Bharat Singh, who had been murdered that same night by dacoits. The ruby had changed hands, but what of Captain Donnan Fraser's merciless retribution? What had become of the ruby after that? The question made Tayte all the more keen to find out.

As he moved around the house, he lost sight of the driveway and the burn. Before long he arrived at the gate that led into the neglected parterre garden, with its views of the Southern Highlands that today were all but masked by the poor weather. He'd seen no sign of a steel hatch, and he was beginning to see why Callum Macrae had said he couldn't find it. It had been dark then, and here he was in broad, if somewhat dull, daylight, unable to find it either.

He kept going, figuring that he had to come to it soon or Sinclair would likely have sent Macrae the other way around the house. He could see another gate ahead, mirroring the one he'd not long passed through. The shrubs and weeds were so overgrown here that he had to step off the pathway to go around them. Then he saw an area that appeared to have been recently trimmed. He went closer, back towards the flagstones, and there it was, set against the house beneath a tangle of ivy that all but obscured it.

Tayte pulled the vines away to reveal two galvanised steel doors that were each about four feet long by three feet wide. There was no chain around them and he could see no lock. He grabbed one of the handles and gave it a tug. It rattled but would not open. He tried the other handle with the same result, concluding that the hatch was secure and clearly locked from the other side. If someone was gaining entry to Drumarthen unseen, then it was not by this route.

He stepped back and looked up. There was no way anyone could get in via the narrow archers-style windows on the ground floor, and the windows on the level above that were so high, the walls so sheer, that someone would need a very long ladder to access them. The thought caused Tayte to look around for such a ladder, but while he thought it was not impossible to conceal one somewhere nearby, he also thought that if there was, Murray, who spent much of his time in the grounds, would have noticed it. Nonetheless, as he made his way through the next gate and continued around the house, he made a mental note to ask Murray whether there were any suitable ladders on the estate that weren't ordinarily locked away.

As far as Tayte could see, there was only one other outside door, which he supposed Murray used most often to come and go in his muddy boots so as not to make a mess in the main hallway. It appeared to be made of solid oak and was locked up tight, which he imagined it was every night and whenever Murray came and went, as Sinclair had recently instructed. He kept going, and quickly came to the front of the house again, having seen no other possible way in. Arriving at the main entrance, he was surprised to see Sinclair standing in the doorway. It was as if he knew Tayte had gone out and was waiting for him to return. When he saw Tayte approaching, he extended an umbrella and came out to meet him. He had a newspaper tucked under his arm.

'You've not chosen the best morning for a stroll,' he said, holding the umbrella over them.

'No,' Tayte agreed, laughing to himself. 'I just wanted to clear my head, ready for some more research today. The weather didn't seem so bad when I set out.'

'Scottish rain may often be fine, Mr Tayte, but it's deceptively wet. I figured you must be out here when I went to your room just now and you weren't there.'

'You wanted to see me about something?'

Sinclair unfurled his newspaper, revealing the headline, 'COMRIE KILLER STRIKES AGAIN! COMMUNITY IN SHOCK!'

'Poor Moira's murder is all over the news today,' he said. 'The police still appear to be clueless as to what's going on.'

'I sensed as much when I spoke with DI Ross on the phone yesterday,' Tayte said. 'I don't think he's had much sleep since Dr Drummond's body was found.'

'No, I'm sure he hasn't. He may appear to be keeping a cool head about it all, but I expect he's just as distressed as everyone else. He knew the victims better than most.'

Tayte shook his head as he continued to take the headline in. 'Thanks for showing it to me,' he said. 'I can't say I'm surprised by the reaction, especially in such a small town as this.'

'Aye, well it's not the only reason I came looking for you. I wanted to see you about Jamie's funeral tomorrow. I just wanted to let you know that the car will be here at ten to take us to the church. I hope the weather improves.'

'Ten,' Tayte said as they went back inside. 'Got it. I'll be ready.'

'I also left a message for DI Ross to let him know we had a visitor last night, and that you've received another letter. I couldn't get an answer on his personal number. He's clearly very busy just now.'

'Yes, I'm sure he is,' Tayte agreed.

'Aye, well I'll leave you to your research. Hopefully your walk has done you the power of good.'

Tayte nodded and smiled. As he made for the stairs he certainly did so with a spring in his step, although on this occasion it was not because of his research, but because he was keen to see if he could find out where last night's visitor to his room had gone. He reached the top step and turned around to make sure Sinclair was no longer there, and then instead of turning left towards his room, he turned right, into the east wing.

'Just watch your step, JT,' he told himself as he went.

⁓

The corridor Tayte had taken was only marginally better lit than it had been when he was there the night before. As far as he could tell, all the doors that led off it were closed, blocking the light from the windows beyond, but it was brighter further down. He supposed a door had been left open somewhere, or perhaps the corridor emerged into a lighter space. He was sure his visitor hadn't gone through any of the doors he could see. It had been so quiet that he figured he'd have heard it open and close if he had. He opened the door nearest him to test it and the hinges squealed, confirming his thoughts. Making his way further along, he took out his phone and switched on the torch to better see where he was going.

The corridor led to another landing area of sorts, only there was no staircase down from here. Instead, Tayte saw a square balcony in the centre with half of its spindles missing. He imagined the other half would fall away with the rest if he breathed too hard on them, and he was immediately glad that he'd turned back the night before, or in the darkness he thought he'd most likely have kept going until he'd tripped over the edge. He was at a junction of four corridors, each of which led off from an atrium that ran down through all the floors of the building. The daylight was coming from a skylight high above him, brightening the otherwise gloomy junction. He stepped closer to the opening at the centre of the atrium and the creaking floorboards reminded him to be careful, as if any reminder were needed. When he peered over the edge, he saw a black-and-white chequerboard floor on the level below that was littered with debris.

To his right, the corridor was very short, terminating at a double doorway that was open and bright. It drew his attention and he stepped gingerly towards it. The doors led into a long and very bright room full of windows that looked out from the front of the house and down on to the driveway below. He supposed he was looking into what had once been the long gallery. There were several dining chairs scattered here and there and another set of double doors at the far end of the room to his right which, given that this room appeared to run parallel to the corridor he'd arrived by, he imagined opened out on to the landing area at the top of the main staircase. He doubted his visitor would have had reason to double back on himself, so Tayte returned to the atrium. There were two other corridors to try. Both were dark and uninviting.

Tayte decided to try the passage that ran towards the rear of the house. It seemed logical that if the person he'd briefly pursued during the night had not turned right when he came to the atrium, then he must have gone left, otherwise the amber light he'd seen would have continued along the corridor in the direction he was heading. He peered into the gloom that quickly swallowed up the light from the atrium, and slowly set off, once more using his phone's torch to light the way. There was little to see apart from the peeling paint and wall coverings, and the worn rug beneath him that was hiding the rotten floorboards. There were also a few wires protruding from the walls, and others dangling from the ceiling here and there where lamps had once been.

Several more doors were set at intervals along the corridor. He tried one but it wouldn't budge. Then he tried another, which opened into a chasm, the floor on the other side having all but collapsed on to the floor below. He quickly closed the door again and kept going. Then he heard a crack beneath him and wished he wasn't so heavy. This was not the kind of environment someone his size should be poking around in.

'In for a penny,' he told himself and continued, testing his weight at every step.

When he came to the end of the corridor, he was surprised to find a half-moon table, on which was set a large vase of flowers. They were artificial, and covered with dust and grime, but even so, they seemed out of place in such a derelict environment. The corridor took him around to his right where it soon terminated at a set of double doors, one side of which was partly open. There was daylight beyond, which was encouraging, so he nudged at the door until it was wide enough for him to fit through. He noticed as he did so that the other door was completely blocked by debris. He looked up and saw why. The ceiling above him had partially collapsed, leaving a gaping hole through which he could see a bright mural, painted in the Italian Renaissance style.

Tayte had arrived at the top of a relatively narrow staircase that only led down. If his visitor had come this way, as Tayte supposed he had, then he would have had no other choice than to take the stairs to the ground floor. It appeared to be a quarter-turn staircase, and Tayte was glad to see that most of the steps seemed to be intact. He grabbed the handrail for support and tested its integrity before descending, keeping to the edge where he imagined the woodwork would offer him greater support. He almost made it to the bottom without incident, but about three steps up he suddenly caught his breath as the step beneath him collapsed without warning and he fell the rest of the way, taking the lower section of the handrail with him.

Tayte groaned to himself as he sat up and began to dust himself down, grateful at least that he hadn't fallen from a greater height. He coughed and covered his mouth with his sleeve until the dust he'd kicked up had settled again. Then he got to his feet and gazed around at the large room he found himself in. Now back on the ground floor, there were more of the same high archers-style windows that ran around the building. Halfway into the room, he could see an enormous stone fireplace, over which there had clearly once hung a large painting or tapestry; the wall covering where it had been appeared bright and relatively fresh by comparison to its faded surroundings. As usual, from what he'd so far seen of the dilapidated east wing, the room was bereft of furniture and ornaments.

A door drew Tayte's eye and he stepped carefully towards it, thinking that his visitor, once here, would have had no option but to do the same. He saw there were floorboards missing in places, some areas large enough to fall through if he wasn't careful. As he went, he soon began to feel the floor bow under his weight. By the time he was in the middle of the room he wished he'd gone around the edge where it might have been safer. He felt as if he were standing on a semi-frozen lake that was about to crack open. He wondered where the floor joists were. The floorboards were exposed, so he began to look for telling nail heads, but the boards were covered in too much dust and peeling paint and plaster from the ceiling above to make out anything so small. He took another step and the floor creaked and cracked beneath him.

Then it collapsed altogether, and Tayte was falling.

The seconds that followed the floor's collapse passed in a blur of dust and darkness that found Tayte lying flat on his back, looking up through a jagged hole above him. He blinked several times and coughed as the sound of his fall continued to echo in the empty space. He wondered whether any of his bones were broken. The fall had certainly knocked the wind out of him, but other than that and a slight pain at the back of his head where it had bounced on the floor, he felt okay. He sat up and saw that he'd only fallen six feet or so. He reached into his jacket for his phone and put the torch on again, blinking to shake the dust from his eyelashes.

The first thing he noticed was that his suit was no longer tan, but pale grey from all the dust he'd disturbed. The second thing was a set of stone steps against the outside wall, leading to the room above. He stood up and went to them, stooping all the way. He figured he was in a part of the cellar, only this part clearly hadn't been used in a very long time. As he arrived at the steps he saw why. There was no opening or hatch above them, and it excited him to think that this area had been sealed off, perhaps a long time ago. He climbed the first few steps and began to push up at the floor above. After several attempts, he knew it wasn't going to budge.

He went back to the area he'd fallen through, thinking he could pull himself up again, but every time he tried he just succeeded in pulling more of the floorboards down with him. He tried the other collapsed areas he'd seen, drawn by the pools of light beneath them, but it was no good. Even the joists were rotten. He turned to his phone, thinking to call the number Sinclair had given him when they first met. The signal strength only showed one bar, which he figured was because he was now beneath the house, surrounded by thick foundations. A second later he saw the signal drop out altogether.

'Patchy reception,' he told himself.

Then he heard a rat squeal somewhere in the darkness, and he quickly turned towards the sound, fumbling with his phone as he shone his torch after it. He figured the rat had to have got in there from somewhere, so he stepped slowly towards it, thinking to take a look around for another way out. If there was one, it would save him having to explain himself to Sinclair after having been told not to go into the east wing.

He quickly reached one of the stone foundation walls. The air here felt cooler, changing from dry and dusty to damp and stale. He followed his nose for several seconds and the musty odour grew stronger and stronger until his torchlight revealed a blank space in the wall ahead. As he drew closer, he saw that it was an archway, no more than five feet high.

'This place just gets more and more interesting.'

He shone his torch into the opening, revealing a narrow tunnel, the end of which he was unable to see. He sniffed the air again and there was nothing fresh about it. It caused him to doubt whether it would lead him out of there. Just the same, with little option other than to call Sinclair for help, he had to take a look, if only to satisfy his curiosity as to where the tunnel led.

As he continued to follow his torchlight, he had the sensation that the tunnel was gradually taking him deeper beneath Drumarthen. There were soon puddles of water at his feet, and every now and then, as he shone his torch ahead, he'd catch sight of scurrying rodents and hear their scratching claws as they receded back into shadow.

'Where does this lead?' Tayte questioned, thinking aloud. 'Why was the area sealed up?'

He knew it must have had a function at some time, or why had those stone steps been built there? As the light fell into another black space ahead, letting him know that the tunnel walls were coming to an end, he figured he was about to find out. When he reached the opening, he found himself standing at the top of another set of six or seven stone steps that led further down into a domed chamber. He shone his light into the space and realised he was in a small tomb, in the centre of which was a single sarcophagus.

Tayte caught his breath at the sight of it. He wondered who had been interred there, although as he began to take the steps down to find out, he thought he knew. The dust here had to be a centimetre thick. It blanketed everything like a fresh snowfall, and the marks he saw in the dust told Tayte that someone else had been here. As he shone his torch down at his feet to light his way, he noticed that he was following in another person's footprints. He squatted down to get a better look at them and thought they looked relatively recent, made with a modern shoe or boot, judging from the tread pattern of the sole. He thought back to the other holes he'd seen in the floorboards he'd fallen through, and wondered whether someone else had found this chamber in much the same way he had.

Approaching the sarcophagus, Tayte saw more evidence that someone else had been there and had taken an interest in it. Where the dust covering the sarcophagus was smooth and untouched for the most part, the area that bore the inscription had been wiped clean so the details could be read. There was a name, followed by the year of birth and of death.

'*Sir Robert John Christie*,' Tayte read. '*1804 to 1873.*'

It didn't escape Tayte that the year Robert Christie died was just three years after he'd arrived in India. Given the time he must have spent there, certainly if his intention was to travel north from Bombay to Jaipur in search of the Blood of Rajputana, and the time it would have taken to travel back to Scotland, it was clear that he had died soon after his return. Christie had been in his mid-sixties when he made the journey, and it crossed Tayte's mind that he might have contracted a disease of some kind while in India, which had proved fatal. The records would confirm it, but the cause of death in this case, unlike that of Cornelius Dredger, seemed unimportant. What was important was that if Christie's trip to India had been a success—if he had managed to find the Blood of Rajputana—he'd had very little time to enjoy it.

'Mr Tayte!'

The sudden, echoing call made Tayte jump. He spun around, back towards the tunnel he'd arrived by, listening. He wasn't sure who was calling him, and the footprints in the dust told him to be wary. Then the call came again.

'Mr Tayte! Are you down there?'

It was Sinclair.

'In here!' Tayte called back, supposing he or Murray must have heard the noise he'd made as he fell through the floorboards.

Tayte met Sinclair at the top of the steps. 'How did you get down here?'

'Murray helped me. He said he heard something so we came to see what it was. I thought maybe we'd found our intruder. What in the world have you been doing?'

'I was trying to find out where my visitor went after he left that letter under my door last night.' Tayte looked down at his suit and brushed some more of the dust from it. 'I had a bit of an accident.'

'So I can see. Are you okay?'

Tayte nodded. 'I expect I'll have a few bumps and bruises, but I'm fine.' In the distance he could hear thumping and grating sounds. 'What's that noise?'

'It's Murray. We saw those stone steps leading to the room above. He's taking a crowbar to the floorboards so we can get back up again.'

'But not just yet,' Tayte said as he stepped aside, revealing the chamber behind him for the first time since Sinclair had arrived. 'Look what I found. Did you know about this?'

Sinclair's eyes grew wider as both men shone the torches from their mobile phones into the room.

'It's a tomb,' Sinclair said, as if unable to believe it. 'No, I had no idea this was down here.'

'I figured as much, or you wouldn't have needed me to tell you who Robert was.'

'So this is Sir Robert Christie's tomb?'

'It sure is, and it makes perfect sense. This was once Robert Christie's house, which he left to his illegitimate son, Angus Fraser, your three-times-great-grandfather.'

'Aye, of course, and given the family rumour that Angus wanted nothing to do with his biological father, it also makes sense that Angus would wish to conceal the man's tomb when he took possession of the house.'

Tayte followed Sinclair back down the steps, wondering exactly why that was. He sensed there was a terrible secret buried in India in connection with the Blood of Rajputana, and he fully intended to find out what that secret was.

'Someone else knows about this,' he said. 'My footprints weren't the first, and the inscription's been wiped clean.'

'So it has,' Sinclair said as he studied it. 'I wonder who was here.'

'So do I. There are plenty of other holes in that floor I fell through. Maybe Murray knows something about it.'

Sinclair shook his head. 'If Murray had found this he'd have told me.'

Tayte couldn't imagine who else knew about this place, but it had to be someone with access to the house. He reminded himself then that someone had been gaining access to Drumarthen to deliver Jane Hardwick's letters to him. Whoever that was might also have discovered Sir Robert Christie's tomb. Unless, of course, that person was Sinclair or Murray. He wondered whether Sinclair was lying to him. It wouldn't be the first time a client or someone he'd been working on an assignment with had done that, and Sinclair hadn't been totally honest with him about his reasons for hiring him.

The sound of footsteps behind Tayte drew his attention, and both he and Sinclair turned away from the sarcophagus to see bright torch-light flickering in the tunnel. A few seconds later, Murray appeared at the opening with a look of wonder on his face.

'I've cleared the way back up,' he said slowly as he gazed around at the chamber. 'What is this place?' he asked, directing his question at no one in particular.

When Sinclair reached the top of the steps, he put an arm around Murray's shoulders and led him back the way they had come. 'I'll tell you all about it over a cup of tea,' he said as they all headed back. 'All this dust has parched my throat.'

Chapter Twenty-Five

Standing at the window in his room, Tayte fastened the buttons on a fresh white shirt as he watched DI Ross's car arrive. It was late morning. The rain was now so heavy that it bounced off the car's roof like hailstones as it crossed the bridge and pulled up close to the front door. Ross climbed out and hurried around to the passenger side, where he flung the door open and took out a large, heavy-looking cardboard box.

Tayte tucked his shirt in, eager to find out why Ross was calling at Drumarthen this time. He ran his fingers through his dark tangle of hair, which was still damp from the shower he'd just taken, threw on another of his tan linen jackets, and went down to find out. As he arrived at the top of the staircase, Murray was already at the front door, letting the detective inspector in. Tayte watched Murray take the cardboard box from him before leading him away in the direction of the dining room.

'This way, sir,' Murray said to Ross as they went.

Tayte followed after them, entering the dining room to find Sinclair already seated at the table with a pot of tea in front of him.

'Inspector Ross,' Sinclair said, standing up as everyone arrived. 'It seems we can't keep you from us. I hope you have better news today.'

Ross frowned. 'I wish I had. Is there any tea left in that pot?'

'Not much,' Sinclair said. Then, turning to Murray, he added, 'Would you bring us a fresh brew, Murray, and a coffee, please, for Mr Tayte?'

'Thanks, Murray,' Tayte said as he watched the man retreat towards the drawing room doorway, still carrying the box Ross had brought with him.

Ross pulled out a chair and sat down. 'I've brought Gordon Drummond's files for you to take a look at, Mr Tayte. I'm sorry it's taken so long to clear it. I can only let you have them for twenty-four hours.'

'That should be fine,' Tayte said as he sat down. 'I can't wait to take a look. Maybe I'll find something in there.'

'I'll be keeping my fingers crossed that you do. I could use all the help I can get where this case is concerned.'

Sinclair drained what was left of his tea. 'I'll have Murray take them up to your room, Mr Tayte.' To Ross he said, 'Now, tell me, inspector, are Gordon's family history records the only reason you're here?'

'No, I'm afraid I bear more grave news. We received a call from a concerned neighbour in the early hours of this morning saying they'd heard what sounded like a shotgun going off in the house next to theirs. No less than four such reports from the area came in soon after that. The house in question belongs to Ewan Blair. He's been shot dead. No one saw a damn thing.'

At hearing the news, Sinclair almost dropped his teacup as he practically fell into his chair. He began to shake his head as the news sank in. 'What in heaven's name is going on here?'

'I wish I knew,' Ross said. 'Chrissie MacIntyre's still missing.'

'That could be a good thing,' Sinclair said, hope in his voice. 'I mean, if your helicopter with its thermal imaging equipment didn't find her, surely there's a chance she's still alive?'

'Aye, there's a chance,' Ross said, but his words lacked conviction. 'If Chrissie was abducted, though, she could have been taken just about anywhere. A helicopter needs to know broadly where to look.'

'What about Callum Macrae?' Tayte asked.

Ross shook his head. 'The lord knows why he's not coming forward. For obvious reasons I'm all the more keen to speak with him. You know, I was beginning to wonder whether Ewan Blair was behind all this when he refused police protection yesterday. It seemed like a daft thing to do under the circumstances. When he said he was leaving the area, going somewhere safe, that just aroused my suspicions further. As it turns out, I couldn't have been more wrong.'

'When Mr Blair came to see me yesterday,' Tayte said, 'he told me the same thing—that he wasn't sticking around to find out who was next.'

'Do you know if anyone else was aware that Blair was planning to leave Comrie?' Ross asked. 'The timing of his murder tells me his killer probably knew.'

'I wasn't here when he called at the house,' Sinclair said. 'I was out buying more whisky. I seem to be getting through more of the stuff than usual this week.'

Tayte didn't like to tattle-tale, but this was serious business. 'Murray was out on the drive while I was talking with Mr Blair. Maybe he heard Blair tell me he was leaving.' Tayte thought back to the argument between Murray and Blair, and how aggressive Murray had been. Did he have a motive to kill Ewan Blair? 'They shared a few heated words before Blair left,' Tayte added.

Sinclair scoffed. 'If Murray was ever going to kill Ewan Blair, he'd have done so long before now.'

'Aye,' Ross said. 'It's old business. Still, I can't overlook the fact that he knew Blair was leaving Comrie.'

Tayte wanted to ask what that old business was, but just as he was about to, Murray came back into the room. He set a tray down on the table and offloaded its contents.

'Thank you, Murray,' Sinclair said.

'It's nae bother,' Murray said. 'Will you be needing me for anything else just now?'

Ross turned his teacup the right way round and poured himself some tea. 'Ewan Blair was murdered this morning,' he said, studying him closely as if trying to gauge his reaction to the news.

Murray drew a deep breath and slowly let it go again. He was speechless for several seconds, and then he said, 'What's going on here is nothing less than tragic, but don't expect me to be sorry that Ewan Blair's dead.'

'Did you know he was planning to leave Comrie today?' Ross asked.

'Aye, I heard as much when I was outside with Mr Tayte yesterday. I didn't go out this morning and kill the man, though, if that's what you think.'

'I think you wouldn't exactly tell me if you had, now, would you?' Ross said. 'Are there many shotguns here at Drumarthen?'

'A rack of four,' Murray said. 'Two are in regular use on the estate. The other two, though fully functioning, are old collector's items.'

'Are they all accounted for?'

Murray's brow set into a crease, as if realising where the detective's line of questioning was going. 'As far as I know,' he said. 'I've not been out shooting in a couple of days. The cabinet was locked as usual once I'd finished.'

Ross stood up. To Sinclair he said, 'Do you mind if we go and take a look?'

Sinclair got to his feet. 'Of course not.' He turned to Tayte. 'Mr Tayte, I don't like to leave you sitting here by yourself. Would you care to join us?'

Tayte stood up, as keen as he supposed everyone else was to see if any of Drumarthen's shotguns were missing. Sinclair led the way, out to the back of the hall, then through a door Tayte had not used before. It led into a passageway that connected a few other doors before opening out into an area that was now clearly being used for storage. There were antiques of all kinds piled on to tables and scattered here and there on the floor. Tayte imagined this was where Sinclair had put some of those items that had been removed from the east wing to protect them, perhaps intending to sell them at some point. Sinclair walked up to a tapestry that was hanging against one of the walls and pulled it aside to reveal another door.

'You have your keys, Murray?'

Murray handed an overcrowded ring of keys to Sinclair, who found the one he was looking for and unlocked the door.

'You can't be too careful where shotguns are concerned,' Sinclair said as he opened it.

Behind this door was a small space, no bigger than a broom cupboard. Just inside, fixed to the back wall, was a tall steel cabinet, the gun cabinet, which Sinclair also unlocked. When he opened it, it was clear to everyone looking on that one of the shotguns was missing. There were only three, not four as Murray had said. The second position along was tellingly blank.

Murray pushed forward, wide-eyed, as if unable to believe it. 'This rack was full when I last locked it,' he said, his voice raised. He turned and looked Sinclair in the eyes. 'I didn't take it. I swear it.'

'Calm down, Murray,' Sinclair said. 'No one's saying you did. Which of the guns is missing?'

'It's one of the antiques. The MacNaughton.'

Ross stepped between them and took a closer look. 'This doesn't look so good, now, does it?'

'What's that supposed to mean?' Murray said.

Ross didn't answer. 'I take it there's more than one set of keys to these locks?'

Sinclair nodded. 'I also have a full set, of course.'

'And where are they now?'

'They're in my cardigan, which is on the back of my chair in the dining room.'

'Mine are always on my person, or by my bedside,' Murray said, volunteering the information before Ross could ask him.

'And there are no other sets of keys?'

'No,' Sinclair said.

He locked the cabinet again and handed Murray's keys back to him. Then they all returned to the dining room and sat down again with their drinks.

Ross shook his head, pulling at his tie as he did so. 'This is a fine turn of events then, isn't it?' he said. 'During the last couple of days, it appears that someone has stolen from this house a pretty secure and well-hidden shotgun, without the need to force any locks, and seemingly having taken nothing else in the process. Then, just this morning a shotgun was used nearby to end a man's life. It's quite a coincidence, don't you think?'

'I really don't care for your implications,' Sinclair said.

Tayte, who had been quietly taking everything in, sipped thoughtfully at his coffee, wondering whether it could yet be proved that the missing shotgun had been used to kill Ewan Blair. 'Has the murder weapon been recovered?'

'No, Mr Tayte. Not yet,' Ross said. To Sinclair, he added, 'Perhaps you should officially report that one of your shotguns has been stolen.'

'I'll be sure to,' Sinclair said, his tone short. 'I take it you picked up the message I left for you earlier this morning about last night's intruder?'

'Aye, I did.'

'And has it crossed your mind that whoever put another of Jane Hardwick's letters under Mr Tayte's door in the middle of the night may have left with my shotgun? What about the CCTV cameras you've had set up? Did they see anything?'

'I'm glad you've asked me that,' Ross said, and Tayte thought he detected a hint of sarcasm in his voice. 'They did. Or I should say one of them did. The camera on the upstairs landing showed someone in a hooded cloak running about with what appears to be an electric camping lamp.'

'A hooded cloak?' Sinclair repeated. 'Did you see his face?'

'No, it was well concealed, as if whoever it was knew those discreet cameras were there.'

'What about the camera in the main hallway downstairs?'

'Nothing at all,' Ross said. 'I might add that the upstairs camera showed no one coming up the stairs, either. If you had an intruder last night, how do you suppose he got in?'

'As I'm sure you can imagine, inspector, there are several staircases here at Drumarthen.'

'Are you telling me you must have left your back door unlocked last night?'

Sinclair shook his head. 'No, I checked myself before I went up to my bed.'

'Then how else could someone have got in without breaking in? The ground floor of this place is like a fortress.'

'Ladders,' Tayte cut in. 'I took a look around outside earlier. Apart from the two doors and the hatch to the generator room, the only way in as far as I can see is via a tall ladder to the first-floor windows. I was meaning to ask whether you keep any lying around outside.'

Murray spoke then, sounding very put-out by the suggestion. 'Of course we don't, Mr Tayte. It would be quite foolish to leave a ladder outside your house now, wouldn't it?'

'But you must have ladders?'

'Aye, of course there are ladders, but they're securely locked away in an outbuilding with the garden tools and machinery. And before you ask, I've already checked the locks.'

'It was just a thought,' Tayte said, sensing the growing tension in the room.

It was clear to Tayte that DI Ross had either Murray or Sinclair pegged for the person on his CCTV camera images, and perhaps more besides. Maybe he was right. It was hard to ignore the fact that no one seemed to have broken into Drumarthen, and that whoever took that shotgun knew exactly where it was and had the keys required to obtain it. What was going on indeed?

Ross drained his tea and stood up. 'Right, I don't want to outstay my welcome so I'll be on my way.' To Tayte he added, 'Do let me know if you find anything useful in Drummond's files.'

'I will,' Tayte said.

As Ross left, he turned back and pointed to Murray as he said, 'I've got my eye on you.'

Neither Sinclair nor Murray proved to be very good company after DI Ross left, so Tayte made himself some lunch and took it up to his room. He was keen to take a look at Dr Drummond's files, hoping there was something in there that might help him to locate the Blood of Rajputana, or perhaps even shed some light on what was going on in this otherwise tranquil part of Scotland, which in the last few days had seen five murders and one possible abduction. That accounted for six members of a syndicate formed around the ruby by Damian Sinclair's late brother, Jamie, who had in all probability not died accidentally, but had also been murdered, leaving only Callum Macrae unaccounted for. Tayte wondered where he was, and he couldn't help but share Ross's opinion that Macrae's sudden disappearance so soon after the family gathering at Drumarthen was highly suspicious.

'Another murder,' Tayte mused as he entered his room and kicked the door shut behind him.

Given the pattern so far, he expected to find another of Jane Hardwick's letters soon. He had to be vigilant. If he was, he thought there was a chance he might get a look at whoever was leaving them for him. He set his lunch plate and his glass of milk down on the desk. As he did so he saw that Murray had already brought Drummond's files up to his room—the box was on the floor beside the desk. He took off his jacket and sat down, then he opened his laptop and took a bite of his sandwich, which today he'd filled with sliced cold sausage and chutney and a few salad leaves, thinking of Jean as he'd added them in, knowing she'd approve.

Once his laptop had fired up, he saw that he had a new email. Noting it was from the Ancestry Shop, he opened it with the same degree of excitement he always felt whenever he was about to view a record he'd been waiting to see. The attachment he was expecting was there: a digital copy of Cornelius Dredger's death certificate. He double-clicked the icon. A second later he was looking at a cause of death that confirmed his earlier suspicions.

'*Found drowned*,' he read aloud. 'So the truth begins to unfold.'

They were just two words, but along with everything else, Tayte knew they were enough to tell him that foul play had indeed reared its ugly head. The truth was in the records, and they spelled this treachery out very plainly to Tayte's mind. When Cornelius Dredger wrote to Sir Robert Christie in October 1869, Tayte was in no doubt that he'd shown his great-aunt's letters to him and told him of his plans to travel to India to recover the Blood of Rajputana. But a month later, in November 1869, Christie had murdered Dredger and taken his letters to make the trip himself, arriving in India in April the following year.

Given that in 1869 Sir Robert Christie was already a wealthy man, it seemed likely to Tayte that his motives were driven by greed. It was easy to imagine the desire that crept over Christie at hearing about the ruby from Dredger, and then having read about it in Jane Hardwick's letters. But then Tayte supposed greed was never far away where the Blood of Rajputana was concerned. Or had Sir Robert Christie somehow believed he had a right to the ruby, and for that reason could not entertain the idea of sharing it?

Tayte began to wonder whether Sir Robert had found what he'd gone to India in search of, and it was Christie's actions after his arrival that now interested him most of all. Where had Christie gone after Bombay? He thought it a good bet that he had gone to Jaipur, where most of the events depicted in Jane Hardwick's letters had taken place. But where in Jaipur? What did Jane's letters yet have to tell that had made Cornelius Dredger, and then Sir Robert Christie, believe they had a good enough chance of finding the ruby to warrant making the long and difficult journey?

Tayte turned to Dr Drummond's family history records, hoping there might be something in the box that could help him to find out. Sinclair had told him that the whole family had been looking into their family history over the years, and none more so than Gordon Drummond, convinced that it held the key to finding the Blood of Rajputana. Perhaps his records would now shed further light on the matter.

Tayte stood and lifted the box up on to the desk. When he removed the lid, he saw that it was full and he knew it was going to take time to wade through everything, but it had to be done. Unlike Sinclair, whose records he'd already seen, Drummond was descended from Lachlan Fraser. Lachlan's brother, Captain Donnan Fraser, had been close to the Christie family, and he was there in Jaipur when on that ill-fated night the ruby was taken from the Maharaja of Kishangarh by the love-struck crown prince. According to the latest of Jane's letters, it was Captain

Fraser who had led the attack on the dacoits and recovered Naresh Bharat Singh's possessions, but again, Tayte wondered what had become of them. What had Fraser done with the Blood of Rajputana? Had it really been seized by the Honourable East India Company as a spoil of war?

Tayte removed the first record from the pile, a folded piece of A3 paper. He sat down again and unfolded it to reveal a plain chart showing Drummond's family tree, going back several generations. It was good work. Most of the boxes contained names and dates of birth, marriage and death—the certificates for which he imagined accounted for the vast number of records inside the box. He scanned the chart, going back through the generations until he came to the point where the Fraser name first appeared. Closer inspection told him it had only survived two further generations after Lachlan Fraser, his grandson along this particular bloodline having fathered two daughters, but no sons.

He set the chart to one side and reached into the box again, removing the next piece of paper, expecting it to be a vital record for either the first or last name on the chart, but it wasn't. It was an envelope, and while that envelope could have contained just about anything, Tayte instinctively knew what was inside it. He held his breath as he opened it and unfurled the contents, revealing yet another of Jane Hardwick's letters.

This letter was dated April 1823, the month following that of the previous letter Tayte had seen. He was keen to read it, but for now he was far too distracted by the question of how the letter came to be in that box. He'd known to expect it because another of the syndicate had been murdered. That was the pattern, and he had been on the lookout, but how could he have seen this coming? The letter was already there in Drummond's research files, where it could well have been since the day Drummond was murdered.

'Or could it?' Tayte mused.

He suddenly found himself doubting that it had been there long at all. Whoever was feeding these letters to him was doing so in the order they were written. That person had to be sure that Tayte would read this letter after the previous letter had been read. It would have been impossible to know when DI Ross would bring Drummond's records to him, if at all. The only person in control of that was Ross himself. A wild thought crossed Tayte's mind then. He shook his head to dispel it, thinking it absurd, but it wouldn't go away.

What if DI Ross put that letter in there?

Tayte reminded himself that Ross had also been around his brief-case the day they went to see Moira Macrae together. He'd had the opportunity to slip one of Jane's letters in there, and he knew all about the family's long-term hunt for the Blood of Rajputana.

But how could he have known about Jane Hardwick's letters?

Tayte wondered then whether Ross had perhaps been invited to join Jamie's syndicate along with the others. He could have found out about the letters that way. He could have pretended to want no part of it, only to go after the letters himself, to have them all for himself in the hope that they would lead him to the ruby, just like Sir Robert Christie. Tayte also thought Ross had seemed very keen to point the finger at the occupants of Drumarthen earlier, but on the other side of that coin, apart from it being Ross's job to do so, Tayte had to agree that his—albeit indirect—accusations were not without foundation.

Tayte's thoughts turned to Murray and Sinclair, and it seemed that poor Murray's name was once again in the frame. He'd taken the box at the front door, and he'd carried it out of sight with him when he went to make a fresh pot of tea. Murray had had every opportunity to put that letter in there. He'd even brought it up to Tayte's room.

Or had he?

Tayte hadn't actually seen Murray carry the box up. He'd merely heard Sinclair ask him to. The box was already there by the desk when Tayte came back to his room. What if Sinclair had brought it up instead? Tayte shook his head and sighed. Once again, he had no way of knowing who had left Jane's letter for him.

He returned to it now, sitting back in his chair with his glass of milk as he began to skim over the words, as he often did on a first read. He was immediately reminded of the newspaper reporter, Mr Albert Faraday of *The Times*, and he made a mental note to see if he could find any more of his articles from the period during which this letter was written. Faraday, who had not previously been mentioned in Jane's correspondence with her brother, now dominated her writings, although the subject matter appeared to be more concerned with Captain Donnan Fraser, which piqued Tayte's interest. He turned the page, still skimming, looking for mention of the ruby again.

And there it was.

Tayte's eyes lit up. Then he took another bite of his almost-forgotten sandwich and turned back to the start of the letter. He began to read it slowly and thoroughly this time, taking in every detail, content that it held the promise of revealing more about Captain Fraser and the Blood of Rajputana.

Chapter Twenty-Six

Jaipur, April 1823

Jane did not delay in recounting to Arabella all she had heard said between her father and the Maharaja of Kishangarh about the fate of Naresh Bharat Singh. Two days later, Jane was with Elspeth, having just left Arabella's room where Arabella had remained with her grief, crying into her pillow, since hearing that her young sowar-prince was dead.

'She'd better clear her plate this time,' Elspeth said. 'She's hardly eaten a thing in days. It can't go on. If it does I shall have to force-feed her.'

Jane hadn't had much of an appetite herself of late. She could only imagine how Arabella must be feeling. When her husband had died, Jane could take comfort in the many wonderful years they had spent together. She felt the finality of such a loss, of course, but she had so many happy memories to call upon in her times of need, and he had passed without the trauma Bharat Singh must have endured if Sir John's account was anything to go by.

'Give her time,' Jane said as they slowly made their way to dinner.

'And how can she not want a birthday party?' Elspeth went on, as if she were caught up in her own inner dialogue and wasn't listening to a thing Jane said. 'She'll only be eighteen once.'

Jane could see that Elspeth was becoming flummoxed over the matter, flapping her fan back and forth more and more as she spoke, despite the breeze that today was circulating nicely throughout the residency. 'She's understandably upset,' she said, finding her own choice of words something of an understatement given the circumstances. Arabella was evidently distressed beyond measure.

'Aye, I expect she'll soon come to her senses and forget all about this native boy, and the sooner the better if you ask me.'

Jane watched her open her reticule, which she was rarely without. Apparently the matter had so agitated her that she needed her opium pills, perhaps to help her to see the situation in a more favourable light, if only temporarily. She removed an unseen quantity of the little pills and popped them all into her mouth at once, needing to take no water with them as she crunched them down. There was no doubt in Jane's mind that her addiction was entirely to blame for the change of character she had seen in Elspeth since they had arrived in India.

'Not that it's any of my business,' Jane said, 'but since supper the other evening, I've been meaning to ask how things are between you and Sir John. As your good friend, you know you can talk to me if there's anything troubling you.'

'Troubling me?' Elspeth laughed to herself. 'Where shall I start? The trouble is that I've no more love for my husband than I have for this godforsaken country. I really don't know which is worse, but I do know that India is no place to raise our daughter. You've seen the state she's in. It's this damned country, and it's my husband's fault for bringing her here.'

Jane hadn't expected such vitriol, but she accepted it as just another example of her friend's changed behaviour, brought about by her opium pills, which seemed to Jane as a crutch to her friend's very existence in India. 'Do you know what's happened to Pranil?' she asked, changing the subject. 'I've not seen him lately.'

'He was dismissed as soon as Arabella made it known to her father that he had been helping her with her foolish plan to run off—dismissed the very evening my husband told her what had happened to her native friend.'

Jane knew that Bharat Singh was so much more to Arabella than merely a friend, yet it seemed that Elspeth could not entertain the idea that he was anything more to her daughter than that. She wanted to tell Elspeth that Arabella had already known Bharat Singh was dead, hours before she confronted her father over the matter, but she knew it served no purpose and would only leave her having to explain how she came to find out.

The conversation between Sir John and the Maharaja of Kishangarh was still fresh in Jane's mind. She had been suspicious of Captain Fraser's motives in avenging Bharat Singh's death since first hearing that it had been Fraser who had recovered Bharat Singh's horse and possessions, proving that the dacoits he and his men had slain were guilty of the murder. It all seemed too convenient to Jane that Bharat Singh should be murdered on the very evening he was coming to carry Arabella away with him—away from her family, and perhaps more importantly, away from Captain Fraser.

As they came to the dining room, where Fraser and Sir John had already begun their meal, Jane was resolved to dig deeper beneath the surface of the events that had taken place the evening Bharat Singh was murdered. She would start with the massacre of the dacoits Fraser had reportedly identified, and she knew just the man to see about it. That was if Mr Faraday was still in Jaipur. If he was, then he was sure to have written about the incident for his column in *The Times* newspaper.

Having tracked Mr Faraday to a ramshackle limestone dwelling near the city's Chandpole Gate to the west, Jane took a short flight of rickety wooden steps up to his door and knocked. She felt instantly sorry for the man. It was such a noisy, smelly area in which to live, almost on top of one of the city's largest bazaars. The midday air hummed with chatter and the heavy odour of sweat from both traders and livestock alike. Getting no reply, she knocked again. A moment later the door opened with a creak, and there stood Albert Faraday, coughing into his handkerchief.

'Mrs Hardwick!' Faraday said, wide-eyed and clearly surprised to find Jane at his door. 'What an unexpected pleasure!' He coughed into his handkerchief again, and this time he wiped his chin with it before putting it into his trouser pocket.

Although in her estimation he had not been much to look at the last time Jane had seen him, today she thought Faraday looked dreadful. His hair was wild and unkempt, his eyes were red and his skin pallid. Judging from his stained apparel, his pale shirt and trousers hadn't been washed in weeks. Here was a man who clearly was not looking after himself in an environment rife with disease, where personal hygiene and attention to proper nutrition were paramount to survival.

'Mr Faraday,' Jane said, still studying the man. 'Have I called at an inopportune time?'

'Not at all,' Faraday said, his tone far more exuberant than his appearance implied. 'Do come in.'

Faraday stepped back, and Jane entered what was without question the dingiest room she had ever set foot in. The already small space had been divided in two by a wall of drab cloth in one corner. The chamber pot she could see poking out from the base of the material told her that Faraday's sleeping quarters were beyond. As he led her further inside, she saw few personal possessions, the room largely being taken up by writing materials, piles of paper and a small desk, upon which, to her surprise, sat a mangy grey-feathered chicken. Faraday stepped up to the desk, threw the now-clucking fowl out of a partially broken lattice window, and then removed his handkerchief again and proceeded to flick the dust off a frail-looking chair.

'Please have a seat,' he said. 'Are you here on business or pleasure?'

Jane almost laughed at the notion that anyone would choose to visit such a man in such a place for pleasure. 'Most definitely business,' she said, making her intentions clear from the outset.

Faraday lost his smile, although it soon returned. 'Any excuse to spend time in your company is a pleasure for me, madam,' he said as he sat down opposite her.

'You're too kind as always, Mr Faraday,' Jane said politely. 'In truth, I was surprised to find you still in Jaipur. From our previous conversations I took it that you prefer to move around.'

'Believe me, Mrs Hardwick, I am as surprised to find myself here as you are. The reason, however, is simple. My health has been too poor these past months to travel. Now, as you can see from the abject squalor in which I am forced to live, I am without sufficient funds to go anywhere. Fortunately Jaipur generates much that is newsworthy. I hope to be back on my feet again soon. Now, what is it that I can do for you? My services are at your disposal.'

Jane remained perched on the edge of her seat, not wishing to become too settled. 'I've come to see you about a matter I'm sure every news correspondent in the area has written about by now—the recent dacoit massacre in the southwest hills.'

'Ah, yes,' Faraday said, rocking back in his chair with a creak. 'A terrible business. Close to fifty dead.'

'Fifty! I hadn't imagined the number was so high.'

Faraday nodded. 'There was not a single man, woman or child left alive. Due to my privileged position with *The Times* newspaper, I was able to see the bodies prior to their disposal, enabling me to better report on their condition. Massacre is the right word for it, believe you me. There were secondary wounds of one kind or another on each and every body I saw.'

'As if someone purposefully wanted to ensure there were no survivors?' Jane asked, considering Captain Fraser's motives again.

'I really couldn't say, Mrs Hardwick. The captain who led the attack clearly wanted to set an example to any other dacoits in the area. That much is certain.'

'Captain Donnan Fraser,' Jane said, considering whether setting an example could very well have been all Fraser had in mind, given his recent orders to put an end to the dacoit problem.

'Yes, that was the officer's name,' Faraday said. 'Do you know him?'

'We're acquainted, although I can't pretend to know him well.'

Faraday sat forward with a questioning smile. 'May I ask why someone as genteel as your good self is interested in these macabre goings on?'

Jane paused before answering, deciding whether or not to confide in Mr Faraday her suspicions that Captain Fraser had another motive for ensuring no one survived the attack. 'What I'm about to tell you, I tell you in the strictest confidence,' she said, having concluded that in her pursuit of the truth, she had to tell someone. 'You're to speak of what I'm about to tell you to no one, nor write about it in your correspondences without my permission. Before I go on, do I have your word?'

'Of course,' Faraday said, eyeing Jane sharply, clearly keen to learn what she had to say. 'And you have my utmost attention.'

'Very well,' Jane began, and proceeded to tell Faraday why Naresh Bharat Singh was travelling to Jaipur the evening he was killed, adding everything she had heard spoken between Sir John Christie and the Maharaja of Kishangarh.

Faraday pressed his fingers together and drew a deep breath. 'In light of what you've just told me,' he said as soon as Jane had finished speaking, 'I'm sure you'll be most interested to hear what else *I* have to tell *you*.'

'Go on, Mr Faraday. What more do you know of the matter?'

'Well, it has been drawn into question whether the people slain that evening by Captain Fraser and his men were dacoits at all.'

'Not dacoits?' Jane said, momentarily bewildered by the possibility.

'Precisely,' Faraday said, smiling—no doubt because he knew that his statement added weight to Jane's suspicions. 'Two people have since come forward, a man and a woman of no relation to one another, but who were related to those that had died in the massacre. This man and woman had been away from their families at the time—the woman fetching water, the man simply returning to his family from his recent travels. I was generously granted an interview with each of them independently. Both appeared genuinely shocked to hear that their families had been taken for savage and violent dacoits when, to the contrary, they each informed me that they and their families practiced Jainism.'

'A tenet of nonviolence,' Jane said. 'A respect of all living things.'

'Precisely, and in which case, they were hardly murderous dacoits.'

She had not wanted to believe it possible, but at hearing this new revelation, Jane was all the more certain that Captain Fraser had set the whole thing up to mask the murder of Naresh Bharat Singh. To remove suspicion over the killing of one person, he was responsible for the deaths of close to fifty. Having gone out that evening and killed Bharat Singh, Fraser had taken Singh's horse, his personal effects and his trove of jewels, which the sowar-prince had no doubt taken from Kishangarh to fund his and Arabella's elopement, and had then pretended to find them after he and his men had brutally slain all those innocent people. Jane could still barely entertain the idea that any man could do such a thing, and yet she could now see it no other way. It all fitted together so well, but how could she prove it?

'Thank you, Mr Faraday,' she said. 'You've been most helpful.'

Chapter Twenty-Seven

Jaipur, April 1823

'Sir John, I must speak with you,' Jane said upon entering the resident's study.

Sir John appeared as flustered as he usually did whenever he was at his desk. His brow was creased, his cheeks were flushed, and now that summer had begun its return to India, his forehead was glistening with sweat, despite the *punkah* that wafted slowly back and forth above him. He pulled at his starched white collar and grimaced at Jane as she approached.

'I'm very busy, Mrs Hardwick,' he said. 'Can the matter not wait until supper this evening?'

'I'm afraid what I have to say will not make fitting table conversation.'

'Very well. What is it?'

'It concerns Captain Fraser and the death of the Crown Prince of Kishangarh.'

Sir John set his pen down and sat back in his chair. 'Does it, indeed. Well, sit down, sit down. Say what you have to say and be quick about it.'

Jane sat down, wondering how best to proceed. She had just come from Arabella's room, where she had spent most of the morning conveying her findings since going to see Mr Faraday the week before. She could hardly take as long to tell Sir John of her suspicions. She reflected momentarily on how Arabella had cared little for what she'd told her, saying that none of it mattered now that Naresh Bharat Singh was dead. But it did matter, and she hoped the man sitting opposite her, a man in a position to do something about it, would feel the same way.

'As you wish me to be brief, I'll get straight to the point,' Jane said, knotting her fingers together, feeling a little nervous in light of the accusations she was about to make. 'I believe Captain Fraser murdered the maharaja's brother and went on to massacre innocent natives to cover it up.'

Sir John leaned forward, his brow suddenly more creased than ever. 'Captain Fraser?' he said, seemingly unable to believe his ears. 'Be very careful, Mrs Hardwick. Those are serious allegations.'

'I'm well aware of that,' Jane said, 'and I can assure you I do not make them lightly.'

'You have some evidence to support this?'

Jane quickly thought over what she knew. She shook her head. 'No, but you must hear what I have to say. Once you have, I'm sure you'll agree that the matter demands further investigation.'

'Go on, go on,' Sir John said as he sat back again, clearly growing impatient.

'Very well. Firstly there's the matter of motive. Captain Fraser, with your blessing, has his heart set on Arabella. I believe he overheard Arabella telling me of her plan to elope two evenings before Bharat Singh came for her, which of course was on the evening he was murdered. The captain had been at the residency all that day, and yet that very evening his duties called him away.'

'That's right. He's a soldier. His time is rarely his own.'

'That may be so, but it's my belief that his time was his own that evening, and that he used it to stop Arabella eloping with the man she loved.'

'I can't say I'm sorry Bharat Singh didn't cart my only daughter off to God knows where that evening,' Sir John said. 'Does that simple fact also make *me* a suspect in your investigations? I had as strong a motive as Captain Fraser—perhaps stronger.'

It had crossed Jane's mind, but as she had previously thought, if Sir John had known of his daughter's plan to elope that night, he would simply have locked her door and barred her windows. 'Of course not.'

'Then why Fraser?'

Jane cleared her throat. 'A few days ago, I went to see a newspaper correspondent of my acquaintance here in Jaipur. He told me that those people Captain Fraser and his men slaughtered soon after Bharat Singh's body was discovered—people who were allegedly dacoits—were in fact Jainists. In other words, they couldn't harm anyone, nor any living thing. Simply put, they were not dacoits at all.'

'So why were Bharat Singh's horse, his ring and all the valuable possessions he was carrying with him that night found at their camp?'

Jane sat forward, gesturing enthusiastically with her hands as she said, 'Don't you see? These people were used as scapegoats. It would have been easy for Captain Fraser to make out that he'd found Bharat Singh's possessions after these poor people were dead, blaming them for his murder as a result, accusing them of being dacoits. And who was left after the massacre to say otherwise?'

Sir John set a quizzical eye on Jane. 'How can you know these natives were not dacoits when every last one of them was killed?'

'Two family members later came forward.'

'I see,' Sir John mused. 'That could prove very useful,' he added, as if coming around to Jane's way of thinking.

'That's what I thought, so I tracked them down, thinking that if I could talk to them I might be able to learn something more.'

'And did you?'

'Yes, and no,' Jane said. 'And this is where my suspicions of foul play were truly aroused. When I located where the woman had been staying, I was told she was dead.'

'Dead? How?'

'She met with a fatal accident, just the day before. It had something to do with an ox-cart. Apparently she was trampled to death.'

'Dear, dear. And the other?'

'I searched long and hard, even soliciting the services of several natives to help me, but I've not been able to find the man my correspondent acquaintance spoke of. He was a traveller, so it's possible he went back on his travels after returning to Jaipur to find his family dead, but so soon? I suspect that he, too, is dead. I believe that Captain Fraser has been busy covering his tracks.'

'I see,' Sir John said. 'You certainly pose an interesting theory, Mrs Hardwick, and I must confess that it holds up rather well. However, if Captain Fraser is guilty of the things you say, he has indeed covered his tracks, and perhaps too well. It won't be easy proving any of this. It may be impossible.'

'I know, which is why I've come to you, as a man of power and influence. Your close association with Captain Fraser may also work to your advantage should you see enough merit in what I've told you to attempt to bring the man to justice.'

Sir John drew a long breath through his nose and sighed heavily. A moment later he said, 'Captain Fraser may have his faults, as do we all, but it is my firm belief that he's an honourable man.' He paused, tapping his fingers together in deliberation. 'I can promise nothing, of course, but leave the matter with me and I'll see what I can do. How's that?'

Jane nodded. 'I only wish for justice,' she said. 'For Naresh Bharat Singh, and for all those poor natives who were killed.'

'I understand,' Sir John said. 'I'll give the matter my utmost attention. Now, if you'll excuse me, I have important affairs of state to deal with first.'

'Of course, Sir John. Thank you for your time.'

The following morning, Jane was in the grand hall helping Elspeth and a host of servants with the decorations for Arabella's birthday party, which was now just a few days away.

'A little higher,' Elspeth called to two of the servants, who were raising a swathe of bright cerise cloth above one of the windows, trying to position it perfectly in line with the rest.

Jane was sitting at one end of a long table that was capable of seating at least forty people, writing place cards for all the key guests. 'I still have my doubts as to whether Arabella will come to her birthday party,' she said to Elspeth. 'To my knowledge, she hasn't left her room once since she heard the young prince was dead.'

'No,' Elspeth said, 'but she'll come around, just you wait and see. What girl could resist her own birthday party, and her eighteenth at that? One more day and she'll be a grown woman, with a woman's head on her shoulders. She'll quickly realise how childish she's been over this native boy.'

Jane wished she could share Elspeth's confidence over the matter, but having seen Arabella draw more and more into herself each day, she could not.

'If it comes to it,' Elspeth continued, 'her father will have the servants drag her out of there. Enough is enough. We can't disappoint our guests.' Her face took on a horrified expression at the idea.

Jane went back to writing her place cards, thinking there was going to be nothing but trouble and disappointment ahead as far as Arabella's eighteenth birthday was concerned. She finished another and set it aside with the rest—only a dozen or so now to go. She picked up her quill pen to continue, dipped it in the ink, then she heard several heavy footsteps behind her and turned to see Sir John enter the room. With him were four armed soldiers in their smart red tunics. Two were carrying a small, but heavy-looking, cast-iron strongbox, painted black.

'Elspeth, my dear,' Sir John said, looking more jolly and showing more affection towards his wife than Jane had yet seen. 'I've something to show you while I'm still in a position to do so.'

'What is it, John?' Elspeth said, going to his side, leaving the two servants holding the swathe of cerise cloth suspended on their ladders.

At Sir John's signal, the two soldiers holding the strongbox carefully lowered it to the floor by its handles. 'A thing of most wondrous beauty,' he said as he produced two keys from his waistcoat pocket: one large, the other small. He bent over the box, set the large key in the lock and turned it to release the locking bolts. 'I'm sure you've heard the commotion outside this morning. This strongbox is to begin its journey to Bombay this very day for onward passage to England. Aside from these fine soldiers, there are close to a hundred more waiting in the courtyard inside the main gate to ensure it arrives safely.'

'I did wonder at the noise,' Elspeth said, 'but really we've been far too busy to pay it much attention, haven't we, Jane?'

Jane stood up and went to Elspeth, her eyes now also on the strongbox as Sir John began to lift the lid, groaning a little from the weight of it. 'Yes, quite busy,' she agreed.

'Inside this box,' Sir John said, 'are the many valuables Captain Fraser and his men found at that wretched dacoit settlement—the murderous scoundrels.'

He paused as he reached down into the box, and as he did so, Jane saw a glimmer of gold within. Then Sir John withdrew another, far smaller—yet clearly strong—box, and closed the lid. He set the one down on top of the other.

'In truth,' Sir John continued, offering the smaller of the two keys to the lock, 'I was in two minds whether or not to show this to you, but such things are a rare sight indeed.'

Sir John opened the smaller box and withdrew something that was wrapped in green silk. It filled his hand. 'I imagine few people will see it in this state again once it reaches England. I expect the Honourable East India Company will make a gift of it to His Majesty the King, to further strengthen the bonds between them.'

He unfurled the silk very slowly, holding his hand up to the light as he did so, gradually revealing the largest ruby Jane had ever seen. Neither she nor Elspeth, it seemed, could contain the gasps that rose from within them.

'There,' Sir John said. 'Didn't I tell you? I'm told the natives call it the Blood of Rajputana, although I expect it will be renamed once it's in England and has been cut.'

'How beautiful indeed,' Elspeth said. 'Don't you agree, Jane?'

Jane nodded. It was beautiful, even in this rough, uncut state. Just the same, she could not help but look upon it with mixed feelings. She knew who it really belonged to, spoil of war or otherwise. At least, she had heard the Maharaja of Kishangarh claim that it belonged to him. She also knew full well how it had come to be there in front of her: it was as a result of Naresh Bharat Singh's murder and the slaughter of a settlement of people whom Jane had come to believe were not murderous dacoits at all.

Sir John held the ruby aloft for a full minute, turning his hand slowly back and forth so that the stone could be seen in its entirety. Then he began to fold the silk back over it again. 'Well, there you have it,' he said as he lowered it back into its place. 'Now the ruby must commence its journey. I've kept its temporary custodians too long from their duties as it is.' He locked the small box again and set it back inside the larger one with the other treasures that had been recovered. Then he closed the lid and proceeded to lock the strongbox again. 'They mustn't be kept waiting a moment longer,' he added, putting the keys back into his waistcoat pocket.

'You're keeping the keys, John?'

'Of course. This box won't be opened again until it arrives in England. The keys and the box cannot travel together.'

'No, of course not,' Elspeth said. 'How silly of me. Such a beautiful thing could play heavily on a man's desires.'

'Quite,' Sir John said. 'It's far safer that the keys remain here. Once in London, the box can be opened by other means.'

Without further prompt, the two soldiers who had carried the strongbox in picked it up again and began to leave.

'I'll let you get about your arrangements for the party,' Sir John said. 'I just thought you'd like to see it.'

'Yes, and thank you,' Elspeth replied, a hand on Sir John's arm and a hint of warmth in her voice, perhaps on account of her husband's rare and thoughtful gesture.

Neither lingered in the moment. Elspeth returned to the two servants, whose arms were surely aching beyond belief by now, and Sir John made for the door. As he did so, Jane went to him.

'Sir John,' she said, almost in a whisper. 'Have you managed to give any consideration to the matter we spoke of yesterday?'

'I have. That said, I have no news for you. I should first like to speak with Captain Fraser, but his duties with these damned dacoits are keeping him away from us. As soon as he's able to return to us, you have my word that I shall quiz him most thoroughly about the matter. Whatever he tells me can be substantiated or otherwise refuted by his commanding officer, or the other gentlemen he keeps company with. We'll soon see if his story adds up. I must, however, be allowed to speak with him first.'

'Of course, Sir John,' Jane said, thinking that Captain Fraser had perhaps rather too conveniently made himself scarce these past few weeks.

As Sir John left the room and Jane returned to writing her place cards, she wondered whether Fraser really was out hunting dacoits. Or was he deliberately staying away from the residency and the young woman he had set his sights on until the dust had settled on his murderous activities?

Chapter Twenty-Eight

After showing the latest of Jane Hardwick's letters to Sinclair, along with the digital copy of Cornelius Dredger's death certificate, alerting Sinclair to the possibility that Sir Robert Christie had murdered him, Jefferson Tayte was back in his room at Drumarthen. He'd spent the last hour going through the late Gordon Drummond's records, and was about a third of the way through the box. So far nothing appeared to be even remotely connected with India or the Blood of Rajputana. He picked up another record and glanced at it briefly before putting it back on to the pile. It was another birth certificate, this time from 1922, offering no connection.

He sighed and sat back in his chair, finding himself distracted by what he'd read in the latest of Jane Hardwick's letters. If the events she had written home to her brother about were true, and Tayte had no reason to suspect they were not, then there could be no denying that the Blood of Rajputana was real. Jane had mentioned overhearing the Maharaja of Kishangarh talking to Sir John Christie about it in the previous letter. Now it was as if Tayte had seen it for himself. Jane's description had drawn such a vivid image in his mind that it was as though he'd been standing in the room with her and Lady Elspeth as Sir John showed it to them.

'And all you gotta do is work out where it is,' he reminded himself, smiling at the seemingly impossible challenge before him.

Tayte also found himself thinking about Captain Donnan Fraser again. After all he'd read in Jane's letters, he found it hard to disagree with her judgement of the man. *No smoke without fire*, he thought. It seemed irrefutable that the massacred people who had been blamed for Naresh Bharat Singh's murder and the theft of his belongings were not the murderous dacoits they had been taken for, and yet Bharat Singh's belongings had supposedly been found among them. Had they been planted there? It was easy to imagine that Fraser could have orchestrated the entire bloody ordeal simply to cover his tracks, as Jane supposed, but had she gone on to prove anything?

When it came to finding out how past events had turned out, Tayte, unlike Jane, had the passage of time firmly on his side. Having been reminded of Albert Faraday, he made a note to consult *The Times* Digital Archive, to see if he could view Faraday's article about the massacre, and perhaps more importantly, find out whether he'd written anything else about the matter.

'One thing at a time, though,' he said under his breath as he looked at the next of Dr Drummond's family history records. *The Times* Digital Archive wasn't going anywhere, and he was conscious of the fact that he only had a limited amount of time to go through these records.

Another thirty minutes passed. Tayte reached the halfway stage with nothing of interest to show for it, but then just about all of the dates on the records he'd seen were too recent to offer any worthwhile connections. He had to look at them all, just the same. He had to be thorough, but he supposed he would find the remainder of Drummond's research more interesting given that the dates on the records he was now looking at were steadily creeping back through the nineteenth century.

He was just reaching for another record when there was a knock at his door. It was Sinclair, and his dark expression told Tayte that he came bearing yet more bad news.

'I'm sorry for the intrusion, Mr Tayte,' Sinclair said. 'I know you're busy.'

'That's okay. What is it?'

'We've just heard that an item of clothing has been found in the woods near Drummond Castle. It matches the blouse Chrissie MacIntyre was last seen wearing before she went missing from her home yesterday. Drummond Castle is several miles from Comrie to the south-west. It's no wonder the police helicopter couldn't find anything when they searched the moorland behind Chrissie's home.'

'That doesn't sound good,' Tayte said, wondering whether it was pure coincidence that the castle Sinclair had just mentioned shared the doctor's name. *The good doctor*, he thought, reminding himself of Chrissie MacIntyre's reaction at hearing Dr Drummond referred to in that way the night he'd met her.

'No, it's not good at all,' Sinclair said. 'The police are out searching the area, but because it's so large and encumbered by the trees, they're asking for support from the community.'

'A search party?'

'Aye. I'm heading over with Murray now. I was wondering whether you'd care to join us. With the weather as bad as it is, I'm sure the police will need all the help they can get. I can lend you a raincoat.'

Tayte was already on his feet. 'Of course,' he said, collecting his jacket from the back of the chair. 'I'd be glad to. Just lead the way.'

It took Murray twenty minutes to drive the seven miles to Drummond Castle, where the search for Chrissie MacIntyre was being organised. The relentless rain that Tayte had observed since opening his bedroom curtains that morning seemed to intensify as they arrived and were directed to an available parking space. Within seconds of getting out of the car, Tayte's loafers and the lower half of his tan suit trousers were soaked through. Clear waterproof cagoules were being handed out, and beneath the cover of an open-sided marquee tent, Tayte put one on in favour of the ill-fitting raincoat Sinclair had loaned him, glad to find that he now had a hood.

From the car park, along with a number of other people who were there to help out, Tayte, Sinclair and Murray were taken back along the road they had arrived by in a small coach that had been laid on to take volunteers to and from each of the search start points. The coach stopped midway into the wooded area where Chrissie's blouse had been found. As Tayte followed everyone else out of the vehicle, he couldn't believe how dark it was. It was barely past three in the afternoon, but because of the heavy rainclouds it felt more like dusk. Above him, he could hear the intermittent roar of the wind as it caused the treetops to sway wildly. Tayte had neither seen nor heard the police helicopter, and he wasn't surprised. He doubted it was safe to fly.

They were organised into groups of around twelve people. Each person was given a bottle of water and instructions not to touch anything they deemed suspicious or in any way worthy of closer inspection, but to inform their group leader, who in their case was a licensed search officer called Paula Campbell. She handed torches out to those who needed them, although Murray had already taken care of that for Tayte, Sinclair and himself. As the group formed a close line and set off into the woods together after their torch beams, Tayte found himself wondering if Chrissie MacIntyre was out there. It didn't bode well that her blouse had been found, and he questioned why she was no longer wearing it. He came up with no good answers.

No one spoke. Apart from the constant static hiss of the rain and the wind, the wood seemed oddly quiet. Tayte could hear no birds singing, no other woodland animals calling to their mates, despite the fact that it was springtime. Every now and then the silence would be punctuated by the snap of a dead branch underfoot, or the occasional sound of a sniffer dog barking in the distance. Beyond that, they walked quietly between the trees, scouring the undergrowth for anything out of the ordinary. An hour in and Tayte found himself wishing he was wearing more appropriate footwear, but it was nothing he couldn't deal with in light of the reason he was there.

Sometime into their second hour of searching, Murray stopped walking and put his hand up, bringing everyone else to a stop with him. 'Officer Campbell!' he called to the group leader. 'I've found something you might want to take a look at.'

Campbell came to Murray's side, where she squatted down to get a better look at the object glowing in Murray's torchlight. It was an orange drink can.

'We've gathered a few empty cans of pop today,' Campbell said. 'They've probably just been discarded at one time or another by irresponsible kids, or adults for that matter.' She took out a clear plastic zip-bag and a pencil, which she inserted into the can's opening before carefully lifting it out from its bed of leaves and twigs. 'You never know, though. They can be a rich source of forensic material.' She slid the can into the bag, then from inside her coat she took out a notepad and a map. 'I just need to record the Ordnance Survey grid reference and we'll be on our way.'

Having also noted down their GPS coordinates for good measure, they were soon walking again. It was a large woodland, and Tayte knew that the odds of them being in the same area Chrissie had been brought to were slim, but he still couldn't help wondering whether he was about to come face to face with the poor woman, or perhaps another piece of her clothing. Given the circumstances, he doubted the day would see a happy ending for her. He believed that whoever was behind this wanted her body to be found. Why else bring her to the woods at Drummond Castle? Why not the vast moorland at the back of her house? Come to that, why abduct her at all? It was out of keeping with the other murders.

Time passed, and at length they came to a shallow ditch that because of the heavy rain had begun to fill with water. The group approached it with caution, pausing briefly to shine their torches over it, fully taking the area in before proceeding. At the edge of Tayte's torch beam he could see a flat overhanging rock. Something colourful beneath it caught his eye and he stepped closer as he focused his torch beam on it. Then he did what Murray had done earlier. He put his hand up and called out to Campbell.

'There's something here!' he said. 'It looks like material of some kind.'

Tayte wondered whether the pale red-and-white cloth he was looking at was clothing. It was hard to tell because most of it appeared to be beneath the overhanging rock. Campbell joined him, as Sinclair, Murray, and the rest of the group drew closer.

Campbell knelt down and tried to get a better look beneath the rock. 'Can you lift this up?' she said, and Tayte and a few others each grabbed a section of the rock and began to raise it.

'Is it clothing?' Tayte asked when he felt the rock had been raised high enough. 'Is there anything else under there?'

'You can lower it again,' Campbell said, and when Tayte turned to her he saw that she had the material hanging from the end of her pencil. 'It's just an old tea towel,' she added. 'There's nothing else there.'

At that point, Tayte heard a dog barking. It sounded nearby, close enough to hear its intermittent whimpering, as if it had been excited by something. A few minutes later, a call came in on Campbell's radio with the news that Chrissie MacIntyre's body had been found.

An hour later, Tayte was with Sinclair and Murray, back in the car park at Drummond Castle. They were sitting beside a trellis table on foldaway chairs beneath the shelter of one of the marquee tents that had been set up, sipping hot drinks while they waited to speak with DI Ross. He'd called Sinclair not long after Chrissie MacIntyre's body had been found, to ask if they would wait there for him. He'd said he needed to talk to them. Most of the other volunteers had left by now, although there were still plenty of people about, mostly police officers and other officials. Tayte wished Ross would hurry up. His damp feet were getting cold.

'What do you suppose Detective Ross has to say?' he asked.

'Whatever it is, it must be important,' Sinclair said.

Murray scoffed. 'Maybe he's found something to incriminate me again. The man's had it in for me ever since he heard I helped get the Frasers' car started that night they all came to Drumarthen.'

Sinclair reached an arm out and placed his hand on Murray's shoulder. 'Don't you fret, Murray. He's just doing his job. I'm sure a case like this could lead any man to clutch at straws over who the guilty party is. He'll be pointing the finger at Mr Tayte here next.'

Tayte looked surprised. 'I hope not,' he said, and before he could add anything, in walked Detective Inspector Alastair Ross.

It was only just after six in the evening, but Ross looked as though he should be heading off to his bed. His gait was laboured and his shoulders were slumped, as if he was too weary to hold them up. His eyes looked swollen and red against his pale complexion, which along with his thinning hair was wet through from the rain that showed no sign of easing up. He took a plastic cup of coffee from a uniformed police officer as he approached, pulling the knot of his tie down until it was barely visible beneath the collar of his coat.

'Thanks for waiting,' Ross said. He pulled a chair over and sat down. 'Ah, that's better,' he added as he slumped back and took a sip of his coffee. He had an iPad under his arm which he now rested on his lap. 'Thanks for turning out today,' he added. 'I'm sorry to have kept you so long, but you know how it is.'

'Aye, and it's nae bother at all,' Sinclair said. 'I'm sure I speak for us all when I say we've been only too happy to help.'

Tayte and Murray both gave Ross a sombre-faced nod.

'I don't mean to shock you,' Ross said, 'but as you're all so close to this, I felt it might be important for you to know some of the details. Poor Chrissie was naked when she was found. Her body wasn't particularly well hidden, either. There's no doubt her killer wanted her body to be discovered. I don't yet know the time of death, but having seen the body, my guesstimate is that she was either killed at her house or very soon after she was abducted.'

'How did she die?' Sinclair asked.

'Again, it's too early to be absolutely sure, but it looks as though she was strangled. There are signs of bruising about her neck.'

'Why naked?' Tayte asked. 'I mean, it's not exactly in keeping with any of the other murders, is it? Until now, whoever's doing this has killed and quickly moved on to the next victim. And why bring her all the way here to Drummond Castle? From what I've seen there are plenty of other places to choose from that are much closer to her home in Comrie.'

'I think you're absolutely right, Mr Tayte. These things have been playing on my mind since I got here. This killer hasn't cared where the victim's bodies have been found before now. He's left each and every one of them right where they died. Why not Chrissie? I can't be certain yet, but I doubt we'll find that Chrissie's murder was sexually motivated.'

Murray spoke then. 'It sounds very personal to me.'

Ross scoffed. 'You could argue that all murder is personal to one degree or another, of course, but I'm inclined to agree with you. I just wish I knew why.'

'The Blood of Rajputana,' Sinclair said. 'That's what the syndicate was about. That's what brought all these people together, my Jamie included.'

'I don't know,' Ross said, sounding dejected. 'All I do know is that someone out there wanted these people dead for some reason, and I need to find out why.'

Tayte dropped his empty drinks cup into the waste bin that was just within arm's reach at the end of the trestle table. 'Do you think all this could have more to do with Dr Drummond than meets the eye? I keep thinking about Chrissie MacIntyre's behaviour the night everyone was gathered together at Drumarthen House.'

'You mean her scoffing when the good doctor was mentioned?'

Tayte nodded. 'She seemed to be scoffing at the suggestion that he was a *good* doctor for some reason.'

Ross sighed. 'Well, if she *was* harbouring a secret about the man, she's taken it to her grave. But what about the others? What connects the Frasers and Moira Macrae to Dr Drummond? What connects Ewan Blair and Callum Macrae, wherever the hell he is?'

That had Tayte stumped. A motive for any single murder was difficult to apply to all the rest. The only things the victims appeared to have in common were that they were family and that, as Sinclair had said, they had all been drawn together to form a syndicate that was connected with a ruby everyone had been trying over the years to find. But why kill these people because of that? Tayte was the one looking for the Blood of Rajputana now, and no one had tried to kill him. Not yet, anyway. As Ross had said, someone wanted these people dead, but what was their motive? Tayte could see why the detective looked so tired.

Ross drained his coffee. 'There's another reason I need to speak with you—particularly with you, Mr Tayte.'

'With me?'

'Aye, another of Jane Hardwick's letters has turned up. It was taped to Chrissie's mouth inside a plastic bag, which is why we know her killer wanted her body found.'

Tayte's jaw dropped at hearing that. He'd always expected as much, but this was the first time one of Jane's letters had turned up on one of the victims. The connotations made his palms clammy. 'So this confirms without doubt that the killer and the person leaving these letters for me are one and the same.' It was an uncomfortable thought.

'Aye, it does,' Ross said. 'Not that it helps any. The CCTV images of the hooded figure at the house are all but useless.' He lifted up the iPad he'd brought with him. 'I'm afraid I can't let you have the actual letter, Mr Tayte. This time it's criminal evidence and it needs to be processed. Given the circumstances, however, I wanted you to see it as soon as possible, so I've taken some photos.' He woke up his iPad and handed it to Tayte. 'There's a photo for each of the pages.'

Tayte took the iPad from DI Ross, and as he curled over it and began to scan the contents, his excitement grew. 'She's written to her brother about the ruby again.' He paused, still scanning. 'There are some more of those Sanskrit symbols. It looks familiar. Maybe they're the same symbols that were written on that note left in my room.' He flicked to the next page. 'That doesn't sound so good,' he added. 'There's a section that says Jane was in fear of her life again.'

'Read it out then, man,' Sinclair said, impatient to hear what Jane had to say.

'I'm sorry,' Tayte said. 'Of course.' Then he began to read Jane's letter aloud in full for the benefit of those around him.

Chapter Twenty-Nine

Jaipur, April 1823

It was the day before Arabella's eighteenth birthday party. Invitations had been sent, all preparations made. Now, at last, Jane was free of involvement in Elspeth's overly fastidious planning and had some time to herself again. She was in her room, sitting at a small desk by the open shutters of her window, which looked out over the city rooftops towards the Aravalli Hills. Having decided to spend the morning writing home to her brother of recent events in Jaipur, she was keen to finish expressing her concerns about Captain Fraser and the murder of the Crown Prince of Kishangarh. Such was her plan, but before her letter was half-written, she was interrupted by a knock on her door.

Jane turned to see who it was. 'Come in!'

As the door opened, a hot breeze blew in through the window, causing her writing paper to flap. It was her personal servant, Rashmi, standing tall in the doorframe in his red turban, his beard split in two and tied behind his neck as it always was.

'Apologies, memsaab,' Rashmi said. 'There is a most insistent man at the gate who wishes to speak with you. His name is Mr Faraday.'

'Faraday?' Jane scrunched her brow. What was he doing here?

'Yes, memsaab. I told him you were not to be disturbed, as you instructed, but he will not listen. Humble apologies once more.'

'It's all right, Rashmi. Thank you.'

Jane set her quill down and stood up, wondering as she closed the shutters what Mr Faraday was doing at the residency. She followed after Rashmi at a pace, thinking it must have something to do with Captain Fraser. Had something else come to light? As she left the building and strode across the main courtyard to find out, she certainly hoped so.

Albert Faraday was standing in the shade just outside the main gate as Jane approached. She thought he looked worse than when she had last seen him, if that were possible, although it was apparent from the tie at his neck and the wilting flower in his lapel that he had made some effort, for what it was worth. He still looked feverish, his skin pale and clammy, despite the heat. He pulled at his collar as she drew closer, putting on a wide smile that was over the top to say the least.

'Mrs Hardwick! It's so good to see you again. Though you do not realise it, you are the very tonic for what ails me. Why, the mere thought of seeing you again has lifted my spirits to—'

'Good morning, Mr Faraday,' Jane cut in, unable to listen to his overblown flattery a moment longer. 'My servant tells me you wish to speak with me. I trust you're here to discuss something important.'

'Er, yes,' Faraday stumbled, still smiling. 'You've not heard the news then? Perhaps it is because I have not yet reported it.'

'News? What news?'

'Why, I should have thought that you of all people would know by now, Mrs Hardwick, living here at the residency as you do. The resident is surely aware by now, although I'm equally sure he must be a very busy man—too busy by far, it seems, to have broadcast this terrible news to the household. It is he with whom I would ask your favour in securing me an interview.'

'An interview?' Jane asked, frustration in her tone. 'About what? Get to the point, will you? What should I have already heard about?'

'The attack!' Faraday said, throwing his arms in the air as if everyone in Jaipur should have heard about it by now. 'The soldiers who left this very spot less than a week ago, charged with the conveyance of undisclosed items to Bombay at the resident's behest, were set upon close to Kishangarh's southernmost border. Many soldiers were killed, their cargo stolen.'

'Stolen?' Jane said, momentarily lost for words as she pictured the black strongbox she'd seen, and the enormous ruby it contained. This was news indeed. But what did it mean? Surely this was no random attack. Whoever was responsible had to know what they were after. 'Do you know who led the attack?'

'Dacoits were blamed at first, of course. Who else would be so bold as to attack a hundred armed soldiers of the East India Company? But rumours spread fast among the natives. I've heard that it was the Maharaja of Kishangarh, taking back what he felt was rightfully his. There's a story behind the gossip, I'm sure of it.'

In light of what Jane knew, it made sense to her that the maharaja had ordered the attack on the soldiers in order to get his ruby back. The Blood of Rajputana, as he'd called it, clearly meant a great deal to him. 'The attack happened near Kishangarh's southernmost border, you say?'

'That's right, but what was the maharaja after? That's what I'd like to know.'

Jane didn't answer. She remained silent with her thoughts for several seconds.

'So, an interview with Sir John Christie? Do you think you can arrange it? I'm sure he knows a great deal more about the matter.'

'The interview. Yes, of course,' Jane said, snapping out of her thoughts at last. 'I'm sure he'll be too busy, but I'll see what I can do.'

'That is all any man can ask or expect to hope for,' Faraday said with a smile and a polite bow of his head.

Chapter Thirty

Jaipur, April 1823

Early on the morning of Arabella's eighteenth birthday, Jane awoke with a start. Her eyes shot open and she sat up in her bed, her pulse suddenly racing. From the pale, pinkish light at her windows, she quickly determined that it was close to daybreak, not quite six o'clock. She had been dreaming that she was amidst the attack on those poor soldiers Mr Faraday had told her about the day before. She supposed it was because she had spoken about it at length with Sir John at supper last evening, the matter still fresh in her mind as she retired to her bed. Sir John had refused Mr Faraday his interview, which was much as Jane had expected. All through supper he appeared to remain deeply shocked by the incident, readily blaming the Maharaja of Kishangarh, against whom there would be serious repercussions should the rumours of his involvement prove to be true.

In her dream Jane kept seeing Captain Fraser over and over again, a turban on his blackened face, his eyes wild with murderous intent, the bright steel of his sabre covered with blood. That was her dream, although in waking she felt it silly to suppose that Captain Fraser could have anything to do with an attack on Company soldiers. These men were not natives, after all—people for whom Jane knew Fraser held little regard— but soldiers of the East India Company, much like himself.

But was it the dream that had awoken her?

Jane shook her head. No, it had been something else. She was sure of it. She folded back her bedcovers, stood and went to the window. All was calm and quiet, and yet she could not shake the unpleasant feeling that something was wrong. She put on her robe and tied the sash as she paced to the door to check the corridor, but before she had taken two steps towards it, she heard a scream and froze. She couldn't be certain, but she thought it was Elspeth.

Jane was at her door in seconds. She flung it open, meaning to rush to her friend's aid, to find out why she had screamed. As she opened it, however, she immediately cowered back, her heart beating faster. A man dressed all in black, his face and head covered in the same midnight cloth, was standing outside her door.

The man's eyes looked as startled at seeing Jane as hers must have appeared to him. In an instant he'd pulled a curved dagger from his belt and had raised it above his head, ready to kill her if he chose to. But he did not. He paused with the dagger in mid-air, and Jane's eyes were drawn to the markings on the inside of his right forearm, which was now exposed. It was a Sanskrit tattoo, etched into his skin in dark red ink.

Noting the intruder's hesitation, Jane quickly kicked her door shut again and turned the key in the lock. She stood against it breathing heavily until she dared open it again. When she did, the intruder was gone. She looked left and right along the corridor, just to be certain. Then a moment later she heard another door open and close further along the corridor as Elspeth came out of her room. Thankfully, she appeared to be unharmed. They met at the top of the stairs, and within seconds they were both surrounded by servants and residency guards, followed by Sir John in his nightcap, gown and slippers. He had a candle in one hand and a heavy-looking bludgeon in the other.

'What on earth's going on?' he cried. 'Elspeth? Did I hear you screaming? Whatever's the matter?'

'Intruders at the residency!' Elspeth cried, frantically gesturing with an ivory-handled letter opener. 'We are besieged!'

Sir John turned to Jane. 'Jane? Is this true?' he asked, as if holding little value in his wife's hysterical opinion. 'Have you seen any of these intruders?'

'Yes. Outside my room a moment ago. Just one man, dressed from head to toe in black.'

'One man, eh?' Sir John turned to Elspeth with a look of disdain. 'Besieged indeed. You need to take a hold of yourself, woman. I trust you also saw this man, hence your screaming?'

'I did,' Elspeth said, still brandishing her letter opener. 'I wasn't sleeping well. I was already awake when he opened my door and came into my room.'

'What in heaven's name did he want in there? And put that blasted letter opener down before you harm someone.'

Elspeth set the letter opener down on a side table between two brightly painted vases. 'There could be more of them.'

Sir John drew a long breath. 'Aye, I suppose there could,' he said. Then, to the guards and servants, he added, 'Conduct a thorough search of the premises, although I suspect whoever was here is long gone by now.'

'Who was it?' Elspeth asked as soon as the three of them were alone. 'What did he want?'

'How the devil should I know?' Sir John said. He paused. 'Heavens! Where's Arabella?'

Elspeth put a hand to her mouth, clearly now as concerned about their daughter as Sir John was. They all rushed to her room, and there she was, still sleeping soundly in her bed.

'Thank goodness,' Sir John said in a whisper, although it seemed that little could wake Arabella from her deep slumber. 'We'd best leave her oblivious to this for now,' he added, turning back to the door.

As they made to leave, Arabella rolled on to her side and her movement drew Jane's eye. There was something on her pillow.

'Wait,' she said, going closer to get a better look.

It was a small piece of cloth, and on the cloth was embroidered the
same Sanskrit word she had seen tattooed on the intruder's forearm. She
picked it up and took it back out into the corridor.

'What is it, Jane?' Sir John asked.

'It's Sanskrit. The intruder carried the same mark. He must have
put it there.'

Elspeth sidled closer to get a better look. 'What does it say?'

Jane studied the markings. 'The Hindi word is *pativrataguna*. It
means virtue of loyalty or fidelity. In other words, a patriot. But to
what or whom?'

'And why put it on Arabella's pillow?' Sir John said. 'What can it
mean?'

'It's clearly a message,' Jane said. 'A warning perhaps?'

Elspeth put her hand to her mouth. 'A warning! You think Arabella
is in danger? But why? Who would wish to harm her?'

'I don't know,' Jane said. 'I'm just guessing. It was specifically placed
on Arabella's pillow, though. There has to be a reason, and the reason
must concern your daughter.'

'Let's not jump to any rash conclusions,' Sir John said. 'Arabella is
safe and sound. If the intruder wished to harm her just now, he would
have done so when he had the chance. Go back to your beds. We'll
discuss the matter further over breakfast.'

With that, Sir John made off in one direction while Elspeth hurried away in the other. As for Jane, she knew she could not go back to
sleep, any more than she thought Elspeth would be able to. She still
had the piece of cloth in her hand. She looked at it again, reading the
Sanskrit as she wondered what the message really meant. She felt sure
it was a warning of some kind. Someone clearly wanted something, and
it seemed to her that Arabella's life was in danger if they did not get it.

The only thing that came to mind was the ruby, which she had heard the Maharaja of Kishangarh tell Sir John belonged to him. But if the rumours were true, didn't the maharaja already have his ruby back? Why then send someone after it now? If the intruder was loyal to the Maharaja of Kishangarh, perhaps even loyal to the Blood of Rajputana itself, then it would appear that the maharaja was not behind the attack after all. In which case, who was?

Images from Jane's dream suddenly flashed through her mind, and she saw Captain Fraser's blackened face again. She shook her head. If he was behind the attack and the theft of the ruby, why should anyone threaten the resident's daughter in order to get it back? Did the maharaja believe that the resident himself was somehow complicit in the attack? The idea seemed preposterous. She had seen Sir John lock the ruby away in that strongbox. Why include it in the itinerary with the rest of the jewels Bharat Singh had been carrying when he was killed if he meant to steal it back again?

Another possibility occurred to Jane. If indeed it was the Maharaja of Kishangarh who sent the intruder she had seen, perhaps he intended to threaten Arabella because he thought Sir John would have enough leverage with whoever did now have the ruby to get it back for him. That notion brought Jane's thoughts around to Captain Fraser again. She sighed to herself, concluding that there were too many questions confusing her mind to make sense of anything just now.

She decided she would go and lie down on her bed until a more reasonable hour, even if she couldn't sleep. She started back towards her room, but as she did so she saw that Elspeth had left her letter opener on the side table. She picked it up and turned back, thinking to return it to her, knowing that Elspeth could not yet have settled back into her bed. She knocked once on her door and entered.

What she saw made her wish she had not.

Elspeth was kneeling on the floor at the foot of her bed with her back to the door. The rug was folded over and there was a length of floorboard sitting on top of it. As Jane stepped closer, Elspeth turned towards her with startled eyes, expressing panic and confusion. She made no attempt to move. She just knelt there, frozen and fearful. In her hands was the Blood of Rajputana.

Chapter Thirty-One

Present day

The morning after Chrissie MacIntyre's body had been found in the woods near Drummond Castle, Tayte was back at the desk in his room. He'd spent the time since breakfast thinking about Jane Hardwick's latest letter while continuing to plough through Dr Drummond's research, ever conscious of the fact that Ross wanted it back today and he still hadn't found anything useful. There weren't many records left to look at. He thought he only needed another half an hour or so, but as it was now almost time to accompany Sinclair to his brother's funeral, he knew they would have to wait.

He'd been thinking about the recent murders, too. He didn't know what was going on or why, any more than he felt DI Ross did, but as there was now no doubt whatsoever that the person behind these murders was the same person who wanted him to find the Blood of Rajputana, he did know it was all the more imperative to work out what had become of it. Sinclair had been right: the ruby had to be found and used to draw this killer out. The stakes suddenly felt higher to Tayte than ever.

That was if it could be found.

He'd read in Jane's letter that the ruby had been sent to Bombay for onward passage to England, but it hadn't made it out of Rajputana.

It had been stolen, the raid on the soldiers carrying it blamed on the Maharaja of Kishangarh. And yet, in Jane's latest letter he'd read that the ruby had somehow fallen into the hands of Lady Elspeth Christie. Tayte wished the letter he'd read on the iPad Ross had handed him the evening before had been complete so that he might have learned how Elspeth came to be sitting there with it in her hands, but he imagined it wouldn't be long before the rest of the letter turned up.

Having also read those Sanskrit symbols in Jane's letter—the same symbols that were on the note the killer had left for him, he'd been reminded of the figure in the hooded cloak who was caught on Ross's CCTV cameras the night one of Jane's letters was slipped under his door. Jane's latest letter had confirmed that Sinclair's Rajputs were real, loyal to the Maharaja of Kishangarh and perhaps now to the restoration of the Blood of Rajputana. That was what puzzled Tayte most. To his knowledge, none of the family had yet succeeded in locating the ruby, and yet people were being murdered, seemingly because of it. For the life of him, Tayte couldn't fathom why.

He checked his watch and noted that the funeral car would be there in less than ten minutes, so he put the record he was looking at on to a tall pile of those he'd already checked and stood up to make his way downstairs. As he did so, curiosity led him to peek at the next record in the box, and he immediately wished he hadn't. It bore the Christie name. He went to take it out, wondering why a record for any of the Christie family was among Drummond's research. He wanted to know if there were any more beneath it, but as he reached in to take the record out he was distracted by a knock at his door. Turning away from the desk, he saw that it was Murray.

'Mr Sinclair sent me up with these,' he said, holding out a long black trench coat and a black tie.

It would have been entirely inappropriate for Tayte to turn up at Jamie Sinclair's funeral dressed in a bright tan suit, but it was all he had, so Sinclair had told him he'd find something more suitable.

'Thanks, Murray,' Tayte said as he took the coat and tie. He tried the coat on, and after struggling with it for several seconds, he added, 'It's a bit of a squeeze, but I guess it'll have to do.'

'Aye,' Murray said, studying Tayte as if wondering how he'd managed to get it on at all. 'Well, we'd best be going down.'

Tayte flicked his shirt collar up and began fastening his tie, which he now wished he'd done before he'd put the coat on. He could barely raise his arms. 'After you,' he said, not wanting to hold things up.

As they left, Tayte was still ruminating over what he'd just seen inside Drummond's box of records. He understood now that they were not simply family history records—not all *his* family history records at least. They were records pertaining to his search for the ruby. He followed Murray downstairs to where Sinclair was waiting for them, and as he went he wondered just how deep Drummond's research ran. How had the doctor come to learn of the Christie name? Tayte had thought himself the first to make that association through Sinclair's four-times-great-grandfather, Sir Robert Christie, but here was proof that Drummond had also known. He recalled Sinclair telling him that he and Drummond had collaborated on their research for a time, and he wondered, as he had before now, whether Sinclair had really known the identity of his Christie ancestor all along.

The funeral service was a small affair, attended only by a handful of friends and family members, and a few locals who had come to pay their respects. As those who were gathered around Jamie Sinclair's grave started to move away and the gravediggers began tipping soil on to the coffin, the cool late-morning air filled with the haunting sound of a lone piper as he filled his bagpipes and proceeded to play 'Amazing Grace.' It charged the atmosphere with such emotion that even Tayte, who had not known Jamie, was touched by it. Sinclair, in his full, predominantly red-and-green Clan Sinclair highland dress, had carried the same stolid expression since the funeral car had arrived to collect them from Drumarthen.

'It was a beautiful service,' Sinclair said to Tayte as they walked the gravel path back through the churchyard beneath their umbrellas. 'It's a pity the weather's so dreich.'

Tayte nodded in agreement, thankful for the loan of Sinclair's old black trench coat, having improved the fit a little by leaving his suit jacket hanging in the hall. 'Those bagpipes really get to me,' he said, dabbing the corner of his eye with the back of his hand. 'It's a tradition back home that they're played at fire and police department funerals. It dates back to the potato famine, when Irish immigration in particular was at its peak.'

'I had no idea,' Sinclair said. 'You learn something new every day.'

They walked slowly and in silence for a while between myriad head-stones to either side of them, both men looking down at their shoes much of the time.

'Is Murray going to be okay?' Tayte asked. 'I was surprised when he said he wasn't coming out to the graveside.'

'Oh, he'll be fine in a wee while,' Sinclair said. 'As I'm sure I told you, Murray was something of a father figure to Jamie.'

'Yes, I remember.'

'Aye, well they were very close. I suppose he couldn't bring himself to watch poor Jamie's coffin being lowered into the ground, that's all it is. We must all deal with such things in our own way. I expect he'll be waiting for us at the car.'

'Is there going to be a wake?' Tayte asked.

'It's traditional, of course, but in light of everything else that's been going on, I decided not to. We'll raise a dram to Jamie when we get back to the house, mind. I hope you'll join us.'

'Of course,' Tayte said as they continued to amble along the path, in no hurry to leave.

Sinclair fell quiet again, and Tayte left him to his thoughts, his gaze returning absently to the headstones, more out of professional habit than interest as he passed beside them. Names and dates began to drift through his mind, and one of those names caught his attention. He stopped beside it, and Sinclair stopped with him.

'*Fiona Murray*,' Tayte read out. 'Any relation to your Murray?' he asked Sinclair, supposing there must be other people with the Murray name in the area.

Sinclair looked down at the headstone. 'Fiona was Murray's daughter,' he said with a sigh, as if recalling her. 'She was a beautiful wee girl—the light in her father's eyes. Murray doted on her, as any father might, not least because of how she came into the world.'

'How do you mean?'

'Poor Murray's wife, Heather, died during the birth. Murray brought Fiona up at Drumarthen by himself, accepting help from no one. He felt it was his duty alone because he blamed himself for his wife's death. His pain eased in time, of course. Fiona looked so much like her mother that I suppose he took comfort from seeing her again through his daughter, as it were. Then Fiona, too, was taken from him.'

'She died young,' Tayte said, noting that she had passed twenty years ago, aged twenty-six.

'Aye, that she was—another victim of alcohol and drugs. Fiona was Ewan Blair's partner at the time. He woke up one morning to find her lying in her own vomit. She'd been dead for hours.'

'Ewan Blair?'

'The very same. He won her over with his charm, and they lived together for a while. He soon had her hooked on cocaine, by all accounts. It turns out that his side of the family knew what was going on, but they kept it from Murray and me. They knew what Blair was getting the poor girl into, and they did nothing to prevent it.'

They moved on. Behind them, accompanying them at a distance back to the church, the piper continued to play. It was clear to Tayte now why Murray had flared up at Blair the last time he'd come to the house, and who could blame him? So this was the 'old business' DI Ross had referred to when he'd visited Drumarthen the morning Blair had been murdered, pointing his accusatory finger at Murray, who was clearly someone with an axe to grind when it came to the other side of the family. It was easy to see how Murray might have blamed not just Blair, but everyone else who knew the danger his daughter was in and yet did nothing about it.

'It's a tragic story,' Tayte said, still reflecting on what he'd heard.

'Aye,' Sinclair said, but left it at that.

As they arrived back at the church, Tayte was thinking about Jamie, considering what Sinclair had said about his and Murray's relationship. Murray had been more like a father to Jamie than Jamie's real father. Now, having already buried his wife and daughter, Jamie had been taken from him, too. It was no wonder he'd chosen not to attend the graveside as Jamie's body was laid to rest. Tayte could see Murray ahead of them now, waiting by the car as Sinclair had said he would be. He was with DI Ross, who had attended the church service.

Sinclair approached him. 'Would you care to come back to the house for a wee drink to my brother, inspector?'

'Aye, I would,' Ross said. 'It's kind of you to ask. Thank you.'

'Not at all,' Sinclair said. 'I'll just thank the reverend, and we'll be on our way.'

Back in the main hall at Drumarthen, Tayte was keen to get out of that tight coat. The persistent fine rain that had been in the air all morning had left him feeling cold and decidedly damp. He was also keen to get back to his room and Dr Drummond's records, but first things first. He'd promised Sinclair he'd join him for a drink to his late brother, and he thought a dram of whisky might help to warm him up. As everyone began to take their coats off, Murray seemed to read his thoughts.

'I'll go and light the fire in the drawing room,' he said.

Sinclair followed after him, keeping his jacket on. 'Thank you, Murray.'

Ross had his coat off ahead of Tayte, who was struggling all the more with it now that the material was wet. It was like wriggling out of a wetsuit, not that Tayte had ever had cause to wear one. Ross came over and gave him a hand.

'It's a wonder you got it on in the first place,' he said as he pulled at one of the sleeves. 'Here, let me hang it on the rack for you,' he added once Tayte was free.

'Much appreciated,' Tayte said, red-faced from the exertion.

Ross returned a moment later holding out Tayte's suit jacket. 'Will you be wanting this?'

'Definitely,' Tayte said. 'I hope Murray's fire doesn't take too long to get going.'

Ross offered Tayte's jacket up by the collar for him to put on, and then they both followed after Sinclair and Murray. They arrived in the drawing room to find Murray bent over the fire, which had already begun to spit and crackle into life. Sinclair was standing beside the drinks cabinet, pouring four glasses of whisky. He brought them to the fireside on a tray and everyone took a glass.

'My Jamie had a troubled soul,' Sinclair said, looking into the flames as they began to take hold. 'A caged bird, but caged no more.' He raised his glass, and then he recited a verse from the song the piper had played at Jamie's graveside. '*Yea, when this flesh and heart shall fail, and mortal life shall cease, I shall possess within the veil, a life of joy and peace.*' He raised his glass higher. 'To my Jamie,' he added. 'God rest his soul.'

'To Jamie,' Tayte said, raising his glass with everyone else, noticing now that Sinclair had a tear in his eye at last for his brother departed, and so did Murray.

Sinclair knocked his whisky back and turned sharply away, perhaps wishing to keep his emotions to himself. He paced back to the drinks cabinet, where he stood in silence for several seconds before returning with the bottle.

'Well, take a seat,' he said, addressing everyone in a more upbeat tone.

For the occasion, four wing-backed chairs had been set up around the fireplace instead of the usual two. Everyone sat down in a close group and Sinclair poured them each another drink. Tayte thought he'd better sip this one, reminding himself that he had more research to do. He settled back, and as he did so he felt something crumple inside his jacket pocket. He tried to recall what he'd put in there, but nothing came to mind, so he reached in and took it out. His jaw dropped.

'What's that you have there?' Sinclair asked.

Tayte set his drink down. 'I don't know, but I have a good idea.' He was holding a few sheets of old and very familiar paper. He unfolded them. There was no name and address, but he instantly recognised the handwriting, which flowed from the top of the first page. 'It's the rest of Jane Hardwick's letter.'

On hearing that, everyone sat up.

'Before you read it, Mr Tayte,' Ross said, 'I should like to tackle the question of what it's doing in your jacket pocket.'

'Someone obviously put it there,' Tayte said. 'It certainly wasn't me.'

'No, I'm sure it wasn't,' Sinclair said. 'But who did put it there?'

Tayte offered the letter to Ross. 'Do you want to have your forensics people look at it? Maybe there are prints.'

Ross shook his head. 'We haven't been able to lift anything useful from any of the others,' he said. 'I doubt this time will be any different. Right now I'm more concerned with how it got there. Can you retrace your steps for me?'

'Sure,' Tayte said. 'It wasn't there when I came down from my room with Murray. I had to take my jacket off to get that coat on. You took my jacket from me, Murray, and hung it up. Then we both went out to the car.'

Ross turned to Sinclair. 'I take it you were already outside?'

'Aye, I was, but I popped back in to fetch another umbrella for Mr Tayte. Then I locked up and we all left.'

'When we arrived back here,' Tayte said, addressing Ross, 'you retrieved my jacket and helped me into it.'

'Well, I certainly didn't put that letter in there, did I?' Ross said. 'But clearly, either someone sitting here did, or someone else has been at Drumarthen while we were at the funeral.'

'The cameras,' Murray said. 'Maybe they picked something up.'

'I'll make a call and have someone check,' Ross said. 'In the meantime, as I'm already here, I'd like to take a look around the place for myself, if you've no objection.'

'Of course,' Sinclair said. 'But Murray had better go with you.'

Ross got to his feet and put his glass down, clearly now in no mood to finish his second drink. 'Come along then, Murray. Let's see what we can find. I'll make that call as we go.'

When they left, Tayte found his thoughts were stuck on the idea that everyone there had had the opportunity to place that letter inside his jacket pocket. It was an unnerving thought, and he hoped that Ross or Murray would find another explanation.

Sinclair deliberately coughed, snapping Tayte from his thoughts. 'The letter?' he said. 'Do you want to read it out, or shall I?'

'Sorry,' Tayte offered. 'I was miles away there.' He unfolded the letter again. 'I'll read it, if that's okay.'

'By all means,' Sinclair said, settling back.

Then Tayte began to read, immediately catching up with Jane again as she confronted her friend over the considerable matter of how she came to be in possession of the ruby, the Blood of Rajputana.

Chapter Thirty-Two

Jaipur, April 1823

'Elspeth?'

Jane looked on in disbelief as her friend continued to stare up at her, the Blood of Rajputana glowing in her hands, reflecting the pale light of dawn at her bedroom window. Her mind was awash with so many troubling questions.

'Where did you get that?' she asked. 'How did you come by it?'

Elspeth did not speak. She began to shake her head slowly from side to side as she drew the huge ruby closer, as if protective of it.

'Elspeth? You must answer me.'

Instead of answering, Elspeth began to tremble and to cry silent tears that rolled from her cheeks and on to her nightgown.

Jane went to her. Her friend cowered back, at first kicking her legs out as though to warn Jane off. Then she relaxed.

'I'm your friend, Elspeth. Is there something you need to tell me?'

Elspeth nodded, her expression suddenly grave and sorrowful. She held up the ruby, and at last she spoke. 'After the intruder came, I wanted to make sure it was still safely where I put it.' She sounded distant, as though lost somewhere inside her thoughts. 'I knew what he'd come here for.'

Jane stepped closer again, and this time Elspeth did not draw away or kick out at her. 'Hide it away again for now,' she said, fearing that someone else might see it.

Elspeth gazed down at the dark hole where the floorboard had been removed. She nodded, and slowly began to lower the ruby, returning it to its hiding place. Once she had, she slid the floorboard back and draped the rug over it, protecting her secret.

Jane offered out her hand and Elspeth took it. 'Now sit on the bed with me,' she said. 'I promise not to judge you, but you must tell me everything.'

Jane had forgotten that she was still holding the paperknife she had come to return. She set it down on the trunk at the foot of the bed, and together they sat, Jane still holding Elspeth's trembling hand.

'I don't know where to begin,' Elspeth said. 'One thing led to another, and . . .' She trailed off, wiping the tears from her eyes.

Jane put an arm around her friend. 'Start at the beginning,' she said. 'I imagine that was the night the young Prince of Kishangarh, Naresh Bharat Singh, came to elope with Arabella.'

Elspeth shook her head. 'It was before then. When my husband told me that Arabella wanted to marry the prince, I immediately offered her servant, Pranil, money to keep a close eye on her. I was concerned she might plan to do something foolish, which of course she did. I told him to report everything he saw and heard to me.'

Jane was put in mind of the conversation she and Arabella had had that evening as she waited on her balcony for Bharat Singh's signal. So it was Pranil who had betrayed her confidence, after all.

Elspeth pulled her hand free from Jane's and began to make knots with her fingers. 'When Pranil told me of Arabella's plan to elope that night, I sent him out to intercept the prince. He was to dissuade him, that's all. To tell him that Arabella had sent him to say she no longer wished to elope with him.'

'Bharat Singh would not believe it?'

'No. The situation got out of hand. Perhaps Pranil took my meaning too literally when I said that he was to stop the prince from coming to the residency that evening. When he returned with blood on his hands, I couldn't get any sense out of him.'

Now Jane was reminded of having seen Pranil outside Arabella's room that evening before she went in to see her. There was sweat on his brow and a nervousness about him that she had previously put down to his fear of discovery should it be found out that he was helping Arabella to elope. He was afraid of being discovered all right, but it was for the murder, intentional or otherwise, of Naresh Bharat Singh.

'What did you do when Pranil returned—when you heard what had happened?'

'I was in such a terrible state, Jane, I really didn't know what to do. I decided to confess, so I went to John and told him everything. I expected to be thrown to the wolves along with Pranil, and it was quite odd, but once I'd confessed, I didn't care what happened to me. My life here with John, anywhere with John, has been so miserable. He could have executed me there and then and I would have offered no resistance. But he didn't throw me to the wolves. He was angry, of course—more upset than I'd ever seen him—but eventually he calmed down. He told me to go about my business as if nothing had happened. He said he would take care of it.'

'Take care of it?'

'Aye, and very soon we all learned how. My husband later told me he'd sent Pranil back out into the hills, to where he'd hidden the prince's body. He was to strip him of everything but the shirt on his back, then find his horse and put everything into the saddlebags. The horse had remained by its master, dutifully waiting for him to awake. Pranil was then to take the horse and tie it up near a small native settlement or encampment of his choosing and leave the body where it would be discovered. John said he would do the rest, and he knew exactly what to do.'

'Captain Fraser,' Jane said, beginning to see the bigger picture.

Elspeth nodded and wiped her eyes again. 'John had someone tip the captain off, telling him that these people Pranil had chosen were dacoits. John knew Fraser would do the rest, eager as he was to make an early impression in his new role to stamp out the dacoit problem in the area. Of course, Captain Fraser was as thorough as John knew he would be. Fraser found the prince's horse at the encampment, and then the saddlebags he'd been travelling with. And of course, he found the prince's ring, which sealed the fate of those poor, innocent people.'

Although she sensed it was coming, Jane put a hand to her mouth in shock disbelief. 'How could Sir John orchestrate such a terrible thing?'

'Aye, it was terrible. I wish now that I'd made my confession to the proper authorities. I had no idea my husband was capable of such things, although I have no doubt he did so, not to protect me, but his own reputation and standing as the Resident at Jaipur.'

'And what of Pranil? You told me he was dismissed as soon as Arabella told her father of her plans to elope and that Pranil was to help her. Was he really dismissed? Is he dead?'

'Pranil is not dead.'

'But how else could Sir John trust to his silence?'

'He and I had something over Pranil that ensured he would never speak of what had happened. He had, after all, murdered the Crown Prince of Kishangarh. Even now I'm sure he lives in fear of the maharaja finding out, and of what he would do to him if he ever did.'

'I see,' Jane said, going over in her mind everything she had heard, and now registering that, contrary to her suspicions, Captain Fraser was guilty of nothing more than an overzealous sense of duty when it came to the slaughter of those people whom he believed were dacoits. He had been no more than a pawn in Sir John's cover-up—Sir John, who was responsible for all those murders, and no doubt the murders of the two family members who had come forward afterwards, one having supposedly met with a fatal accident, the other having disappeared.

'And the ruby?' Jane said. 'Does Sir John know you have it?'

Elspeth began to fidget. She was silent again, and Jane could see that the question had made her all the more uncomfortable. A moment later, Elspeth stood up and went to the end of the bed. She reached down and picked up her paperknife.

'John knows nothing about it,' she said as she returned. 'That ruby is mine!'

The knife was suddenly in front of Jane's face, so close that she was forced to lean back. 'What are you doing, Elspeth? I'm trying to help you. Can't you see?'

'You can't have it!' Elspeth said. 'I need it to get away from here—to get as far away from him as possible.'

'From Sir John?'

'Yes, from John, and this wretched land. I need it for Arabella's sake as much as my own. This is no place for a young girl.'

Jane sat up again, defiantly close to the knife. Although it was a blunt-edged letter opener, she was all too aware that it had a sharp point, which Elspeth could thrust into her if she chose to. She put all question of how Elspeth came to be in possession of the Blood of Rajputana aside for now, focusing only on the knife and what was to happen next.

'And what exactly will you do now that you're discovered?' she said, her voice no longer soft and caring, but angry to think that Elspeth cared so little for their friendship that she could threaten her life so. 'Will you thrust your knife into my heart and add one more death to your conscience? We've been friends since we were nothing more than children. Can you do it? Is the gemstone worth that much to you?'

The paperknife was already shaking in Elspeth's hand as she continued to hold it out, now inches from Jane's chest. Her eyes were a flood of tears and confusion, and Jane knew her friend could not follow through with this insane idea that had suddenly possessed her. A moment later, Elspeth dropped the knife and it clattered to the floor. Then she fell on to the bed and began to sob heavily into the bedcovers.

Jane took a deep breath to calm her nerves. She began to stroke Elspeth's back. 'We'll sort this out, don't worry.' Slowly, Elspeth turned around and sat up as Jane drew her friend into her arms, adding, 'Everything will be all right.'

'I'm responsible for the deaths of more people than you know,' Elspeth said. 'How can I live with myself after what I've done?'

'What have you done?' Jane asked. Again, she had a good idea by now, but she wanted to hear it from Elspeth. 'Tell me how you came by the ruby.'

They separated, and Elspeth avoided eye contact with Jane as she began to explain.

'The other day when we were dressing the grand hall for Arabella's birthday party, and John brought that strongbox in and showed the ruby to us, I knew I had to have it. It represented a new life for Arabella and me. I have no money of my own, John has seen to that. I knew the ruby could change things, and I had an idea how to get it. I went out and found Pranil again. He was already begging in the streets, the poor, foolish man. I threatened him with the thing he feared most. I said I'd tell the Maharaja of Kishangarh that he'd murdered his brother if he didn't do exactly as I said. On top of that, I promised him he'd come out of it a wealthy man.'

'You told him about the strongbox,' Jane said. 'You told him what the soldiers who left the residency that day were carrying with them?'

Elspeth nodded. 'Aye, I told him. I was sure Pranil had not looked inside the prince's saddlebags the night he killed him, or we might never have seen him again. I told him of the treasures that were to be had, saying nothing of the ruby, of course. I simply told him he would have his share if he did as I said, and that he would have his life.'

Jane was scarcely able to comprehend what she was hearing. 'So you were responsible for the attack on those poor soldiers—for the deaths of half their number?'

'Have you seen my reticule, Jane?' Elspeth asked, avoiding the question. 'I always leave it by my bedside at night, but it's not there.'

'No, I've not seen it,' Jane said, imagining that Sir John had confiscated it to stop her from taking any more of her opium pills. 'Please answer the question.'

Elspeth paused before answering, once again making knots with her fingers. She nodded. 'I was responsible.'

'How?'

'Pranil. I didn't care how he went about it. I told him there was another box inside the strongbox, and that he must bring it to me. I told him I had to have it, and I steered him towards the kind of people who would happily attack those soldiers for what they carried.'

'The dacoits?'

'Aye, the dacoits. Pranil had only to speak in certain circles of what I'd told him. Such news travels fast among the natives. Very soon it reached the right ears and Pranil was picked up and made to tell what he knew, which he readily did, of course. He mentioned nothing of the smaller box I told him to bring to me. He was wise enough not to draw attention to it.'

'How did Pranil manage to get the box? Surely there's little honour among such thieves.'

'It was a risk on Pranil's part, with no guarantee of success, but to try was better than the alternative—a long and painful death at the hands of the Maharaja of Kishangarh. Pranil explained that after the attack the dacoits spent hours opening the strongbox, with axes and gunpowder. When they saw what was inside they immediately began to rejoice, welcoming Pranil into their fold. They lit campfires, danced and drank in celebration, overlooking the smaller box containing the ruby for the time being. It was during that time that Pranil slipped away with it and brought it to me. I opened it with my husband's key that night while everyone was sleeping. Then, as you now know, I hid the ruby beneath the floorboards here in my room.'

'Where is Pranil now?' Jane asked. 'What happened to him?'

'Pranil is somewhere between here and Calcutta for all I know. He took his share of gold from the dacoits before he fled their camp. I told him to use it to leave Rajputana and never return.'

'I see,' Jane said, wondering what best to do next. Elspeth was her good friend, after all, yet surely her actions could not be ignored.

'What will become of me, Jane?'

Jane honestly did not know. She feared what Sir John would do if he found all this out. Would he try to cover the matter up, as he had before? Jane thought he would. After all, this was no longer just a matter of his good name and reputation. Sir John was responsible for the slaughter of all those innocent people—Jainists, who meant harm to no one. How far would Sir John go to save his own skin should Elspeth be forced to explain everything that had happened to the proper authorities?

And where did that leave Jane?

She concluded that it left her in a very dangerous situation. She was just telling herself that if she told anyone it would be Mr Faraday so that he might report the matter in his newspaper, when a distant, yet very distinct, gunshot sounded, interrupting her thoughts and causing both her and Elspeth to jump in alarm.

Elspeth sprang to her feet. 'Jane!' she cried, her eyes wide with alarm. 'The intruders are back! The maharaja's men have returned!'

They went to the door together. As Jane opened it, a second shot was fired. She thought it came from the direction of the main gate, from the courtyard perhaps. Hurriedly, they left the room together, heading for the stairway.

'Heavens! What if they've come back for Arabella?' Elspeth said as they came to her room.

Jane couldn't see why they would. As Sir John had previously said, if the intruder she had seen earlier wished to harm or abduct Arabella on this occasion, he would have done so when he had the opportunity, before the alarm was raised. To her mind he had come merely to leave the note—the threat—and perhaps to look for the ruby while he was about it. Nevertheless, Elspeth seemed determined to satisfy herself that Arabella was still safe and sound in her bed. She ran to her bedroom door and threw it open. In that same instant Jane saw her raise a trembling hand to her mouth.

'No!' Elspeth cried.

Jane quickly caught up with her. 'What is it? What's wrong?'

Elspeth did not need to answer. Jane could plainly see that Arabella was no longer in her bed. 'Arabella!' she called, scouring the room, but Arabella was not there.

'They've taken her!' Elspeth said, just as a third gunshot sounded. 'Quickly Jane! Outside. The guards must have found the intruder and opened fire.'

They took the main stairs down into the grand hallway, running as fast as their legs and their cumbersome nightgowns would allow. When they reached the courtyard outside and the main gate came into view, they both fell to their knees in shock, their strength suddenly failing them as a look of abject horror washed over both their faces. There before them was Arabella, dressed in the gown Jane had last seen her wearing the night she was to elope with Naresh Bharat Singh. Her body was hanging a few feet from the ground, suspended from the arch that spanned the main gate, her neck tied with a length of the same cerise pink silk her mother had bought for her birthday celebrations. Arabella, Jane's charge, whom in many ways she had come to think of as her own daughter, was dead.

Sir John and a number of guards and servants were already at the scene. One of the guards had a pistol drawn, and Jane supposed it was he who had fired the shots they had heard, to raise the alarm. She was instantly reminded of the four lizards she had seen in the garden soon after her arrival in Jaipur—four lizards for an upcoming death.

'Arabella,' she whispered, tears filling her eyes.

Her head began to shake from side to side, unable to believe what her eyes were telling her, and yet she understood well enough. No intruder had done this. The Maharaja of Kishangarh's men had not murdered Arabella over the Blood of Rajputana. Arabella had taken her own life, unable to bear the burden of loss she had carried since learning of her young sowar-prince's death. And she had chosen the morning of her eighteenth birthday to end her life, to spite her parents for their part in denying her love.

At length, Jane stood up again. She turned to Elspeth, whose head was now buried between her knees as she rocked back and forth, clearly racked with pain and anguish at this most unexpected and terrible turn of events. She began to soothe her friend, her hand gently circling her back.

'Elspeth? Shall I help you back to your room?'

Elspeth continued to rock back and forth, sobbing into the ground. She gave no reply for several seconds. Then she lifted her grief-stricken face and said, 'It's all my fault, Jane. I did this.'

Jane helped her friend to her feet. She shook her head. 'You mustn't blame yourself,' she said. 'Who could have known what was in Arabella's mind?'

'Help me go to her, Jane. I don't think I can manage by myself.'

Jane put an arm around Elspeth, and together they walked slowly towards the main gate, where Sir John was now standing on a munitions crate with a dagger in his hand. As they progressed towards the scene, Jane watched Sir John reach up and begin to cut the material as two guards held Arabella's legs, ready to break her fall. Jane could feel Elspeth's body shaking as they arrived. A moment later Arabella's body fell, and Jane saw Elspeth's reticule dangling from her neck. Elspeth had said it was missing. Now it was clear that Arabella had taken it, and she had no doubt swallowed the opium pills inside it to help her to go through with her suicide.

Sir John leapt off the crate and dropped his dagger, the same jewelled dagger the Maharaja of Kishangarh had presented to him. 'Arabella,' he said as he went to his daughter, though he knew she could no longer hear him. He held her lifeless body in his arms. 'What have we done to you?'

'John?' Elspeth said, her voice faint and distant.

At hearing Elspeth, Sir John snapped his head around, his eyes red with sorrow and grief, his jaw clenched tightly as if trying to hold back his emotions, or his anger. 'This is your doing, woman!' he barked. 'Arabella was the only good thing between us.'

Elspeth had stopped crying. Jane now saw a sudden calm wash over her as her face lost all expression. She imagined she must be in shock at the sight of her daughter lying dead on the ground before her. Elspeth fell to her knees beside Arabella's body. She reached out to stroke her hair, but her hand was quickly slapped away.

'Do not touch my daughter! You no longer have the right!'

'I did it for her,' Elspeth said. 'For our darling daughter.'

'Be quiet, woman,' Sir John said, momentarily gazing up at Jane with questioning eyes that asked how much she knew.

'Perhaps we should have allowed them to marry,' Elspeth continued, her fragile voice now sounding all the more distant, as if thinking wishful thoughts aloud.

'Do not blame me for this,' Sir John said. 'I—'

'No, I don't blame you, John. It's my fault alone that our daughter is dead. I should never have brought her here in the first place.'

What happened next came so fast that Jane and all those present were powerless to prevent it. She watched in horror as her friend picked up the jewelled dagger that had been dropped just a few feet from her, and without a moment's hesitation, drew the blade sharply across her throat.

Chapter Thirty-Three

Present day

'It's tragic,' Tayte said to Sinclair, scarcely able to believe the events that had played out through Jane Hardwick's letters. He checked the pages in his hands, looking for more. He shook his head. 'That's it. That's all there is.'

'For now,' Sinclair said, alluding to the possibility that, although Jane's letters appeared to have reached a conclusion of sorts, there had to be more.

'Yes, for now,' Tayte agreed.

He couldn't believe for one minute that Jane had left the ruby where Elspeth had put it, under a floorboard in her room at the Jaipur Residency which, as he understood it, was now a high-class hotel. Cornelius Dredger had gone to Robert Christie, confident that his great-aunt's letters held a clue to the ruby's whereabouts—a clue strong enough to lead Robert Christie to murder, and to go to India himself in search of it. Tayte doubted any man would have gone to such lengths unless he was confident of success. Then there was the syndicate, created to fund a more recent trip to India, again citing Jane's letters as the key to discovering the ruby's whereabouts. Except that at the family gathering DI Ross had told the syndicate members that it had been nothing more than a con to solicit money from them. That still puzzled Tayte.

'As far as Jane's account goes,' he said, thinking aloud, 'she was the last person to see the Blood of Rajputana. With Lady Elspeth dead, Jane was the only person who knew where the ruby was.'

'The question is,' Sinclair said, topping up his whisky glass again, 'what did she do with it? I suppose it's possible she left it where it was, but—'

'I don't think so,' Tayte cut in. 'It was far too precious a thing. Even if Jane had no intention of keeping it for herself, surely she would have done something with it. If she'd left it where it was, in light of what had happened, she couldn't be sure of remaining at the residency and having access to it for much longer. As you said, Mr Sinclair, there must be more to come. There has to be some further clue to tell us what Jane did next.'

Apart from wondering what had become of the ruby now that it had changed from Elspeth's possession to Jane's, Tayte also began to think about Sir John Christie and his son, Robert. It was clear now to see how Robert came to be in Jaipur in 1825, when his and Aileen's son, Angus, was born. Tayte imagined that at hearing the terrible news that his mother and sister were dead, Robert had gone to India to support his father, who could easily have made the introduction to Aileen via Lachlan Fraser's brother, Donnan.

'It must have been a terrible time for the Resident at Jaipur,' Tayte said. 'On that same fateful day, he lost both his daughter and his wife.'

Sinclair gave a sombre nod. 'And if Jane chose to divulge what Elspeth had told her about Sir John Christie's part in the massacre of all those innocent people, I imagine things soon became far worse for him.'

Tayte nodded. 'Although any impact was relatively short-lived. We already know from *Burke's Peerage* that Sir John died just a few years later in 1826. Maybe these events took their toll on him. If what he'd done was made public, it seems likely that this is why your three-times-great-grandfather, Angus Fraser, wanted nothing to do with his paternal bloodline. In all likelihood it wasn't so much because of who his father was, but because of his grandfather, Sir John. It's easy to see that what happened back then could have blackened the Christie name beyond redemption.'

'Aye, it's no wonder Angus chose to distance himself. Who in their right mind would want to be associated with such a heinous act if they had a choice?'

'And because he was illegitimate,' Tayte said, 'Angus had that choice.'

'He chose well, if you ask me,' Sinclair said. 'Although where did that leave his father? I can't condone Robert Christie's actions when it comes to the murder of Cornelius Dredger, but I have sympathy for the man when it comes to his son. Robert loved him enough to leave him this house, and yet Angus evidently wanted nothing to do with him.'

Tayte couldn't bring himself to share Sinclair's sympathy for Robert Christie. He saw him largely as a greedy man, who had taken Dredger's letters at the cost of the man's life. As far as Tayte was concerned, Robert Christie had made his bed and had to lie in it, whatever Angus's reason for wanting nothing to do with him.

His thoughts turned to Jane Hardwick. 'I should like to know what became of Jane, too,' he said. 'Her life beyond these letters of hers might yield a clue or two as to what she may have done with the Blood of Rajputana.'

'Good thinking,' Sinclair said. 'Did you get around to finding out when Jane died?'

Tayte thought back to his first day at Drumarthen, to when he'd learned that Sinclair could find no death record for Jane in the British parish registers, suggesting the possibility, even the likelihood, that she had chosen to remain in India. 'No, I didn't,' he said. 'The details of Jane's death didn't seem so important at the time. Perhaps they aren't now, but I'll be sure to take a look.'

Sinclair held the whisky bottle up and shook it. 'You're out,' he said. 'Can I top you up?'

Tayte thought about it briefly, but as much as it would have been easy to sit there by the fire talking to Sinclair, he had work to do, and he was all the more keen now to get back to it. 'That's very kind of you,' he said, getting to his feet, 'but I need to finish looking through Dr Drummond's records. I'm sure Detective Ross would like to take them with him when he leaves, and I'd like to carry out the research we've just discussed.'

'Of course,' Sinclair said. 'It's probably for the best anyway. Afternoon drinking always gives me a headache.'

Tayte smiled and made for the door, noticing that Sinclair was pouring himself another glass of Scotch just the same. As he left him to it, he was already wondering what those Christie records he'd seen among Drummond's files pertained to.

Tayte pounced on Drummond's records as soon as he was back in his room. He reached in and pulled out the Christie record he'd glimpsed before the funeral and his eyes quickly devoured it. He was looking at a copy of Sir John Christie's record of death, issued in Christie's home county of Fife in Scotland in 1826. It told Tayte that Christie had returned home soon after those terrible events he'd read about in the latest of Jane's letters, and it told him a great deal more. His eyes hovered over the cause of death, where he saw that, like his daughter Arabella, Sir John had hanged himself.

Tayte could only assume that the grief of losing his wife and daughter in such a tragic manner had proved too much for John Christie to bear, but the document he found next added even greater weight to his theory. It also cleared up any question he had over whether Sir John had been brought to account for the cover-up he'd engineered to save his wife and the good name of his family, which had led to the massacre of so many innocent people.

Tayte was now looking at a copy of a newspaper cutting from *The Times*, and he was once more reminded of the reporter of Jane's acquaintance, Mr Albert Faraday. Tayte expected to see that Faraday had authored the report, but he was surprised to see that he had not. The report was dated May 1824, more than a year after the events Jane had written about, which was plenty of time for news to have reached London from Jaipur. It had been written by someone called Alfred Crumb.

'HUNDREDS SLAIN!' Tayte read. 'RESIDENT AT JAIPUR CONFESSES ALL.'

He read on, seeing the headline for the sensationalism it no doubt was, having already read that the number was closer to fifty. He noted that Sir John had suffered something of a mental breakdown following the tragic events of his daughter's eighteenth birthday, and that when recovered sufficiently to speak of what had happened, he had confessed to orchestrating the plot that led to the slaughter of those peace-loving native people. There was no mention of the Blood of Rajputana, which led Tayte to suppose Jane had not disclosed its whereabouts, leaving everyone to believe that it had been taken in the raid on the soldiers carrying it to Bombay.

'So what did you do with it, Jane?'

Tayte had to know. If the ruby could be found, then he had to find it so that it could be used to flush a killer out and help bring him to justice. He put the Christie records to one side and looked back inside the box. The remaining records were now no more than an inch thick, so he took them all out and began to flick through them, noting that most were for Drummond's Fraser ancestors dating further back, to the late 1700s, offering no value to his search.

As he began to put everything back into the box, it struck him that those two isolated records pertaining to Sir John Christie seemed out of place among Drummond's files. Christie was not a part of Drummond's family history, and there were no other Christie documents. If

Drummond had known about the connection, surely there would have been more. He would have gone on to find Robert Christie, who was a key piece of this puzzle. Had other Christie records been removed the day Drummond was murdered? Were these two records the only ones to have been left behind, either deliberately or by mistake?

Tayte had no way of knowing. He finished putting the records away and slid the lid into place, thinking that DI Ross could have them back now. If those Christie records had been left there for him to find, then he'd learned all he was meant to learn from them. He went to pick the box up to carry it downstairs, when a beep from his phone told him he had a text message.

Jean . . .

It struck him that he'd forgotten to call her that morning as he usually did. He didn't think she'd be too upset because he'd called her before he'd gone to bed the night before. She knew he was okay. He took out his phone and checked the display, and his shoulders slumped when he saw that the message wasn't from Jean. He didn't recognise the number. He opened the text and was initially confused.

'*One more to go,*' Tayte read out.

Then everything fell into place. The text had to be referring to Jane's letters. It had therefore been sent by whoever had been leaving them for him—the same person who had killed Chrissie MacIntyre and was no doubt responsible for all the other recent murders in Comrie. Or was the message referring to one more murder? Tayte couldn't be sure.

The last letter, or the last murder? Tayte thought, suddenly aware that he was breathing more rapidly. Perhaps it meant both, but what then?

He stood perfectly still by the desk for several seconds, wondering why this person had sent the message to him, and why now? What did this change in the killer's pattern mean? He made for the door, knowing only that he had to show the text message to DI Ross as quickly as possible.

Sinclair was still sitting by the fire, cradling his whisky tumbler, when Tayte entered the drawing room. The bottle on the table beside him looked about as full as it was when Tayte had left him.

'Has Detective Ross come back yet?' he asked, a little out of breath from having run most of the way there.

Sinclair sat up as soon as he saw Tayte. 'Murray called me just a few minutes ago. Apparently they've found something and are on their way back now. They should be here any minute. Whatever's the matter with you? You look as if you've seen one of Drumarthen's ghosts.'

Tayte held out his phone. 'I've had a text message.'

'Who from?'

'I think it's from whoever's behind all this.'

He handed his phone to Sinclair, who read the short message and immediately put his whisky glass down. He took his own phone out from his pocket. 'I'm sure I know that number,' he said, his brow knotting as he spoke.

'I took it to mean there's going to be one more letter,' Tayte said, 'but it could also be referring to another murder. Callum Macrae is still unaccounted for.'

'Aye, he is that,' Sinclair said, the two phones now side by side in his hands, 'but as it appears that Callum Macrae sent you this message, I'd say he means for you to expect one more letter. You see, unless he plans to come after us, he's run out of syndicate members to kill.'

'Macrae sent the message?'

Sinclair held the two phones up so that Tayte could see the displays. 'See for yourself. I have Callum's number in my address book. Maybe Ross was right about Callum all along.'

Tayte checked the phones. The numbers were identical. It puzzled him to think that Macrae had used his own phone to send the message, knowing it would easily identify him. He wondered whether that was all somehow part of the plan, but before he could explore the idea further, his thoughts were distracted by voices out in the main hall. A few seconds later, Murray and DI Ross entered the room.

Sinclair got to his feet. 'I'm glad you're here, inspector. Mr Tayte has just received a text message from the man you're after.'

'Have you now?' Ross said, addressing Tayte with raised eyebrows. His expression darkened. 'What does it say?'

Tayte read out the message. *'One more to go,'* he said. 'That's all there is.'

Ross held out his hand. 'Can I see it?'

'Sure.'

Tayte handed his phone over and Ross studied it briefly. Then he took out his notepad and pencil and wrote the details down.

'I'm a little perplexed by this,' Tayte said. 'Why would Macrae send the message from his own phone? He didn't even withhold the number.'

'I don't know just now, Mr Tayte. It's odd, that's for sure. Maybe he wants us to know it's him for some reason, or maybe he didn't send the message. Perhaps whoever's doing this was simply using his phone. If it's still powered on, we should be able to find it. In which case we'll know soon enough.'

Murray spoke then. 'We know how he's getting in.'

'Aye, you said you'd found something,' Sinclair said. 'What is it?'

'It's best you come and see for yourself.'

Ross went to the door. 'I'll leave you to it, Murray. I need to go and find this phone.'

Tayte followed after him. 'I've finished with Dr Drummond's files if you want to take them with you.'

'Were they of any use? Did they tell you where the Blood of Rajputana is?'

Tayte snorted a laugh. 'No, they didn't tell me that. They're in my room. I can—'

'I'll collect them later,' Ross cut in. 'When I've more time.'

'Of course,' Tayte said, and with that, Ross left.

When Tayte turned back into the room, Sinclair was standing right behind him. 'Would you care to come with us to see what Murray's found? We'll have some lunch afterwards. You must be famished.'

'Sure,' Tayte said. To Murray, he added, 'Please, lead the way.'

It took no more than a few minutes to get where they were going, having followed Murray along a number of corridors on the ground floor, turning this way and that as they went. They were in the treacherous east wing, where everyone had to watch their step whenever they left the flagstones and the flooring changed to rotting floorboards. Murray seemed to know where it was safe to tread, so Tayte kept in his shadow until they arrived at a large oak door towards the back of the house, which looked as if it had been there since the place was built. Murray lifted the catch and opened it. He flicked on a light switch, illuminating a narrow stone stairwell that spiralled away below them.

'This leads to the old wine cellar,' Murray said for Tayte's benefit as he made his way down.

'And more besides,' Sinclair said, raising his eyebrows at Tayte as he invited him to go next.

Tayte grabbed hold of the thick rope that ran around the walls as he went. The air became cooler the further he descended.

'We've not used this room for a very long time,' Sinclair said from above him. 'Not for wine, that is, and thankfully not for its other purpose.'

'Other purpose?'

'You'll soon see.'

Tayte emerged at the bottom of the steps into a low, dimly lit room about fifteen feet square. There was no longer any evidence of wine storage, no racks against the walls, which were bare apart from a few sections of oak panelling. What little of the original wainscoting remained looked as if it would crumble away at the slightest touch. Tayte's eyes found Murray, who was standing in front of another oak door, this one quite narrow and very plain.

'Here we are,' Murray said, and Sinclair stepped beside him.

'I thought you checked this area,' Sinclair said.

'Aye, I did. The door was locked then, and it's locked now.'

'Then why do you suppose this is how our visitor's been getting in?'

Murray knelt down and ran his hand over the flagstones. When he held it up Tayte could see that it was damp and there was something clinging to it.

'Pine needles,' Murray said. 'They weren't here when I looked before, when it was dry. They'll cling to anything when they're wet, and with all the rain we've had . . .'

'I see,' Sinclair said. 'So someone must have brought them in on their shoes.'

'Aye. There are more leading to the steps.'

'Is the lock damaged?' Sinclair asked, turning the handle. He gave the door a tug to see if it would open.

'No, it's sound enough. Whoever's been here must have had a key.'

Tayte noticed that there were no bolts on this door, although there clearly had been at some time in the past; large, heavy bolts, if the paler outlines at the top and bottom of the door were anything to go by.

'Where does it lead?' he asked, his fascination with the door having grown while he'd been listening.

Sinclair turned back to him. 'Outside,' he said. 'Behind this door there's a tunnel that comes out in the woods.'

'An escape route?'

Sinclair nodded. 'It's an elaborate priest hole of sorts. Many old houses had them, especially those built during a time when its occupants might have had need of an alternative, secret way in and out—like when they were under attack from their neighbours or were facing religious persecution.' He waved a hand around the room. 'When the wainscoting was intact, there was a secret panel hiding this door. The same was once true in the room above us, where we've just come from. Anyone who happened to find that secret door would arrive down here to find nothing more than another room that led nowhere. They'd soon be on their way again, continuing their search elsewhere, which was the point, of course.'

'So who has the key?' Tayte asked.

'There are two. Both are kept in a drawer with several other old keys for locks that are no longer in use.'

'Aye,' Murray said. 'And that's just the thing. I went to fetch them before we came back to the drawing room to tell you about it.' He reached into his trouser pocket and withdrew an old iron ring. He held it up, dangling a single key before them. 'One of the pair is missing.'

'There's no question then,' Sinclair said. 'This is how our intruder's been accessing the house so freely, but however did he get hold of the other key?'

Tayte thought about that, and he recalled the night of the family gathering again. Apart from Sinclair and Murray, who had no need to come and go at Drumarthen in secret, only Ewan Blair and Callum Macrae were gone from the dining room long enough to have taken the key, and Blair was dead. Then he remembered that the first of Jane's letters to be found at Drumarthen, other than the letter that was already in Sinclair's possession, had turned up before the family gathering, suggesting that the key had perhaps been taken earlier. But if it had been taken by Callum Macrae, how would he have known where to find it?

Tayte voiced his next thought. 'Who else in the family knew about this secret tunnel? Would Callum Macrae have known about it?'

Sinclair seemed to think on his answer. A moment later he said, 'I should think just about everyone had heard about it, or would at least expect there to be one. They were quite common in such houses.' He paused, and then began to shake his head. 'As to the specifics, however, I don't know how Callum could have known where the key or the tunnel was. Unless someone told him, of course.'

Tayte chose not to voice the next thought that popped into his head. If Macrae was behind this, then given what Sinclair had just told him, it seemed likely that he wasn't working alone. His eyes flicked from Sinclair to Murray and back again, holding on to that thought for a moment. Then he said, 'Shall we open the door and take a look?'

'Of course,' Sinclair said, gesturing to Murray, who set the key in the lock, gave it a turn, and pulled the door open.

The air that greeted them carried a damp odour that was laced with the smell of iron and undergrowth from the wooded area Sinclair had said was at the other end of the tunnel. Tayte couldn't see more than a few feet inside, so he followed Sinclair's lead and they both shone their phone's torches into the darkness, illuminating a low and narrow tunnel that seemed to rise gradually before them.

'It looks tight in there,' Tayte said.

'It only had to accommodate one person at a time,' Sinclair said, 'and people were typically smaller when this was built. Shall I lead the way?'

Tayte followed Sinclair and Murray into the tunnel, stooping so low that he felt as if he were bent double at times. Apart from the cobwebs and the occasional spider, there wasn't much to see beyond Murray's back and the stone floor and walls, which were stained with rusty brown streaks where the rainwater had soaked through over time. He could hear dripping sounds and he imagined he might see a rat or two at any minute.

They kept going, shuffling along at a steady pace until Sinclair called out from the front.

'I can see the opening.'

Tayte had been aware that they were rising all the time, gradually climbing to ground level. The air became fresher, and he could soon hear the wind and the rain in the trees outside. It was suddenly brighter, and then he came to a few steps that ran up to a horizontal iron gate. He heard it being pushed open with a low rusty squeal, and he was soon following Murray up and out into the daylight and the shelter of the woods. He could make out the house through the gaps in the trees and hear the nearby course of the burn that was swollen from all the rain.

Sinclair was holding something out. 'Look at this,' he said. 'It's been cut through.' It was a length of old chain, which had clearly been used to secure the gate. 'It's more evidence, as if any were needed, that someone's been using this old tunnel to gain access to the house.'

'Callum Macrae's as guilty as sin, if you ask me,' Murray said. 'I wouldn't be surprised to learn he's been stealing things from the house, too.'

'Aye,' Sinclair said. 'He told me my brother's debt to him was now my debt.' He handed the length of chain to Murray. 'Make all this secure. Then come and join us for some lunch.'

As Tayte followed Sinclair back down into the tunnel, he wondered about Callum Macrae. He still thought it odd that he would use his own phone to send that text message. It was a foolish mistake to make, and Tayte didn't think that whoever was behind this would do such a thing unless he intended to. That person, Macrae or otherwise, had a plan, and that worried Tayte.

Chapter Thirty-Four

They had buttered bread rolls and a dish called Cullen skink for lunch, a thick soup of smoked haddock, potatoes and onions. It was a favourite of Jamie's, according to Sinclair, so on the day of his funeral Murray had prepared it in his honour. All Sinclair had to do was warm it up and butter the rolls. As they ate, Tayte brought Sinclair up to date with his research, letting him know how things had turned out for Sir John Christie, courtesy of the records he'd found among Gordon Drummond's files. As keen as he was to continue trying to establish what Jane had done with the Blood of Rajputana, he was never at his best on an empty stomach, and he sensed that Sinclair wanted his and Murray's company on this day of all days.

Murray was sitting opposite Tayte at the dining table, still eating. He'd joined him and Sinclair part way through their meal, having secured the door in the old wine cellar with planks of wood that he'd nailed to the frame, making sure no one could use it. He was about to put another spoonful of soup into his mouth when the house phone rang in the hall. He started to get up, but Sinclair stopped him.

'Finish your lunch, Murray,' he said. 'I'll get it.'

When Sinclair returned with the phone, he sat down again and told the caller, 'Hold on a moment, I'm just putting you on speaker. I think this is something we all need to hear.' To Tayte and Murray, he added,

'It's Inspector Ross.' He pressed a button and set the phone down on the table. 'Alastair, could you repeat what you've just told me.'

'I said Callum Macrae is dead,' Ross said. 'We managed to triangulate the signal from his phone. It led us to his garage where we found his body, which, I might add, he clearly wanted us to find.'

'How did he die?' Sinclair asked.

'He appears to have killed himself with what I suspect is the same shotgun he used on Ewan Blair. Perhaps you can tell me if it's the one that's missing from Drumarthen. It's engraved with the same maker's name—MacNaughton, Edinburgh—and there's a small chip above the trigger on the right-hand side of the stock.'

Murray gave Sinclair a nod. 'Aye, that sounds just like the one we're missing.'

'Are you sure he killed himself?' Tayte asked.

'I'm not entirely sure of anything just now,' Ross said, 'but he left a note. It was beneath his mobile phone on the desk he was sitting at when he pulled the trigger. The shotgun was on the floor between his legs.'

'Can you tell us what the note said?' Sinclair asked.

'As his mother's already dead, I don't see why not. It said they were all guilty—that they had it coming to them.'

'That's it?' Tayte said. 'Nothing else? No reason why he decided to kill himself? I thought he wanted the ruby—the Blood of Rajputana.'

'That's all it says, Mr Tayte. Maybe he wanted us to think it was about the ruby to confuse what he was really up to. I don't know. There could be more to it. We found another of Jane Hardwick's letters on his desk, just as that text message you received said there would be.'

'The last letter,' Tayte said. 'Can I see it?'

'Not the original,' Ross said. 'I've taken a photo, though, as I did before. I'd have brought it over, but forensics have found something I need to look at. I'll text the photo through to you shortly. Maybe it'll help you find that ruby.'

'What's the point?' Tayte asked. 'I mean, if Macrae was behind this, surely it's over.'

'Just keep going for now, Mr Tayte. Maybe there's more to it. Now, I have to be going.'

'Did Callum kill my Jamie?' Sinclair asked before Ross was able to end the call. 'Can you tell me that?'

'I really don't know, Damian. I'm sorry.'

With that, the call ended and Tayte sat back with a sigh, unsure what to make of this recent turn of events. As he saw it, there were too many possibilities to contemplate. Had this been Macrae's plan all along, a simple matter of revenge for reasons yet to be established? Or had Macrae been working with someone else, who had now staged his murder to make it look like suicide? For that matter, his apparent suicide could just as well have been staged by whoever was really behind all this, simply to draw attention and make it look as if it were all over. But what of the Blood of Rajputana? Was it really all just a decoy?

Tayte didn't think so. That the killer felt he had a strong motive to want his victims dead, Tayte didn't doubt, but he also believed that where there was the promise of such great wealth as the Blood of Rajputana offered, there was also the propensity for greed. There was no question in Tayte's mind that someone still wanted that ruby.

His phone beeped. He took it out and checked the display. 'It's the text from Detective Ross,' he said as he opened it. 'It's the last of Jane Hardwick's letters.' He studied the image, expanding it so that he could see it more clearly. 'It's dated August 1823,' he said. 'Four months after the previous letter.' He cleared his throat, and then he read the letter out.

My dearest brother,
I must apologise for not having written to you sooner following the terrible events of April, and for the brev-ity of this letter now that at last I have, but I have fallen on difficult times. Following the death of my

good friend, the Lady Elspeth, and of our daughter, Arabella—for that is how I came to know and love her—I have been forced to seek alternative accommodations, altho' I was permitted to remain at the residency long enough to attend their coffins and do what had to be done. My change of fortune as a result of leaving the residency has taxed me greatly, having necessitated the need to find work so that I might earn my living expenses. I am well, however, and have now taken a position with a respected Jaipur family, providing translation services, for which I am most humbly grateful.

Of Sir John Christie, I have little news, having seen him but once since I left the residency. It was at the funeral service, and I must report that his demeanour was understandably as wretched as my own, as first Elspeth's and then Arabella's coffins were laid together in a quiet corner of the British cemetery here in Jaipur, where I am informed a fitting tomb is to be erected. I have also heard that Sir John was removed from office soon afterwards. What will become of him I do not know, and for himself I suspect he no longer cares.

I find myself racked with guilt over everything that has happened. Could I have said or done anything which might have altered this most tragic course of events? I can only imagine how these thoughts must continually torture Sir John, and I hope in God that he soon finds his peace. How different things might have turned out had Arabella not been denied the love of her young sowar-prince. How all this could have been prevented if Naresh Bharat Singh had been allowed to continue his journey the night he came to elope with Arabella. But their hearts are together again now. That much I have seen to.

Dearest brother, I regret to say that I shall not see you again. I have decided to remain in India, as there is much need of education here, and in truth I have never felt a greater sense of belonging anywhere on this earth. Time will judge my decision, but for now I am sure of it. To-morrow I am to take my first English language student, and it is my hope that this vocation will flourish in me and continue to do so for many years to come. All that remains is for me to wish you a good night, and ask that you do not worry over me. I shall write again soon.

Your loving sister,

Jane Hardwick

Tayte lowered his phone. '*Do what had to be done,*' he said, slowly repeating Jane's words. 'What do you make of that?'

'Last respects?' Murray offered. 'Maybe she just means she had to look at their faces one last time before their coffins were sealed.'

'Perhaps,' Sinclair said, 'but what of that last part? I think it must be significant.'

'So do I,' Tayte said, aware that he was expecting to find some clue from this letter, the last letter, as to what Jane did with the ruby. 'Their hearts are together again,' he added. 'She can't mean in the spiritual sense because she goes on to say that she's seen to it herself. That sounds more physical to me, but how could she possibly accomplish that? Naresh Bharat Singh wouldn't have been interred with Arabella. His body would have been taken to his brother in Kishangarh. I don't think the line can be taken literally.'

'So she's speaking metaphorically,' Sinclair said.

'Yes, and if this is about the ruby, as it almost certainly is, then we can suppose it's the ruby that Jane's really referring to here.' A moment later Tayte threw his head back and smiled as the obvious answer suddenly struck him. 'We know from her letter that Jane didn't sell the Blood of Rajputana because she says she had to go out and earn a living after she left the residency. So she has the ruby, which she takes to represent Bharat Singh's heart. He was bringing it to Arabella the night he was murdered. It was meant for her. When it fell into Jane's hands she made sure no one else would have it—no one but Arabella, as her young sowar-prince had intended.'

'Of course,' Sinclair said. 'By doing what had to be done in Jane's eyes, by placing the ruby as the representation of Bharat Singh's heart inside Arabella's coffin, she was seeing to it that in a manner of speaking their hearts were brought together again.'

'Precisely,' Tayte said. 'The Blood of Rajputana was entombed with Arabella. It makes perfect sense when you think about it. That has to be what Cornelius Dredger drew from these letters, and what Sir Robert Christie clearly came to believe, enough for him to have killed Dredger before travelling to India in search of it.'

Tayte was now all the more keen to continue his research. He stood up. 'If you'll excuse me,' he said. 'I'm going up to my room to explore this further.'

Sinclair rose with him. 'Perhaps we could explore it together. Why don't you bring your laptop down here?'

'I'll do that,' Tayte said, glad to know that Sinclair remained keen to continue in light of what DI Ross had just told them. Whether this was over or not, he wanted to see it through. It was the only way to be sure.

When Tayte returned to the dining room with his laptop, Sinclair was waiting for him, having set two chairs closely side by side for them to work at. Murray was no longer there.

'Didn't Murray want to join us?' Tayte asked.

Sinclair pulled his cardigan sleeves up over his forearms, as if keen to get stuck into the research. 'He's giving the dishes a quick wash. He said he had some clearing up to do after securing that door in the old wine cellar, too. There's always something for him to do around here, I doubt we'll see him again before suppertime.' He paused and eyed Tayte with enthusiasm. 'Now, where do we start?'

Tayte sat down and fired up his laptop, wondering just that. 'First of all, I think we need to determine whether Sir Robert Christie's travels in India in 1870 were a success.'

'By which you mean, did he manage to find the Blood of Rajputana?'

'Exactly. It's something I've wondered before, of course, but until I read the last of Jane's letters, I didn't really know where to begin trying to answer that question. Now, on the other hand, we know everything from Jane's letters that Christie knew. If the ruby really was entombed with Arabella Christie in 1823, as we're supposing from her letters, then that has to be the best place to start.'

'Aye,' Sinclair agreed. 'Jane's letters would have led him to the British cemetery in Jaipur. But how do you propose to discover whether Robert was there?'

'I don't think we have to prove whether Robert was there or not,' Tayte said as he began tapping the keys on his laptop. 'It's the ruby we're interested in, or rather where the ruby was.'

'Inside Arabella's tomb.'

'Precisely. The way I see it, that's all we need to focus on. If Robert's trip was a success, he'd have had to partake in a little grave-robbing. That kind of thing doesn't usually go unnoticed, especially when it concerns the graves of prominent families such as the Christies.'

Tayte accessed a website he'd used to good effect before when looking into Robert Christie—the Families In British India Society, known as FIBIS. He navigated to the section inviting him to 'Browse Records' and clicked on the FIBIS database folder entitled 'Cemeteries, monuments and memorial inscriptions.'

'That has to be as good a place as any to start,' he said.

When he clicked on the folder he was presented with a list of possible locations to search. He scrolled down, and was pleased to see there was a folder for Jaipur. He opened it. There were two items: 'All Saints, Jaipur' and 'Jaipur Graves.' The first was clearly a church, the second perhaps a general list of graves in the area.

Sinclair was closely following the information with Tayte. 'It's a pity Jane Hardwick's letter didn't mention the name of the church she attended for Arabella and Elspeth's funeral.'

'There are only two options,' he said. 'It shouldn't take long to check them out.'

He clicked on the first, which presented him with sixty-four results. The year he was interested in was 1823, so to save time he quickly scanned the rightmost column, which bore the heading 'Date of Death.'

'That's no good,' he said a moment later. 'The oldest records here are from the 1870s.'

'Maybe All Saints Church hadn't long been built by then,' Sinclair offered.

Tayte nodded. Then he tried the file for 'Jaipur Graves,' hoping for better luck. He frowned when he saw that there were only twenty-one records, the oldest being from 1863, which was forty years too late to be of any interest.

'Now what?' Sinclair asked.

'Now we try another angle. It's possible that the year we're interested in is just too far back for this area. It would have been good to find a burial entry for Arabella Christie, which would have given us the name of the graveyard we're interested in, thus helping to narrow down our further searches, but it may not matter.'

Tayte went back to the 'Browse Records' section, and this time he opened the 'Publications' folder. Inside that was another folder with the heading 'Newspapers and periodicals.'

'I think it's safe to assume that Robert Christie wasn't caught in the act,' he said, 'or I doubt he'd have made it safely back home again, which we know he did.'

'He's entombed in my basement,' Sinclair said.

'Exactly, so there's no use searching for Robert Christie by name. What we're looking for is an event from the time he was there. He arrived in Bombay in April 1870. Allowing several months for his onward journey overland to Jaipur, he'd have arrived late in 1870, or perhaps even early in 1871. It's possible that one of the news publications of the time reported an incident.'

There were twenty-six newspapers and periodicals listed. Tayte scanned them, looking for anything that might be related to Jaipur or Rajputana. He saw publications for Bombay, Calcutta and Madras, but nothing specifically for Jaipur. There were publications which covered India in general, such as *The Times of India* and *Allen's Indian Mail*, but when he looked at those he quickly came to realise that he was looking in the wrong place for the type of information he was after.

'These entries are all for births, marriages and deaths,' he told Sinclair. 'I don't think the FIBIS organisation is going to be able to help us this time.' He opened another Internet browser. 'I'm sure I've seen an online archive for *Allen's Indian Mail*, though. It's worth taking a look.'

He ran another search, entering the name of the publication along with the first of the two years he was now interested in: 1870. The top result showed free access via Google Books to content that had been provided by the Bavarian State Library. He clicked it, and within seconds he was looking at the title page of the first publication that year, which was on Wednesday, 5 January 1870.

'Search in this book,' Sinclair said, pointing to the option on the left side of the screen.

Tayte had seen it. 'I'll just try searching for the Christie name to begin with,' he said. 'There shouldn't be too many entries, and I don't want to risk missing anything.'

There was a match found on nineteen of the publication's pages. Tayte read out the first. *'This is the second tiger Colonel Christie has brought to bag in seven days.'*

'I think we can discount that one,' Sinclair said.

The next was also about Colonel Christie and his tiger-hunting, so Tayte read on, discarding each and every match he came to until the list had been exhausted.

'On to 1871,' he said as he opened the subsequent publication from Google Books.

This time there were sixteen matches with the Christie name, and Tayte was disappointed to see yet more news in the first two of Colonel Christie's hunting exploits. Next was a match in the Madras civil section, then one for a Captain H. T. Christie in the 'Military Furloughs' section. There was a match under 'Passengers Departed' and two more for the aforementioned captain. Tayte was beginning to think he would exhaust all these matches, too, when he saw an entry that caused him to catch his breath. It was under the heading 'Jaipur' in the miscellaneous column of the publication dated Tuesday, 14 March 1871.

'This has to be it,' he said, narrowing his eyes on the report as he read the highlights out to Sinclair. *'Heartless vandalism,'* he said. *'Christie tomb desecrated.'*

Sinclair was reading it with him. 'It doesn't say much, does it?'

'No,' Tayte agreed. 'But I think it says enough.'

The report was no more than a few lines describing the incident, blaming it on continued unrest among the natives following the Indian Mutiny of 1857, which had later become known as the Indian

Rebellion. Perhaps it didn't say much, but it was everything Tayte hoped to find.

'Civil unrest be damned,' Sinclair said, voicing Tayte's thoughts. 'That was surely Sir Robert Christie's work.'

'The timing fits,' Tayte said. 'What are the odds of the Christie tomb surviving close to fifty years, only to be desecrated around the same time our man happens to be in the area?'

'I should say they were very slim.'

'And why doesn't the report mention any other damaged graves? We know from Jane's letter that the Christie tomb was in a British cemetery. If this was due to civil unrest, why was this the only tomb that had been desecrated?'

'As you say, Mr Tayte, the report says enough. It tells us all we need to know. My four-times-great-grandfather, Sir Robert Christie, went to India and literally dug up the Blood of Rajputana from his own sister's grave.'

Tayte closed his laptop and sat back in his chair. 'The question now is what did he do with it?'

'Aye,' Sinclair said, thoughtfully rubbing his chin. 'I suppose he could have sold it, although if he had, surely something so large and so precious would have shown up by now. Unless it was cut up, of course.'

'I'm not so sure he'd have sold it,' Tayte said. 'We know from Robert's tomb that he died in 1873, two years after the desecration. It might have taken him almost that long to travel home again. By then he would have had very little time to do anything at all with the ruby. It seems likely that he knew he was sick, dying even, in which case what benefit would there be in selling it? He was already a wealthy man. He didn't need the money.' A shiver ran down Tayte's spine then, as an obvious answer hit him. 'What if he left it to his illegitimate son, Angus Fraser?'

The idea seemed to render Sinclair speechless.

'It makes perfect sense,' Tayte said. 'Robert left this house to Angus. He clearly wanted to do good by him. Robert was a dying man with no other family to leave anything to, so Angus got the house, and perhaps a whole lot more besides.'

'So maybe Angus sold it,' Sinclair said. 'He'd have needed money to keep this place going.'

'Didn't you say that Angus was left a tidy sum by his stepfather?'

'Aye, that's right. So he didn't need the money, either.'

'And as you've said, such a ruby coming on to the market would have drawn interest. I'm sure the Blood of Rajputana would be more widely heard of by now if it had been sold.'

Another thought crossed Tayte's mind, and he voiced it. 'There was no mention of such a ruby in Sir Robert Christie's will—only the house and its contents. What if Angus was supposed to find it at Drumarthen, but for some reason he didn't?'

Sinclair drew a deep breath and thoughtfully let it go again. 'Then it's still here?' he said, and they both stared at one another as the single most obvious place for it to have remained hidden and untouched all these years hit them.

'Sir Robert Christie's tomb,' they said together, as both men stood up, eager to go and take a look.

Chapter Thirty-Five

Tayte had seen the inside of a great many crypts during the course of his work, but few unsettled him as much as the long-forgotten crypt beneath Drumarthen. Perhaps it was because the place had been sealed off and had gone untended for so many years, or perhaps it was the presence of that solitary sarcophagus in the centre of the chamber and the way the dust seemed to drape over it like a ghostly veil. Either way, he was keen to get on with what had to be done and get out of there again.

They each had a crowbar in one hand and a torch in the other as they approached along the low tunnel that led to the chamber. Murray wasn't with them. Sinclair had tried to contact him, both by shouting for him and then calling his mobile phone, which he usually only carried with him when he was out on the estate, in case Sinclair needed to speak with him. They had even gone back to the old wine cellar to look for him, but he wasn't there, so Sinclair had fetched the crowbars from the tool shed himself.

'Should we be concerned about Murray?' Tayte asked, still wondering where he was.

'I'm sure he's just fine,' Sinclair said. 'He's probably outside somewhere and he's forgotten to take his phone with him. That's all it is.'

They came to the stone steps at the entrance to the chamber, and as he and Sinclair descended towards the sarcophagus, Tayte shone his torchlight over it. Maybe it was the dry, dusty environment that made his throat feel so parched, but he thought it was more likely on account of the discovery he hoped they were about to make. They stopped beside the sarcophagus and Tayte set his torch down, shining the beam up at the ceiling to spread the light out. Then he ran the palm of his hand over the top edge of the stonework to clear the dust away, trying to see where the lid joined the main body.

'Here's our way in,' he told Sinclair as he raised his crowbar and set it into place.

Sinclair copied him at the other end, working the flat tip of his crowbar into the seam that ran around the sarcophagus. 'Ready when you are.'

'Okay then, on three,' Tayte said, bracing himself. 'One, two, three!'

Both men leaned on their crowbars together, pushing at the same time, trying to raise the stone lid and slide it back. It moved, but not by much. Now, however, there was more of a gap to work their crowbars into.

'Again,' Tayte said. 'One, two, three!'

This time the lid lifted and slid a couple of inches, revealing a dark crack along the top edge. Tayte half expected some unholy stench to ensue, but the air didn't smell any different from the dry, stale air in the rest of the chamber. He didn't really know what to expect from the contents—the decay of human remains wasn't something he'd found cause to study before—but as he and Sinclair set their crowbars into place again, he imagined he was about to find out.

'One more push should do it,' he said, still wondering what sights were about to meet his eyes as he began to heave on his crowbar again.

Then he jumped as the otherwise eerily silent chamber was suddenly filled with the echoing melody of the latest show tune he'd installed on his phone. He dropped his crowbar with a clatter that kicked up the dust, looked apologetically at Sinclair and answered the call.

'Jefferson Tayte,' he announced as he stooped and picked the crowbar up again.

'Mr Tayte, it's DI Ross. I have some news and I couldn't get an answer on the home number. I've tried Damian's mobile, too, but it goes straight to voicemail.'

'That's okay,' Tayte said. 'I'm with Mr Sinclair now. We're in the basement looking for the ruby. You're breaking up a little.'

'That would explain it then,' Ross said. 'I'll be as brief as I can in case the signal drops out altogether. My news concerns Callum Macrae. I thought it might be important for you to know that it's unlikely Callum Macrae killed himself.'

'It is?'

'Aye, the time of death's all wrong. Callum was already dead when that text message was sent to you. It doesn't necessarily mean he didn't kill himself, we're still looking into that, but there's no way he could have sent the message. I believe Callum was murdered, just like the rest, and I believe that message was sent by his killer.'

'I see,' Tayte said. 'So he's still out there.'

'Maybe not out here so much as in there, if you catch my drift.'

Tayte did. Ross's message had been received loud and very clear. If Callum Macrae hadn't killed himself, then someone else had killed him, and unless Sinclair's Rajputs were real and among them in present-day Scotland, there were few potential suspects left. He supposed he could rule DI Ross out. If Ross was behind this, why would he let on that it was unlikely Callum Macrae had killed himself? It would surely be in his best interest to leave Tayte and everyone else at Drumarthen believing the killer was dead—that they were safe. As far as Tayte could see that only left two suspects, both of whom were there at Drumarthen with him.

Tayte's eyes wandered along the sarcophagus to Sinclair and the crowbar he was holding. He wondered whether Sinclair had been pushing the idea that these loyal Rajputs were behind this in an attempt to draw suspicion away from himself. Jane's letters made them real, but could they really be seeking the Blood of Rajputana today, almost two hundred years after Naresh Bharat Singh had stolen it? There was no doubt in Tayte's mind that Sinclair needed money, whether he cared to admit it or not. Was this all about Drumarthen? Such a ruby could be used to restore the house to its former glory. Or had he made one too many bad investments in London?

Tayte had to remind himself then that this wasn't all about the money that could be made from the sale of the Blood of Rajputana should it be found. People had been murdered—family members who'd had little to no chance of finding the ruby for themselves. What threat had their search for it really posed? Surely not enough to warrant their murders. Just the same, with his eyes still on the crowbar in Sinclair's hands, Tayte couldn't help but wonder whether he was in that chamber with the killer right now. The thought sent a shiver down his spine.

'Thank you for the information,' he said to Ross, sounding calm, trying to play it cool. 'Do let us know if there are any further developments.'

'I'll be sure to,' Ross said. 'I've plenty keeping me busy for now, but I'll be over as soon as I can.'

As the call ended, Sinclair said, 'I take it that was Ross. What did he say?'

Tayte was reluctant to tell Sinclair that Callum hadn't sent the text message, which in all probability meant that he had been murdered just like all the rest. It was information he wanted to keep to himself for now, because if Sinclair was behind this he supposed it was better to let him go on thinking that his plan to frame Callum had worked. But how could he not tell him? What if Sinclair was innocent? If he was, then he also had every right to know that the killer was still at large.

'He told me he believes Callum Macrae was murdered,' Tayte said, carefully watching Sinclair's reaction, supposing that such news would come as a blow to him if he were behind all this. 'He was already dead by the time that text message was sent to me.'

Sinclair's only physical reaction to the news was a slow rise and fall of his eyebrows. 'That's a worry, then,' he said. 'Still, I'm sure Murray has the place locked up tight as a drum.' He shook his crowbar. 'Ready?'

Tayte wished all the more that he knew where Murray was. From what Sinclair had told him about the death of Murray's daughter, Murray had a reason to dislike every one of the victims. But was it enough to kill them? And why now? If murder was in his mind, why wait so long after his daughter's death to enact his revenge? It was, however, hard to ignore the fact that Murray had access to the missing shotgun, and to the house in general. It would have been easy for him to leave each and every one of Jane's letters.

As Tayte set his crowbar into place, ready to give the sarcophagus lid one last heave, another thought occurred to him, the most unsettling of all. What if Sinclair and Murray were in on this together—Sinclair for the money he could use to rebuild his family home, Murray for revenge? Was he in the house with two cold-blooded killers?

'Mr Tayte?' Sinclair said, clearly having noticed Tayte's hesitance. 'Ready?'

'Sorry,' Tayte said, concluding that he had little choice for now but to continue. 'On three,' he said again. 'One, two, three!'

Both men leaned on their crowbars and pushed again, and this time they kept pushing. The sarcophagus lid began to slide until it became unbalanced. Then it crashed to the floor with a crack and a thud, filling the room with so much dust Tayte had to cover his mouth with his sleeve so as not to breathe it in. When the dust began to settle he peered down into the sarcophagus and saw the pale grey skeletal remains of Sir Robert Christie, wearing full Highland dress in the now-faded ancient Christie tartan colours of orange, black, white, blue and yellow.

Tayte turned away again, partly out of respect and partly because he didn't have much stomach for looking at dead bodies, however old they were. 'He's your ancestor,' he said to Sinclair. 'I'll leave the rest to you, if you don't mind.'

Sinclair had already started searching for the ruby. He gave a nod and continued to rummage inside the sarcophagus with both hands, his enthusiasm to know whether it was there written all over his face. Tayte watched him move slowly along the sarcophagus towards him, his features souring with disappointment more and more with every step he took.

When he was standing beside Tayte at the foot of the sarcophagus, he shone his torch over it and took one last look inside. Then he shook his head and said, 'It's not there.'

Tayte had begun to expect as much. 'I guess we shouldn't be too surprised,' he said.

'We shouldn't?'

'No, I mean how could your ancestor have trusted anyone enough to carry out such a wish? The temptation to take the ruby for themselves would surely have been too strong. At least, I expect that would have been going through Sir Robert's mind. After all, he himself had killed a man merely for the letters that pointed to the ruby's whereabouts.'

'That's a fair point,' Sinclair said. 'So what else do you think he might have done with it?'

'I don't know,' Tayte said. 'Let's get some fresh air. I don't know about you, but I've definitely had enough of this place. Maybe it'll help us think.'

As they made their way out, Tayte also thought it would be good to get back up into the main body of the house, closer to the front door. A big part of him was relieved that the ruby wasn't in that sarcophagus. If Sinclair *was* behind this, Drumarthen's basement was the last place he wanted to be when the Blood of Rajputana was found. As far as he was concerned, the sooner DI Ross got there the better. For now, though, he figured he would just have to keep going and hold out until the detective inspector arrived.

Chapter Thirty-Six

By the time Tayte and Sinclair arrived back in Drumarthen's main hallway, Tayte's thoughts had turned to the paintings he'd previously heard about. He'd been told they were the cause of a long-running family feud between the Sinclairs and the Macraes, and they were from Sir Robert Christie's time. That made them worth exploring further. Perhaps between them they held some clue to the ruby's whereabouts.

'What else can you tell me about those paintings Moira Macrae wanted?' he asked as they reached the foot of the stairs.

They stopped walking and Sinclair sat down on one of the lower steps. 'There were only three paintings left to Angus in his mother's will. I really can't see what all the fuss has been about. They were painted by a Scottish portrait artist called Andrew Geddes. His work is well known, so I suppose they're worth a bob or two. He died in the 1840s.'

'That was three decades before Robert Christie died,' Tayte said, shaking his head. 'To have any significance they would have to have been painted around the time of Robert's death or perhaps soon after.' A moment later, he added, 'Unless it's not the paintings themselves that are important.'

'How do you mean?'

'I mean there could be something written on the back of them, or hidden inside the frames. It's possible that Robert had written a secret message to his son on these paintings somewhere and asked Aileen

Fraser to leave them to Angus in her will. Maybe she still cared enough for him to fulfil his dying wish.'

'Aye,' Sinclair said with renewed hope in his voice. 'And it's not so much to ask a mother to leave a few portraits to one of her sons, illegitimate or otherwise, despite how Angus's siblings might have felt about it.'

'No, it's not,' Tayte agreed. 'We know from the research both you and Gordon Drummond carried out that Aileen outlived Robert by more than ten years, so there's every chance we're on the right track here. I think we need to go and take a look at those paintings. Do you know where they are?'

Sinclair threw his head back. 'Now you're asking. So many things have been moved around over the years, it's hard to keep track of it all.'

'But you do still have them?'

'Oh, aye, I'm sure of it. I expect Murray will know where they are. I'll try his phone again.'

Sinclair took out his mobile phone and made the call. Several seconds later he shook his head and said, 'He's still not answering.'

'Should we go and look for him?'

Sinclair stood up. 'I'd sooner go and look for those paintings. I'll leave him a message to get in touch.' When his call went to voicemail he said, 'Murray, please call my mobile as soon as you get this. We could use your help.' He put his phone away again. 'Now, let's go and see if we can find them. It shouldn't be too difficult. I don't recall seeing them in a while, so I expect they must still be hanging in the east wing.'

Tayte followed Sinclair to the back of the hall. 'We'll have to be careful then.'

'Aye, careful as ever in the east wing, and more so the higher up we go. A mishap on the top floor could see you back down here again in no time at all.'

They checked the ground floor first, which was relatively easy-going as much of the flooring on this level, particularly at the heart of the house, was made of stone. Where the rooms they entered had wooden floorboards, as with the room Tayte had previously entered when he'd found Robert Christie's tomb, they exercised all necessary caution. They came across only a handful of paintings, one or two of which were portraits of past family members, but none had been signed by Andrew Geddes.

They worked their way back to the main hallway and went up to the first floor, taking the corridor Tayte had previously used on the morning he'd gone exploring. He didn't recall seeing any portraits in the rooms he'd looked in, but they checked them all again to be sure. When they came to the atrium they went straight on, now treading a path Tayte was unfamiliar with. Looking into the rooms in this area, he imagined they had once been bedrooms, and it was here that two paintings drew their attention. Both were portraits, hanging between windows that were too dirty to see through.

'There,' Sinclair said, pointing to the lower right-hand corner of the first canvas. 'Andrew Geddes.'

Tayte had gone to the other painting. 'Same here,' he said, checking his footing on the floorboards as he stepped back to take them both in. One was of a seated, dark-haired woman wearing a deep red, empire-line dress, pensively looking up towards the right side of the image. The other was of a man in a green hunting cape, looking straight out of the picture. Neither were very large. Their condition appeared to be very good.

'Can we take them down?' Tayte asked.

'Of course,' Sinclair said, lifting the portrait of the man down for them to take a closer look. 'They can stay down, too. I'll have Murray put them up in the west wing where they'll be safer.'

Tayte lifted the other painting down and they stood them side by side beneath one of the windows where the light was better. 'Do you know who the subjects are?'

'I'm almost certain the woman is Aileen Fraser,' Sinclair said. 'As for the man, I'm afraid I have no idea. Given the time period in which it was painted, and because it was one of the paintings bequeathed to Angus, I suppose it could be one of his brothers. If he spawned the Macrae bloodline, maybe that's what all the fuss has been about.'

Tayte turned the paintings around. There were a few marks on the back, but nothing that resembled any kind of message. He wanted to take the canvases out of the frames to see if Sir Robert Christie had written anything on the back of them, but just as he was about to ask Sinclair if that would be okay, he checked his thinking. Then he began to shake his head.

'Supposing there *was* a message inside one or all of the paintings left to Angus,' he said. 'How could he have known about it?'

'That's a good point,' Sinclair said. 'It would have to stand out in some way.'

'Precisely,' Tayte said. 'And nothing here does. You said Angus was left three paintings.'

'That's right. Shall we see if we can find the other one?'

Tayte nodded. 'I think we have to. If only to rule it out.'

They left the room, checking several others before moving up to the next floor, where they found a handful of other paintings, none of which were by Geddes. This floor was entirely new to Tayte, and the condition of the house in this section was by far the worst he had seen. There were the typical signs of peeling wall-coverings and flaking paintwork, but it was much worse here. The obvious neglect was further accentuated by entire sections of floor that were missing, giving clear views down into the rooms below.

'We took up some of the boards on this floor before the rot got to them,' Sinclair said by way of an explanation. 'This section of the house has been out of use the longest, so we used the good boards to repair the rooms that were in use in the west wing.'

'I see,' Tayte said, opening a door that led into a dark and uninviting room.

'If you can believe it,' Sinclair continued, 'once upon a time this used to be the master bedroom.'

Tayte shone his torch into the room, illuminating a large space that contained an old four-poster bed and a few items of bedroom furniture. There were also two more paintings here, although Tayte couldn't make them out very well from where he was standing.

'At least the floorboards are okay,' he said as he stepped inside.

Sinclair scoffed. 'Don't you believe it.'

There were drawn curtains at the windows, which Tayte thought had once been a rich silky green colour. Now the moth-eaten cloth was pale and covered in years of dust and grime. He went further in, testing every floorboard before he trusted his weight to it. It all seemed sound enough, and although he was a heavy man, he figured that the four-poster bed had to be far heavier. It gave him confidence. He reached one of the tall curtains without incident, sensing that Sinclair wasn't far behind him. He went to open it, thinking to let some natural light in, but as he pulled at it the entire pelmet and framework came crashing down around him with a thud that sent a plume of dust into the air.

Tayte coughed. 'Sorry,' he said, throwing Sinclair a smile. 'At least now we can see what we're doing.'

Sinclair seemed more interested in how Tayte was than the old curtains. 'Are you okay?'

Tayte nodded. 'Luckily, it just missed me.'

He turned away from the window, back into the room, his eyes seeking out the paintings he'd seen. One was adjacent to the bed on his right. The other, to Tayte's left, was much larger. It hung above a grand inglenook fireplace, over a smoke-blackened beam. They were both portraits. As before, one was of a man, the other was of a woman. The smaller portrait to the right was closest so they went to it first. It was a dark picture of a man in a black, almost indistinguishable coat, which highlighted his face and the white of his shirt collar.

'I do know who this fine gentleman is,' Sinclair said. 'That's Angus's stepfather, Lachlan Fraser.'

'It's by Andrew Geddes,' Tayte said as he began to scrutinise it. Then a sound outside the room distracted him. 'Did you hear that?' He tilted his head back towards the door, listening.

'Hear what?'

Tayte went to the door and looked out along the corridor. 'It sounded like a creaking floorboard.'

'I can't say I did,' Sinclair said as he joined him. 'Murray? Are you there?' he called, but there was no answer. Turning back to Tayte, he said, 'It's a very old house, Mr Tayte. Given the state it's in, I expect you heard another piece of plaster falling from the ceiling somewhere.'

'It sounded just like a floorboard to me,' Tayte said as they returned to Lachlan Fraser's portrait.

Tayte carefully lifted the painting down and turned it around, hoping to find something on the back that might at least give them their next direction, but as before, there was nothing to suggest any kind of message. He propped it up against the wall, and he and Sinclair went over to the other painting. He recognised this portrait as that of Aileen Fraser, although she was older than she appeared in the portrait he'd seen on the floor below. Standing on the stone hearth in front of the fireplace, both men had to crane their necks to look up at it. When Tayte's eyes fell on the signature his chin dropped. There was no name, just three initials.

'RJC,' he said, turning to Sinclair.

Before Tayte had arrived at Drumarthen House, the initials would have meant little to anyone who saw them. Now, however, following his research into Sinclair's four-times-great-grandfather, both he and Sinclair knew exactly whose initials they were.

'Robert John Christie,' Sinclair said, spelling it out. 'It seems that Sir Robert was something of an artist himself.'

'Yes, it does,' Tayte said. 'I saw plenty of books on art in the library you showed me. Maybe some of them belonged to him.'

'It's really quite good,' Sinclair said. 'Not that it's a patch on the Geddes portraits, of course, but it's a fine piece none the less. I'm sure I must have seen it before now, but there are so many paintings at Drumarthen—at least there were—that I don't particularly recall it.'

'He's made an amateurish error with that book the subject's hand is resting on,' Tayte offered.

'Yes, I can see that. It's very much out of proportion with the rest of the image.'

'I wonder when it was painted,' Tayte said, stepping closer until he could read the book's title. It didn't escape his attention that the subject matter concerned India. '*The History of British India Volume I* by James Mill,' he read out. 'It's almost as if the artist purposefully made the book too large just so he could fit the title in.'

He lifted one corner of the frame away from the wall, and as with so many paintings that had been hung at Drumarthen, the wall covering beneath it was far brighter than that which surrounded it, telling him that the painting had been hanging there for a long time. Perhaps since Angus Fraser inherited the house. He went over to the bed and looked back at the image. His eyes were immediately drawn to the book, the spine of which was red, black and gold, with gold lettering.

'That book really does stand out,' he said. 'In fact, I'd go so far as to say that it stands out more than the subject of the portrait. It's good work, as you say, so why ruin it by detracting from it like that?'

'Tell me what you're thinking,' Sinclair said. 'Do you suppose Sir Robert was trying to send his son a message via that book? Judging from Aileen's apparent age, it could well have been painted close to Robert's death.'

Tayte couldn't be sure, but from where he was now standing by the bed in the former master bedroom, which would have been Angus Fraser's bedroom, he couldn't imagine a better place to hang a painting that was intended to grab Angus's attention and send him a message.

'I think it's highly possible,' he said, thinking that the error with the book had to be deliberate given the otherwise obvious skill of the artist. 'The house came with a collection of old books, didn't it?'

'Aye,' Sinclair said. 'A considerable collection at that.'

'Well then, let's go and see if that book's in your library.'

Chapter Thirty-Seven

The afternoon light was beginning to fade by the time Tayte and Sinclair entered Drumarthen's makeshift library. As Tayte looked up at the high grey windows, he thought there could only be another hour of daylight left. Then half the house would be in darkness. With no electricity on the upper floors of the east wing, if their search for the Blood of Rajputana was to take them back there, he imagined that unless they went soon it would have to wait until morning. That would mean spending another night at the house, which was a prospect Tayte didn't relish given there was every chance he would spend it under the same roof as a murderer.

Sinclair switched on the lights. 'That's better,' he said, looking around at the shelves of books. 'Now, where might a book about the history of British India be?'

Tayte went over to the first tall bookcase to his left and began to look. 'Let's take a side apiece,' he said. 'If we haven't found it by the time we reach the other end of the room, we can use that ladder to check the books higher up.'

They each began to walk slowly along the bookcases. Tayte scanned the shelves on his side for any references to India or history in general. He passed a fiction section, and then the large number of books on art that he'd seen before. After that he came across several leather-bound titles on natural history, and others on poetry. As he drew closer to the back of the room, he hoped Sinclair was having better luck than he was, although his silence was far from encouraging.

The books on the far wall were not in the bookcases that had been saved and brought down from the original library. They were on shelves that had been crudely put up to accommodate the rest of the collection. When he reached the back of the room, Tayte also noticed that there were several cardboard boxes, presumably filled with books for which there was no shelf space left. He opened one and his hope lifted when he saw that it contained several old volumes of Ridpath's *History of the World*, but there was nothing in there concerning British India. He opened another box, aware that behind him Sinclair was now climbing the ladder.

'I think this is the section,' Sinclair called. 'There's a number of books here about India.'

Tayte went to the bottom of the ladder and read out one of the titles from the section Sinclair was referring to. '*A Handbook for India* by John Murray.' On the shelf above it he saw several volumes entitled *The History of the British Empire in India* by Edward Thornton. As Tayte's eyes wandered further up he saw books on soldiering in British India and many more concerning the East India Company. A moment later, he noticed Sinclair reaching for a book which formed part of a row of similarly coloured red, black and gold spines.

'Here it is,' Sinclair said as he pulled one of the books out and passed it down to Tayte.

'*The History of British India Volume I* by James Mill,' Tayte read out. 'It's the same book.'

Sinclair reached the bottom of the ladder. 'Aye, the exact same. The colouring on the spine is identical.'

Tayte opened the book, wondering whether there was something inside it that Sir Robert Christie meant his son to see all those years ago—something that might tell them what he'd done with the Blood of Rajputana.

'There's an inscription,' Tayte said, pointing it out to Sinclair as soon as he turned the title page over. He felt his pulse quicken as he read it out. '*To my beloved son. I regret that I could not be the father you deserved, but please know that my heart is with you, as it is with your mother. It lies at the heart of Drumarthen. Look for it there. RJC.*'

At face value Tayte thought Robert Christie's message was a sentimental one, letting his son, Angus, know that he loved him, and that even though he was dead, his presence could still be felt at Drumarthen if he chose to look for it. That was likely how anyone else who came to read the inscription would see it, but knowing what Tayte knew, he clearly saw it for what it was.

'I think we can safely say that Robert's reference to his heart is really another metaphor for the ruby,' he said. 'As it was in Jane Hardwick's last letter. I'm not too sure about the next part, though. *My heart is with you* suggests that the ruby was with Angus at the house, but I'm confused as to why it would also be with Angus's mother, Aileen.'

He began to wonder whether Aileen was also entombed at Drumarthen, if there was another sarcophagus yet to be discovered, but he quickly ruled that idea out. He'd seen all the family death and burial records in both Sinclair's and Drummond's research files. He clearly recalled that Aileen was buried in the Fraser family plot alongside her husband, Lachlan, far from Drumarthen.

Sinclair held his hand out. 'Can I see it? I'd like to read it for myself.'

Tayte handed the book to Sinclair, who proceeded to read the inscription in silence. A moment later, he read out, '*It lies at the heart of Drumarthen.* If I hadn't already looked inside his sarcophagus I'd say he was referring to his tomb, but it can't be that.'

'The heart of Drumarthen . . .' Tayte said, thinking. 'The heart of the house . . . When we think about the heart of any house, it's often the kitchen that comes to mind.' He paused and began to smile to himself. 'Or perhaps around the fireplace,' he added, his tone bright.

'At least, that's where families from Robert Christie's time would gather on cold evenings.'

Sinclair gave Tayte a knowing look. 'The painting that led us to this book is hanging above a fireplace,' he said, suddenly sharing Tayte's enthusiasm.

Tayte nodded. 'And it's a painting of Angus's mother, Aileen Fraser.'

'*As it is with your mother,*' Sinclair said, repeating the line from the inscription.

Tayte was keen to go and find out if they were right before the light faded. 'I think we need to head back to the former master bedroom and take a good look at that fireplace,' he said, feeling both excited to know that the Blood of Rajputana could be there, and at the same time fearful of what would happen if it was.

Chapter Thirty-Eight

Back in Drumarthen's former master bedroom, Tayte and Sinclair went to each of the tall windows and opened the remaining curtains, taking care this time to do so without bringing them all crashing down. Because the windows here were so large and so many, they soon had enough light to comfortably see by, despite the time of day and the overcast weather. They stood looking at the fireplace in silence for several seconds. The opening was around ten feet wide by five feet high. There were narrow stone seats at either end with recesses in the back wall to either side of the iron fireback, which bore the embossed image of two stags and a thistle. Before that was the fire basket and firedogs.

'Let's lift the basket out,' Sinclair said. 'Maybe there's space enough to hide something beneath it.'

They each took an end and lifted the basket out on to the hearth along with the firedogs. The area beneath offered no encouragement. The flagstone base looked solid, giving no suggestion that any part of it could be lifted up to reveal a secret hidey-hole. They explored it further just the same, tapping at the stone and feeling along the cracks where one section met another.

'The cement's solid,' Tayte said, shaking his head. 'Maybe there's another recess behind this fireback.'

They grabbed a corner each and slowly tilted the top edge away. It was so heavy that it didn't have to be secured to the wall at all, which gave Tayte hope. It was quickly apparent, however, that there was nothing behind it but a solid stone wall. Tayte wasn't really surprised. If there had been a recess behind it, he imagined it would have been too easy for someone other than Angus Fraser to find it. They moved on to the visible recesses, looking and feeling to see if there might be a loose section of stone that could be drawn out, but everything was fixed in place. The same was true of the stone seats at either end of the inglenook, and the walls they were set against.

Tayte followed Sinclair back out on to the hearth. He was glad to be able to straighten his back again. 'I guess that just leaves the chimney,' he said, switching on the torch Sinclair had loaned him. He bent down again and peered up inside. 'It looks big enough for me to stand up in,' he added. 'Can you see if you can find something for me to stand on?'

'There doesn't seem to be anything suitable in here,' Sinclair said, looking around. 'I'll try one of the other rooms.'

As Sinclair left him, Tayte took off his jacket and laid it over the frame of the four-poster bed. As soon as Sinclair was out of the room he rushed back to the fireplace. In the brief time he'd just spent looking up inside the chimney, he'd seen that it soon widened out, creating shelves to either side where he thought someone could have placed something they wanted to hide. He felt sure that the clues he'd seen, the painting and the inscription in the book, meant that he was looking in the right place, and there were few if any other parts of the inglenook left to explore. If the Blood of Rajputana was here then he wanted Sinclair out of the room, if only to give him time to find it and come up with some kind of plan to keep himself alive.

He ducked under the blackened beam again and shone his torch up into the darkness. The smell of old soot was strong, and the draw of air being pulled up into the chimney began to ruffle his shirt as he rolled up his sleeves and reached for one of the shelves. Standing on his toes he could reach it easily enough. He couldn't see on to the shelf so he began to pat his hand around, feeling for whatever might be up there. He felt several lumps of what he imagined were pieces of debris from the chimney. Nothing was large enough to be the ruby he'd heard was the size of a man's fist.

He put his torch down to free up both of his hands, shining the beam up into the void. He tried the other side, and as soon as he did, his hand met with something flat and hard. He pulled himself up and stretched further, reaching higher until he was able to feel the outline of what seemed to be some kind of box. It was cold to the touch and he imagined it was made of metal, something that could easily withstand the heat from the fire below.

Tayte's heart was in his mouth as he steadily drew the box closer to the edge of the shelf. Very soon a corner began to slide into view. He could see it clearly now in the glow of the torchlight. He flicked at it again and again until it began to topple over. Then he grabbed it with both hands and heard the contents rattle inside it. He held the box still, listening in case Sinclair had returned. When he was sure he hadn't, he brushed the soot away and examined the box further.

There was a clasp, but no lock. What need would there be for one given where the box had been hidden? He held his breath as he opened it, and there inside was a dull, yet undeniably red stone. It had been placed there by Sir Robert Christie for his son to find, and yet Angus clearly had not found it. In wishing to ensure no one else found it, Robert had been too cryptic with his clues for Angus to work them out—clues that were so much easier to understand when you knew what you were looking for. Gazing at the dull red stone, Tayte thought it was not quite the size of a man's fist, not his fist at least, but it was nonetheless impressive enough for him to know he was looking at the ruby known as the Blood of Rajputana.

'Here we are,' Sinclair called from inside the room.

His voice startled Tayte, snapping him from his thoughts. Without thinking, he grabbed the ruby and dropped it down the neck of his shirt where it caught amidst the material tucked in at his waist. He closed the box again and bent down to see Sinclair approaching.

'I've found something,' Tayte told him, keeping the box out of view for now. He wanted to gauge Sinclair's reaction before he showed him exactly what he'd found.

'Is it the ruby?' Sinclair said. There was excitement in his voice, but that much was to be expected. 'Here, I found this footstool. It should be strong enough to take your weight.'

'It's okay,' Tayte said. 'I think I can reach it.' He put his head back up the chimney. 'There's a box,' he called, hurriedly trying to think.

If Sinclair was to show his true colours then he had to believe Tayte had found the Blood of Rajputana, in which case he couldn't very well show him an empty box. If he did, Sinclair might also wonder why anyone would go to the bother of putting an empty box back once they had taken the ruby from inside it. Tayte felt around the shelf again until he found a piece of rubble large enough to fool Sinclair into thinking the ruby was there. He put it inside the box and began to rattle it.

'I've got it!' he called. 'There's something inside. It has to be the ruby. We've found the Blood of Rajputana!'

With that, still shaking the box, Tayte bent down again to come out from the fireplace, but as he did he knew at once that Sinclair was not behind this. He saw another figure in the room, standing right behind Sinclair, dressed in what he imagined was the same hooded cloak DI Ross had described from the CCTV images. He had a shotgun in one hand, and a heavy-looking marble sculpture in the other, which he began to raise.

'Look out!' Tayte called to Sinclair, who was full of smiles at the discovery Tayte had made, oblivious to the figure standing behind him.

Tayte's call was too late. As he fully came out from the inglenook, covered in soot, he could only watch as Sinclair began to turn around, just as the marble sculpture was driven hard into the side of his head. Before Sinclair's body hit the ground, the shotgun in the hooded figure's other hand began to turn on Tayte.

Chapter Thirty-Nine

So many questions began to spin through Tayte's mind that he started to feel dizzy. Who was beneath that hood? As far as he knew, besides himself and Sinclair, the only other person in the house was Murray. Was this why Sinclair's trusted family retainer had distanced himself from them and had failed to answer his calls—so he could follow them around the house until they found the ruby? Or was someone else there at Drumarthen with them? Given the hooded cloak the figure standing before him was wearing, Tayte couldn't help but think of the Rajputs Sinclair had told him about, whom he'd also read about in Jane Hardwick's letters. Had they really come to restore the Blood of Rajputana to its rightful place after all these years?

As the shotgun turned on him, Tayte tried to glimpse the figure's face, but it was in shadow beneath his hood. He had no idea who it was. All he did know was that Sinclair was down, dead for all he knew, and unless he did something fast, he was going to be next. There was blood around Sinclair's head where it had been struck, staining the floorboards black in the fading light. As much as Tayte wanted to go to him, to try to help him if he could, he knew he would not be allowed to. He had to get out of there.

As the shotgun began to draw level with Tayte's chest, all he could think to do was to throw the heavy metal box at it. He hurled it hard, right at the muzzle. At the same time he started to run for the door, hoping he would make it. He saw the box hit its target. There was an explosion as the shotgun went off, loosing one of its cartridges at the floor ahead of him.

Tayte knew it wouldn't take the hooded figure long to fire off the other cartridge, but he was almost at the door. Beneath him as he ran, he could feel the old floorboards, now splintered and further weakened from the first shotgun blast, crack and give way, but they held. Then he was at the doorway, passing through it just as the second shot blew a hole clean through the door.

The corridor beyond the room was almost in darkness now, but having been there twice with Sinclair, Tayte knew his way back to the stairs they had used. He wanted to get off this floor. If he could make it to the ground level, maybe he could reach the front door. He ran hard, hoping his luck with the floorboards would hold out. A voice in his head told him he needed to call Ross, but he was starkly aware that he no longer had his phone with him. It was in his suit jacket, which he'd hung over the bed frame in the room he was running from. He had to get to the front door. If not there, then he had to find somewhere to hide.

Tayte figured the box would buy him a little time. The man in the hooded cloak would have to pick it up and take a look inside. He would expect the ruby to be there, but he'd quickly discover that he'd been duped. Then he'd know Tayte had it. Why else would there be a piece of rubble in the ruby's place? For that reason alone, Tayte understood all too well that the man would not give up the chase. As he reached the end of the corridor he also knew his head start had run out. Behind him in the near-darkness, he could already hear the floorboards thumping and creaking as his pursuer came after him. Tayte ducked into the corridor on his left and the light fell further. He wished he had a torch, but that was also back in the room where he'd had no choice but to leave it.

Further along, the pale grey glow from a window revealed the top of the stairway he was heading for. He was running almost blind towards it now. He knew he had to slow down or risk a fall. He could still hear his pursuer coming after him, and he figured it wouldn't be long before he caught up with him. If he could only reach the stairs. There were several ways he could go from the landing below, most of which were unfamiliar to him, but in the low light he imagined he could find somewhere to hide.

He reached the top of the stairway, where several steps were missing. It meant he had to descend via the railing support and it was painfully slow going. He slid one foot carefully between the rails and then another until he could use the steps again, then he jumped the last few, cracking on to the boards beneath him as he landed, taking one of the corridors at random. Part way along it, he opened a door to his right and went inside. His heart was pounding hard, and now that he'd stopped running, he could feel the adrenaline coursing through him, making his hands shake as he quietly closed the door and pressed an ear to it, listening, not daring to move or make a sound.

All Tayte could hear was his own heavy breathing. He tried to calm himself, taking slow, controlled breaths until he felt his pulse begin to slow down again. He could feel the ruby beneath his shirt, pressing into his waistline, and he was glad to know it was still there. He took it out and put it into his trouser pocket where he thought it would be safer. Out in the corridor all appeared to be quiet. That was good. He thought maybe the man had taken one of the other corridors. A second later, he heard a creak and knew he hadn't. It was followed by the sound of a door opening further back towards the stairway he'd just left. His pursuer clearly knew which way he'd gone, and now he was trying all the doors to find out which room he was in.

Tayte turned away from the door and looked around, squinting in the dusky light from the bare windows. As with most of the rooms in the east wing, there was little to see. There was no furniture and no furnishings, just more cracked plaster and bare floorboards, many of which were missing. He was glad to see that there were double doors at both ends of the room, giving him an alternative way out should he need it.

Another sound drew his attention then, as the next door along the corridor was opened and closed. He had to move. He didn't want to, but he figured his best chance was to double back, taking the doors to his right, but just as he took a step towards them he saw one of them begin to open. His heart was suddenly in his mouth. He turned back, grabbed the door knob and flung the door open, just as his pursuer entered the room. Another blast from his shotgun echoed out, but Tayte was already running again, deeper into the house towards what he hoped was the main staircase and the front door.

There was light up ahead, which he imagined was the atrium he'd come across the night this hooded man had slipped one of Jane's letters under his bedroom door. Tayte was desperate to reach it, where he knew other passages would be open to him, but he didn't think he'd make it. The man chasing him was already out in the corridor, and Tayte was all too aware that he was probably lining up another shot at him right now. He tried to hold out and keep running, but his nerves soon got the better of him. He burst through the next door on his left, quickly closed it behind him and continued running through what was now total darkness. Moments later he heard a splintering crack beneath him and he was suddenly weightless, falling through the floorboards momentarily before catching himself by his elbows.

Tayte did well to stifle the cry that rose within him as the shock of what had just happened registered. The ground floor below him had a very high ceiling. Had he fallen all the way through he figured he'd have been lucky to survive, not that he was out of danger yet. His elbows were supporting him, but he didn't know how long he could hold out for. He tried to lift himself up, but the added pressure on the floorboards around him caused them to crack further under his weight. He heard another sound then and he stopped struggling. The man chasing him was at the door. He was opening it.

Tayte sank lower, putting more strain on his already aching arms. He had his back to the door now, but he sensed the man was standing somewhere behind him. He hoped the darkness would save him. Perhaps he wouldn't be able to see him. Then a torch clicked on and its beam began to scan the room like a searchlight, shattering Tayte's hopes. Instinctively, he dipped his head as low to the floor as he could. Behind him, floorboards began to creak as the man came further into the room, his torch beam highlighting heavy red curtains that were drawn, shutting out what little light the day still had to offer.

The torchlight flicked across the room and fell on another door to Tayte's right, which was open, and the sight of it seemed to excite the man because he was suddenly running again. Out of the corner of Tayte's eye, he watched him go to the door and pass through it, clearly believing Tayte had gone that way. When the man was out of sight, Tayte gave a long if quiet sigh, thankful that the torch beam had passed above him.

He waited several long seconds before he moved again. When he was sure his pursuer was far enough away, he raised himself up on to his elbows again and began to push himself higher, but by now his arms felt so weak that he knew he wasn't going to be able to climb out unassisted. He began to kick his legs, trying to get some momentum going as he pushed, but that only made the rest of the floorboards around him creak and crack all the more. He wanted to shout for help, but that would only get him killed.

Better to chance the fall, he thought as he tried to peer down through the gaps around him to see what was below.

He couldn't see much. It would be a gamble, and while it wasn't a decision he wanted to make, he knew if he didn't do something soon his arms were going to give out anyway. Several more seconds passed. His arms began to shake. Very soon he was going to fall whether he liked it or not. He began to brace himself, using the last of the strength in his arms to draw them closer to his body. Then he heard a floorboard creak out in the corridor he'd entered the room by. His pursuer had returned.

Tayte cursed himself for making so much noise trying to get out of that hole. He was all the more determined now to drop through the floor, whatever the outcome, but when the door opened he craned his neck around and saw Murray standing in the frame, his face lit by an electric camping lantern. He wasn't wearing a hooded cloak. He had on the same old blue corduroy trousers and jumper he always seemed to wear.

'Mr Tayte?' he called. 'Are you in here?'

'Murray! I'm over here!'

The light drew closer until it was right in Tayte's face. 'Mr Tayte! Are you okay?'

'I will be if you can help me out of this hole. I don't think I can hold on much longer.'

'I'll be back in a minute.'

'Wait! Where are you going?'

Tayte got no answer. Instead he heard the sound of creaking wood coming from somewhere behind him. A moment later Murray returned with a floorboard which he'd clearly just pulled up. He put his lamp down and tested the boards in front of Tayte. Then he laid the loose floorboard down in front of him to help support his weight.

Murray grabbed Tayte's upper arms. 'You push, I'll pull,' he said. 'Ready?'

Tayte gave a nod, and with all the strength he could muster, he pressed his elbows down hard, raising his body as Murray helped to lift him up high enough for him to fall forward over the plank he'd just laid in front of him. Tayte was then able to use his arms more freely to wriggle and kick his way out of the hole while Murray continued to assist him. When he was clear, he stood against the wall with his hands on his knees, panting.

'Thanks, Murray,' he said. 'Now we have to get help. And we need to get out of here. It's not safe.'

'Where's Mr Sinclair?'

Tayte shook his head. 'I don't think he made it. We were upstairs looking for the ruby. The person in the hooded cloak from the CCTV images showed up and hit him hard in the head. There was a lot of blood.'

'I need to go and see if he's okay.'

'Right now we need to get help, or we'll both be next. Whoever hit him is running around Drumarthen with a shotgun, bent on killing me for that ruby.'

'You found it?'

Tayte was about to answer when it dawned on him that, despite Murray's help, he could still be the one who was behind all this—the same man who had been chasing after him with that shotgun. He was of similar height and build to the hooded figure, and it would have been a simple matter to take his cloak off and leave it outside the room along with that shotgun. The lamp Murray had with him was different, but that didn't mean much. His pursuer had been gone a while. He could easily have fetched another, and then been drawn back to the room by the noise Tayte had been making as he'd tried to get out of that hole. Was Murray trying to gain his trust in order to put him off his guard?

'The ruby,' Murray said. 'I asked if you found it.'

Tayte's eyes narrowed on him. 'Exactly where have you been all afternoon?'

'I was struck, too,' Murray said. He raised a hand to the back of his head. 'When I came round, I found myself tied up in one of the basement rooms where I'd been tidying up.'

'How did you untie yourself?'

Murray fished in his pocket and pulled out his penknife, flashing the mother-of-pearl handle at him. 'I cut myself free. And I can't say I like your tone, Mr Tayte. Just where are you going with this?'

Tayte stepped away from the wall. If Murray was behind this, penknife or not, without that shotgun in his hands he figured he was more than a match for him when it came to a straight fight. 'Do you have your phone? Mr Sinclair told me you carried one in case he needed to get in touch with you. He tried your number a few times, but he couldn't get an answer.'

Murray shook his head. 'It was taken from me.'

'But not your penknife?' Tayte said, thinking it rather too convenient that Murray's assailant had taken his phone, yet left him with a means to free himself.

'I suppose he was only after my phone,' Murray said as he put his penknife away. 'I expect he wanted to make sure I wasn't able to call for help, and he overlooked my knife. Luckily for you, I might add.'

With everything that had happened, Tayte didn't know what to believe. His mind flashed back over the events of that week, and it was easy to convince himself that Murray was behind all the murders, in revenge for his daughter's death, and now, he might also have killed Damian Sinclair for Drumarthen, which he stood to inherit, possibly along with the Blood of Rajputana, too.

Tayte stepped away, heading for the side door the hooded figure had previously left the room by. He was taking that ruby with him, too. He didn't know who he could trust, so he would trust no one.

'I'm getting out of here by myself,' he told Murray. 'You can go up and check on Mr Sinclair if you want to.'

All Tayte wanted was to get out of that house alive. DI Ross could take it from there. He stepped back again, distancing himself further from Murray, checking the floor as he went to avoid repeating his earlier mistake. The light began to fade around him as he left the glow of Murray's lamp, his eyes on him the whole time. Then, as he reached the door he was heading for, something stopped him. It was something hard and it was pressing into his back. He turned around, and there in front of him was the hooded man.

The muzzle of his shotgun pressed hard into Tayte again, and with more of a shove this time, pushing him back into the room. Tayte still wasn't convinced that this man could be one of the Rajputs Sinclair had spoken of, but who was he? The only other person Tayte could think of was DI Ross. Whoever it was, Tayte was all too aware that he was about to find out, or he figured he'd have been shot already. As they drew closer to the light from Murray's lamp, the hooded figure gave Tayte another shove with the shotgun, pushing him towards Murray. Then, as he turned around, the figure lowered his hood at last.

At first Tayte didn't recognise him. Then he was reminded of the photograph Sinclair had shown him, of the athletic-looking, dark-haired man who had been playing extreme paintball in his swimming trunks. His hair was much longer now, and Tayte was also reminded of the figure he'd seen looking up at the house from the other side of the burn the day he'd arrived. Standing before him was the man whose funeral he'd attended just that morning, while all along he'd really been roaming the corridors of Drumarthen dressed as one of Sinclair's Rajputs, leaving that Sanskrit note and Jane's letters for him to find. It was Jamie Sinclair.

Chapter Forty

Ignoring the double-barrelled shotgun in Jamie's hand, Murray stepped towards him. He raised his lamp higher and began to study him, as if he couldn't believe his own eyes.

'Jamie?' he said, looking confused, clearly still doubting it could be true. Then, as he continued to stare at Jamie in the lamplight, he began to nod his head. 'My God. It *is* you.'

'Surprise,' Jamie said, his tone flat.

It gave Tayte the impression that Jamie would rather Murray had not known he was behind this, as though he now had to explain himself to someone he knew would be disappointed in him. Tayte had heard that Murray was like a father to Jamie, far more so than Jamie's real father had been. He supposed that was why. He said nothing, opting to listen to what these two had to say to one another instead.

'It's a surprise, all right,' Murray said, his features souring. He sounded angry now. 'Just who did we bury today? Whose death have I been mourning?'

'No one you know.'

Murray shook his head. 'What have you done, Jamie Sinclair? Why?'

Jamie didn't answer the question. 'You're not supposed to be here,' he said, shaking his head. 'I needed you out of the way. You should have stayed where I left you. The police were supposed to find you tied up in the basement, none the wiser about what had happened here. I gave you the perfect alibi.'

'I don't need an alibi,' Murray said, the level of his voice rising. 'I've done nothing wrong!'

'That's not how the police will see it. You'll be blamed otherwise. It's not too late.'

'Too late for what?'

'I can tie you up again. I'm about done here.'

Murray screwed his face up. 'Are you completely out of your mind?'

'You'll get Drumarthen,' Jamie said. 'All this will be yours if you'll just turn a blind eye.'

'Is that why you're doing this—so I can have Drumarthen?' Murray said. 'Is that why you killed all those people?'

'They deserved it. Every last one of them.'

'Then I'll ask you again. Why? It can't all have been for that ruby. Why did you kill them?'

Jamie was silent for several seconds, as if carefully contemplating his answer. 'I'll tell you everything once you've agreed to let me tie you up again. I need to know you'll be okay.'

'You'll tell me right now, Jamie Sinclair, or you'll have to shoot me.'

In the silence that followed, Tayte could see that Jamie was uncomfortable with the decisions he now had to make. If he chewed his lip any harder he'd make it bleed. Tayte didn't doubt that Jamie would shoot him in a heartbeat, but it was plain to see that he had plenty of affection for Murray. That made it difficult to know which way this was going to go. A lot was riding on Murray, who appeared to be deeply hurt by Jamie's actions, and the suggestion that he should turn a blind eye for his own personal gain. Murray had to be careful what he said. To Tayte's mind, Jamie Sinclair was a man who needed extensive psychiatric help. There was no telling how far Murray would be able to push him before the connection between them snapped.

Murray went over to the outside wall between the curtains and leaned against it, waiting for answers. Tayte went with him, trying not to draw too much attention to himself. With that shotgun still in Jamie's hand, he certainly wasn't about to tackle the man unless he had to.

'I'm listening,' Murray said.

Jamie came closer, the muzzle of his gun still raised towards them. 'Then you'll let me tie you up again?'

'Then we'll see. You can start by telling me how you faked your own death.'

Jamie drew a long and thoughtful breath. Then he stared at the floor and slowly began to speak. 'Gordon helped me. I gave him no choice. I had something on him from way back. I told him I needed to disappear, and that if he didn't help me I'd ruin him. What he didn't know at the time was that he was the reason I wanted to fake my death.'

'How do you mean?' Murray asked.

'I mean I wanted to kill him. I wanted to be sure I'd get away with it, too, and no one suspects a dead man.'

'Why did you want to kill him?'

Jamie scoffed. 'The good doctor wasn't as good as most people seemed to believe. He had a dirty little secret—a very dirty secret. You remember my best friend, Conall MacIntyre?'

'Chrissie's boy. Aye, of course.'

'Well, Gordon Drummond used to interfere with him. He'd often visit Chrissie after her husband left her, and she'd tell herself his interest was in her, but it wasn't. She knew why he was really there and she did nothing about it—a lonely woman going along with whatever the *good* doctor wanted, just for his company. Drummond liked boys—boys like Conall and me, and God knows who else. He was the reason Conall MacIntyre killed himself.'

'So you took revenge, both for Conall and for yourself?'

Jamie nodded. 'All these years I've lived with the scars of what Drummond did to us. I couldn't take it any more.'

'Why didn't you tell someone about it?' Murray said. 'If not your father, then you could have told me. I'd have—'

'Why do you think it hurts so much?' Jamie said, cutting Murray short. 'Do you not think I've regretted keeping quiet every single day of my life since Conall died? If I'd spoken out, Conall might still be alive. But I felt so ashamed, and who would have believed me, an errant fifteen-year-old boy, over the word of the good Dr Drummond? Yes, I killed him for Conall, and for myself, and I don't regret it one bit.'

'All right, Jamie. Calm down now,' Murray said. 'So you threatened to expose Dr Drummond if he didn't help you. Not wanting to take the risk of what might have happened if you did, I take it he went along with your plans?'

'Aye, he did. I rented a penthouse apartment in Glasgow where I knew there'd be plenty of potential candidates to literally take the fall for me. I'd single out someone on the street who looked most like me— same height and build, et cetera. I'd befriend him long enough to get a blood sample, which is where Drummond came in. He knew people who could tell him their blood type. If it matched mine, I'd befriend him some more. If not, I moved on. The homeless problem in Glasgow is huge, and single males account for almost half the number. I have a common blood type. It didn't take long.'

Murray's face twisted at the idea. 'He was an innocent man, Jamie. He'd done you no harm.'

'He was a means to an end, and he had a good time before he went, if that makes you feel any better about it. It was easy to get him blind drunk, and what homeless person would turn down some new clothes to wear—my clothes? The rest was easy. I slipped my wallet into his pocket, tangled him up in my net curtains to disorient him, and then I shoved him over the balcony, leaving it to Drummond and my brother to positively identify me from the mess they scraped off the pavement.'

'But how did you get out of there?' Murray asked. 'The police said your apartment door was locked and bolted from the inside.'

Jamie grinned. 'Building. Antennae. Span. Earth,' he said. 'I BASE-jumped after him. By the time his body hit the ground, I was floating away, unseen by the few people who were out at that time of the morning. If any misdirection were needed, my homeless friend amply provided that too. Of course, I needed money for all this. That apartment wasn't cheap.'

Tayte spoke then. He hadn't planned to, but he'd been wondering where the syndicate featured in Jamie's plans. It just came out. 'Which is why you started that syndicate of yours. For the money.'

Jamie snapped his head towards Tayte as if he'd forgotten he was there. 'You keep your mouth shut!' he said, stabbing the muzzle of the shotgun towards him as he spoke. 'This is between Murray and me.'

'Easy, Jamie,' Murray said. 'I'm still listening. So you needed money, and you formed a syndicate to get it, spinning them all some fanciful story about a trip to India.'

Jamie nodded. 'I already knew who Robert Christie was. I'd found his tomb in the basement some time ago. It was the missing link for Gordon Drummond. Along with Jane Hardwick's letters, he was then able to do the research that told us Robert had gone to India and had likely been the one who desecrated Arabella Christie's grave. I was in little doubt that he'd found the Blood of Rajputana, but I couldn't work out what he'd done with it.'

'How come you didn't bust open Sir Robert's sarcophagus and take a look for yourself?' Tayte asked, knowing it was the obvious first place to look.

Jamie laughed to himself, sarcasm written all over his face. 'You mean apart from all the noise I'd have made, and the risk of discovery?'

'There must have been opportunities when the house was empty.'

'Oh, aye, there were plenty of opportunities, but what would have been the point? I mean, how could Robert have trusted anyone to put such a valuable thing in his sarcophagus after he was dead? I'm surprised you bothered looking yourself.'

Tayte didn't answer. He'd reached the same conclusion after he and Sinclair had opened Sir Robert's sarcophagus, but they'd had to be sure.

'I thought the ruby must be at the house somewhere,' Jamie continued. 'I just didn't know how to find it. That's where you came in. You're a clever man. I thought once you knew what I knew, you'd be able to work out the rest for me.'

'I looked at Drummond's files,' Tayte said. 'There was nothing in there about the desecration of Arabella Christie's grave.'

'There wouldn't have been, would there? That's because I took those records out the day I killed him. I left some of them in case you needed a helping hand, but I couldn't give you too much to go on too soon. I needed time, which is also why I had to drip-feed Jane Hardwick's letters to you.'

'Time for what, Jamie?' Murray said. 'Time for murder? They were your family, for Christ's sake.'

'Don't give me that,' Jamie said. 'They were nothing more to me than unfinished business. I hadn't planned on killing Drummond so soon after my apparent death. I was going to wait until after my funeral—do it once the dust had settled. Then I heard that my brother and you, Mr Tayte, were going to see him. I was there at his house when Damian telephoned. I was already nervous. Gordon was the only one who knew I was still alive. I was worried he might talk, so I had to do it there and then, before you arrived.'

'But why kill the others?' Murray asked.

'Because they had it coming to them, and I knew I could get away with it. I planned to start a new life somewhere with a new identity, but I wanted to settle the score here in Comrie first. It was killing Drummond that gave me the idea. If I could get away with his murder, why not the rest? I was a dead man after all. Who would suspect me? I'd wanted to hurt them all for a long time. Now I had my chance. I killed Mairi Fraser for cheating on me, and her husband, Niall, who was supposed to have been my friend, for taking her. I wanted Moira

Macrae dead for so many reasons, not least for driving my father into his grave over those paintings. I'd hoped I could someday reconcile my differences with my father, but Moira denied me that chance. Ewan Blair I killed for you, Murray.'

'I didn't ask you to,' Murray said. 'I've never forgiven him for what he did to my daughter, but I came to my own terms over it a long time ago.' He paused and drew a long breath as though to calm himself. 'And I suppose you killed Chrissie MacIntyre because she kept quiet about Drummond's abuse of her son? Is that why you taped her mouth shut and left her naked body in those woods near Drummond Castle?'

Jamie didn't speak. He just nodded his head.

'And what about Callum Macrae?' Murray continued. 'I know he used to bully you at school, but that was a long time ago.'

'Aye, but it didn't stop after we left school. He's made my life hell over the years, physically and mentally. Sure, he was always beating on me with his mates, but sometimes he'd hurt me in other ways. You remember I once had a budgie?'

'Aye, you doted on that wee bird.'

'I cared for it more than I cared for most people,' Jamie said. 'One day I thought the tide had turned with Callum. He said I'd shown him how strong I was for taking his punishments and not telling anyone. For that, he said he wanted to be my friend. He made me part of the gang, so I took him and his mates home after school that day. That was his idea, of course, and it was all just a trick. He knew about my budgie—knew how much it meant to me. When we were up in my room, his mates held me while Callum took the bird out of its cage and slowly wrung its neck in front of me. He said if I told anyone, he'd do the same to me, and I believed him. I killed him for the pain he caused me, and because I could.'

'Does the same go for your own brother, Jamie? Mr Tayte says you struck him. He's lying upstairs in a pool of his own blood. Is that right?'

'Damian had it coming to him, just like the rest of them. If not for him my father might have loved me. If not for him, I'd have inherited this house. As far as our father was concerned, Damian's the reason I never existed. Well, now I don't exist, and Drumarthen's yours. All you have to do is look the other way.'

Tayte wasn't sure whether Murray was thinking about it or not, but the silence that followed worried him.

'I've told you everything,' Jamie continued. 'Now what do you say, Murray? You get the house. I get the ruby. We both live happily ever after.' Jamie turned to Tayte then. 'Speaking of which, I think it's high time you handed it over.'

'And then what?' Tayte asked. There was no use denying he had it.

'Just hand it over. Then we'll see.'

Tayte reached into his pocket and slowly drew it out. He held it up in his clawed fist and started moving it slowly back and forth. 'You want this?' he said, following Jamie's eyes as they tracked the ruby's movement. 'You want to use it to start a new life for yourself? Well, go and get it.'

With that, Tayte turned and tossed the Blood of Rajputana towards the hole he'd made when he almost fell through the floor. It landed on the boards with a thump, then it rolled, and just as Tayte was starting to think he hadn't tossed it hard enough, it tipped over the edge and vanished. He'd expected Jamie was going to shoot him whether he handed him the ruby or not. He wasn't about to make it easy for him.

As Tayte turned back, Jamie was already following after it, moving towards the hole. When he reached it, he stood at the edge and looked down briefly. Then his eyes were back on Tayte. They were suddenly full of hatred. He raised the shotgun and pulled it close to his side as if to brace himself, ready for the recoil as he fired. Then just before he squeezed the trigger, Murray threw down his lamp, casting the room into semi-darkness.

In the next instant, Tayte saw Murray leap at Jamie with the agility of a man half his age. Murray knocked the gun barrel away towards the window. There was a flash from the muzzle as the shot exploded out, and a deafening blast that was accompanied by the sound of shattering glass.

'Murray!' Jamie shouted, but Murray was no longer listening to him. As Jamie recovered and tried to line up his next shot, Murray shoved him hard. Jamie fell back towards the hole.

'There's my answer,' Murray said, as beneath him the already weakened floorboards cracked and splintered.

Then suddenly both men were falling.

'Murray!'

It was Tayte calling his name this time. He threw himself to the floor to spread his weight out. As Murray fell beyond Tayte's sight, he reached a hand down into the hole and grabbed Murray's arm. Murray slipped lower, and Tayte thought he'd lost him, but then he felt Murray's hand lock tight around his wrist.

'Hold on!' Tayte called. Then he began to pull Murray back to safety.

Standing at the edge of the hole a moment later, Tayte knelt down and held the lamp out to see what had become of Jamie. In the pale glow he was immediately drawn to Jamie's contorted expression, and then to the outline of his twisted body, lying still and lifeless on the flagstones thirty feet below.

Chapter Forty-One

The following morning, Tayte was with Murray on the drive outside Drumarthen beneath a cloudy if brighter sky, his briefcase and luggage at his feet, all packed and ready to go home. He and Murray had not long returned from the hospital where they had been told Damian Sinclair was going to be okay, and Tayte was glad to know that the otherwise peaceful Highland town of Comrie wouldn't have to read about the murder of yet another of its residents in their morning newspaper. Sinclair was being kept in for concussion, and he'd needed stitches, but his wound was largely superficial. He would be home again in a day or so, facing the unpleasant task of burying his brother for a second time. Tayte supposed it would be no easier for him to deal with, despite knowing what his brother had done.

On the other side of the burn, Tayte heard the car he was waiting for as it approached the house. DI Ross had offered to take him to the train station for his journey back to London.

He turned to Murray with a warm smile on his face. 'Well, thanks for all those interesting meals,' he said. 'Oh, and for saving my life, of course.'

'I could say the same to you,' Murray said. 'I always imagined I was going to die at Drumarthen some day, but I'm grateful it's not just now.'

'So am I,' Tayte said.

As the car began to cross the bridge, Tayte shook Murray's hand and picked up his briefcase. Murray went to pick up the rest of Tayte's luggage, which wasn't much, but Tayte stopped him.

'That's okay, Murray. You've done more than enough for me already. Go and put your feet up by the fire and have a wee dram of the laird's finest Scotch. I'm sure Mr Sinclair won't mind. If he does, tell him to take it out of my cheque before he sends it.'

Murray gave him a sheepish smile, the first Tayte had seen from the tough little Scotsman since he'd arrived at Drumarthen a week ago. He didn't reply. He just nodded, turned away and headed back to the house, his expression telling Tayte that he intended to do just that. Tayte watched him go, shuffling along in those same old clothes. Murray had come close to inheriting a potential fortune, but even if he had, Tayte doubted it would have changed him one bit.

The sound of tyres on the gravel drew Tayte's attention as Ross's car pulled up. 'Good morning,' Tayte said as he opened the door and threw his things in the back. He climbed into the front passenger seat and immediately felt a weight lift from his shoulders, just to know that his assignment was over. It had been a week he would never forget. 'Thanks for the ride,' he added as Ross turned the car around and headed back over the bridge.

'It's the least I can do,' Ross said, turning out on to the road, which was soon canopied by budding trees. 'If you hadn't persisted with this, we might never have known who was behind it. Jamie Sinclair might have decided to stay dead and disappear if he felt there was nothing left in it for him. Your work in finding that ruby flushed him out.'

'Just as Mr Sinclair hoped it would,' Tayte said, 'although I'm sure he'd have liked a different outcome.'

'Aye, I'm sure he would.'

It wasn't long before they were out on the main road, heading east along the A85 towards Perth. They passed through the market town of Crieff and Tayte's thoughts turned to the poor man Jamie had murdered at the start of his killing spree. 'What will happen about the man who was buried in Jamie Sinclair's place yesterday?'

'His body will be exhumed,' Sinclair said. 'Proper identification will be sought. Missing Persons may be able to help us, although as the man was homeless that may be unlikely. There are other records that can be checked, though. We'll do everything we can to find out who he is so we can inform his family.'

'And the ruby?' Tayte said. 'I suppose the Blood of Rajputana now belongs to Mr Sinclair. Finders keepers and all that.'

'I very much doubt it. Under Scottish law any ownerless object found by chance like that, modern items excluded, becomes the property of the Crown. Unless Damian can prove he's the ruby's legal owner it will be claimed as treasure trove.'

Tayte knew Sinclair would have a hard time proving ownership of the ruby. Perhaps through his ancestor's paranoia over someone else getting their hands on it, Sir Robert Christie had made sure no one knew he had it. He could have left it to Angus Fraser in his will along with the house, making it easy to prove ownership now, but then he would have had to explain how he'd come by it. He could hardly have done that. He'd killed a man and robbed a grave to get it. Had he claimed to have found it, on the other hand, under Scottish law it would likely have been taken from him.

Tayte couldn't see how Sir Robert had any other choice than to hide the Blood of Rajputana at Drumarthen for his son, or perhaps future generations of his family to find, but it seemed that his efforts had been in vain. As far as Tayte was concerned, he thought it was for the best. From what he'd heard and read about the ruby during his brief time in Scotland, enough greed-driven blood had already been spilled over it.

The journey continued in silence for several miles until Ross announced, 'Almost there. We're on the outskirts of Perth now.'

Tayte nodded, not really taking much in. His thoughts had turned to his family, and he became so lost in them that he was completely unaware that they had arrived at the train station until the car came to a stop in the car park and Ross nudged him.

'Mr Tayte? We're here.'

'Sorry,' Tayte said. 'I was miles away.' He shook Ross's hand. 'Thanks again.'

'Don't mention it. You have a safe journey now.'

Tayte smiled and got out of the car. He collected his things from the back seat, and as he closed the door and watched the car pull away, he took out his phone to call Jean. How he yearned to be home with her and his son again. Before he'd taken the assignment, he'd been keen to tackle something other than the usual run-of-the-mill jobs he'd had since moving to London. Now, after all that had happened, he thought such jobs were perhaps not so bad after all.

He dialled Jean's number, his thoughts continuing to drift. He began to reflect on Jane Hardwick's letters and the tragic story they told. Jane was now long dead, but her letters had served to breathe life into her again, if only for the time it took Tayte to read them. He hoped she had succeeded in her ambitions to teach in India, as the last of her letters had suggested, and that she had lived a long and happy life in the country she loved so much. Maybe it really was time to hang up his hat and start a teaching career himself, as his brother Rudi had suggested on his and Jean's wedding day. While he waited for Jean to pick up, he smiled as he headed for his train, wondering just what that future might look like.

Acknowledgments

My thanks as always to Katie Green for helping me to tell this story in the best way possible, to Gillian Holmes and Gemma Wain for editing this book, to Laura Deacon and the team at Amazon Publishing for all the hard work that went into producing it, and to all the proofreaders who have helped to ensure that this book is as error-free as possible. Special thanks to former Inspector Pat Rawle for continuing to help with my enquiries, and of course to my wife, Karen, whose continued support makes everything possible. I would also very much like to thank you for reading *Letters from the Dead*. I hope you enjoyed it.

About the Author

Credit: Karen Robinson

Steve Robinson drew upon his own family history for inspiration when he imagined the life and quest of his genealogist hero, Jefferson Tayte. The talented London-based crime writer, who was first published at age sixteen, always wondered about his own maternal grandfather. 'He was an American GI billeted in England during the Second World War,' Robinson says. 'A few years after the war ended he went back to America, leaving a young family behind, and, to my knowledge, no further contact was made. I traced him to Los Angeles through his 1943 enlistment record and discovered that he was born in Arkansas . . .'

Robinson cites crime-writing and genealogy amongst his hobbies—a passion that is readily apparent in his work. He can be contacted via his website, www.steve-robinson.me, his blog at www.ancestryauthor.blogspot.com, and on Facebook at www.facebook.com/SteveRobinsonAuthor.